THE
SUN
STILL
RISES

AN ANTHOLOGY IN MEMORY OF
LANI FORBES

COPYRIGHT

Contents

The Sun Still Rises

Foreword

If you've ever had a dedicated advocate for the dreams you hold dearest or a friend who would stand with you in life's storms, then you have been blessed indeed—even more so if this person offered tender tendrils of hope when you had none. There was one such exceptional woman who touched many readers, communities, students, and families in her life, and her name was Lani Forbes.

In 2021, following the birth of her son, author Lani Forbes discovered that she had an aggressive form of cancer. Her community poured out compassion and care as she began navigating her altered world. Despite the many difficulties she faced, Lani didn't stop living her life to the fullest. She wrote and edited books, co-authored works and articles, taught writing and editing, brainstormed beginning a podcast, and more. She didn't let a day pass without making the most of it. All the while, she continued to be a ray of sunshine to people in the writing industry. The stories she wrote of wildly brave people overcoming unimaginable trials were true in her own life.

We were all deeply saddened when she passed away in 2022, but the community she created formed lasting friendships and her stories continued to touch readers' hearts. Her friends and colleagues in the writing industry helped with the next book launch, and she still has one more in the works soon to be published.

And now this amazing, tenacious, talented community has collaborated—twenty authors in all—to keep the legacy of Lani Forbes alive. We've banded together, volunteers giving countless hours of writing, editing, and creative work to design this gift for her young children in tribute to Lani. Each author captured a thread of the spirit that Lani gave us in this compilation of young adult fantasy stories, aptly named *The Sun Still Rises*. Inside are tales set in worlds with dragons, magical jewels, and fantastic powers, with themes of breaking curses, healing wounds, and making painful decisions with heavy costs. Just as Lani gave her time and energy to encourage and help others, all profits from this book will go to her family.

Our hope is that this anthology will encourage everyone who reads it and carry forward a small nugget of Lani's love. Of special note: at the back of the book is a personal message Lani herself penned for each of you before she passed away.

Signed,

The Lani's Legacy Leadership Team

Soul Threader

Ellen McGinty

One-thousand threads pulse inside me as my feet thud against the slick cobblestones, out of time—as usual. I can't be late, not for this.

Drums thunder across the mountains, signaling the arrival of Princess Kogane and the royal procession, two days earlier than planned. Mother will be furious. I've not scrubbed the slimy bathhouse tiles, wiped the windows, or arranged the welcome lilies. The last artisan who invited the imperial family to test their art, and then disappointed them, lost not only their rank, but their head.

I round the last corner and slam face-first into a wall of knotted silk. My sister's calloused fists grab my tunic as she staggers back from my thundering pace.

"Mirelle," she gasps, throwing a hand against her heart. "Why are you here and not at Fever House? It's filthy! The princ—"

"So, it's true?" I bend over, waiting for my heart to stop slamming against my ribs. "The artisan hearing is today. Why didn't anyone tell me?"

"Mirelle!" Lala hurls my name like salt over her shoulder. "Mama informed the whole bathhouse yesterday when handing out chores. Where were you?"

My gaze steals over my sister's tanned face, sinewy arms, and wide lips pinched into a familiar frown. Lala means well, trying to keep our family stitched together, but she can't replace Papa. I straighten, coming only to her shoulders. The breath I'd lost racing down the mountain finally settles in my chest, but I can't swallow the lump in my throat. "Threading."

"Boiling saints!" Lala shoves me with the strong slant of her palm, her voice dropping to a harsh whisper. "Are you trying to get into trouble? Threading the soul isn't an art you dabble in for sport. It's forbidden outside the capital."

"Papa was a threader." The words taste like bitter ash from Mt. Kildar, the same mountain that heats our bathhouse and saturates the water with the richest quality minerals in the world: iron, sulfur, aluminum. One day in the Fever House baths and your skin is smoother than silk, your muscles no longer ache, and even tiny scars start to fade.

For generations, we learned to churn the hot springs, to cool the waters and spread the minerals with their healing properties. But some of us, like Papa, could *thread* the water, send strands of our very being into the boiling stream and touch the soul of another living thing. Scars completely disappeared, fractured bones mended, broken hearts healed—but every thread is costly. Papa had withered away, down to his last thread when he kissed me goodnight five years ago.

"We can't count the threads of our life, but we count who they connect us to," he said with a wink, smoothing my wild hair with a worn hand. How I wish that I still had that warm hand to hold.

Lala loops my arm in hers and tugs me at a run down the slick stone road wending to the hot spring bathhouse. "Let's go."

I race along the town's stone walls as thick clouds of steam rise like dragon smoke from an open geyser in the courtyard. Tears prick at my eyes, and I rub them with a bony fist, blaming the steam. I have to be a threader, not just of water but souls and heart ... like Papa. That connection is all I have left of him.

The Fever House greets us in its four-story glory of charcoal walls, slanted bamboo, and tiled windows curved like so many appraising frowns. I duck my head beneath the banner entrance, ignoring the empty carriages parked in the front courtyard. Mama's sharp orders bark from the hallway as servants scurry with practiced poise, hustling towels, baskets, and scrubbing buckets down the narrow passages. The warm glow of the lanterns carries the scent of sandalwood.

"You're late. Are you the threader?" A voice shakes me like the autumn wind, cold and wild, a hint of laughter riding on its edges.

My head jerks up. I'd expected Mama and her warm, dark eyes, but the eyes that light on me are pools of hazel milk, the unseeing eyes of Prince Kogan.

I fall to my knees, face smacking the floor with a too hard jolt. *The prince?* I'd missed more in Mama's announcement than the time of the royal artisan test; I'd missed which royal! Princess Kogane hadn't come but her brother, Prince Kogan. "Your Highness." The words scratch my throat.

"Answer," he says, a pinch of desperation in his sharp tone. "Are you the threader?"

My throat goes tight. Only Mama and Lala know about my threading in secret on the mountain. Had rumor spilled the edges of our small town? I can't be taken to the capital like Papa and the threaders of old; it would destroy what's left of my family. Still, a tingle of curiosity pricks my spine, daring me to look into the prince's eyes again. After all, the blind prince wouldn't notice, would he? But a slight cough from Lala reminds me to keep my head ... literally.

"The art of threading is ancient, Your Majesty," Mama says, her voice a note higher than usual. "None practice it anymore. But there are healing qualities in our waters—"

"Whispers reach every corner of a kingdom," the prince says ruefully. "There is a threader still practicing in secret, and I've traveled a long way to observe this ancient art. My inspector will relay the terms."

An attendant at the prince's side steps forward. "The artisans of Fever House claim to possess miracles in their waters," he drones. "We have dozens of requests from hot spring houses claiming such wonders, but none have succeeded in becoming a cultural heritage—a title worth more than a hundred years of the state's financing. It's an honor to care for a place of miracles, that is ... if such things truly exist. Prince Kogan will accept proof of your family's art with a demonstration: the healing of his eyes."

Heal his eyes? How many threads would that take? Could it even be done? Blood sinks to my trembling legs, going numb against the wooden floor. My eyes snap to the twisted scars marring the prince's face, hidden beneath long bangs and the shadows of the hall.

"Begin now," the prince commands, a tic in his rough jaw. The dim amber glow of lamplight catches dozens of tiny scars along his neck and jawline, as if he'd insisted on shaving himself with an unsteady hand. My gaze lingers, traveling to the jagged pink web across his brow. I'd been nine, the same age as the prince, when rumor of his accident flooded the village. The spoiled child was terrorizing the kitchen staff when a vat of boiling water fell ...

A thick finger thumps my back, reminding me to stand. I jump to attention, eyes searching for Mama and Lala, but they're already leading the prince's reception down the hall toward the baths. The royal inspector straightens, eyeing me with suspicion. I meet his gaze before turning down the hall toward the hot spring rooms, my face flushing from more than the steam clogging the air.

Threading only works in the water when the soul is laid bare. Nothing foreign can enter the water: soap, makeup ... clothes. Dread and heat flush my cheeks as we enter the room of Heavenly Tears. Five tiered pools stretch up the center of an elaborately carved cypress room, steam curling into every cranny, the wood slick with white foam, and the hush of water ruling out every sound except the wild beating of my heart. Wooden dragons spiral across the ceiling, water dripping from their fangs. I'd always thought it beautiful, but now it feels like a trap.

Heal his eyes? Threading for practice was one thing. Staying connected to Papa. But healing this stranger under threat of losing our home ... our heads? The royal family was supposed to test our healing waters, not demand the impossible.

My eyes pivot to my bare feet sloshing in the waters overflow as the prince enters the room dressed down to a linen garment below his waist. Usually, we bathe naked, like we came into the earth, but the royal family must be an exception. The room stills as my sister and two other women lift wooden paddles and dip them into the water's edge with a hum.

Turn water,
Like leaves of autumn roll into spring.
Turn water,
Heal scars and eyes as we sing.

I stir the water with a long cedar paddle, aiming a song at the azure pool below. Words roll across my lips, humming an ancient tune recorded with memory and kind eyes. The water churns against the wood, thick, unruly, stubborn—like me. I grip tighter; the paddle is taller than me and nearly weighs the same. I carved it from the ruby heart of a cedar tree with Papa. They say the waters of Fever House heal people. Like salt cleanses a wound, the water cleanses bodies ... and souls, if the threader's song is right.

But my song has never healed, not since Papa passed away.

Images of the creatures in the mountains crowd my mind, frogs with broken legs, a flying squirrel with a torn wing, the wild piglet with a broken heart that refused to eat. I'd sing over the open waters streaming from the mountain's side, but the threads of my heart didn't listen. The waters didn't heal as I spun them and sang.

Likewise now, nothing happens. The water isn't healing the prince. His scars are more ample than spots on a frog ... and more costly. Pink lines of flesh glow beneath the water as I stir my paddle, words humming across my lips. The royal inspector's eyes bore into the back of my skull and Lala shoots me a pleading look. We turn our paddles through the water, distributing the minerals and keeping the temperature just cool enough so that the prince doesn't overheat. The minerals could help him over time, the water giving his body strength, but he needs more than empty promises.

My toes curl over the edge of the pool as I watch the prince lean his head against the wooden ledge, unseeing eyes closed. A twinge of sorrow ruffles his brow, furrowing the scars for one brief moment. His eyes squeeze shut as if to lock away the pain behind them before his face smooths into a mask again.

My jaw clenches, locking away my own pain, the threads of soul Papa had spent in service to the capital until he gifted me with the last one as he kissed me goodnight—the magic of a soul threader. I focus on the threads of magic in my soul, the tiny parts of myself that I can give to another, to heal or to harm.

The threads pulse faint against my fingertips, inking through the damp cedar board and into the water, tiny silver threads. Each one carries a weight, heavy like breath tugged from your lungs, only this comes from the heart. Threading is costly. The magic that heals him drains me, so I must be careful.

Something stirs in me ... whispering that this should not be. Giving fills. Emptying fills.

Hadn't the waters of Fever House taught me this? Volumes pour from the heart of the mountain, ever warm, sanctifying our skin ... our hearts ... but it doesn't run dry. They say a black dragon lives in the mountain with a princess made of snow. She cools the water, he warms it, and together their breath gives us air and life.

Heal. Mend. Remove all that is broken. I must prove that I can thread the waters or my family will lose more than their honor.

But the scar tissue tightens, knitting the prince's shoulders into a hunch. He grimaces, resisting the pain and the silver threads. I turn the water, cooling it, mixing the minerals, willing the threads of my soul to mend like yarn. *Let him see.*

Prince Kogan doesn't wince as the pink scars across his eyes pucker, shrinking and drawing inward. Pain ripples up the wooden paddle, squeezing my heart with the effort. But I strengthen my grip, my tune, the anchoring of my feet, and will the scar to fold inward until it disappears.

I stumble across a word of song, earning a fearful look from Lala. Beads of sweat pool across her brow. If we fail the artisan test, we could lose the house, the spring Papa's family had passed down for generations, and even our lives.

I sing louder with my sister and the others, steaming water folding over my paddle. Then as the last ridge of wrinkled scar tissue fades from view, the prince slips down into the bath. His head tilts beneath the steaming water, bubbles popping to the surface—unconscious.

I drop my paddle, breaking my song with a cry for help.

It wasn't only his scar that folded inward; his heart had too. Silver threads traveling inward, removing *all* that is broken as I'd asked them to. Why hadn't I sensed the real scar first, the one on his heart?

The royal inspector barks out orders and sentinels step forward, grabbing Lala and pulling her and the others away from the pools. I duck, knees brushing the slick square frame, and plunge my arm into the steaming water. In seconds, my hand is red and my arm burns as I latch onto slippery smooth hair. Frantic, my hand dives deeper until my chin touches the water, and then my face submerges. I grab the prince by the arms and pull.

I drag his limp form out of the pool and heave him onto the side steps. Water drenches my cotton tunic as I lean over him, listening for breath. Steam clogs the chamber, spiraling like a typhoon of heat and salt and sulfur. The scars on the prince's face are gone. Trembling, my hand brushes his smooth face and trails to his neck where I check for a pulse. His chest rises and falls but ... his heart isn't beating.

Remove all that is broken.

Prince Kogan opens his eyes, blinking at the wooden ceiling dripping with condensation. Brown eyes like a dappled autumn forest find mine. Lips turn in a slow frown, his eyes too, wilted with disappointment. He touches his face, fingers brushing across his silken skin, up the ridge of his smooth nose and across an intelligent brow.

"You healed my eyes," he says, distant, detached.

"The waters of Fever House have healed Your Majesty's eyes," I say. But I can't share in the relief that spreads across the room. Was I just imagining that his heart stopped or ... ?

Water drips from my chin and onto his tanned shoulder, and I straighten, giving him room to sit upright. My heart aches as I stare at his eyes. Beautiful, like a forest of fireflies and yet lonely.

The prince stands, looking around the room, at each face as if he'd never seen a face before. Never seen a smile, the twitch of laughter on lips, or the soft glow of a lantern.

My mother nods approvingly at me. Lala's shoulders slump with relief. But ... I haven't healed him. I see it in the threads of soul that stitched his scars, that knit together skin and blood, but not the one muscle that mattered above all—his heart.

Healing the prince may have saved Fever House, but it didn't save him. I curse my foolish heart as the prince extends a hand to me. Taking it, I stand, but not before snatching the nearest water ladle from the cold pool. At the last moment, I splash the cold water onto the prince's head. Threads of my magic go forth as I will them to unknit his wounds, to let them be open and free. Scars blossom across his face, blistering the perfect brow, creating canyons and ridges where gentle skin had formed seconds ago.

"I'm sorry," I whisper, meeting his eyes one last time. His eyes shift from warm brown to palest milk. And I send the threads to his heart, asking the water to work its magic, asking for a deeper, lasting healing. Magic leaps to my fingers with the ease of water, like I'd seen with my Papa, filling the need instead of covering the pain. The prince may thank me in the end ... or not. But if I had to choose between my eyes or my heart, I know which I'd pick.

Prince Kogan staggers backward. Guards seize me and pull me away, rough hands squeezing to the bone. My legs slip, buckling under me as I'm dragged outside beneath the setting sun. A cry of protest lodges in my throat as my heels drag against the amber glow of cobblestones. *Please spare my family ... please.*

"Wait," the prince calls out, blindly bracing against the entrance pillars, a loose black robe thrown over his shoulders bearing the insignia of dual dragons. His bare chest heaves, out of breath, as he leans an arm against the gate, sweat glistening across his scarred skin. Milk pale eyes search the sky and the misty courtyard before settling over the shuffling guards jerking me to my feet. Mama and Lala spill into the stone yard, falling to their knees before the guards and the royal inspector.

"Have mercy," Mama cries. "The prince was healed once; it can be done again."

"No."

My head jerks up at the crisp voice. The prince is now arm's length from me. He gestures for the guards to release me, and they do so immediately.

"My kingdom has many artisans," he says, his voice a welcome cold against my feverish skin. "Artisans that sew living fables from strips of cloth, knead soil into richest porcelain, and now, ones that heal scars made not of flesh and bone but heart and soul. Fever House has earned its rank as an artisan of the kingdom, and a place of healing."

I rub my arm where the guards had held too tight. My eyes fix on the cobblestones and the steam curling round my ankles. Everyone is watching me. Watching ... *us*, if that's a word I can use with a prince.

"Forgive me," the prince says, low so that Mama and the others do not hear. "It's bad manners to keep you out in the dark. Would you like to go back inside? I've a question for you."

"You can ask it here," I say, turning my eyes to his and feeling the threads of my soul connected to him.

"How did you know"—he pauses with a smile, all crooked and light-hearted—"that it was my heart that was broken?"

"I almost didn't see it," I admit, thinking of how the worry of losing my family's Fever House nearly stopped me from doing what I knew I should. "Every scar tells a story of who we are, past, present, and future. My papa always said that it's never too late to repair a broken past. We don't erase the wound, but we fill it with good."

The prince turns his head to the side, his smile fading like a distant ripple. "I saw your face."

"I'm sorry it was not something grander for your first glimpse of the world."

"It was all the light I needed," he says.

Prince Kogan offers me his arm. My stomach swoops as I take it, my heart pounding faster than it had racing down the mountain. I peek over the prince's shoulder to catch a glimpse of Mama and Lala gaping through tented fingers, though their jaws aren't nearly as dropped as the royal inspector, who's turned birch white. Together, the prince and I step inside Fever House where we dine with my family until it's late, spinning stories and souls.

At the end of the night, the prince takes my hand, enveloping it in his warmth. "Thank you. Now I know that it's never truly dark, even when my eyes don't see. True healing and *seeing* comes from the heart, and the connections that thread us together on this warm earth are the strongest light of all."

"You can see," I say, meeting his eyes ... or rather his heart and the threads connecting us.

The prince lifts my hand to his lips with a kiss that radiates warmth down my arm and blossoms like fire across my cheeks. "I can now."

Pixie Dust and Princes

Julie Hall

It's official. I'm going insane.

My mind is a million miles away from my calculus test as I tap my pencil against my paper and watch a purple pixie flit around the room. It lands on the head of the student to my left. Keeping my head dipped, I pretend to concentrate on the math problems, but I can't seem to unglue my eyes from the tiny winged creature as it does pirouettes in my unsuspecting classmate's hair.

Yep. Definitely insane. Because mentally sound people don't see things that aren't there, hear voices when no one's around, or feel rushes of electricity up and down their spine.

After a few moments, my classmate reaches up and scratches his head. Dodging his hand, the pixie jumps into the air. Giggling, she flutters her delicate dragonfly wings and a fine mist of sparkling dust sprinkles over his face, causing him to sneeze.

Ripping my gaze away from the little troublemaker, I force myself to refocus on my test. On the off chance my insanity is only temporary, I'd still like to get into a decent university later this year. That means I need to keep my grades up, but it's not a minute later before the pixie is dancing over the derivatives and integrals on the page in front of me. I try to discreetly shoo her away, but she starts chucking balls of pixie dust at my face, which sets off a round of my own sneezes.

With a high-pitched peal of laughter, she finally shoots into the air and toward the window, zipping straight through the glass as if it isn't even there. Outside, she meets up with two other pixies, one blue and the other green. They fly in frantic circles before zipping away into the forest that borders our school.

A throat clears next to me and I jolt. When I look over, my teacher is standing beside my desk.

"Finished already, Greer?" Her gaze tells me she knows I'm not.

Biting down on my lip, I shake my head.

"Then perhaps keep your eyes on your paper rather than letting them wander. I promise you won't find the answer to question four etched into the trunk of a tree out there."

There's a smattering of smothered laughs and giggles from the room around us as I mumble an apology. My face feels hot as I get back to work, powering through the rest of the test. When the bell rings, I turn in my test with the rest of the class and filter into the hallway.

Sloan, my best friend since she moved to our town in second grade, comes up behind me, bumping my shoulder lightly as we make our way to our lockers.

"What was up back there?" she asks. Below her full fringe of auburn bangs, her gaze is questioning.

"Nothing," I lie.

Concern clouds her eyes. "You've been having a lot of 'nothing' happen to you the last couple of weeks."

I could make up another lie—it's what I've been doing since the hallucinations started three weeks ago—but I'm drained. My slow slip into madness has been surprisingly exhausting, and I don't have the mental energy to come up with another excuse for my weird behavior, so I settle on a half-truth.

"I've just got a lot going on right now. Can we not talk about it?"

A line forms between Sloan's brows but she nods, giving me the space I need. I'm relieved she's not pushing it because I'm right on the edge. One little nudge and I might break down right there in the hallway.

If only things could go back to how they were three weeks ago.

I didn't think much of it when I started seeing things that can't possibly be real. At first I'd catch a flash of something in my peripheral but when I turned my head nothing was there. Then it was just small things, like flowers being more vibrant or animals appearing more human-like in their expressions. I've always been a creative person, an artist at heart, so I just chalked it up to an overactive imagination, but when the otherworldly creatures started to appear and fantastical or natural elements bled into the fabric of everyday life, I knew something was very wrong with me.

We reach our lockers with plenty of time to make our next class.

"Want to head to the Necto this weekend?" Sloan asks, breaking the somewhat awkward silence that's filled the air between us.

The last thing I want to do is go dancing at the local club. The lights and decibel level of the music are sure to make my symptoms worse, but the hopeful look on Sloan's face keeps me from coming right out and saying no.

"Yeah, maybe. That could be fun." I shrug, forcing my face and voice to look and sound more excited than I actually am.

I must be convincing because a genuine smile breaks out on Sloan's face. Ugh, I'm the worst friend in the world. I've totally flaked on her the last few weeks, and her happiness over something as small as the possibility of hanging out weighs me down with guilt.

Now I really *do* have to go to that club with her.

Sloan turns to her locker, putting away books and grabbing others, and gabbing about a new red dress she bought last weekend.

I tune her out as the back of my neck starts to chill and warm electric currents crawl down my spine. A sensation that's become uncomfortably familiar to me.

Glancing over my shoulder, I search the hallway, expecting to see more pixies or perhaps vines crawling over the ceiling or maybe even a small troll planting toadstools on the floor—all hallucinations I've had over the last couple of weeks—but nothing appears out of place.

I'm about to turn back to Sloan when I see him.

A tall guy with black hair and ice-blue eyes stands casually with his shoulder propped up against the wall a little ways away, and he's staring right at me.

I dip my head, trying not to be overly obvious that I'm staring back, but the side of his mouth quirks up in a knowing smirk anyway.

Who is this guy?

His face has sharp angles and symmetrical lines that are offset by full lips. I'd describe him as pretty if he wasn't so edgy. His dark hair is shorn at the sides and longer at the top. The tips are dyed electric blue and a ring pierces through one of the dark slashes over his eyes.

He seems older than eighteen, but I suppose he can pass for a student. One thing is for sure, dressed in a leather jacket and ripped low-slung jeans, there's no way he's a teacher.

Maybe he's someone's older brother? But then what would he be doing hanging out in the hallway between classes? Perhaps a transfer student from Europe or something? He has a foreign vibe that doesn't fit in here at Jefferson High.

I may have no idea who he is, but I'm positive I've never seen him before. There's no way I'd be able to forget someone who looks like him. Already his image is burned into my mind.

"Who's that?" I ask, glancing back at Sloan. Between the two of us she's the social butterfly. She basically knows every student in our grade and the one under us.

Sloan zips her bag and then skips her gaze over my shoulder. "Who are you talking about?"

I almost laugh. "Tall leather-clad dude behind me. Black and blue hair with an eyebrow ring."

He sticks out like a sore thumb. Who else could I be talking about?

Sloan's eyes widen when she hears my description. She looks over my shoulder again but then frowns. "I don't see anyone like that."

What?

I whip around, not concerned with being obvious anymore, but Sloan's right, he's gone.

"But ... he was right there."

Fantastic. I'm hallucinating people now.

"Sucks I didn't see him too because he sounds hot."

He was, I almost say.

Sloan gives me the side-eye as we walk down the street toward Necto.

"You're flawless tonight," she says, seeing me fidget with the bracelet and then wrap my jacket more firmly around me.

I shoot Sloan what I hope is a confident smile as my boots and Sloan's heels click against the pavement.

I *am* nervous, but not about how I look. Just this morning, I woke up to find my bedroom had been completely transformed. Moss hung from the frame of my canopy bed, the carpet on my floor replaced with the unnaturally bright green grass, and one whole wall of my room was missing, opening up to a woodland scape that rivaled any fairy-tale forest. I squeezed my eyes shut, hoping that when I opened them the hallucination would be gone, but even after rubbing them and blinking several times nothing had changed. I avoided my room for as long as possible today, but when I went back in to change to go out tonight, it still looked the same.

Whatever is happening to me is getting worse. My parents are loving and wonderful and it's past time to tell them about it, but I don't know how.

I sigh, concerns heavy on my heart as we near the street corner. The Necto is less than a block away, and the beat from the trance music they're playing thumps in my ears. Something catches my attention and I look to the side, catching what I think is a person ducking into the alley across the street. My skin chills, but I shake off the feeling like I'm being watched.

This isn't the best part of town, but it isn't the worst either. Even so, I pick up my speed and Sloan matches my steps. We're around the corner and waiting in the small line to get into the club within moments. Sloan gets let in in front of me, and I hand the beefy bouncer my ID. He looks over it a long time, which is weird. It's my real ID. It's an eighteen and up night, so there shouldn't be any issue.

After what feels like an eternity he hands me back my driver's license, flashing me a creepy smile. A silver and gold grill covers his front teeth, and when I look into his eyes, they flash green. I step back with a gasp, but that only makes the bouncer smile more broadly.

"Have fun, Princess," he says as he unhooks the velvet rope, giving me entrance to the club. I swear his eyes never leave me as I skirt past him and scurry through the door.

It takes a couple of seconds for my eyes to adjust to the flashing lights inside the club, and when they do, I wish they hadn't. Vines hang from the rafters of the ceiling with unnaturally bright flowers clinging to the green foliage. The air, which should smell like a mixture of sweat and alcohol, is scented with the sharp tang of citrus instead. Pixies of all different colors zip through the air above people's heads, and when I scan the crowd of dancing bodies, I start to pick out things that don't belong. Humanoid creatures with antlers growing out of their heads, some with green skin and pointed ears. Others with eyes that are too big or features too perfect to be human.

My heart races and I start to get light-headed.

It's happening. It's happening right now and I can't do anything to stop it.

"This is wild, right?"

With a gasp, I turn to Sloan who's now standing next to me. Her gaze roams over the chaotic revelry, her mouth slightly agape and an expression of awe on her face.

"What do you mean?" I ask. We've been to the Necto a ton of times. This shouldn't be new to her.

She glances at me with a crease between her eyebrows. "You're joking, right?" She motions outward. "I don't know who did these decorations, but they are epic. I think those are real orange trees they hauled in here. Those oranges are huge."

I didn't even notice the smattering of fruit trees placed all over the dance floor.

Sloan laughs. "I don't know what kind of dress-up party we stumbled across, but this is legit." She points to someone in the crowd. "Does that dude have hooves? He actually looks like a satyr. Come on, I gotta go ask him where he got his costume."

She starts to head in the half-man half-goat's direction, but I grab her arm.

"Wait. Are you telling me you can see all this?"

Sloan gives me a look. "Umm, yeah. Of course." Her smile drops. "Are you feeling okay?"

"And you can see them as well?" I point to the pixies buzzing through the air.

Sloan nods. "How do you think they made them look so lifelike? They've got to be suspended by wires, right? Genius!"

I take in a deep breath and get a whiff of lemon this time. If possible, I'm even more confused than before. How are my hallucinations bleeding into reality?

"Oh, dang. That guy is fine." Sloan pretends to wipe her mouth and then asks, "Am I drooling?"

I look in the direction she's staring and there he is again. The guy I hallucinated at school. He's standing with his back against the bar, his elbows propped up behind him. Instead of a leather jacket and ripped jeans, he's wearing a fitted black vest with gold embroidery and no shirt underneath, and tight black pants that hug his thighs. His boots come up to almost his knees and are covered in straps and dagger sheaths. A circlet of gold leaves rests on his head. The outfit would probably look outrageous on most guys, but he's pulling it off.

He's more than pulling it off, he's owning it.

And once again he's staring right at me.

"You can see him?"

"Seriously, Greer. Now you're really starting to scare me."

Okay, so he's not a hallucination. That's good, right?

"Oh," I say, trying to recover. "I just mean that it's crowded and kinda dark in here."

"Not dark enough that I wouldn't see that fine piece of—" She cuts herself off and sticks her bottom lip out in a pretty pout. "Well, shoot. He's obviously checking you out and not me. He hasn't taken his eyes off you." She sighs dramatically. "If only I had your white blonde head of hair and perfect skin. Your teal eyes don't hurt either."

I roll my eyes. Like her thick auburn hair and amazing hourglass figure doesn't attract guys like bees to honey. She's definitely the standout beauty between the two of us. Especially in her tiny red sequined dress and three-inch heels.

I sneak another peek at the guy and he's still staring. Seeing he caught my eye, he inclines his head, inviting me to join him.

"Yas, girl. Go shoot your shot." Sloan gives me a gentle shove in his direction. And being the dork that I am, I stumble over my feet before righting myself.

So embarrassing.

"Don't worry," Sloan calls to me over the music. "I don't think he saw."

I shake my head and shoot her a glare. He was looking right at me. He'd have to be blind to not have seen that. I'm more determined than ever not to go over there, but when a cool hand cups my elbow and a deep voice rumbles, "Let's dance," in my ear, I know he's come to me instead.

My tongue feels glued to the roof of my mouth as the dark stranger leads me into the thick of the dance floor, right under one of the orange trees. I glance back at Sloan once and she smiles and waves at me before disappearing into the crowd.

The song that is playing is slow and sultry. The guy slides his arms behind me and reels me in. We're close enough that I have to tip my head up to look into his eyes, which is rare for me because I'm so tall, but not so close that I'm uncomfortable.

The music is unfamiliar but hypnotic. It feels like it's sinking into my skin, making my body malleable as I sway to the rhythm.

"Who are you?" I finally ask, looking into his pale blue eyes. They remind me of a frozen lake.

"Prince Rafe of the Winter Court."

I huff a laugh. "Excuse me?"

He leans into my space. His lips brush against the shell of my ear, making it feel like the temperature inside the club just jumped up at least ten degrees. "I don't believe you misheard me."

Straightening, he looks down on me with a small smirk of amusement.

This dude is taking his cosplay role pretty seriously. But sure, I'll play along. "You don't look like a prince."

His mouth quirks into another smirk. "How should a prince look?"

Definitely not so sinfully gorgeous.

An image of the stodgy members of the British monarchy comes into my head. This guy definitely doesn't fit that mold.

I shrug. "You know ... regal. Disciplined. Controlled."

He chuckles, and the sound makes goose bumps break out on my arms. "It's obvious you've never met any fae princes before. We're anything but controlled. We encompass the essence of Faerie and are as wild and savage as the realm itself."

Fae? Faerie?

I look into his eyes and although there's a touch of amusement there, I can tell he's serious.

Swallowing, I lean back, putting some distance between myself and the self-proclaimed Winter Prince.

This goes beyond cosplay. This guy is delusional.

Either that, or ...

His gaze is penetrating as he watches me process.

I shake my head, refusing to even entertain the idea that what he's saying is true. Maybe he's telling *his* truth—his delusional truth—but that doesn't make it real.

He catches something over my shoulder and his face hardens. Dropping his arms from me completely, his hand goes to his side where there's an empty scabbard. He swears under his breath.

"Time to go," he says.

My first reaction is disappointment, and I want to kick myself for it. Rafe is a veritable stranger, and an unhinged one at that. I have enough crazy for the both of us; adding his to the mix would be a disaster. But even so, there's something about him I'm drawn to. Something that makes my heart beat in the most delicious way. My hands itch to run through his hair.

Rafe grabs my hand and starts to lead me through the crowded dance floor.

"I thought you had to go," I say as he pulls me along.

"*We're* going," he clarifies.

Now wait a second.

I plant my feet and Rafe stops, looking back at me.

"I don't have time to argue, Princess."

"I'm not a princess."

"You are. You just don't know it. And we have to get you to Faerie, right now. We've run out of time."

I open my mouth to argue when a boom shakes the club and a waterfall of multicolored pixie dust rains down from the ceiling like a torrential downpour.

At first, shouts of excitement sound, but once the sparkling dust reaches the crowd people start dropping.

Someone hits the ground beside me and I gasp. Ripping out of Rafe's grip, I crouch down to check on him, noticing at least half the club goers are lying prone across the dance floor. The only people remaining standing are the ones with pointy ears, different colored skin, or parts of an animal.

I feel the guy's pulse next to me and it beats strong.

"Aurora Dawn, we have to go," Rafe says as he pulls me back to my feet.

A rush of adrenaline floods my system. *Aurora Dawn*. Why does that name feel familiar?

I yank free from Rafe again. "That's not my name," I hiss at him, only now realizing he never actually asked my name.

"It is," he says. "It's your fae name."

"Fae?"

"You're not human. You're fae, like me," he says and then with a wave of his hand his ears transform into gentle points, the angles of his face sharpen, making his face even more impossibly beautiful than it was. Weapons appear in his once empty holsters.

My breathing picks up, and I'm about three seconds from hyperventilating when I spot a familiar pair of red pumps and sequined dress.

"Sloan!" I shout and weave through the unconscious forms on the ground toward her.

My friend lay on the edge of the dance floor with an arm haphazardly thrown over her face. I've almost reached her when Rafe wraps his arms around my waist and lifts me into the air.

"Stop," I yell, trying to pry myself free. "That's my best friend."

"She's fine," he says as he throws me over his shoulder and then starts to push through the otherworldly creatures toward the front door. He shouts orders at them as he goes. Things like, "Bar the doors," "Put the trolls on alert," and "Make sure we're not followed." The creatures he speaks to snap into motion to follow his instructions.

I don't care about any of that though because my friend is knocked out and vulnerable back there.

When we reach the front door and Rafe doesn't even break his stride, I start to go ballistic, hammering my fists against his back and shouting insults so vile my parents' ears would bleed. We round a corner into an alleyway a couple blocks from the club and Rafe puts me down. Pressing me back against a brick wall, he puts a hand over my mouth to shut me up.

"Stop," he says. A trickle of frantic energy bleeds into his gaze and I realize that was as much a plea as it was a command. "Your friend is fine. She just succumbed to the pixie dust like every other human in there. She'll wake in an hour with a headache and no memory of tonight, but otherwise unscathed."

I glare at him, my hands gripping his wrist. My knee is in just the right position to put him down, but I hesitate.

Against all reason, some deep instinct tells me that I need to trust Rafe. That my life depends on it.

"If I move my hand, do you promise not to scream?" he asks, and I nod.

He removes his hand but doesn't back away. We're touching from thighs to chest. The way he's looking down at me makes my stomach flip.

"Do you mind giving me some breathing room?" I ask, even though my body isn't sure that's actually what it wants. My fingers twitch, and I have to curb the urge to reach up and run a finger over his full bottom lip.

He shakes his head, and his eyes clear. "Right," he says and then takes a small step back. He's still close enough that he can grab me if I try to bolt, but he's giving me the space I need to think straight.

"You need to tell me what's going on."

Rafe checks the alley to make sure we're truly alone and then asks, "Do you know what a Changeling is?"

I shake my head.

A look of frustration crosses his face. "Like I said, you're not human. You're fae."

I scoff, but he continues anyway. "When you were born, there was a prophecy that put your life in grave danger. Your parents, the king and queen of the Summer Court, decided to hide you in the human world to protect you. They swapped you with a human child when you were only a day old."

"I'm not fae. I don't look anything like you," I argue, eyeing his pointed ears.

"When we get to Faerie the glamour that was placed on you will lift. You'll still look like you, but you'll notice subtle changes. Your skin will be more luminescent. Your features will be perfectly symmetrical. And yes, your ears will be pointed."

I touch one of my cheekbones. My face isn't currently symmetrical? I shake my head. Whatever, that's not what's important here.

"You're telling me my parents aren't my parents? No way. They would have told me if I was adopted."

But even as the refusal leaves my mouth, doubt starts to creep in. I don't look like either of my parents. I'm a tall blonde with teal eyes. My parents are both brown-eyed and on the short side. My skin is free of any marks, but my mom's nose and cheeks are covered with cute freckles I always wished I had. My frame has been described as willowy, yet my dad is on the hefty side and my mom is curvy. We used to joke that I was a genetic anomaly.

"Your human parents' child died hours after birth," Rafe says. "You were replaced with her while they were still in the hospital. As an infant you looked close enough to the child they lost that with a little bit of confusion magic they never even knew you weren't their flesh and blood."

I want to deny everything he's saying, but it all makes an awful sort of sense.

"And what I've been seeing the last couple of weeks?" I ask, almost daring him to make sense of my hallucinations.

"Faerie is a different realm and a home to all types of fair folk," he explains. "But pieces of Faerie are always bleeding into the human world. You're close enough to your eighteenth birthday that the block the king and queen put on your magic all those years ago is starting to fade, so you're beginning to see the real world. The world only those with fae blood can see."

I probably shouldn't be relieved, but I am. Somewhere along the way I stopped disbelieving Rafe. It might be because I want to believe there's an explanation for what's been happening that doesn't involve me going insane, but witnessing a rainfall of pixie dust put down half the club and Rafe's pointed ears staring me in the face don't hurt his argument either.

I nod and if Rafe is surprised I finally stopped arguing with him, he doesn't show it.

"You keep saying we have to get to Faerie, why?"

"The Wild Ones have risen up and are searching for you. I have to get you back to the Summer Court before you are discovered."

"Summer Court. You're bringing me to the king and queen there?" I'm not ready to admit they are my birth parents yet.

Rafe nods.

"But you said you're the Winter Prince."

"I am," he says. "We have an alliance with your court, and I was commissioned to find you and bring you home. It was pure luck I found you before the Wild Ones." He cocks his head, his eyes drinking in my face. My unsymmetrical face. "Or perhaps it wasn't luck at all, but rather fate."

The way he's looking at me makes my face heat, but I force myself to focus.

"Who are these Wild Ones and what do they want from me?"

"The Wild Ones are various species of fair folk who have rejected the rule of any of the courts. They will do anything to destroy us and put all of Faerie under the rule of their dark king. As to what they want from you ..." Rafe hesitates.

"Just tell me," I beg.

"To kill you," he says, and a brick of lead settles low in my gut.

"Kill me? But, why?"

"It's part of the prophecy. You're meant to unite all of Faerie and secure the Seasonal Courts' rule forever. The Wild Ones will do anything to stop it."

A roar tears through the air around us, making my eardrums ring.

Rafe spins, keeping me behind him as a beast prowls toward us. He pulls a sword from the scabbard at his waist. "Aurora Dawn, stay behind me."

"My name is Greer," I say, but stay put.

The beast that's closing in on us is easily the size of a grizzly bear but with the body of a black wolf. Rafe, at least, has a weapon against the creature, where I have no defense against something like this.

"I'm bringing her to her parents. There's nothing you can do about it, Striker. Yield now, or die," Rafe says.

A wheezing sound comes from the beast and I realize it's laughing. I'm further shocked when the giant wolf answers Rafe, its voice growly but distinguishable.

"The only creatures dying in this wretched alley are you and the hidden princess."

The beast jumps into the air and Rafe swings into motion, leaping to intercept the creature that's at least three times his size with a jaw full of jagged teeth and hooked claws.

They clash in a flurry of steel and fur and then crash to the ground.

I hold my breath as I watch in horror.

Rafe slashes at the wolf with his sword and a dagger he's pulled from his boot, but the creature has animal instincts and a longer reach than the Winter Prince. Their motions are so fast and furious that I can't track them with my eyes. Their forms keep blurring, making it impossible for me to tell who has the upper hand.

Should I run for help? But who could possibly help Rafe in this type of fight? A human would be shredded by the giant wolf in seconds.

The sounds coming from the wolf and Rafe fray my nerves and I'm just about to bolt, desperate to find help, when there's a high-pitched yelp and the wolf collapses on the dirty ground. Rafe's sword sticks out of its side.

With his back to me, Rafe stands over the body of the felled creature, breathing heavy. Reaching forward, he grabs his weapon and pulls it free with a sickening wet sound. Blood drips from the sword to the black asphalt below him.

"Rafe?" I say, my voice tentative.

He turns toward me and I see two slashes across his face, leaking blood down his cheek.

I rush to him. "You're bleeding."

He reaches a hand up and prods the wound, wincing a little when his fingers connect with the ripped flesh.

"I'll be all right. I heal quickly. We have to get to the Faerie portal before we're attacked again."

He takes my hand and together we sprint through the alley and down streets. I don't know where he's taking me, but after he saved my life, I'm willing to trust him.

By the time we reach the outskirts of the woods, I'm panting from our run and coming down from my adrenaline high.

"It's just a little farther," he says as we pick our way through the trees. I'm thankful I opted for boots tonight instead of something strappy.

After about ten minutes of traversing the forest, Rafe stops.

I look around, not seeing anything.

Next to me Rafe has gone statue still. His eyes are closed and the only thing moving is his mouth, but the words he utters are too quiet for me to hear. A moment later a flash of light blinds me, forcing me to squeeze my eyes shut. When I open them again after the light dissipates, an undulating wall has formed between the trunks of two trees.

"The portal to Faerie," Rafe explains. "Only a fae of royal blood can open or close it."

It's a semi-translucent wall with iridescent colors shifting over its surface. I can still see the forest through it.

"Let's go," he says and starts forward.

"Rafe, wait."

He stops and glances back at me, his face expressionless.

"If I follow you into Faerie, my life will never be the same."

Will I ever see Sloan again? My parents? My hopes and dreams have always been grounded in this world, not another one.

He must see the panic in my gaze because his eyes soften. "No, Princess, it won't. But just because the future is uncertain doesn't mean it won't be the greatest adventure of your life."

A rakish smile spreads over his face, giving me the impression this fae lives for adventure. I'd be lying if I said a seed of excitement hadn't just been planted in my heart as well.

Faerie. Who knows what mysteries and wonders I'll discover there.

Taking a deep breath, I take Rafe's outstretched hand and step through the portal with him into the unknown.

The Flame of Stars

Crystal D. Grant

There used to be more stars in the sky. But one by one, they are fading. Just like the people of my tribe.

I stand before the village torch and stare into the blaze that weakens with every life lost. Soon the flame will go out and the sky over my village will be void of stars. My people will be no more.

The cries in the wooden hut behind me cut my spirit. Another life taken by the dark plague. *Eternal One, will you do nothing?*

A soft, wet nose presses against my fist. I look down into the brown eyes of my dog, Bravor, and stroke his black fur, wincing at the wails of the grieving parents.

I should pay my respects. Chicco was one of my regular attendees during story time. But his family will wish to receive nothing from me, the village outsider. So I remain where I am, clutching the star amulet around my neck.

Somehow, mine remains bright. I am among the few who have remained healthy while so many amulets have been darkened with the plague. The tribe is but a shadow of what it used to be.

A young man joins me at the torch, his tanned face pale and pinched. He no longer sports the broad, muscular frame that brought him so much pride and female admiration. His black hair hangs limply around his ears. Dark circles frame his tear-shaped eyes. His amulet still shines steadily, but not with the same intensity.

"What is it, Kebo?" I can't help but ask, afraid of the answer.

He swallows and looks up at the sky. "Dari grows worse."

A band tightens around my chest. Kebo's whole family carries the plague. His father has passed, and now he faces losing Dari—another one of my faithful listeners.

Did the Eternal One not care for his people?

The village priests would be shocked at my boldness. They spend their days pouring out their prayers and offerings before the One who can heal them, yet nothing happens. It seems He is no longer satisfied with our offerings. Why doesn't He answer?

"Grandfather speaks of going to the Eternal Flame."

I suck in a breath. "He hasn't the strength for such a trip."

Kebo sighs. "But the people grow desperate, Ayza. The strong must stay to guard the village."

A chill dances up and down my skin. The shadowlings lurk outside the village perimeters every night, waiting for an opening to break through the line of defense. They know we grow weak. I hold my amulet tighter.

I've heard the legend of the star that rests on earth yet still burns. Just an ember will spark life back into the whole village.

So the story is told.

I struggle to believe it, especially as I watch people die. Death seems to follow me.

My parents traveled to this tribe two summers ago when I was but thirteen, hoping for a better life. Instead, my mother was one of the first victims of the plague, and my father fell before a shadowling a few seasons later.

I became a poor orphan, the girl with no dowry. I was given a blanket and a sleeping place in the community tent, but nothing more.

I finger the dark hair sweeping my jawline. My braid was cut off to signify my lowly status. No warrior would wish for a wife who brings nothing but a mouth to feed. As the resident storyteller, I earn enough silver pebbles to trade for food and clothing, but I remain alone, distant from the rest. This may be my tribe, but they are not *my* people.

Still yet, my heart grows burdened. Just because I have been left alone does not mean I want others to suffer the same fate.

But if no one can be spared, who will go?

A seed of an idea takes root in my mind, taking my breath away with its boldness. There is nothing I can do for anyone here. My help is not always welcome.

But what if I can do something outside of the village? What if I can earn my tribe's respect and save us all?

I gulp and look down at my dog, who stares up at me as if he senses the direction my mind has taken. He will stay by my side, no matter where I go. The thought brings me comfort. No one else will miss my absence.

Kebo turns to me suddenly. His amulet flickers. "Ayza, you must remain healthy. I cannot bear the thought ..."

The depth of his dark eyes startles me. He has always been a friend—despite his family's misgivings and my detachment. But surely he does not feel anything more?

As much as it pains me, I harden myself against his emotion. Any girl would be proud to have Kebo's affection, but I cannot claim it. My mind is already made up.

"I'll be fine, Kebo." I give him a small smile to ease his worry, then walk away to prepare for my journey.

I leave before dawn, skirting the nighttime guards. My leather bag is full of dried buffalo meat, as well as a rolled-up map, drawn from memory of the stories told. My woolen cloak covers my one-shouldered tunic and the dagger at my hip. Bravor trots beside me silently.

Fear sends my pulse racing as I approach the border of the encampment. The faint light of dawn stretches in the eastern sky, but will it be enough to deter shadowlings? What if they still wait in the darkness for a sign of weakness to enter the village?

A black line of trees signals where my village ends. I clutch the strap on my bag with white fingers. What am I doing?

Saving my people. And I can't do that if I cower in fear.

The thought bolsters my courage enough for me to straighten my shoulders and march into the woods.

All is still and calm. I tiptoe through the fallen leaves with bated breath, listening and peering through the tangled mess of trees for a sign of the shadowlings.

I've never laid eyes on them, but I've heard the reports. Black cloaks mingle with the darkness, shrouding invisible forms that float over the earth. Two cold, indigo points gleam from underneath the hood, where eyes are assumed to be. They attack when all is dark and still, filling their victims with paralyzing fear. It is said they can fill a soul with so much darkness the essence of life is forced out.

The thought sends a shudder through my form and Bravor presses closer. Sucking in a deep breath of the early morning air, I set my chin and continue on.

After two days of nonstop walking, I still do not encounter shadowlings, not even at night when I settle down to sleep for a few hours. Which is strange, but I don't question the respite. Instead, I thank the Eternal One for His protection. But boredom, sore feet, and bone-deep weariness become my companions.

The silence is deafening, and I miss Kebo's chatter. He is the only one who talks to me as an equal. To the adults, I am the girl with no means. To the children, I am the storyteller. But to Kebo, I am a friend, even though I have nothing to offer.

By now, the tribe will have found my message, but I've no fear of pursuit. If anything, they will believe they've seen the last of the outsider.

Bravor is a constant source of security and company, save when he scampers off to pursue a wild hare. Sometimes he brings one back to me, so I rarely go hungry. At night, I sleep under a star-studded sky that takes my breath away. Will our piece of the sky ever shine like that again?

I aim for the Blue Mountains on the horizon, where stories claim the Eternal Flame rests on a small mount lit with an ethereal glow. As I draw closer, I search for a glowing mountain, but all is shrouded in shadows. A prick of disappointment, followed by fear, jabs at me. Am I going in the right direction? What if there *is* no Eternal Flame?

But I press on. I cannot go back to the tribe with empty hands.

Soon I approach a cluster of foothills. They are not steep, so I decide to go over, rather than skirt around them. The climb is long and hot, and I soon shed my cloak, tying it around my waist.

At the top, I pause to behold the view. My heart pounds like a drum. The mountains stand tall and proud, and there, right in front of me, is a small peak that pulses with a soft, blue glow.

I've found it. Sweat pours down my smiling face and I bite back a squeal. Soon I will carry the flame back to my village. Soon I will save my tribe.

I take a step, but a low growl from Bravor gives me pause. I peer down into the valley below. My blood runs cold. Multiple dark shapes lurk in the shade of nearby trees and ledges.

My lungs betray me, and a weight drops on my shoulders. I drop to my knees, tears stinging my eyes. Why had I not considered the mountain might be guarded by shadowlings? How can I ever hope to pass them with only a dog and a dagger?

I bury my face and tears in Bravor's thick fur while he stares down at the creatures. Time is lost, along with the hope I had carried. What am I to do?

After a while, I stir and look again. The creatures are still there. If anything, there are more of them now as sunset approaches.

I clench my fists, tempted to scream out at the faint stars mocking me above. Instead, I whisper, "Why did You allow me to come all this way for nothing?" I swipe a runaway tear. "Why do You care so little for us? Why do You not come?"

The skies are silent. The red sun sinks below the horizon, bathing the area in twilight. A snap sounds behind me. I jerk around.

A shadowy figure emerges from the edge of the hill, floating over the ground. Indigo eyes pierce my soul. My skin tingles with ice-cold fear.

Another shadowling appears to my right, its dark cloak lost in the surrounding dusk. A whimper escapes my throat when a third arrives on the left. I stumble back to the edge of the hill. Bravor lets out a snarl and bounds before me, his fur bristled. All three advance and my dog pounces. My foot catches a root and I tumble down the hill with a scream. Bravor's howl fills my ears before I hit the bottom.

And darkness swallows me.

I awake on a cot in a small room with a crackling fire. Someone hums in another room. My cloak covers me and Bravor lays at my feet. I sit up with a groan, though I feel none of the pain I expected. The humming stops and a man enters the room with gray-streaked dark hair and a thick beard. "Are you well, lass?"

Panic robs me of my voice for a moment. What happened? Where am I? Who is this stranger?

The man smiles. "I am Sol. Do not fret over the shadow creatures. They cannot harm you here." His voice is hoarse and low, but gentle. "That was quite a fall you took. Best watch your step if you hope to reach the Eternal Flame."

I shrink back. "How could you know where I am headed?"

"Why, Bravor here filled me in."

I gape at him. "You understand my dog?"

"Well, Ayza, it's either that or you talk in your sleep." He winks and leaves the room.

Startled at his use of my name, I gasp and stare at Bravor. "Did you tell him?"

Bravor cocks his head at me, and I roll my eyes at myself. I must have hit my head harder than I thought.

"Let's get out of here." I pull my cloak back on, grab my bag from the table beside me, and leave the room.

Sol is seated at a small, wooden table. My stomach betrays me with a loud growl at the spread of fruits and nuts.

"Please, nourish yourself before you leave." He holds a hand out to the empty chair.

It is foolish to stay in the home of a stranger, but I am famished. Bravor will defend me if necessary. So I sit.

"How did I get here?" I demand.

"Does it matter?"

I shrug. "I'd like to know."

His dark eyes gleam. "Ah, the wish to always know. But some things are meant to be unknown. The important thing is that you are safe from the shadowlings. That is sufficient for the moment."

What a strange, exasperating man. But funnily enough, I do not feel unsafe. Maybe a little frustrated at his roundabout way of answering questions, but not fearful. I reach for a plate of blueberries. A cup of something hot and delicious warms my belly. It smells of cocoa beans and cozy nights.

Sol folds his arms on the table and allows me a few moments to eat. His silence is unnerving, but not in a threatening way, so I shrug it off. Bravor flops down on the floor, but my traitor dog chooses to lay beside the stranger instead of me.

When I am nearly finished, Sol speaks again. "So, why do you aim for the Eternal Flame?"

I wonder at the wisdom in telling him, but there seems to be no reason not to. "My tribe suffers from the dark plague and needs a spark from the Flame."

"Did you come all this way for them?"

"I'm here, aren't I?"

He cocks his head. "One can often do the right thing but with the wrong motivation."

I take another sip, trying not to squirm in the chair under his scrutiny.

"Why are you here alone?" Sol reaches down and pats Bravor on the head. "A dog is a fine traveling companion, to be sure, but why did you not ask for help?"

My lips tighten. "No one would help me if I asked." Not even the Eternal One it seems.

He cocks a brow. "Not one?"

Kebo comes to mind and guilt crowds my annoyance. "Maybe one, but he's too ill."

"It's not too late to ask for help."

I frown at him. "Who? You?" He looks more robust than Kebo's grandfather, to be sure, but he is still an elder.

He laughs out loud. "I've taken many a journey in my days, and I know my way around the mountains." His laughter fades and he leans forward, pinning me to my seat with his gaze. "You don't have to be alone, Ayza."

My insides shiver. I still don't know how he knows my name, but something tells me he would just say I don't need to know.

I eat the last of the berries and pull my bag over my shoulder. Sol rises with me and reaches for the plate of nuts. "Here, you will need to keep your strength up for the rest of the journey." He pours them into my bag. Then he takes a flask and fills it with water from a pail and gives me a wink. "Let's go, shall we?"

Unsure how to refuse his offer of help, I follow him mutely. Bravor plods after me on his padded feet. When Sol stops and looks down at me, I feel compelled to thank him, but it comes out strained and awkward.

His face creases into a smile. "All you have to do is ask. We will see you to the Eternal Flame, little one. But be sure you've taken this mission for the right reasons, or it shall fail."

His words are cryptic, but I don't wish to waste time asking him to explain. I step outside and down the path leading from his porch. Bravor is back at his usual spot by my side. I turn a corner and inhale.

Before me stands the little mountain, glowing so that it seems to beckon me. Sol's cabin sits at the very foot of it. In my excitement, I spin to call out to Sol. When I don't find him behind me, I run back around the bend, where he must have already fallen behind. But there is no sign of him. The path is empty. Puzzled, I go all the way back to the cabin, Bravor on my heels. The little cabin is dark and closed up. Sol is nowhere to be seen.

Relief wrestles with disappointment. I did not want the strange man to join me, but his shallow promises still sting. Why did he offer to help if he had no intention of fulfilling it?

Turning my back on the cabin, I resolve to do what I set out to do in the first place: take a spark back to my village. Alone.

The glowing mountain is small and looks easy to climb, but not for a dog, so I find a safe place for Bravor and order him to wait. He lays down under a ledge, his gaze trusting and loyal.

Then I start to climb. Soon I am puffing and sweating, but my mind is too busy to notice. First it goes ahead to where the star is. Will it be easy to spot? How will I claim a spark?

Then I think of the village. Has the plague claimed any more lives? How is Kebo? And Dari? Will I make it in time to save her?

Soon, I reach the peak—a flat plateau covered in blue grass. My heart skips in anticipation as I walk to the center of the mountain and look around. But there is nothing there. No star. No flame. Not so much as a rock. It's not even glowing up here anymore.

I shake my head as my fingers curl into fists. "Eternal One, I do not understand," I grind out. "Where is it?"

Silence is the only answer I get, and it hits me then. There is no flame to take back home. My journey brought me to an empty mountain. I have no way of saving my people.

A sob breaks through the tightness in my chest. How can I go back home and face them? How can I return home and watch one by one as they all die, until the plague finally takes me?

I sit and wrap my arms around my legs. Fear and despair wrap themselves around me, as strongly as if a shadowling had me in its grip. "Eternal One, please help me," I whisper past trembling lips.

"Ayza."

The familiar voice—low and hoarse—brings me around. Sol stands a few yards away, his eyes brimming with compassion. Before I can respond, a band of shadowlings approach from behind him.

"Sol, look out!" I jump up and grab my dagger.

But Sol faces them head on with an outstretched hand. "Be gone."

Light radiates from his being, shooting from his hand and disintegrating every one of the dark forms. Then he turns back to me. The light settles in his eyes, shines from his skin, captivating me, drawing me closer.

Shock and realization hit me at once as the story of the Eternal Flame becomes clear. It was Sol all along. He is the star—the Eternal One Himself, dwelling on the mountain.

And now He stands before me. Shame fills me at all the times I questioned and challenged Him. I drop my gaze. Why would He even bother with someone of such little faith?

"I told you, all you had to do was ask, Ayza." His voice is warm and soothing, with not an ounce of scorn.

I shake my head. "But why me?"

"Because you are not afraid to talk to me or ask me hard questions."

My brow furrows and I look up. "But the elders say we shouldn't question You."

Sol holds up a finger. "To question my existence or ability, yes. But that is not the same as asking for the sake of understanding or knowing Me. So long as you continue to trust Me." He rests a hand on my shoulder; I can feel the strength residing in it. "What do you wish to ask, child?"

"Why do You not answer our prayers?" I hold my breath at my boldness.

Sol sobers and a shadow passes over his face. "It is not always for my children to know My intention, but that does not mean I do not hear or answer."

"But why do You allow Your people to die?"

"Death comes to all who live on this earth, and it is harsh and painful." His eyes cloud over as if the thought hurts him. "Children are left without mothers. Wives are bereft of their husbands. It's a harsh reality of this imperfect world created by the choices made."

I stiffen. "So we are being punished?"

"No, Ayza, I am not so cold. But I do allow life to continue on its natural course. And sometimes bad things happen. Life is hard. It's tough. But if you believe in Me, trust Me, I will share every part of it with you."

He gazes deep into my eyes. "Do you question My existence, Ayza?"

"No." I always knew He existed, but the truth burns within me now.

"And do you trust me?"

My throat closes up and I lower my head. "I want to," I whisper. "Will you help me?"

He nudges my chin up with his finger, still smiling. "I will." Then he leans forward and kisses my forehead. Warmth fills my being and I know I will never again doubt He loves and hears me.

Sol reaches for my hand and places something smooth and warm in my palm. I look down to see the clearest stone I have ever seen. The edges are as smooth as glass and within its depths, a blue flame burns.

"You were willing to risk your life to save an old man from shadowlings." Sol smiles. "You are worthy of carrying the spark back to your village."

Sol leads me to the edge of the mesa. "Tell them what you have learned here, Ayza." His voice drops in fervor. "They make their prayers and their offerings, yet they miss what really matters. I yearn for their hearts, to commune with them so that they might know Me. Tell our people what we can share."

I nod, suddenly anxious to return. Does Kebo know he can talk to the Eternal One? Will the elders want to hear it from me, the village outsider? How can I teach the children who come to listen to the stories I tell?

He puts his hands on my shoulders. His touch reminds me of my father's, warm and safe. "I will always be with you, Ayza. Never doubt that." Then He steps back and gives me a single nod.

The time has come for me to leave, but it takes every ounce of willpower to turn away from Him. My soul longs to stay in his presence. But I have been given a mission. My tribe needs me, needs to hear what they can share with the Eternal One.

I look over my shoulder, but He is already gone. Sorrow lances me, but I am comforted by His last words. And I do not question them.

It is the evening of the third day when I approach the line of trees near home. Bravor gives a happy yip and runs on ahead. I reach into the bag and clutch the stone, its warmth filling me. My steps are quick and sure in my anticipation to see them all again, to place the glass stone in the torch so that it will heal.

But screams pierce the air, cutting my joy short. I break into a run and dash through the trees. Then I slide to a stop to behold the scene.

Shadowlings have broken through. They storm through the village square. Bravor stands guard before Kebo, who is on his knees, clutching his chest. The head elder cowers on the ground by the flame. Fear—rank and cold—hangs everywhere.

Anger fills me and I march onward. The shadowlings will not claim these souls, not after all I've gone through to bring back the spark. I lift the stone up high over my head and shout. "Be gone!"

The stone lights up, filling every corner of the village. The shadowlings shriek and then disappear, leaving blessed silence and relief behind.

The people rise from their hiding spots, murmuring in shock and staring at me in wonder. But I stare at the stone. It is gray and empty now. The spark is gone.

I look up as Kebo approaches. His frame is thinner now than when I left, his skin still tinged with gray. His amulet is dim. The plague still grips the people and there is no more spark to light the torch.

What have I done?

"Ayza, you came back." Kebo's voice is soft, but his expression intense. "And you've saved us."

I shake my head. No, I didn't. I've failed. There is no way to save them now.

Sol's voice drifts in my memories. "Be sure you've taken this mission for the right reason, or it shall fail."

My fingers drift to where my amulet hangs. It still shines brightly. My breath quickens. Will it work? Am I willing to give my light so that the others can live?

The answer comes quickly. Yes, I am. The people must be given a chance to know the Eternal One. If I can't share it, He will find a way to reach them.

I walk to the torch, aware of the people following me. Swallowing my tears and hesitation away, I hold up my amulet and speak out loud. "Eternal One, please take my light so that they might live."

There's a gasp behind me. For a moment, nothing happens. Then my amulet flashes. My light grows and stretches out for the torch. The torch flickers and brightens, drawing strength from my amulet. Soon the village flame glimmers and burns in all its strength.

And my amulet goes dark.

I glance around as the people murmur. Kebo takes a deep breath with wide eyes, his skin glowing with health. Men and women hold up their hands in shock. Dari emerges from her hut and runs to Kebo's mother. The elders stare up at the torch in amazement.

It is done. My people are healed. I meet Kebo's eyes and give him a smile, hoping he can see how much I appreciate his friendship. Then my legs give out and I crumple to the ground.

"No!" Kebo cries and gathers me in his arms. "What have you done?"

I swallow past a dry throat, knowing my time draws near. My amulet is flameless. But I feel no regret. Only love for the people standing around me.

Kebo's face contorts, and he grabs his own amulet. "I won't let you die for us. Take my light for hers, Eternal One."

I shake my head. "No, Kebo. You must stay so that you can know the Eternal One."

The head elder kneels at my feet, his face haggard. "You have brought us to shame, Ayza. Forgive us, Eternal One, for how we've treated this girl." He holds his amulet up.

One by one, the people standing over me offer their own amulet. I do not understand what they are doing, but soon the amulets begin to glow. Small streaks of light reach out for me, absorbed by the lifeless amulet on my chest. Then the lights fade, and I glance down. My amulet shines again. And so does everyone else's.

Kebo lets out a glad cry and crushes me to his chest. I breathe in his strength, trying to wrap my mind around what has just happened.

The head elder reaches for my hands and helps me to my feet. "Dear Ayza, you brave girl. We are so sorry for the way we shunned you. Please pardon our faults."

I think of the way Sol smiled at me, despite my weaknesses and my shame, and I smile back at the elder. "Of course, I forgive you."

Dari squeezes in and wraps her arms around my waist. Her mother draws close and clasps her hands together. "I too, am at fault. Please take a cot in my cabin. That is until you are ready to claim your own hut." She casts a sly glance at Kebo, who beams back. My cheeks heat, but I nod to accept her offer.

Chicco's parents stand to the side, and I go to them. "I am sorry for your loss."

The father gives a sad smile. "I am thankful no more children will die of the dark plague."

"What happened, Ayza?" the head elder asks.

I look around at the people. Kebo, Dari, and their mother. The elders. Chicco's family. I open my mouth to do as Sol asked. I share my story with my tribe.

My people.

Wielder of Light

R. M. Scott

Summer solstice brought gifts.

And curses.

I walked to the cliff's edge of my mountain hideout and gazed at the overlook. Black locks of hair blew in front of my eyes, the rest tied back with a leather band. I missed home, but the hurt from rejection curled inside me.

The obsidian fortress of the Cursed, wielders of darkness, blended into the volcanic cliffs of The Kingdom of Renaissance. It sat above the ocean's edge, purposely engineered to catch the first shadow of the setting sun. Its jagged edges proclaimed ownership of the isle. Behind the fortress, labyrinths of city stretched beyond where I'd ever gone.

My gaze trailed across the bay to the Island of the Dawn. Atop it glimmered the luminescent limestone temple of the Gifted, a single tower reaching toward the sky.

I glanced down at my hands, half-expecting light to spark at my fingertips. I'd developed a gift, an ability to heal by wielding light, on my seventeenth solstice, but it came with a grave cost. Since that day, I'd stayed hidden for two months in the wilds, unable to flee or return home, lest I suffer a fate worse than death.

The ashen sky brightened with a few more rays of sunrise. It was almost time for the morning hunt of ravens. I didn't have long to practice before I'd have to hole away again.

I rubbed my hands together. Static warmth built between my palms, increasing at their centers. I pulled them apart. A peach glow, its outer edges a creamy white, emanated visibly. I focused on making it spin. The glow flipped within the vortex. Its strength increased as it caught momentum and spun faster and faster.

Wielding like this in the open was dangerous—I knew that. If found, I'd be locked away in the temple and forced to heal the majority, the Cursed. I'd absorb their suffering and hold it in my body. It was a life sentence, leading to inevitable insanity or seizing death.

Once, wielders of darkness had to carry this curse. When they wielded darkness, it caused disease and injury, but that was before they'd learned to enslave wielders of light to hold their pain for them.

But this tiny ball of light in my hands could keep me safe—if I could figure out how to expand it into a star.

Stars contained enough light to fill every molecule of my being. If I could create that, I wouldn't be able to absorb the Cursed's pain. I'd be full of light instead and turn into an unbreakable healer. But stars were only found in fables in ancient storybooks.

Still, every fable carried a fraction of truth. A possibility.

One that might've been buried away to keep the Gifted held down. Or so I hoped.

It was only taking a lot longer to make a star than I thought it would.

I continued practicing with smaller light, training until Elex, my only friend, came to shadow me to try for the star. Otherwise, my location would be given away by my bright light, and I'd be captured.

The light within my hands spun faster. I pushed my hands closer together, condensing the light into a ball. My hands vibrated from the pressure, but I held strong, forcing the orb smaller and smaller until it completed into a tiny fleck.

Small, but it held power to heal.

My power.

I closed my hands around the light orb and guided it into the pocket of my gray tunic that fit snug to mid-thigh. A brief happiness spilled through me. I'd made the orb quick and without a hiccup. I was improving.

I climbed down from the cliff's edge, traversing the volcanic rock. My leather boots kept my footing steady with textured soles, and my thick wool leggings acted as a buffer to scratches and slices.

"Lera," a familiar voice called.

A smile broke through my isolation. Elex stood at the mouth of my cave in a green hooded cape. A leather belt hung low across his tan tunic. A coin purse and knife scabbard looped around the belt and rested over his hip. He grinned, showing perfectly straight teeth. His jawline had grown defined and his build thicker. If I hadn't known him since childhood, I'd assume he was like any other Cursed, waiting to turn me in and collect an award for catching a Gifted.

But he didn't believe what others did—that all Gifted were soulless, empty vessels meant to hold suffering until broken. At least not after he'd learned I was one.

"When are you going to come live in the Quarters?" He lowered his hood and uncovered loose dark curls. Their pitch-black coloring matched the freckles resting under his lime-green eyes.

I turned and looked toward the waves. He'd found an abandoned apartment in the heart of the city. Scoped it out for me. It was a sweet gesture, but in truth, it was impossible to hide me. "You know I can't. Even if you offered me the world, I couldn't come back."

"But I miss seeing you in the city. It's not the same without you. You know I'd protect you." He half-smiled, and an endearing longing gathered around my heart.

We had grown up in the same grouping, those born between spring and autumn solstice. Sat by one another in classes. Snuck into the basement of the great library beneath the fortress to read fables. One summer, we'd gone almost every morning before school dawned, finding new books to dust off, some a thousand years old.

Though no one had ever caught us with those forbidden books, we had had one close call, and, as always, we had protected one another. After we'd found the storybook with the star, we'd been separated and interrogated over what we'd read. He'd defended me. Said I'd read nothing of stars, and I said the same for him.

I met his gaze, full of persuasion. "I can't go back. I'm worth nothing more than a vessel now to the people of Renaissance."

Elex reached in his pocket and pulled out a cloth bag. He handed it to me, his outstretched hand shaking barely enough to notice. "Not to me."

I took the bag and shoved it in my other side pocket. The weight gave away its contents, the same flaxseed bread and goat cheese as last time.

His mouth turned to a straight line. "I'd hide you. With my curse, I could."

Elex could dim any light, make it disappear. Make my shine less hard to find, but I didn't want to be locked away or hidden.

Freedom was worth more.

I shook my head. "No, they'd break you for it. I couldn't stand it."

If caught, he'd be surrounded by a group of the Cursed. They'd wield darkness and throw it at him until it consumed him. It would turn him into a soulless wanderer. A mindless body that meandered the wilds until death found him.

I nudged his side. "Besides, I have an orb. Before we practice, let's go for a quick hunt."

His eyebrows narrowed. "Lera, the ravens are getting closer. Each day. Closer. They might spot us."

"But look." I took the orb out of my pocket, then tossed it into the air. It started floating toward the field. Then, as if alive with divine intelligence, it changed path, weaving its way through the tall ocher grasses.

"Come on." I grabbed his hand and felt his hesitation as I tugged him forward, but he came. He always came.

We ran over lava rock interspersed with brush, grasses, and limestone, following the tiny twinkle.

I laughed, the warmth of Elex's hand comforting. The lessened worry on his face livened my energy.

We were free. Together.

The twinkle stopped and lowered below the grasses. Its glow brightened, the never-failing signal that it found an injury it could heal.

I slowed and let go of Elex's hand. Walking carefully, I approached the marked location. I pulled back the grasses. Hidden within lay a rabbit. Its limbs stretched out, flat as it could be.

Elex picked it up by its gray ears. Puffs of white hair jutted out of its chin. "It looks dead."

"My light's never wrong. Life energy is constantly working to heal us, and the light can sense it. The rabbit's still alive." I held out my hands and called the light back with a silent mental request. It snapped back to my palm. I closed my fingers around it. Then I stepped forward and applied the orb against the rabbit's chest. Feeling resistance, I waited, holding my hand steady until the light absorbed into its fur.

White light emanated around the rabbit. Then its racing heartbeats thrummed against my fingers.

I smiled, feeling its life awaken with my touch.

The seemingly dead rabbit opened its shiny gray-blue eyes and wiggled its nose.

I laughed and offered my hands. Elex placed the rabbit within them.

The rabbit cuddled against my chest. Its ears tickled my chin. Deep satisfaction rolled through me, a life force connection of earth and sky.

Elex tilted his head. "I swear it was dead. It must've startled and froze. Maybe from the mechanical ravens released before dawn?"

I ran my fingers over its furry back, the touch warm and calming. "Yes. I've heard that a rabbit's heart can stop out of fear. It would be almost dead but not quite."

Carefully, I lowered to a crouch and set it down.

The rabbit hopped once, then bounded through the brush, disappearing.

"Well," Elex said. "Now that you've finished the hunt, are you ready to try for the star again?"

I stood and looked at him. His eyes seemed brighter than before, but the worry had returned. "Yes, I have to."

"It's getting more dangerous. Last time, they released the ravens early. They knew, Lera. Someone must've spotted the light."

My head lowered. He had the most to lose for helping me—he'd proven he was the best at wielding the darkness in our grouping. He'd released more fog than some of the masters, earning an open ticket to any trade in the city. "I'm sorry. This time, cloud me first? I'll be more patient."

He sighed. "You know I hate this. It's riskier than hiding you out."

I gave a smirk. "But you still show up every third day to try."

He looked to the sky. "Maybe stars are only a fable, Lera," Elex said, his voice pained. "We should be more calculated. Lower risk. Keep you safe as long as possible. One day, I might rise up and be able to change the law to free the Gifted. My curse is strong."

But no happiness could thrive under anticipation of being the temple's healer—locked away without a morsel of freedom to explore and use my gift. "Elex, surviving years in hiding is less likely than the fable carrying a morsel of truth. Just admit it. You felt the power when you read the story."

His shoulders relaxed as if giving in. "I wouldn't keep trying if I didn't."

We'd found the book with the star hidden beneath a trapped door among artifacts. When we'd opened it, light shot out of it, pure white like starlight.

In it, there was a drawing of a young man holding a star, called the Unbreakable Healer. He'd washed ashore the forbidden isle of the Cursed. He should've been thrown back to the sea to drown, as any intermingling between the Cursed and the Gifted was forbidden, but a young maiden nursed him back to health in secret.

Together, their powers increased like no powers before them. Instead of light and dark weakening each other as opposites, they strengthened each other.

Eventually, the girl could wield darkness so powerfully that she could harness the sky.

And the boy could craft a star in one movement and heal without taking on suffering.

Enlightened, they built the temple and taught healing through balance.

I sighed. It was as if that magical realm could still exist. "Remember how angry the Cursed elders were when they thought we found that book?"

"Stars are evil's way of provoking doubt in official teachings." He rolled his eyes as he repeated their warning.

I grimaced. "Why would they try so hard to convince us stars weren't real if they are only fables?"

Elex released a long breath. "It felt wrong to me, like a secret meant to be set free."

I nodded. "It's almost like the book found us."

We stared at each other for a moment, a silent debate of how much to believe in the power of the story.

Elex took a wide stance. "If we're going to do this, we'd better get started. Ready?" he asked.

I exhaled slowly and cleared my thoughts. "Yes."

Elex rubbed his hands together, then parted them, palms facing me. Dark clouds emerged and flowed toward me. He held steady, releasing until a dark fog surrounded me in a cool, misty shield. Then he stopped, lowered his hands to his sides, and waited.

On cue, I rubbed my hands together. A small light ignited between my palms. To give it high-frequency energy to grow, I imagined home before I'd come into my gift. Walks with my sister, Leila, to the boardwalk to watch the ships dock. Helping Mother bake croissants filled with blackberries and cream. Learning to forge steel with Papa.

The light spun, and I fed it all the good energy I could muster. It grew, its creamy peach rim deepening to a thick milky white.

I was getting closer.

I smiled, but then the memory of Papa's face when I told him I'd created light came back. And next, Mother's shouts of wishing I'd died instead of disgracing them. And finally, Leila's tear-streaked face as I said goodbye before I ran.

The orb's spin slowed.

"No, no," I cried. "Elex, how do I keep the light from fading?"

"The story said true power comes when you open your heart, Lera."

I focused on the orb, trying to open up, but my heart's door slammed shut. I directed my thoughts from the pain and to Elex's hand as we had run. I conjured warmth. Security. How he never gave up on me.

But the orb didn't move.

Instead, the ache of homelessness rose up, the yearning for a place to belong. The empty throb in my belly rotated with stabbing pains. The unyielding yearning for a companion, a word, or a touch growled from loneliness.

I remembered the sweet applause of acceptance after I'd recited my first curse against the Gifted at six, the first of seven poems of the beliefs of the Cursed. Joy and hugs after Father enveloped me in fog during my purification ceremony at ten, a ritual to protect against developing a gift.

But I'd become what no one wanted, a wielder of light, an outcast.

Emotions corded around my neck, making it hard to swallow. It was too much. All too much to overcome. And it only built every day, worsening like shadows appearing in the night in the corner of the eye, my heart racing, mind cracking.

I was breaking.

I clenched my teeth and closed my hands around the orb. Tears rolled down my cheeks. I squeezed the light, molding it into a tiny ball. Then I slipped it into my pocket for later. For light in the cave. For comfort when I was the most alone.

"Do you want to try again?" Elex asked.

I shook my head and wiped my tears. "No, I can't. It's ..."

"Lera, never abandon hope."

My eyes met his, and desperation coiled inside me. "Maybe this is pointless. Maybe we don't have enough skill to make a star. Maybe you're right, a place hidden away in the city is the best option."

My eyes started to well again, and I brushed the wet away before more tears could fall. "The rejection is too much, Elex. I can't sustain the feeling of love long enough before it cuts in."

Elex stood still, the cool breeze tugging at the ragged edges of his cape. "I'm here for you."

It wasn't enough, but I couldn't tell him that. Not when he'd risked his life for me. When he still did now. His devotion should be enough, but the hurt was more. My heart only ached and twisted in ways it shouldn't.

The Cursed only wanted me to use me.

The daydreams of finding a new home, sailing to a fertile isle with mango trees and clear streams brimming with rainbow fish, was an illusion. I'd be lucky to jump into the sea before the ravens targeted me.

"One more try? Please, Lera?" he whispered.

His plea stirred a reckless abandonment inside me, reaching for a last chance. "Yes, but don't cloud me this time."

"Lera, they'll spot you."

"Just don't, Elex." My voice came out harsh, but it was the only path I hadn't yet tried. I had to give it my everything.

If caught, I'd tell the Cursed Elex had found me. At least he'd get the reward for my capture.

I took a deep breath and caught Elex's gaze. His brow crinkled in concern, but he didn't question me.

I rubbed my palms together. A faint glow emerged, weak and beaten down. I closed my eyes and drew back the memories of youth, of painting the walled rock around home with sunlit yellow and cranberry red.

Mother had laughed. Father didn't appreciate it as much but still let it be until the second rain washed it away. I let the memory of Leila's birth spill in. How I'd felt it then, the warm glow of new life entering this realm. Her tiny fingers wrapped around mine.

I opened my eyes. The glow had strengthened into an orb. I focused, centering my energy on making it spin, infusing it with heart, the strongest power. I awakened the love I still had inside for my family, though they rejected me. The abiding love for Elex, for staking out the abandoned apartment, for my grouping as we learned and grew together.

The light brightened and spun, its speed and brilliance increasing tenfold, building momentum with each turn.

But like clockwork, the hurt moved in. Renaissance, my home, wanting to cage me. From young ages, children were taught that the Gifted were meant to hold the pain of others. My sister would be turned against me in her next year, just as my parents had been, and the generation before them. But instead of trying to quell the hurt, I let it flare up hot. I let it enter and stay.

Anger burned through me at the injustice, and the light grew more vibrant, its edges turning sunrise orange.

"Lera," Elex called. "You need cover. Can I help now?"

I didn't want him to calm this, to cradle it. I released more, holding the light in my hands until it burst with crimson flares.

The orb grew hotter and hotter. My hands caught on fire and blazed. I screamed in pain.

"Lera, stop." Elex raised both his hands and released dark fog. The chilled air flowed toward me, then split. It encircled, blanketing me and my light.

But instead of before, he kept releasing, strengthening his force.

He knew I could burn out. Turn into a lifeless meanderer by way of overusing light.

My body heaved. I'd pushed too far.

And yet, Elex still tried to protect me, though I could take him down with me.

Elex continued to release his curse to thicken the blanket. The fog strengthened into clouds, which then hurled into a powerful wind.

My hair whipped. The flare hovered between my hands, its heat making sweat pour from my brow.

Elex's fog darkened, giving more power to withhold mine.

But I didn't fight it. I sucked it in. All the darkness, all the hurt.

The clouds roared and crackled.

The fire between my palms turned violet. My body heat rose until dizziness came. My breaths came out hot. My tongue felt on fire. Yet, I did not stop. I absorbed the hurt.

White light beamed from between my fingers. Its power strengthened, feeding off Elex's energy. It grew brighter. The light would shoot straight into the heavens, giving away my location, but not before it might explode.

And Elex's storm surged louder, more powerful, creating more clouds that raged about me.

My body shook from the opposing pressures.

We were the eye of the storm.

Dark fog closed in around me.

Boom!

Lightning erupted out of my hands, connecting to Eli's clouds like a thunderstorm.

My body weakened, and I hunched over.

Then, the light between my hands sucked in the storm, like a white hole, compressing it to a tiny star. I closed my fingers around it in a fist. "We did it. We made a star."

Elex dropped his arms. "Lera," he said, his voice weak. He swayed, the color in his face drained, and fell to his knees.

I stumbled my way to him and collapsed beside him. "No, Elex! I didn't mean for it to hurt you."

"I am the fool," he whispered. "Thinking I can keep you safe." His eyes filled with tears. Two escaped and ran down his cheeks.

I lifted my gaze to the cliffs. A murder of ravens released from the fortress. Their black forms filled the sky above. Metallic caws screeched like obsidian on glass.

It was over. We both knew it.

I'd be taken.

"You're a good friend, Eli. Helping me as you do."

He lowered his head and leaned against a rock. His eyelids drifted closed. "Friend. What is ever worth more?"

My gaze lowered to the dusty overlay of his shined boots. Elex. The only one who still believed in me. "Nothing."

"You are my gift, Lera. The only light I've ever known."

I held out my fist. Then, rolling it over, I opened it, revealing the tiny star. "I can use it. Save myself from the temple. I'll tell them you came to stop me but were too late. They'll let you go. We'll both be free."

He laughed, but it ended in a choked gasp. "That only happens in storybooks, Lera."

Dark shadows rose from the bottoms of his eyes. They expanded into a cloud cover, reaching to overtake the whites.

"Elex!" My voice came out desperate.

He closed his eyes. "You're too powerful, Lera. Your light won this time."

My heartrate ramped up, beat like the waves pounding the rocks during a storm. I didn't mean to hurt him. Didn't realize it'd gone that far. He'd used too much darkness to stop my star. It'd consume him, make him a soulless wanderer.

The ravens flew toward us. Their mechanical wings flapped an eerie hum. High-pitched screeches sliced over the crashing waves. Red orbs on their foreheads glowed like eyes but acted as range finders. We were caught.

There was only one star. Only one of us could have it.

Elex deserved it more than me. Had more life to live. More chance. His test score could grant him immunity, raise him up to be on the High Council. He could marry any woman in Renaissance after attending the elite school of ministry.

He could have it all without me.

But with me, he'd be forsaken.

I couldn't lose him. No matter the price.

I rotated my wrist until our hands were palm to palm. Then slowly, I pressed them together, the star trapped between.

Connection.

White hot light shot out of our hands.

"Heal, Elex. Take the star, all of it."

"No, Lera. It's yours," he mumbled, too weak to fight it.

"Not anymore."

Starlight spread up his arm and over his chest, casting a healing glow. The color in his pale cheeks grew pink.

As he healed, his darkness washed through me. Worry, deep and tormented. Flashes of markets, food, extra quantities bought for me. The last of his crowns spent on an onyx bracelet, one infused with enough darkness to keep my light at bay, but that I refused to wear. Fears of being unlovable. The shame and doubt of not being able to do more for me. Regret.

My eyes opened. His care for me was apparent in his suffering, though overlaid by dark thoughts. "Elex, I ..."

"I didn't want you to see it." His voice trembled.

I intertwined my fingers with his, pressing our palms together. My light had healed his darkest secrets. "I accept it. It's you. I would hold all your pain."

Then, our hands began to glow again. Starlight burst between our palms. It spread up my arm, continuing over my chest and condensing around my heart.

Elex's eyes weighted with sympathy. He grimaced.

And my pain, the suffering I'd gone through the past two months, it reared with ugly intensity but then vanished.

My eyes widened. Elex had somehow absorbed my pain. The Cursed weren't supposed to be able to, only the Gifted. It must've been a lie. A way to keep it one-sided. To control it. "I'm sorry you had to feel that. I didn't intend to ..."

He gave a weak grin. "You missed me though you'd never admitted it."

"I did." I squeezed his hand, then let go.

We stood, but a new power was transmitted between us. An electric pulse ran down my spine. Our hurt had merged, and together it had transformed us into balance. The newness of it felt reminiscent of home. A heart full of acceptance. A moment of strength, determined to exist fully, a thrust of life and first breath.

"Do you feel that?" I asked. "As if our worth doesn't need to be proven. Instead, it's innate power."

"Yes." He nodded and looked toward the sky.

The ravens circled above. Targeted streams of electric venom would soon rain down on us. We would be frozen by neurological stimulants, our hearts stunned, similar to the rabbit.

I rubbed my hands together, and so did Elex.

We'd go down fighting.

As I pulled my palms apart, a star emerged, bright but with a dark shadow, a fiery sun. Enough force to blast through the murder.

Eli rubbed his hands, and within them a storm surged, containing a tiny crackle of lightning, a light within his darkness. Enough power to scatter them to separate isles.

We looked at each other, understanding crossing between us.

We were the next storybook, the girl with the star and the boy who could harness the sky. The ones that would bring balance back to the isle.

I turned and faced the ocean.

Ravens dove from above, electric venom pouring out their mouths, but I wasn't afraid anymore.

Inevitably, I'd have to face both the fortress and the temple.

I reared back and threw the star at the ravens. It blazed as it catapulted into the sky; then it stopped, just below the oncoming attack.

It remained still, beaming a beautiful light. A sunburst of rainbows emerged on the misty clouds, mesmerizing but dangerous.

Elex reached forward and released his storm. A thick shield of fog surrounded us. If storybooks were true, it would protect us from the star's power.

The star's white light brightened. Then its core spun, supercharging a magnetic pull. Its gravity drew the ravens in.

They tried to fly back. Their metal wings squealed against it.

But the star didn't fail. It pulled with a slow, steady force.

The ravens screeched. They drew closer to the star's fire. Their calls heightened to an ear-deafening blast. The red glow of their orbs brightened until the sky turned the color of blood.

And still, the star stayed steady.

Their venom poured down about us in electric rivers, rolling down Eli's shield.

But the star didn't waver.

The ravens succumbed to its light, scratching metal on metal as they evaporated in its heat. The starlight mixed with their glow, changing the heavens to an idyllic pink.

And the star, as if knowing the task was complete, burst.

Tiny particles of sparkly dust rained over us.

Elex reached for my hand. And I held it.

Together, we'd reclaim the isle.

The Moon Cake

Carrie Anne Noble

"Get down, Simeon," my fiancé's three sisters chorused as he danced a jig atop the high stone wall.

Moonbeams lit half of his blond head and lithe body, the half on our side of the wall separating our land from the land of the Gray Goblins. I never minded his antics, but tonight, I had a sinking feeling in my gut. We should have taken the long way home from the tavern with our friends, the safe, winding path through the town's common gardens.

He performed a perfect cartwheel, landing on his feet without faltering upon the narrow ledge. "I decline your invitation, dear fair but boring sisters."

"You're seventeen, not three," his eldest sister said.

I said nothing. Let his sisters be the killjoys. Secretly, I prayed he'd listen to them as I started to chew away at a fingernail.

"It's my birthday. I will celebrate as I choose." Grinning, he raised his arms and started to sing. We all knew the song. As children, we'd sung it in our secret forest forts, far from the wall. It had given us little thrills of terror to mock the Gray Goblins with our small voices. To sing it here, at the border of their dark land, was folly of the worst kind. They were enemies we had no power to fight. If the goblins heard Simeon's mockery from their side of the wall, how easily might they reach up to claim Simeon by grabbing his ankles and giving a quick tug.

Up there in the moonlight, he looked like the indomitable young hero of a fable, or a fearless god sent to earth to win the hearts of mortal maidens. My heart beat wildly with a mixture of fear and adoration. I wanted to kick him and kiss him in equal measure.

As he crowed the final note, Simeon leapt and spun. Lost his balance. Tumbled over the wall and out of sight with a muffled shout.

For a moment, my heart stopped. I felt the hush of his voice in my bones like winter itself was reaching through my skin.

I pressed my hands against the cold stone and called out his name, again and again, so forcefully that my throat and chest burned. He did not reply.

He was gone. Gone.

"O gods, o gods, o gods," cried his sisters with their faces bowed to the earth, but the gods did not come to their aid.

I fell to my knees with them, unable to speak or weep. I tore the sleeves off my dress. The garnet betrothal ring, given to me by Simeon on my recent birthday, caught on the fabric as an immeasurable hole opened up inside my soul.

How could the very light of my life have gone into the darkness forever?

The Gray Goblins never returned the people they snatched from among us to work in their mines. They would certainly not return a strong young man who'd all but offered himself to them. Simeon's adventurous, mischievous nature had charmed me since we were children. Never had I thought it would be his undoing. And mine.

My hand and heart had been given and could not lawfully be given again. My fate would be to live unwed with my family until death, or to join the holy order of women whose husbands or fiancés had been stolen away to Tenebros—women who spent every day, all day whispering prayers for light to come someday to eradicate that shadowed land.

I mourned my separation from Simeon for three days. When I ran out of tears and prayers, I rose from my bed, knowing I could never join the convent of the Waiting Ones. I had never been as bold as Simeon, but I was too bold to let him go without making an effort to get him back.

I loved Simeon too well to wait for a someday. But how could one girl save someone from the world of darkness and the foul, powerful creatures who dwelled there?

Autumn arrived riding the back of a chill wind. The Day of Visiting was nigh, and all the townsfolk were preparing to observe a solemn day of fasting and silence.

It had been seventy-one days since Simeon had fallen into Tenebros.

The cold of the stone doorstep seeped through the soles of my leather slippers as I stood watching the neighbors drape their white mourning robes over the hedges. Across the dry dirt road, a dozen robes of varying sizes already flapped like unhappy ghosts, pegged to a rope strung between trees. These garments needed the kiss of sunlight and the caress of the pine-scented air that swept down from the mountains. They'd been tucked away in chests and cabinets for almost a year, safeguarded from beetles and moths. Held captive in darkness like the ones we prepared to remember on the Day. Unlike the freshening robes, the people we missed and mourned, including my Simeon, were doomed never to see sunlight again.

Everyone should have done more than simply airing out their robes, for Visiting Day was the one day of the year when the Gray Goblins permitted humans to pass in and out of Tenebros, their realm. Nothing grew in that sunless place, and the thin, boiled rat soup the goblins gave their prisoners kept them alive to work in the mines for a year or two at best—if the constant cold didn't kill them first. The human captives desperately needed nourishing food and woolen clothes in order to survive—and in order to keep the goblins from stealing yet more of our people to replenish their workforce. There was nothing we could do to stop them, no charm or weapon with which we might ward them off. Brothers, fathers, aunts, cousins ... anyone could vanish from bed in the middle of the night, snatched without warning, without a sound.

Or they might go as my beloved Simeon had. Foolishly. Needlessly.

For all the trouble he'd caused me, I still loved him beyond measure, the way the Moon is said to love the Sun.

In the months since Simeon's disappearance, I'd sold the precious contents of my dower chest, from the carved wooden spoons and Great-Gran's silver candlesticks to the bridal gown Ma had been embroidering since my twelfth birthday. The toll required by the goblins on Visiting Day could only be paid in pure gold coins. With the leftover money, I'd purchased fabric to make Simeon clothes, and foodstuffs to fill the two baskets I'd be allowed to carry into the prison.

As Visiting Day grew nearer, I slept less and less. To take Simeon a few provisions, to hold him for a moment, then to leave him behind for another year—or until the afterlife we hoped to share—seemed unthinkable. I'd watched my neighbor, Widow Baines, die day by day for want of the stolen husband she'd adored. She'd withered like a blade of grass in a drought, never leaving her tiny cottage once he'd been taken.

She'd surrendered. Given up on Owen Baines, no matter how much she claimed to have loved him.

To surrender Simeon was something I would not do.

I had to save him. But how? The goblins were many and strong, and if given the smallest reason to suspect a visitor was up to trickery, they'd use their axes to fell the offender like a sapling. It had happened before. The law prevented the goblins from taking visitors captive, but it did allow them to "punish" any visitor suspected of scheming to liberate a slave.

Early in the morning, I paced the lanes around my parents' cottage, desperate to think of a way to rescue Simeon.

"I hear you're going to visit the shadowed place, Eseld Kerrow," old man Priddy said, taking hold of the hem of my dress as I passed by his cottage doorstep, the place he always sat to smoke his pipe as the sun rose.

I turned to face him. His aged countenance bore a hundred beautiful wrinkles, but his brown eyes shone like a child's on a festival day. "Yes," I said. I didn't want to say more, because if I did, the fear of going into Tenebros and the thought of returning without Simeon would fall on me like a wave made of granite. Everything I had to do felt impossible.

"How brave are you, lass?" He patted the step beside him, and I sat. A tendril of sweet-smelling smoke swirled upward from the bowl of his pipe.

"Brave enough, I hope."

"Good. Because I'm thinking you first need to make a journey up Seissylt Mountain to talk to the Moon, and that mountain's a cruel one."

"What?"

"I been watching you since you were a chick. I reckon you're not the sort to let your man go so easy. I reckon you've enough pluck to get yourself up that mountain and talk to Her. I only told one other youngster the way, years ago, and he didn't make it up there. Turned out he didn't love his wife half enough. But you, I've seen you with Simeon Griffith. Seen that look that passes between ye. Your love's no ordinary thing, and that's a fact. I been holding this secret, this plan that came to me in a dream, waiting for the right one to pass it on to ever since the other youngster failed. Dream said it can only be shared twice, this secret. That being said, I think you've the mettle for it. And me being old as I am, it'd make me right merry to see one last good thing on this earth before I leave it."

My face must have reflected my bafflement because he chuckled and said, "Lean close and let me whisper the particulars in your ear. There are crows about that like nothing so much as collecting secrets for the goblin folk."

Hand over hand, I pulled myself up a jagged wall of rock. Seissylt Mountain had been the death of experienced adventurers, and it had not been kind to me. It tripped me with tree roots, sent me sliding backward on patches of pebbles, bruised my elbows, and skinned my knees raw. My path was sprinkled with blood, a desperate traveler's unholy offering. I was glad the mountain wouldn't ask for greater gifts from me, for I had almost nothing left to my name.

Before heading to the mountain, I'd traded Simeon's betrothal ring for boots sturdy enough to withstand the journey. I sold my hair to the wigmaker so I could purchase a leather satchel and traveler's rations. I exchanged my empty, skillfully carved dower chest for coins to pay the troll that kept the bridge leading onto the mountainside.

A pair of magpies swooped close enough to stir the air around my aching forearms as I hauled myself onto a grassy ledge. Was their presence a bad omen or a portent of good fortune? I was too weary to remember the lore.

For a moment, as the stars came out to blink wonderingly at the earth, I lay still on my back and thought of Simeon.

I'd loved him since we were small enough to hide among the stalks of wheat in Farmer Myrick's fields, and he'd loved me since I'd saved him from drowning in the River Clydwell on his eleventh birthday. Obviously, Simeon's brush with a watery death had failed to dampen his foolhardy spirit.

I forced myself onto my swollen feet and started to walk again. I'd lost count of the number of days I'd been scrabbling upward. Soon, the top of the mountain came into view. My chest heaved as I strained to take in enough thin air. A beam of moonlight made the path ahead glimmer as if strewn with black diamonds. She was close, the Moon. Her round, gray edges extended beyond the mountain's crest like a halo, and I could hear her whispering her old, old song.

When I planted my feet on Seissylt's pinnacle and looked the Moon in the face, she smiled coolly and said, "Daughter, I have watched you struggle against the mountain for many a night. Why have you come unto me? Is not the good silver light I shed upon your home enough for you?"

My lungs were too short on air for fine speeches. I fell to my knees and said simply, "I've come to beg for help, my lady."

A pearly mantle of moonlight fell over me and renewed my strength.

"I dislike giving favors to humans," said the Moon. "Too soon, they forget to be grateful. But since you've come far, I will hear your request."

I stood to plead my case. "The boy I love is a prisoner of the Gray Goblins, and—"

The moon interrupted. "He was reckless, your beloved. I saw him tumble over the wall that divides the humans' land from the darkness of Tenebros. He brought about his own doom. He ought not to have danced upon the wall so brazenly."

"His behavior was unwise, but young men often find it hard to resist acts of daring."

Her light shifted as a cloud passed between us. "The world is full of men, daughter. Find one more cautious."

"There is room in my heart for no other," I said. "For I love him as much as I have heard you love your husband the Sun and your sky-full of Star-children."

"Nevertheless, I cannot help you. There are rules. Laws as old as time. I am forbidden to shed my light upon that shadowy kingdom, even for love's sake."

"I did not come to ask you to break the old laws," I said, then whispered to her the plan Priddy had whispered to me.

She glowed almost warmly. "So be it," she said.

A moment later, with her gift enfolded in my hand, I skipped down the mountainside like a young goat.

While my friends kept the happy customs of the harvest, I sewed and baked through the final hours before Visiting Day, filling the two big wicker hampers I'd soon bear into Tenebros. My hands were scarred by needle-pricks and oven burns, but my heart remained steadfast—in spite of Mama's anguished pleas for me not to venture into the shadowed land. I promised her I'd return. I reminded her that the goblins were forbidden to take visitors captive. I asked her to keep busy by altering her old wedding dress to fit me, for as soon as Simeon was safely home, we'd hasten to the priest to be married. Mama looked at me like I'd gone mad. She bit her lip in silence, but I knew the thought she held inside: the goblins never, ever freed prisoners.

On the last morning before Visiting Day, I hummed to myself as I worked at Mama's kitchen table. Pale golden dough stuck to my hands. I flung flour onto it and rolled it thin, then cut a circle round as the moon. I took a stone from my pocket and placed it in the center of the circle; then I pleated the dough into a pretty little ball that fit in my palm. I made a few more dough circles, but these I filled with berries. The cakes looked delicious and identical.

An hour later, I set the cakes in a tiny basket and nestled them among preserves and flatbreads, atop folded woolen undergarments, thick knitted socks, and a linen shirt with clumsily crafted buttonholes.

A tall Gray Goblin stopped me at the gate and looked me over with huge, obsidian eyes. He stank of decay and wore nothing but a ragged, knee-length tunic as gray and filthy as his flesh. He searched the hampers carelessly, disordering the contents with long fingers sheathed in gloves made of something slick and pale. Did he fear our things might contaminate him, or were they a status symbol among his kind? A trophy made from ... ? I shuddered and tried to cast off the grim thought.

He finished his search and, with a grunt, ordered me to join the queue of other visitors. In the dimness, I recognized the candle maker's wife, the cheese monger's eldest son, a sheep farm lad, and an old woman who sold flowers in the marketplace. Their faces were grim. They gripped the handles of their hampers as if the wicker might save their lives. Only the old woman dared to speak to me.

"Oh lass," she said, shaking her head. "You're here for that rascal Simeon, are you? Two years I been coming here to see my grandson, but don't you keep this up. Your boy'll never get out. Might as well move on. Forget this like a bad dream."

I nodded in reply. *Never*, I wanted to say. *Never will I give up on Simeon.* If she saw the stubborn hope on my face, she didn't bother to comment. The way she set her jaw told me she thought I'd lost my mind, going there for someone whose name I didn't share.

A goblin motioned for us to follow. He held up a lantern stuffed with poisonous, green-glowing mushrooms, the only form of light the goblins used in their land. The lantern offered enough illumination for us to see the path but nothing beyond.

My heart galloped wildly as we marched deeper and deeper into ever-shifting shadows. Black mud sucked at the soles of my shoes with every step. Just as my eyes became accustomed to the darkness, the prison barracks appeared suddenly before us, black stones piled on black stones. A door wide as a house creaked open, and we were ushered into a courtyard thrice the size of our village square. On the walls here, the glowing mushrooms grew out of every crack and crevice. Waiting on long benches were skeletal figures with dust-coated skin and swollen eyes. They wore tattered clothes crusted with dirt. How could these have been our loved ones, these gaunt, ruined husks of humans?

When I saw Simeon, I ran to him. I dropped the hampers at his feet and embraced him. He smelled like a bog, and his clothes were damp. A scruffy hint of a beard had grown on his cheeks and chin.

"You shouldn't have come," he said as tears made downward paths through the filth on his face. "Oh, Eseld! Your hair—"

I interrupted him. "No, I shouldn't have come. You did this to yourself, Simeon Griffith. You don't deserve me at all." I pointed to the bench and said, "Now sit."

Grinning sheepishly, he obeyed. I sat shoulder to shoulder with him, keenly aware that it was a miracle to be together again. In the months since he'd fallen, he might have been killed. He could have died of a fever or starvation.

A goblin crept close and shook a spear at me.

"No talking," Simeon translated. "It's the rules."

"He can stuff his rules," I whispered, and Simeon laughed quietly. "I've been working for weeks to fill these hampers. And I've been waiting to see you for months. If I want to talk, I'll talk." I opened the closest hamper and fished out the little basket of cakes. "Here. Try these."

"I'm so hungry that even your baking sounds good to me." He nudged me with his bony elbow, then peered into the basket. "These look like moon festival cakes. But Visiting Day is nowhere near the festival."

"Doesn't matter. Taste them."

He bit into a cake and sighed with pleasure. Berry juice dripped from his lower lip. "Not bad."

"Have another."

"I should save them. They have to last a long time, my love."

"Please." I picked up one of the remaining cakes and held it to his mouth. "For me."

He bit down with a crunch. "Ouch," he said as a beam of light burst out of the cake. "My tooth! What the—"

Light exploded in front of Simeon's face. From the cake, silver shards shot in all directions and bounced off the walls. Each ray split into two, then three, then six, a hundred, until the courtyard could hold no more and beams spilled out of the barracks.

When the light touched them, the goblin guards cried out in anguish. Their bodies crumbled.

Everywhere within sight was as bright as the brightest moonlit night. The prisoners cheered. They rushed to the door, hand in hand with friends or visitors. Simeon pulled me after them. We leapt over smoldering piles of ashes that once were goblins. We ran to and then through the gate in the wall, out of Tenebros and back toward our village.

We stopped beside the village well. Simeon cranked up a bucket of cold water and we drank our fill. Afterward, he kissed me.

"Sorry about your tooth," I said, examining the chip in one of his front teeth.

"What was that? Did you put actual *moon rock* in those moon festival cakes?"

"I climbed Seissylt Mountain and spoke to the Moon," I said proudly. "She said she couldn't shine on Tenebros. It's against the old laws. But there wasn't a law against *someone else* taking moonlight there. The Moon likes a bit of mischief and tales of true love, so she gave me a piece of herself ..."

"And you brought it into Tenebros to destroy the goblins. You saved me, Eseld. You saved our people."

"I noticed. Now, let's go home. We're getting married tomorrow and you need a bath or two. Also, you're done dancing on walls forever."

"Truly? Forever is a long time," he said teasingly.

"If I thought you were serious, I'd throw you over my shoulder and carry you back to Tenebros."

"No more wall-top dancing," he said, leaning in to kiss my cheek. "I swear by the Moon."

I gave him my sternest look. "Such a vow is not to be broken, Simeon Griffith."

"I'm well aware of the power of the Moon, believe me."

We wove our way through the crowded village lanes. Everyone had come out to celebrate. In the village square, a bonfire blazed as folks young and old tossed their mourning robes into the flames. They danced around the fire and sang a new song, one about light overpowering darkness. One about love conquering evil.

I glanced at the mountains in the distance just as the Moon peered over their edge. She winked at me.

And I winked back.

The Gossamer Ascent

Elizabeth Van Tassel

Jett crouched on the precipice overlooking the city and dusky beige hills in the distance as the evening shift workers arrived. Her stomach twisted in resentment. The bright gilded dome being built above the skyline was nearly completed.

Her long, dark hair tickled her neck as she squinted at the guards through her binoculars. Twelve of them lined the central quad streets along the alabaster buildings in Almonia. A heaviness settled. The time was almost at hand—either to be confined under the city's huge dome or to escape.

A courier in a tan uniform saluted, then delivered the clear crystal box down the long pathway to where her father stood. Jett leaned forward to better see the sharp golden spike through the crystal. Her hair's ebony strands brushed her cheeks, as if they knew they were illegal—each curl a silent mark of rebellion.

Her father took the box with a nod and carried it into his central building that housed his office.

Jett's mouth twitched. How could her father sell out his own family to the governor, just to broaden his rule? It seemed like a project to help with the drought and atmospheric troubles, but she knew the governor really wanted full control—every citizen locked down, like a bird in a cage.

That golden connector made the magic function. Once her father activated it, the spike would harness all the suppressed magic flowing within the city, which was plentiful, and channel it into the dome, completely locking them off from other civilizations.

The officials said their regulations offered protection, but Jett knew the governor. In other cities, he increased his control incrementally, over simple choices at first. Water scarcity softened the people so they were willing to suppress the magic their hair held in exchange for extra water rations and financial rewards. They didn't realize that by relinquishing their individual giftings, they each ceded power to him. It was easy to identify the submitters: they had little or no hair.

Once he had control, he'd kill any opposition.

The resistance couldn't be trapped under the dome. Not only would they be outlaws, but easily spotted as dissenters. The hair that gave them powers—to send messages, images, and thoughts—also gave them away. But there was still hope. Jett had a plan.

The sun set as the message came. Her long hair tingled at the roots and the ends sparked. The static disclosed a time and place to meet.

Before she moved out, Jett overheard her father planned to bring the spike home, so the public show had to be a ruse to tease out any insurgents. But that also meant she had to be the one to break in and steal the spike. She knew every crevice of that place.

To save hundreds of others like herself, she would have to betray her family.

She waited until the moon settled behind clouds to creep down the hill into town. Under the cover of night, she climbed her favorite oak tree and dropped over the wall into a courtyard filled with fountains and fruit trees. The scents of orange blossoms reminded her of sweeter times. She crept toward her father's office, avoiding any guards throughout the palace. As she drew near, she heard her parents arguing.

"Laird has joined the guard and we must respect that, Sophia." Her father's voice boomed in the hallways. "You cannot keep pestering him about Jett. She is not his responsibility. She may know how to listen to the wind, but she will *never* obey the governor. She made her choice."

"But Stephan, she's your daughter. How can you tear apart our family?" Her mother's voice gave Jett chills. She risked a peek in the window and choked back a sob—her mom's tawny hair had been cropped above her ears.

She leaned against the cool stone building. Her father's words burned like acid on her heart, but her mom's capitulation was even worse. *My whole family is taken in. Gone.*

Her parents went down to the kitchen, still arguing, and for a moment his office was empty. The spike sat encased in a clear box. Jett didn't hesitate; the activation ceremony couldn't be held if the spike was gone. Her ruse, long in the planning, had to work. She lifted the glass cover with care, then caught her reflection. There was another figure behind her.

She drew in a sharp breath and swiveled, keeping her hands behind her as she eased the duplicate from its hiding place. "Laird."

Her twin, opposite in every way. Compliant from his shorn blond locks to the governor-approved pure white clothing. The only deviation was the green from his eyes directing daggers at her.

"Don't touch it, Jett. There's nothing left for you here."

She made the trade with deft movements behind her back, even when the tip of the spike stabbed her finger as she slipped it in her pocket. "You used to know what was really important. What happened to you?"

Laird stepped around her to check on the spike. He seemed to believe the one present was the original.

Jett gently swished her hair with her hand and sent a sound outside the window, hoping to distract Laird.

As she backed away, he matched her every step.

"Jett, don't test me."

If he called the guards, she was done for. She stopped. Maybe all this wasn't necessary. Could her brother finally take down the wall that had grown between them? For a heartbeat, she breathed. Closed her eyes. Waited. It was what she wanted most.

"That's better. Let's talk."

For a moment she let herself believe in the impossible, nodding to him.

He wiped perspiration from his bare forehead. Maybe he was nervous too. Their days of whispering jokes into the wind or dropping words from scaled heights were no more. All that remained was the growing chasm between them. Unless ...

His voice cooed like a gentle bird, but his eyes were hard. "It's not too late, Jett. I'm sure I can help you contain your hair." He stepped toward her.

"So, nothing has changed for you, Laird?"

He shook his head. "You are the one who has hesitated. You don't want to give up your whole life, your family. So, you ... will comply." Another step. "Or go to prison."

She blinked. All he wanted was to get rid of her. That meant there was no redeeming their life together. She had to move quickly, or she'd be trapped. A sigh escaped; then she ran from the room.

Laird didn't pursue her, and he also didn't signal the guard since she'd left the spike. Or so he thought. The copy held no magic. They had until tomorrow for the governor to realize the farce. Without the spike, the dome's seal wouldn't be completed, and the spell could only be attempted once per decade. This could buy them time. Maybe, by then, even the shaven would rebel. That was her dream.

In that moment, her past was lost, and a new future was set in place.

Jett sat with her back to the cold exterior of the bank, shaking a sharp pebble from her sandal. Her chest heaved from running to avoid troops all night. She shoved the pack on her shoulder and felt for her rations, risking a small bite. No one would search for her in the financial district. *They'd expect me to flee the city.* Jett had another plan.

She peered above the nearby crates as dawn rose, the golden rays touching the white city with its rosy-pink fingers. The light hues of the marble facade warmed her aching heart. Jett loved the open square, with the clock tower that she and her brother used to run around. Later today, there would be merchants offering fruits, pastries, and woven goods. And gems excavated from mines that the governor wanted to exploit.

Across the plaza, she spotted a shadow creeping along the archways, hiding by the stacked crates. She had until the sun rose fully to wait for her rendezvous. A slight breeze blew some hair in front of her face.

Suddenly, a stranger sat on her right, tossing his long sandy bangs aside. *How did I not hear him?* Her stomach was queasy with excitement.

"The pathway is not determined," he said, a glimmer in his dark eyes. He looked strong but had deep creases in his cheeks, worn by years of avoiding the troops and living in the camps.

"The sun will shine once more," she answered. *Yes, one day her people would be free again.* Both ran their hands over their hair in silent salute. Those with the locks would rescue the shaven.

"So, you are my aid."

"Shhh. Jason, right? The guard will return at dawn, so we must work quickly. Did you bring the gold?"

"Two bars." He withdrew a sack and pulled back the corner for her to inspect. The governor's insignia was stamped into the metal.

Jett quieted the rush of expectation. It was far too distracting. "Adequate. Admirable even. How did your people find these?"

"The troops have a deposit near the mines by the ridge, about two miles from the dome's perimeter lock. We descended three days ago and, well, liberated a substantial amount."

It was best not to ask more. She felt the day warming as the sun's rays hit the center of the square.

"What about your task?" Jason's brows furrowed. He crouched on his knees and kept alert, surveilling the area. "Did you locate the walkway?"

She nodded. The hidden path.

Troops began arriving for the dawn patrol and a chill tiptoed down her spine. Laird was present. Not today. Not now. What if he detected the switch she'd made?

"Who's the tall one?"

"That's my brother." Dressed in pure white with gold stripes at the collar and arms, her lanky brother was of course freshly shaven. He raised his cap. *No.* She could see the blue serial numbers shining from his scalp. *That's new.* He had signed in fully, then. He must have received the numbers this morning. That meant the governor and his people had full access to his memories, his complete knowledge base. To her, in a way, too.

Jett directed her hair toward her brother and gently blew a word into the cup of her hand. Forgotten. His shoulders shook at this last gesture. They had been twins—an invisible thread stretched between the two. But she shook her head and cut the line to her heart. Once and for all.

"We'd better get moving soon."

A bright light shone in the middle of the street, almost landing on Jason's dark shoe. Jett kicked at his feet with a warning glare. When everyone was all in white, those who deviated were obvious.

She scratched the claw mark on the lower left side of the column. It was time.

"Let's go. The tunnels begin under the bank," she whispered.

Jason didn't know she had the magic spike. He didn't need to yet. But he was agile and moved with an easy confidence.

"You've planned well for the group's departure, Jason. Especially since the elders weren't all available and your time was limited. I know this path. Once we have clearance, they'll be able to navigate to safety, if we're not discovered."

"Have you ever seen them before, the dwellers beneath the city? I've only heard stories from my father, from times of old. He said they're like animals." His hands trembled as he slipped off his pack and lit a small lantern.

"No time to worry, we're all in, Jason. Sir Velm and his night-people are intelligent and strong. And yes, they are part beast. But they hold the only path to our freedom. All they require is respect, and payment of course."

"Did you get the artifacts? Father said they held the key to the cata-
combs below us."

Jett smirked. "Sometimes it pays to be a good listener." She toyed with
a tendril. How many times had she tried to comply, tried to shave her
locks to keep from shaming her family? It didn't matter. Her hair just
grew. Immensely. Prodigiously. Daily. It refused to stay cut. She used
to try and get it to comply, but now she couldn't force her hand to do
the singular motion necessary to slash it off. And the magic in her hair
knew her heart's true desire. Her heart wouldn't let her cut it again in
complicity to the governor or anyone else but her own wishes.

Jason's gaze landed on her fingers, intertwined with her impossibly
long, dark hair. "There's some open rebellion. Bet those pretty curls got
you into trouble."

"Yes, but they also come in very handy." She smiled. "I overheard my
mother talking about a time when our people were on friendly terms
with those who lived in the dark, and the true nature of some ceremonial
jewelry. When I saw the scrolls on my father's desk, I knew they connected it with the gems at the reserve. That's when I started making plans."

His eyebrows raised and a crooked smile lit his face. "And you worked
your own magic to get them."

"Indeed." Jett removed her necklace and ring from the museum's
antiquities section. She placed the amulet against a small hole in the wall
and pushed her ring in the custom slot, rotating both twice to the right.
The door creaked open, slowly, but her ring was stuck; it didn't fully
turn in the crest. Any confidence she'd felt evaporated as, far above them,
sirens began to blare. She prayed the troops had a delay before being
alerted.

No such luck. She heard footsteps and pulled Jason inside the cavern,
the door closing just as a squad arrived. Her brother would still be able

to guess her path, but not, perhaps, her mission. They were safe, but for how long?

Darkness surrounded them.

She held his hand and whispered. "Wait." She blew into her hair and the long ends illuminated like a thousand tiny lights. She waved her curls left and right, sending pinpoints of light like tiny darts into the walkway and walls above them.

Something further down began to wiggle.

"What's that?" Jason said.

Hundreds of moths took flight, creating a rustle as they moved, like small mirrors circling higher and higher. "The light in my hair is telling them to allow us passage. They will carry the message."

"To whom? Or—what?"

This was a test. Couldn't he understand? "I've only met one of their scouts in a different location, but he told me if we don't respect the sanctuary of the dwellers, we won't be able to meet."

"I thought you had been this way before."

"I have been through the entry but was never invited into their sanctuary as will be required for our escape."

"Great." Jason gazed upward and let a sigh escape.

A large figure approached, greeting them with a low growl. He shoved long, shaggy brown hair aside to reveal a face with human features, despite the thick brown fur that covered his arms and legs, then slowly bowed. It was Sir Velm, chief of the earth-dwellers. They'd met while she was searching for the cause of the drought.

With a peek at Jason, who seemed frozen in place, she matched the bow and urged him to do the same.

"Oh, it's you, Lady Jett," the creature said. He held himself with a regal stance. "And who did you bring?"

"Sir Velm, this is Jason Partune. He is coordinating passage for our people."

"He brought payment?"

She nodded and indicated for Jason to produce the gold.

He cleared his throat. "Here it is, as promised, Sir Velm." Jason held out the first gold bar to Sir Velm and warmed it with his breath. It shone and glowed like a flame.

"This flaming gold is rare and costly. You have honored us. We will allow passage."

"We have about four hundred traveling through here later tonight. Are you able to protect them?" Jett touched his arm. "We did set off the outside alarm and my brother, Laird, may know. If he figures it out, we will be at risk."

Velm answered with a slow growl, exposing his pointed teeth. He scratched his ear and raised his shoulders. Then he looked above Jason's head.

A single moth landed on Sir Velm's finger. It had dusty brown highlights, a blue smear on each wing, and clear window-like features in the center. Words and images raised on the clear portions of the wings. He whispered and it took flight, each beat of the moth drawing more light until the whole flutter followed it to the heights. They illuminated a large circular cavern carved out of the stone.

"How do they fly so high?" Jason wondered out loud.

"Their quiet, shimmering ascent shows the only way forward. But you ask the wrong question." He pointed toward the top of the large cave. "Sometimes there's more transpiring within the silence. The moths are essential to how we communicate with our troops in the maze of tunnels beneath the ground. They, in fact, are the connectors for us all and have a vital role in our community, and now yours as well."

They proceeded in silence, giving Jett time to absorb the importance of this moment when her future seemed held by a small night-creature. Jett had grown used to darkness. Jason, however, seemed strong and capable outside but had drawn his knife to separate his boot from something he'd stepped in. He was poised like a prowling tiger. That was good, useful at least. He would be alert and lead the groups later this evening, after he and Jett confirmed the deal.

A large silver door wavered in the moving lights from the moths. Jett had never been allowed so deep in their cluster.

Hope surged despite her effort to control her emotions.

They'd rescue their own kind, and with the golden spike, she could find a way to remove the dome. Once the dome was disabled, perhaps the shaven would awake and no longer be held in the governor's thrall. If she couldn't save her family, she at least hoped to be a catalyst for the rebellion.

"You are the first outsiders to ever set sight on our city. It is because of your listening, Jett, that we will give you and your people safe passage. What the governor disdains we dearly value, for those that live in the dark know your voice should not be silenced. You can offer discernment and wisdom—which we highly revere."

The doors glowed, then slowly rolled left and right in succession. A whole cityscape opened before her in dull, smoldering light. Buildings and dwellings with rounded edges rose from the ground like sandcastles at the beach. She held her breath.

Jason spoke what she was thinking. "We understood you just had an encampment. But this—this is a world of its own."

"For certain." Sir Velm narrowed his eyes, searching their faces for any disrespect. "You thought we were less than because we live aside from glaring stares of our kind." He whistled.

Twenty affirmations greeted him in response, the growling men moving next to Sir Velm. They took an aggressive posture.

"I meant no disrespect. In fact, I'm really amazed at it all," Jason clarified. He looked over at Jett with apprehension.

"If your companion here won't abide by the rules, then this deal is dissolved. You will leave now."

"I didn't mean to violate the rules. Please reconsider."

Jett shivered, a combination of nerves and wonder. What could she do to smooth the situation?

The city wound deeper and deeper underground. She rubbed her right leg where she'd sewn the spike into her pants. It warmed to her touch and vibrated. The magic was strong. Keeping it secret meant no one society had the power to control the other. She didn't want to give her allies the power to negotiate with the governor. The two worlds need never meet, or at least not until their safe escape.

"Sir Velm, thank you for your trust. Jason misspoke," Jett began. "It has been my honor to be invited into your city. We are experts at listening and hold you with the greatest respect." Those years playing with word tossing were paying off. "We bring light for your city and give you tools and jewels for adornment. It will provide subtle differences to enhance your lives. The gold Jason has uncovered will power your mills or whatever else you choose. Together, we can free a whole civilization about to be trapped under the dome."

The group still looked menacing and stricken by the offhand comment Jason had made.

Jason pulled his jacket tighter.

Jett wished she felt safe but supposed that might never again be possible. However, their alliance would bring an opportunity to forge a path forward. She had to make it work. She looked upward and whistled lightly into her hair and sent a message higher up.

A moth separated from the cluster and flew down, alighting on her shoulder.

The men stopped. It amazed her that these fierce people would watch the gentle dance of wings and flight.

The moth tickled her cheek, climbing slowly by her ear. She heard whispers she couldn't quite understand. She answered with a gentle tone, telling the moth about what she had risked, how she had left her family and life behind and how they truly needed its help. The wings fluttered, as if understanding her words. She moved it to her hand, admiring the patterns emerging in the speckled light.

"Please make a way for us, will you?" Jett inhaled slowly, waiting for a sign.

Three words wavered, then lit in the glistening wings. *You are chosen.* Her eyebrows raised as she tried to figure out the message. The moth danced on her shoulders and hid behind her curls. It emerged slowly from her thick waves of dark hair. The moth had changed. It was covered in small lights like the ones her hair could make. It flew higher and brushed the other moths, the light spreading and arching across the large cave.

Everyone watched the lights brighten the whole cavern little by little, like a small comet with a long tail crossing a dark sky.

Jett's gift, the power held in her hair, had somehow been harnessed by the single moth and spread to its whole community. She wasn't sure if it was for communication or illumination, but the result was breathtakingly beautiful.

Her light had started a reaction.

No, a silent revolution.

Sir Velm leaned over her shoulder. "Then this is it. We obey the signs. You have my people at your disposal. Let us commence planning as time is short."

The two removed their packs, their bargaining chips contained within. The spike was safe, buzzing against her leg.

"You did it! We have an alliance," Jason whispered and patted her back. She swallowed hard. She'd succeeded, yes. But she'd lost her family. She wiped away a tear as discreetly as possible. If only they'd been open to the truth. Her own brother was gone now; she couldn't change that.

While the light kept spreading, a thought drifted in her mind. The swirling brightness carried by the magical moths could spread endlessly. Each tiny speck of light was like each person they would rescue. Then freedom would arch and rise higher and higher like the words on the wind she'd caught her whole life.

The words and magic of her hair were bringing more than antics or fun. This time, her gift would be the key to saving a whole community no longer destined to be silenced.

As she watched the lights arching higher and the smiles on their hosts' faces, she wanted to hold onto the elusive moment. Her gifts, which had been such a burden and even threatened her welfare, now provided the linchpin for a new life filled with possibility.

The Weaver and the Dragon

Lauen Hildebrand

The cart bounced and Keito grabbed the seat, his wide straw hat sliding over his face.

"Careful, boya. You won't see the tower faster by breaking your head," Ojiisan said.

"Yes, Ojiisan." Keito pushed the woven hat back on his head. He spread his feet, clinging to the bolts of brocade piled high in their cart. He couldn't sit down, not when his first glimpse of the Dragon King's Horn was so close.

His grandfather understood. Ojiisan leaned forward and pulled a lever. The lumbering metal box that pulled their cart—Grandfather still called it "the mule"—slowed with a hiss of steam, and the rocking stabilized.

"Now it will take longer!" Keito cried.

Ojiisan laughed. "Longer than finding the pieces of your head and stitching them together? If I attach one wrong, your okaasan will have my hands. A weaver cannot risk such calamity."

Keito studied the pines and mesas still hiding the Horn, then settled down on the seat with a sigh. Ojiisan smiled and pushed the lever. With a clatter of gears, they lurched forward again.

Keito squirmed on the seat. A few more hours and they'd be in Ryuki-Kerai. He could picture it from cousin Miroku's stories—the city, bustling with farmers, merchants, and artisans who supplied the needs of the samurai in the palace. The palace itself, where Miroku and the other apprentices lived and trained, built halfway up the strange rock column. And towering above both, the sun-burned Horn with dragons circling its peak.

A shadow moved across the sky, and Keito whipped his head up, but it was only a vulture hanging on the current. The bird flapped great wings and drifted away. Keito settled back against the brocade and sighed.

"Where have your thoughts flown, boya?" Ojiisan smiled at Keito, his eyes barely visible under his straw hat.

"To the DragonFriends. I'm excited to meet one."

"You already have, Kei-chan. Your cousin."

"You know that's not what I mean, Ojiisan."

Ojiisan pretended to scowl, and Keito adopted a more respectful tone. "Miroku Niisan is only an apprentice; he hasn't been chosen yet to bond with a dragon. I want to meet a *real* DragonFriend." He dropped his voice until it was covered by the clanking metal mule. "And a real dragon."

"You will." Ojiisan rested his hands on his knees. "There are many in Ryuki-Kerai. Besides"—the wrinkles in his face shifted as he smiled—"the Hata family makes the best brocade for the sash of a warrior. Be proud they wear our cloth, flighty Kei-chan, for even you are part of this greatest alliance."

The cart creaked up an incline, and as they cleared the summit, Keito gasped. A pinnacle of rock—reddish bronze in the burning sunlight—rose alone and proud from the valley floor. The thick column towered eight hundred feet into the air, then cut off as though slashed by a katana. Dark specks soared about its peak, and sunlight flashed on great wings.

"The Dragon King's Horn," Keito breathed.

Ojiisan pulled the brake, and the mule shuddered to a halt. A many-windowed palace with curving, red-tiled roofs clung like an enamel brooch to the cliff face. A slightly larger speck wheeled away from the palace, veering up, up, up into the sky where it hung suspended before the blazing sun. Keito's eyes stung as he tried not to lose one glimpse of the majestic outline.

The dragon paused, wings outspread, a perfect silhouette against the crystalline blue. A figure—so small it seemed almost imagined—bent forward over the dragon's neck. Then the dragon dropped and, in a few wingbeats, vanished behind the Horn.

Keito blinked happily, spots of white swimming before his eyes.

"A beautiful thing to be part of," Ojiisan whispered. He released the brake, and the mule rumbled down the slope.

Keito kept his eyes toward the Horn, even after the pines hid it from view. Something had awakened in his chest, a happiness and an ache combined. He was proud he belonged to the best weaving family in the American territories; happy when he sat beside Ojiisan, learning the family trade; much, *much* too old to train as an apprentice at Ryu-ki-Kerai. And yet—seeing the spreading wings framed against the sky, an impossible desire had hatched, awakened, taken flight in his soul.

"I want to be a DragonFriend." He barely breathed the words, then shuddered at the audacity of the wish. "Please, ancestors, do not send misfortune for my presumption. Only ... know I mean it, too."

He glanced at the brilliant sky, then pressed himself back against their cargo and watched for his next glimpse of the Horn.

I am alone. The hard rocks and sharp trees stretch as far as I can see. I should keep going—"Run," that was the last command the samurai gave me—but I do not know where to go, and I am past the point when I can run.

I am alone. I felt the moment my mother died. Her pain had echoed through our bond, lending speed to my escape. Then I felt nothing, so she was gone. I could not feel the samurai either. He must be dead also. If he wasn't, he would have come for me.

I am alone. I tried to leave the streambed, to avoid the spiny plants that tear my scales as I pass, but the hot stones burned my paws, and without the stream I have no point of reference, no way to tell if I'm moving in circles. Also, I have no place to hide. So I returned.

Now, I pause and lap up the gurgling water. Some drips back into the stream, distorting my reflection, the only face I've seen since I left the samurai. I raise my head and resist the urge to call out, to cry aloud in hope that someone, anyone, will find me. Because I am alone, but I cannot be found.

That was the second-to-last thing he told me as he clutched me to his chest and ran—away from my dying mother, away from his best friend whom he'd sworn to protect. His bond let him speak to my mother, just as ours—hers and mine—let me speak to him. And so, as I silently screamed for my mother, clung to him in terror, twisted, fought, and begged him to go back, I heard his voice in my head, a point of safety in that terrifying night. "We can't go back. They are after you, ryu-chan. And I will not let them have you."

He ran a long time through the dark before my mother's pain winked out; then he stumbled and nearly fell. He paused and lowered me to the ground. Behind us, war cries filled the night.

"I'll draw them away," he said. "You must run. You are not safe until you reach the Horn." He placed a hand on his katana. "Understand? Don't let anyone find you. Run!" Then he staggered away, followed by the whoops of our pursuers.

I obeyed. I ran.

And now, I can run no more. I sink beneath a stunted bush, pull myself into a tight ball, and hide my eyes from the blistering sun. I am alone.

Keito caught two more glimpses of the Horn as their cart lumbered toward the valley. As long as the Horn was visible, he stared eagerly at it, memorizing every line and shadow. When it was hidden, he spun visions of how he'd meet his first dragon. Perhaps he'd be standing on a bluff at sunrise, practicing the sword forms Miroku performed, and with a *whoosh* of wings, a dragon and rider would land beside him.

"I've never seen such control in one so young," the samurai would say. *"Who is your sensei?"*

"Halt!"

Keito jerked from his daydream and scrambled to his feet. Ojiisan seized the brake. Two guardsmen stood in the path, pikes in their hands.

Ojiisan scowled. "What is this? The shogun's guard halting craftsmen on the road?"

"Your pardon, Ojiisan." The taller guard dipped his head. "We take no pleasure in stopping honorable men, but you cannot follow this path today."

Keito looked up the roadway. Ahead, the track vanished into a grove of aspen and pine. Near its edge, a dozen guardsmen moved about something hidden by the brush.

Ojiisan huffed. "The main road is not available for travel?"

"We apologize, Ojiisan," the guard said stiffly. "If you turn aside at that cutoff"—he pointed to the left—"you will find a dry creek bed running down into the valley. From there you may rejoin the road."

Ojiisan glanced past the guards at the milling warriors. "Is there danger an old weaver and his grandchild should know about?"

The guards exchanged a look.

"There is no danger to you," the taller guard said. "You had best move on. You'll add an hour to your journey to Ryuki-Kerai."

Ojisan muttered under his breath but swung the mule aside. Keito gripped the bolts, craning for a glimpse of what the guardsmen were doing. Had outlaws attacked the roads? *Did any of the samurai bring their dragons?*

The group shifted briefly, and Keito gasped. *No.* He clutched the piled brocade. No, it couldn't be. He leaned forward, straining for another glimpse to disprove what he thought he'd seen. There—the crumpled wing, the outstretched neck, the single golden eye staring at the shimmering heavens. The iron bolt protruding from the scaly chest.

Their cart dipped below the gully rim, and Keito dropped onto the seat. "Ojiisan—someone's killed a dragon!"

The hours passed as slowly as the turning cartwheels. Keito couldn't stop picturing the dead dragon. Who could have killed it? And why? He tried to focus elsewhere, to erase the image of that iron bolt dropping the creature from the sky, but the high banks hid all view of the Horn, and the sun-parched landscape offered little distraction.

The cart rounded a curve, and Keito straightened. Here the lefthand bank dropped away, and beside it stood a figure in long red robes. Gold embroidered the wide sleeves. He raised his eyes to the approaching cart, and they shone black as obsidian beneath his weathered brow.

"Whoa, there!" Ojiisan pulled the brake, leaning back as the mule halted. He bowed to the approaching figure in red. "Greetings."

"Greetings, Ojiisan." The man held himself erect as a pine. His dark eyes seemed to slide straight through Keito before dismissing him. A medallion hung about his neck, containing the shogun's crest and the symbol of the dual forces that created the world. *He's a magician.*

"Are you headed to Ryuki-Kerai?" the magician asked.

Ojiisan bowed. "Could we offer you a ride to the city?"

"I do not return there this night, not until my task is complete." His dark gaze flicked from the hills to Keito. "Are you excited to see the dragons, boy?"

Keito swallowed and nodded. "I ... saw one dead two hours back."

The magician pursed his lips. "Yes, I seek the ones that killed it. Have you seen anything since then?"

Keito shook his head.

"Only the grasshoppers," Ojiisan supplied.

The magician nodded. "May the rest of your journey be equally un-eventful." He swept past and up the track.

Ojiisan watched him go, then unfolded his legs and climbed stiffly from the cart. He placed both hands on his back and leaned backward. "Boya, check the mule since we've stopped."

Keito shook disturbed thoughts from his mind—those dark eyes unsettled him—scrambled off the seat, and hurried to the mechanical mule. On its round metal side, about where a real mule's belly would be, was a hinged iron door. Keito pulled his sleeve over his hand and opened the hatch. Heat washed from the opening, and he squinted inside. The grate holding the fuel was still burning well, but he tossed more coal onto the crimson bed, then secured the door.

Next, he grabbed a metal loop at the mule's "shoulder" and pulled out the dipstick. He wiped it on his *jinbei*, then plunged it back into the water tank. When he pulled it out, the tongue showed damp to the third mark. "It has three *shō*!"

Ojiisan squinted down their path. "We'll need to refill it."

"I saw a stream just beyond that rise." Keito pointed.

Ojiisan nodded. "Good. Take the gourd. I'm going to have a word with nature." He shuffled off into the brush.

Keito found the water gourd and headed up the ridge. He spied the stream easily from the crest and hurried toward it. The tang of damp clay met his nose as he slid down the bank, squatted beside the rivulet, and helped himself to a long drink.

He filled the gourd next. As the chilly water swirled inside, a pebble clattered on the opposite bank. He looked up, expecting a toad or desert hare. Instead, golden eyes—larger than his own—blinked at him from a scaled head. Keito gasped, dropped the gourd, and scrambled back. The creature also jerked away, pressing itself deeper into the bur oak's shadow.

Keito paused, sitting in the mud. "Are you ... a dragon?"

The creature crouched, watching him closely, wings curled tight against its back. Was it afraid of him?

Slowly, Keito rose to his knees. "You *are* a dragon! A baby one."

The dragonet bared its teeth.

"No, it's okay, I'm just a kid too, and I'd never hurt you. Not that I could."

The dragon looked past Keito's shoulder, then back at him.

"Why are you alone? Are you lost?"

The dragon bobbed its head, as if annoyed at the obvious question, then jerked its nose behind Keito again.

"Are you looking for someone?" Keito guessed.

The dragon shook its head and jabbed its nose past Keito's shoulder.

"Where did I come from?"

The dragon cocked its head, as if Keito was an idiot.

"Oh!" Keito exclaimed. "Is anyone with me?"

The dragon nodded.

"Just my Ojiisan. We passed a magician, but he's gone already. We're taking a load of brocade to Ryuki-Kerai. My family are weavers. We can give you a ride if you need help getting home."

The dragon seemed to consider this. Slowly, watching Keito closely, it crawled from under the bush. The creature was almost eight feet from nose to tail and big around as his brother's mastiff. But its shoulder only reached Keito's hip, and its glossy, folded wings rested even with his chest.

Keito could hardly believe he was meeting a real dragon. He clenched his hands, resisting the urge to touch the blue-rimmed scales. Such a familiar gesture from a non-DragonFriend would be rude. He stood and bowed. "I am Hata Keito, your humble servant."

The dragon bobbed his head.

Keito retrieved the dripping gourd. "If you'll follow, I can show you our cart." He backed up and waited. The dragon twitched his wings, then gathered himself and hopped across the streambed. He trotted up to Keito.

"Do you fly?" Keito asked. It would be amazing to see even a baby dragon fly from this close.

The dragon cocked its head, one golden eye looking straight up at Keito.

"Or ... are you still too young? How old *are* you?"

The dragon pointed at the sun with his nose, then swept his head across the sky.

"A day?" Keito frowned.

The dragon scratched a claw on the earth seven times.

"*Seven* days?" Keito gasped. "You *are* just a baby. How did you end up here all alone? Was it ... was the dragon I saw ... ? "

The dragonet looked at him, then nudged his hip and gestured up the slope.

"Oh, yes." They should go. Whatever the dragon's story, he couldn't tell it in signs. *But ... surely he must know the dead dragon.* What could've happened?

He clutched the water gourd and scrambled up the bank. The dragonet bounded after him, limping slightly. Keito winced. Crusty blood streaked his scales, and scratches marred his sides and flank. Whatever had happened, it hadn't been good.

The dragon slowed and returned his stare. Keito gulped and looked away. Ojiisan would know what to do, and they were only four hours from Ryuki-Kerai. They'd soon have the dragon safe where it belonged.

The boy trots ahead of me, diligently looking away. He is embarrassed for staring. I do not mind; he seems kind and honest. I wish I could speak to him, but he isn't a DragonFriend, so I cannot.

He crests the ridge and rounds a boulder. I follow. A cart sits in the gulley, its bed piled high with bright colors. The wind brings me a human's scent, older but reminiscent of the boy. His grandfather.

I start down the slope and pause. A second human is down there too, male, but younger. A strange spiciness, like the incense my mother's DragonFriend burned in his helmet, accompanies the second man-scent. Is he samurai too?

I squint at the blurry cart—my smell is better than my vision—and try to find the second man. Only one stooped figure is near the cart. But the wind cannot lie ... I swing my head into the breeze and make out a splash of red, further up the gulley. Even as a blur, he carries himself with authority. I reach out to him in thought. Hello?

He doesn't hear me. There's a distinct sense of listening when I speak into a DragonFriend's mind. But the red figure pauses, looks back, scans the cluttered slopes. I crouch beside the boulder, fear surging back to life. If he could not hear me, he should not have felt me.

Keito hurries down the slope. He didn't notice my halting. No, stop! I uselessly call to him. Don't tell them—

"Ojiisan!" Keito shouts, waving the gourd. "I found the water and guess what else. A lost baby dragon!"

"He was hiding in the creek bed and he looks hurt and he talked with signs and—"

Ojiisan pushed back his hat. "Slower, boya." He caught Keito's shoulder and gazed up the empty ridge. "What did you find?"

"Yes," a deep voice cut in. "Tell me what you found."

Keito whirled. The magician stood a few paces off, his dark eyes boring into the boy's.

Keito swallowed. "I ... it was only ..."

The magician strode forward, crimson robe flaring, and seized Keito by the chin. "What did you find?"

"Oh great magician." Ojiisan's voice was low. "Please remove your hand."

Keito swallowed, the motion constricted by the harsh grip. A scrabbling came from the left, and he glanced toward the ridge. Halfway down it the dragonet stood frozen, wings half-raised, looking uncertainly between the group and the hills.

The magician pushed Keito away and bowed to the dragonet. "Greetings, *ryu-sama*. I have been worried for your safety since we discovered your dead okaasan."

He stepped forward, and the dragonet stepped quickly back.

"Do not be afraid. I'm here to rescue you." His hand drifted beneath his robe.

The dragonet tasted the air, wings quivering. His eyes sought Keito's. Keito shivered. What was happening? The shogun's magician should protect a baby dragon, but Keito still felt the grip on his chin, saw dark eyes boring into his. Nothing about this man felt trustworthy.

"Come." The magician took another step forward. "Let's get you home." He withdrew his hand from his robes, and Keito recognized what it held.

"Run!" he shouted.

The dragonet whirled and dashed up the slope. The magician uttered an oath and fired after it, a small iron bolt ricocheting off a rock. The dragon vanished beyond the ridgeline.

The magician whirled on Keito, already re-cocking the device. Keito had seen these before; a larger version hung in his brother's quarters. Four sleek tubes each held an iron bolt with a gunpowder charge at their base. It was not a long-distance weapon, but up close, he'd seen it pierce a bison's skull.

"Why did you tell it to run?" the magician hissed.

Keito trembled. "I ... didn't want ..."

The magician brought up his weapon and fired.

Keito ducked and clapped his hands over his ears. He waited, shivering, for the pain to hit. He felt nothing, but something grunted and thumped to the ground behind him. He whirled. "Ojiisan!"

His grandfather sat against the cart wheel, his face pale, the iron bolt protruding from his thigh. "I'm ... all right, Kei-chan."

The sharp *click* of the gun being cocked sounded behind Keito. He looked up into the magician's cold face.

"You have a choice, little DragonFriend. Find the dragonet and bring it to me or"—he swung the gun to point at the old weaver—"your Ojiisan dies."

Keito looked from his groaning Ojiisan to the ridge where the dragon had vanished. "What if ... I can't find it?"

"Pray to your ancestors that you do. You have until sunset. Go!"

Keito ran. He scrambled up the hill on all fours, shale biting his palms. Tears blurred his vision, but he raced down the other side without wiping them away. Where should he go? What should he do? If he backtracked to the guardsmen, he wouldn't reach them in time. He *must* find the little dragon, but even then, how could he ask a baby to return to an evil magician?

Did the magician kill the dragon on the hill? Was the dragonet already running from him? Keito halted and scrubbed his eyes. He needed his Ojiisan. Despite all his daydreams, he *wanted* to be a weaver, wanted to sit beside his grandfather and learn the secrets of silk and loom.

"I just want my family," Keito choked out. "Please, I just want to go home with my whole family."

Something tugged at his *jinbei*. He whirled. The baby dragon stood behind him, earnestly looking up. He stepped back, stepped forward again, a question in his face. Relief surged through Keito. He dropped to his knees and wrapped both arms around the dragon.

"I don't know what to do!" He sobbed. "I'm not brave or strong like I thought. Ojiisan is in danger and there's no one who can help and I'm all alone and *I don't know what to do.*"

The dragon had tensed when Keito hugged him, but now he stepped forward, laid his neck about his shoulders, and drew him close. The boy clutched him tighter and poured out the magician's deadly threat.

The boy clings to me, his words running together in a flood, but the meaning is clear. He needs my help.

An hour ago I was lost and alone. Five minutes ago I was yet again. But now I am not. The boy cannot hear me, and while my mother's bond taught me much, it did not teach me how the bond is forged, the vows spoken or the ritual performed that allows dragon and man to know each other's hearts. But I do not need that here. I know my heart, and I know this boy's need.

I pull back my neck, bring my face close to his, and lick away his tears.
"That tickles!" He sniffs. "Does this mean ... do you know what to do?"
I nod and walk up the slope, back toward the waiting magician.
Keito hurries to catch up. "Can you show me the plan? I can help."
I look up at him with one eye. There is no plan, just a simple choice.
My mother and her samurai made it first, giving up their last moments
together to protect me. They showed me what friendship between man and
dragon should be. They made my choice easy.
I shake my head. No, I cannot explain. But when you and your Ojiisan
make it to Ryuki-Kerai, tell the others that I, too, lived up to the oath of the
DragonFriends.
I continue up the slope. After a few paces, a hand rests on my shoulder.
Yes, the boy understands, even if he doesn't know. Step matching step, we go
to face the magician.

Keito stood with the dragon and looked down at the lonely cart. Ojiisan
sat beside a wheel, his leg stretched out and wrapped in his cloak. The
magician paced before him, the red of his robe a bright stain in the gulch.

Keito rubbed the dragon's shoulder. The scales' edges were soft,
smooth and waxy. *I keep forgetting how young he is, yet he doesn't act like a*
child. Keito chewed his lip. What was the dragon planning? The creature
stood tensely beside him, the slight flicker of his nostrils the only sign
that he breathed. Keito wished he could soothe him, but his own heart
pounded fearfully in his chest.

A shiver ran through the dragon from his tiny horn nubs to his tail;
then he started down the slope.

The magician looked up, and a dark smile parted his lips. "You've brought back my young friend. Come, I am eager to be better acquainted."

The dragonet shuddered again but continued down the slope. Keito's heart beat faster. This was it. A few steps more and the dragonet would enact his plan. Should Keito try to help?

They halted in front of the magician. The baby dragon looked up at the leering magician, then slowly lay down at the man's feet, tucking his wings tight around his body.

The magician smiled. "Welcome, *friend.*"

Keito caught his breath. Wasn't he going to attack?

The magician squatted and lifted the dragon's chin. The dragonet squeezed his eyes shut but didn't resist.

"You should be excited. You are about to witness a new era between man and beast."

Keito shuddered. Do something. *Do something.*

The magician rose. "You've fulfilled your end of the bargain, boy. As soon as I've created a bond with this one, you and your grandfather may go."

Ojiisan hobbled to his feet. "Why not now?"

"Because we wouldn't want the dragon running off again before I'm finished." The magician smiled, and the baby dragon flinched. "Go care for your Ojiisan, boy."

In a daze, Keito supported Ojiisan and helped him onto the cart. Was this really it?

Ojiisan squeezed his arm. "Stoke up the mule. Get us ready to leave."

Keito nodded. He started to clamber off the cart, then paused. "Ojiisan, I thought the dragon would fight or ... run ... or something. But he's

... he just came back, and I didn't even ask. I don't understand. What's he doing?"

Ojiisan looked to where the dragon crouched on his belly, tail wrapped about his feet. The magician paced around him, muttering a low chant and drawing characters in the dust.

"It's the way of the DragonFriend—protect the weak, no matter the cost," Ojiisan whispered.

Keito gasped. "But he can't. He needs to get home!"

"Shh." Ojiisan squeezed his shoulder. "He is honoring his family and name. We must honor his choice. Go now."

Keito stumbled off the cart and toward the mule. He dumped the long-forgotten gourd into its tank, then moved to its belly to check the fire.

The magician's chant rose, and purple energy streamed up from the circle of characters. Keito didn't want to watch, but the ritual drew his gaze. The dragon crouched, eyes tight shut, his nostrils quivering. *The way of the DragonFriend.*

As if he sensed Keito, the dragon opened his eyes and locked gazes with the boy. Even without words, Keito could see the terror, the pain, in the young dragon's eyes. But also resolve, pride, even fear-laden joy.

"You're a true DragonFriend," Keito whispered.

The dragon bobbed his head, a salute from one friend to another, then shut his eyes and laid his head on his paws.

Keito's fingers curled around the furnace's handle. No. No! He wouldn't let the dragon lose his freedom without a fight.

The magician completed his circle and faced the baby dragon, his eyes lit by the glowing *kanji*. "And now, little one, you are mine."

"No!" Keito yelled. He yanked out the fire grate and flung the crimson coals into the magician's face. The man shrieked. The purple script flared high. The stench of burning flesh filled the air.

I was losing myself, my will being drawn in by the red man, sucked up like water on desert ground. The magic pulled me and it hurt and I knew this bond being forced upon me would never be a bond of friend to friend, like my mother shared with her samurai, but rather of master to slave. The magic wrapped around me, ready to seal the deed, then—

"You are mine."

"No!"

The word slices through the chains, even as something snaps into place inside me. A second consciousness, a second voice, appears beside my own. My eyes fly open.

The magician staggers back, clawing at his face. He reaches for the weapon at his side. I leap.

He's turned away, facing Keito and the cart, his right shoulder toward me as he raises the gun. I crash into him, teeth closing on his wrist, my weight forcing his arm up and away from the boy, from my friend. The magician cries out and staggers. Something explodes between my teeth, rattling my skull and upending earth and sky.

I blink and shake my head, trying to clear the ringing in my ears. I'm lying on something warm and crimson. Smoke and sulfur stain the air, mingling with the fading tang of magic.

Footsteps pound up behind me.

"*Little dragon!*" *Keito skids to a halt at my shoulder and gapes down. "Is he ... ?*"

I push myself up off the limp crimson form. Its head is thrown back, eyes glassy. A black bolt protrudes from beneath its chin.

He is indeed dead, Kei-chan.

The boy shudders and pulls the robe across the dead face. "*I suppose we should bring him back to Ryuki-Kerai. Though I'm not sure how to put him on the cart, what with Ojiisan's leg ...*"

I shake my head. It will not hurt to leave him for a few hours. We can send back riders to fetch the body.

"*True.*" *Keito pauses, then turns wide eyes on me. "Did you just talk in my head?*"

I stare at the boy, again aware of the warm second presence humming within my mind. I tentatively reach out. Yes?

I can feel him hear me even before he leaps and claps his hands. "*We can talk! I'm talking to a dragon! What happened? How did we ... ?*"

"*Kei-chan!*" *Ojiisan shouts from the cart. "Are you hurt? Is the red crow dead?*"

"*Ojiisan! The dragon talked to me!*"

Ojiisan pushes his hat back and stares at me. Slowly, he grips the pile of brocade and wobbles to his feet.

"*Ojiisan, be careful! Your leg.*" *Keito dashes forward and seizes his arm.*

The old weaver grips his shoulder, but his eyes remain on me. "*So. You've chosen my Kei-chan?*"

I slowly nod. I'm still not sure what happened—if I chose him or if, somehow, we chose each other. But I understand what the bond means, and I do not regret it. He has the heart of a warrior.

Keito flushes. "*He says I have a warrior's heart, Ojiisan, and ...*" *He falters, but I encourage him. "He is honored to have me as his friend.*"

Ojiisan bows deeply. "You honor our family greatly. I am a poor, foolish grandfather, but I do not think you could find a better friend."

Nor do I.

"Come." Ojiisan settles on the seat. "If my DragonFriend grandson will rebuild the fire he threw in that coyote's face, we should reach Ryuki-Kerai shortly after dark."

Keito nods and hurries to obey. I crawl up the heap of brocade and find a place at the top. When Keito returns, I drop my neck so my head is level with his.

He reaches up and strokes me. "Thank you for saving Ojiisan."

Thank you for saving me.

"Is that what it means? To be a DragonFriend?"

I think back to my mother, the love she had for her samurai and his care for her. I believe so.

"Oh." He wriggles on the seat. Ojiisan adjusts some dials and steam huffs from the mule.

Do you regret this? We will be bonded for life. That's a long time to put the needs of another ahead of your own.

Keito shakes his head and rests his hand on my neck. "Not when they would do the same for me. Not when they're my friend."

Ojiisan releases the brake, and with a shudder that sets the fabric swaying, we start down the slope toward Ryuki-Kerai, city of the Dragon-Friends.

A companion story to "To Share the Sky" by A.C. Williams

Where I'm Supposed to Be

Callie Thomas

Rain spattered against my cloak as I stood in the mud, surprised that the place from my childhood bedtime stories was real.

Her sign tapped the side of the wagon as it swung in the breeze. I caught the lettering, hand-carved and in clear print: *Madame Luna's Magical Curiosities.*

Exactly how my mother had described it so many years ago.

The dull green paint of the exterior was chipped and peeling, revealing the dark wood underneath. Thick clouds of fog swirled from the wagon's undercarriage like wisps of smoke curling through the wheel spokes.

In the lone window hung a drape so dark it dampened the glow from within—and hid the secrets inside. Narrow stairs led up to a curved door, black symbols scrawled along the edge. Ancient words I couldn't comprehend added to the mystery.

I flinched when the door flew wide.

"Are you lost, child?" An elderly woman leaned out the door. The dim light from behind silhouetted her plump frame.

I flicked my hood back, the drizzle of rain cool on my cheeks. "I'm where I'm supposed to be," I said with a calm I didn't feel. "I've come to purchase an item."

"A customer! Why didn't you say so sooner? Come in, come in." Her long skirts swayed as she moved from the door, beckoning me to follow.

I stomped up the steps, then knocked off the muck that had clung to my boots from the bog and stepped inside the wagon's large interior. Waves of tingles coursed through me when I passed through the door frame. My cloak and wool frock were instantly bone dry.

I was in the presence of magic.

Another step and another illusion. The room was double the size of my family's living room and kitchen combined, with only two long tables positioned in the center of the space. Shadows slithered from the dark corners of the wagon, obscuring the objects that littered the tabletops. The floor creaked as I shifted closer, the noise echoing around me. With an unexpected gust from outside, the door slammed shut, summoning the candles on the tables to life.

"Don't be afraid. If you're here, you were supposed to find me. Look around and let me know if you have any questions. You can only—"

"—choose one," I finished for her, my eyes scanning the weapons on the table to my left.

"Hmm," Madame Luna said, muttering under her breath. Her gaze bore into my shoulder blades.

My mother's voice spoke in my mind, reminding me of everything she had seen when she had come to purchase her magical item. Her words were comforting. I hadn't heard them these last few months since she passed away.

"The bow of accuracy, the sword of resilience, the dagger of truth, the spear of agility, the axe of courage, and the whip of fire." I said each item under my breath, remembering the names by heart, my fingers trailing over them.

"You did not come here for those," the old woman stated, appearing as silent as a ghost at my side.

The candlelight highlighted her small nose and thin lips, painted a bold wine. Her ample cheeks were full, stretching her skin and smoothing her wrinkles. Dark honey eyes searched my face, shining with curiosity. If it wasn't for her straight silver hair, I would have thought her to be thirty years younger.

But how could she be the same age now as when my mother visited this wagon thirty-seven years ago? The answer was always magic.

"You're right," I agreed. Yet my gaze still locked on each weapon, etching their beauty in my mind. The turquoise handle of the dagger, the bronze glint of the axe, the ruby embedded in the handle of the sword that burned in the light. I couldn't rush. Once you left Madame Luna's, purchase or no purchase, you could never come back.

All sales were final.

Turning toward the other table, I jumped, startled by my own reflection in the floor-length mirror. There were two ornate gold mirrors side by side, and though I stood before the one, both showed my wild red hair curling around my confused expression. How could both mirrors show the same image?

"The mirrors of illusion are not for sale, I'm afraid. Someone has already purchased them."

She stepped to my right, standing before the second mirror that still reflected my wide blue eyes, too afraid to blink and miss a moment. With a snap of fabric, she whipped a white sheet over the mirrors, hiding them from view and drawing my attention back to her. She grinned at me.

"You are familiar," she drawled out.

"Am I?"

"Have you come to hear your fortune?"

I cringed, and she chuckled.

"Afraid of the future before you ... or of the past that won't let go?"

Her words pierced me, too close to the truth. As we stared at each other, I was suddenly overcome with nerves. My hand plucked at the loose thread of my cloak. What if she remembered? Would she realize I was nothing but my mother's shadow?

"Another table, perhaps?" Madame Luna stepped back, waving her crooked fingers at the items across from me.

Stay focused.

Just another assortment of random objects to the novice eye, but I knew their power was extraordinary.

"Do you know these too?" she asked, humor lacing her words.

I reached out my hand, pale and smooth compared to hers, and listed each item as I went. "The chalice of healing, the crystal of memories, the elixir of affection, the fife of peace, and the brush of beauty."

She lifted a brow. "You missed one."

I scanned the table, repeating the names in my head. Thousands of times I had heard the stories—I hadn't forgotten one. "Impossible."

She gently grabbed my wrist, moving my hand to the open spot at the end of the table and pushing my fingertips down into the coarse fabric. Fabric I couldn't see. "The cloak of invisibility. It's new and very expensive."

My mouth parted with a sigh. Tucking my fingers into the folds of the fabric, they disappeared. Where could I go unseen? Would this protect me if King Bartholomew accused me of performing magic? It didn't matter that I wasn't a witch; they would still execute me.

Just like my mother.

My breath hitched at the thought, and I jerked my hand back. Like ripping open a wound, my heart ached with each beat. Would it ever stop hurting?

"What is your name?" she asked over my shoulder.

Lost in my sadness, I replied without thinking. "Clover."

"Ah-ha!" she exclaimed.

I winced. Information freely given was useless, for the items on the tables didn't come with a price tag of gold or silver. No, you had to pay with a piece of yourself: memories, thoughts, or information to be forgotten forever.

I had hoped the similarity between my mother and me would pique Madame Luna's interest, but now I had lost that, too. There had to be something she wanted from me for a trade. To hide my blunder, I touched the engraving of marigolds on the brush, pretending to inspect it as if I hadn't lost my leverage.

"As I told your mother so long ago, that brush is wasted on you. Your beauty shines bright from the inside. Come now. Let's not waste any more time. What are you looking for? It surely doesn't sit here on my tables."

I took a deep breath, faced her, and prepared for the moment of truth. I had hoped to lead up to it, but it was now or never. "What can bring the dead back to life?"

Her mouth turned down at the corners. "Oh, sweet Clover. There is no magic here that can do what you wish. Only Ruah knows what is beyond this plane and into the next. It's up to you to find peace."

"I don't want peace. I want her back," I ground out, staring at my boots. "They say there is a wishing pool at the top of Mt. Cynale. Do you think—?"

"No. I meant what I said. Nothing here can do what you wish. And the path to that pool is fraught with danger. You seek death if you seek the wishing pool. Have you nothing to live for?"

Unexpectedly, Laurent's face flashed in my mind with his thick curly hair and brown eyes the color of rich earth. His smile was soft, shy almost. I blinked away thoughts of the shepherd's son. We were strangers, exchanging basic pleasantries on market days. He could barely bumble through a sentence without his face flushing scarlet when he ordered a bushel of apples from our stall each week.

Why would I think of him?

"What would she want for you? To spend your life looking for her?"

My last memory of her unfurled like the soft petals of a bud, blossoming in color whether I wanted it to or not. Pressing my fingers into my eyes, I willed it to stop, but instead it transported me there.

A loud knock shook our cottage walls.

"Open up by order of His Royal Highness Bartholomew Dylan Fergus Reginalt Abel, King of Cadell and ruler of the five territories."

Mother's blue eyes flew wide. She took the small sack of beans from around her neck and pressed it into my trembling hands. What we feared had come true—they had come for the beans of transformation.

The guards didn't wait for us to open the door, barging in with their swords drawn. Chairs were knocked over and the table overturned, our plates shattering across the floor. My mother didn't cower when they grabbed her, her eyes sparking with rage. A man knocked me back, and I slammed into the wall, almost losing my grip on the magic beans.

"Do what you want with me, but don't touch her," she seethed.

Two of the guards shrunk back. "We only have orders for you, not the girl."

"What crimes do you charge me with?"

"Witchcraft as reported by an anonymous royal adversary. How do you plead?"

She met my eyes from across the room and blinked three times: I love you. *"Guilty."*

It was a lie. She wasn't magical; it was the beans. But if they knew, they would burn everything, including us both.

"By chance, did Jacklyn ever plant those beans she purchased from me? They would grow whatever her heart desired."

Hearing my mother's name jarred me out of my thoughts, and my eyes narrowed.

"Yes. She did. We were the only farm to have yielding crops in the middle of winter." I spun away, clenching my jaw. I tried not to think of the weapons on the table. "Did you know what would happen?"

"Information doesn't come without a price," she singsonged, and I realized I had given away another snippet of information for free.

Anger fueled me, spinning me back in front of her, my cloak whipping about my shoulders. "I bet you knew exactly what would happen to her when she planted those seeds. She might as well have dug her own grave, and you helped."

Instead of arguing back, her eyes turned soft, and she pressed a hand over her heart. "I promise I never knew. The things I make and the visions I see, they are gifts from above. Once they are given, they are lost to me forever. I remember my customers and what they have purchased, but how they use their item is beyond my control."

"And the information you steal?"

"I never steal, you stubborn child," she snapped, her back straight. The candles flickered, and she added, "I will not stand here and be insulted. Leave."

I had ruined everything.

Falling to my knees, I buried my face in my hands and sobbed. Now I would leave with nothing. Months of traveling on foot, following the stars, and scouting the wagon tracks had been for naught. I hunched my back, curling into myself as my shoulders shook.

Or maybe I knew it was finally time to say goodbye.

She isn't coming back.

"Clover."

Sniffling, I lifted my head, Madame Luna's face blurry through my tears. I croaked, "What do you sell that can heal a broken heart? The chalice of healing?"

Her hand rested on my head, the warmth of it comforting. "Ruah says internal wounds heal differently than physical ones. Only time can heal those."

"And th-th-this Ruah? Would he—?"

She laughed, stroking my hair. "To converse with Ruah would be a grand thing, indeed. But I am not worthy."

Dejected, I let my hands fall to my lap, tears glistening on my palms. "Then my trip was pointless."

"Was it? You have not left yet."

"I have nothing else to give you. I gave you all my secrets for free."

"A secret freely given, as to a friend, is purer and more precious than one that is bartered. Here," she offered. In her palm rested a pendant of a pressed four-leaf clover—like one of the many that grew in the fields of our farm—attached to a silver chain.

I scrunched up my nose, but I accepted it anyway. Perhaps that was all I was worth—a plain old clover you could find in any field.

"Don't make a face," she said, looping it over my head before I could stop her. "It's a lucky clover. It wasn't what you came looking for, but it's what you need. Soon, you will stand on your own two feet again without the past hovering over you. Your future is waiting for you. Jacklyn died protecting it."

My heart clenched as my finger glided over the clover. "What does it do?"

"Let it guide you."

"Where?"

"To happiness."

"How will I know?"

"You'll know." She winked.

"What do you I owe you for the necklace?"

"Consider it a present from a friend. Hold it and remember how lucky you are to live. If you don't want to live for yourself, live for her and her sacrifice."

"Lucky ..." I ran my thumb over the encased clover.

"Now, off with you. I sense another customer on the way." She placed a comforting hand on my shoulder, guiding me to the door that swung open on its own. "You are the first person I wish I could break my rules for. Maybe we will see each other again, young Clover."

And with those words, she shoved me out the door.

I expected to fall on my face, but I stumbled onto the cobblestone, the walkway outside our tiny cottage. Spinning around, I saw the cracked frame of our door, now closed. I had left it open the day I decided to find Madame Luna's wagon.

Or maybe I hadn't left at all?

Frantic, my fingers searched through the fabric of my cloak, grasping the clover pendant like a lost memory. It was real.

Entering the cold house reminded me of just how alone I was. It was up to me to take care of the farm and orchard. Righting a chair, I put things back in their places. As I lit the wicks of the candles, sweet memories flooded my mind. My mother's rocking chair where she knitted. Her favorite shawl hanging by the fireplace mantel. It was as if she was reminding me that she was still close by.

I knew the truth. I didn't need to bring her back to feel her presence. I would always have her memories. I sat in her chair, wondering what to do next.

Touching my pendant, I closed my eyes. "I'll make you proud, Mother."

A knock at the door startled me. With a heavy heart, I approached, worried it could be the guards returning.

Instead, it was a red-faced Laurent, holding a crate of eggs, milk, and fresh cheese. His long bangs curled across his forehead, covering one eye. He opened his mouth to say something, then shut it fast, his teeth clicking together. If it was possible, his face grew even redder.

"Hello, Laurent."

"I—uh, we—uh, this is for you." His words rushed together as he pushed the box into my arms. "My ma saw the light in your cottage and sent me over. I—we haven't seen you in a few months, so we assumed you'd be hungry since you've missed so many market days. It was like you had disappeared, and I stopped by a few times before, but you weren't here, which made me worry—"

"As you can see, I'm well," I interrupted before he ran out of air. I shifted the awkward crate in my arms, trying to get a better grip.

"Oh, here. I should have brought that in for you." He snatched the box back. "How thoughtless of me."

I surveyed the broken china on the floor. "Really, you are too kind. It's a mess since Mother ..."

My throat clamped up, emotions strangling me. The memory of that day began to repeat in my mind. Alone. I was so alone.

Tears flowed freely down my cheeks, surprising me with their ferocity.

"Clover," he whispered. The crate thudded at his feet, and he clasped my shoulders. "You mustn't cry. *Please.*"

But once I started, I couldn't stop, crying until every last drop was spent. I didn't know when his arms wrapped around me and pressed me to his chest. Or when he started rocking me back and forth, making soothing noises. Or when I dug my fingers into the wool of his tunic, desperate to keep him close.

"You're not alone," he murmured into my hair, sounding more sure of himself than he ever had.

My heart pounded in my ears. He was right. The pendant heated under my cloak, and a feeling passed through me, a rightness, that I was exactly where I was supposed to be.

The Golden Curse

Jill Williamson

It must be a mistake.

Empress Evaleen stood beside her bed, staring at the flecks of gold on her pillow. She pressed her palm against her chest as if the action might quell the sudden race of her heart. "Fetch Chancellor Roua. Now!"

The maid shoved the breakfast tray onto the table and fled the room, pushing past the guard, Voana, who filled the doorway.

As a woman, everything about Voana was a little too much. She stood a little too tall. Her eyes, nose, and head were a little too big—chest a little too flat, teeth a little too crooked. Yet as a guard, she was formidable.

Voana approached. "Something wrong, ma'am?"

Evaleen gestured to her disheveled bedsheets. "What do *you* see?"

The guard inched closer, brow furrowed as she examined the bed. "Looks like dirt, ma'am. Maybe scraps of leather?"

Evaleen released a pent-up breath. "That must be it. I informed my tailor just yesterday that my leather belt was falling apart."

Light bloomed through the windows as the clouds moved past the morning suns, and the flecks on the white linen sheets sparkled. Dread pooled in Evaleen's stomach. Surely it couldn't be gold.

The door burst open and Chancellor Roua rushed inside, her emerald robes billowing. The maid slipped in behind her.

"Remain calm, Your Eminence." Roua lifted a monocle to one eye and studied the bed for an agonizingly long time, her brow pinched. She spun around and seized a spoon off the breakfast tray. This she jabbed at one of the gold flakes.

"It has every appearance of gold, ma'am. I'll have it examined to be certain." Roua claimed the empty cup and saucer from the tray. She scooped flakes onto the saucer and covered them with the cup. "Try to eat something. I'll send for the physician."

Roua bowed and rushed from the room, leaving Evaleen alone with the maid and guard. If doctors were coming, there was no point getting dressed.

"Well? Fetch me a fresh cup," Evaleen snapped. "I intend to have my breakfast."

The maid curtsied and fled.

The morning passed by in tedious agony from the presence of far too many ignorant servants. Chancellor Roua assembled a conglomeration of medical experts: physicians, healers, medicine men, alchemists, apothecaries, surgeons, dentatores, herbalists, and midwives. All agreed that the skin on the back of Evaleen's shoulders was flaking, yet no one would confirm that the golden curse had come to their empress. They were cowards, all of them. Had Evaleen not been terrified, she might have thrown them all in prison.

In the end, Evaleen had no choice but to summon Grand Master Finhaut, who had once served her father as chancellor. He took one look at Evaleen's shoulders and said, "It's the golden curse, ma'am."

At this, the assembly muttered, low enough that Evaleen could discern no clear words yet loud enough to push her irritation too far.

"Out!" she screamed. "All but the chancellor, Grand Master Finhaut, and my guard."

Everyone scattered, and in moments, Evaleen again had a modicum of peace.

"It's a myth," Roua said. "Over 250 years have passed since Empress Aosta ruled."

"The golden curse is no myth," the grand master said.

A flash of cold ran up Evaleen's spine. "I cannot simply wait around until I am solid gold and the Kupio come to melt me down."

"That would never happen," Roua said.

"Yet that's what legend says happened to Empress Aosta." Evaleen's heart had never beat so quickly. On top of that, her hands were shaking, and she felt as if she might burst into tears at any moment.

What had she done to deserve such a fate? She was too young to die. Plus, she had no heir. What would become of her dynasty? Would Kupion invade?

Only when she had mastered her emotions did she speak. "What can be done?"

"The answers you seek are in the royal vault," Finhaut said.

Evaleen reached for her robe. "Show me."

They climbed a spiral stone staircase to a cramped tower. Finhaut bade the guard retrieve a tiny silver box from a high shelf. Roua used her sleeve to wipe off a thick layer of dust.

The box had been cast from silver with intricate whorls and flowers. It was so tarnished it looked black. On the top, thick with grime, was the inverted shape of the royal signet ring.

Evaleen set her ring in the indentation and pressed down. The box clicked open, revealing five small pearls and a scroll that said:

Those inflicted with the golden curse must travel to the wishing pool in Romont and bathe in its waters. Take the pearls with you. They can help.

Evaleen had so many questions. "What does this mean?"

"You must go to Romont and take the pearls with you," Finhaut said. "The message is clear, ma'am."

Clear as gold. "How did you know this was here?"

"The pearls were taken from the pool where Empress Aosta died," Finhaut said. "It is written in the annals."

Rage curdled in Evaleen's chest. "If Empress Aosta died in the wishing pool, why should I bathe in it? Clearly it did her no good."

"I know not, Your Eminence," the grand master said.

Evaleen turned to Roua. "I don't suppose you have a better idea."

The Chancellor shook her head. "I'm sorry, ma'am."

Evaleen carried the box back to her chambers. She read the scroll and examined the pearls repeatedly. How in all the lands could five tiny pearls help?

She held them and wished for healing. When nothing changed, she considered having one ground into powder for a tonic, but destroying one felt too risky. She summoned her advisors and commanded them to find an explanation that made sense.

They found none.

In the end, she had no choice. She must go to Romont.

The journey would take the better part of three days. Evaleen ordered Chancellor Roua to prepare a grand procession. Should this be the last her people saw of her, she wanted them to recall her magnificence, wealth, and power.

Yet the chancellor brought forth dire news. "Kupio raiders are outside your gates, ma'am. They want to speak with you. Peacefully, they say."

A surge of terror coursed through Evaleen. "We both know they're *not* here for peace." Her mind raced until she settled on an idea. "Let them wait," she said, feeling quite clever. "I will go in disguise with only five guards." There would be no parade, but throwing off the Kupio was more important.

Evaleen admired herself in the mirror. The peasant disguise made the coming journey feel like a jolly game, which pleasantly overshadowed the dread of the golden curse.

The door opened and the guard, Voana, entered. She bowed deeply. "I mean no disrespect, ma'am, but I beg you take someone else to Romont as your fifth. My brother is ill. I am his keeper, and I dare not leave him unattended."

Fire burned through Evaleen. "I've been sentenced to death, and you wish to desert me?"

"No, ma'am," said the guard, her eyes rimmed in red. "It's just that my brother is dear to me and—"

"Your empress is not so dear?"

"That is not what I meant, ma'am, I—"

"Kupio raiders are camped on my doorstep, seeking my demise," Evaleen snapped. "I must reach the wishing pools of Romont as soon as possible and will not take a quivering maid as my chaperone. Refuse to serve me and you will be executed for treason. The choice is yours."

The guard swallowed, jaw clenched. Finally, she nodded. "I will accompany you to Romont, ma'am."

"A wise choice," Evaleen said.

Within the hour, the small party had sneaked out the garden gate. They now rode two abreast through the capital city. When the lead guard steered his horse toward the river road, Evaleen drew her mount to a halt.

"Market Street is the fastest way out of the city," she said. "Plus, it's so crowded no one will notice us."

"It's not safe," Voana said. "With the ever-increasing taxes and reduced guard, Market Street has become a hovel of smugglers and thieves."

"We'll take the river road," the lead guard said.

"You dare accuse me of not knowing my own city?" Not one guard would meet her reproachful glare, so she nudged her horse between theirs and led the way herself. "We will take Market Street, and that is final."

As predicted, Market Street was busy this time of day. Vendors sold wool, lace, tea, wine, and other spirits. All highly taxed export goods, Evaleen couldn't help notice. These people were stealing from the crown. She wanted to confront them, but now was not the time.

She entered a spot of congestion. A sea of people grew thick around her horse. "Move aside!" she yelled. She squeezed her knees and clicked her tongue. "Come on, go!"

The horse whinnied and tossed its head. A hand clutched her leg. She glanced down and saw a hooded person unlatch her saddlebag. Another took hold of her reins.

"Stop!" she yelled. "Thieves!"

Someone pulled her off the horse and into the crowd—two men dragging her toward a market stall. Before Evaleen could think of how to escape, Voana intercepted them. Her guard tripped the first man from behind and kicked the second in the chest. When both men fell, the guard dragged Evaleen away through the crowd.

"We must go back for my saddlebag and horse," Evaleen said.

Yet the guard did not stop until they reached a tenement at the end of a narrow alley. "We'll wait here for the others," she said.

But the others did not come.

As the time passed, the back of Evaleen's neck grew stiff, making it hard to turn her head. She stepped in front of the guard and lifted her hair. "What do you see?"

A drawn out silence, then, "Your neck is gold, ma'am," Voana said.

Evaleen sucked in a breath. There was no time to waste. "We must leave. Now," she said.

"We don't have any supplies or transportation," Voana said. "And I have little money."

"I cannot return to the castle, not with the Kupio waiting." Evaleen tapped a silk pouch tied to a cord around her neck. "I have the pearls. They're all I really need."

"A friend of mine owns a stable on the outskirts of town," Voana said. "We can rent horses there."

The guard led the way to the stables. They found her friend Tigdur shoeing a horse in the yard.

"Vo!" the man said. "Last time I saw you, you were knee-high to a cricket. How's your brother?"

Voana's eyes misted. "Not well, I'm afraid. He has lenamia. The doctor says he could pass any day."

"Oh," Tigdur said. "How dreadful. I'm terribly sorry. If there's anything I can do, please—"

"You can give us two horses," Evaleen said.

"I beg your pardon?" Tigdur said.

"We're in a hurry to reach Romont," Voana said. "How much to rent two horses?"

"You, I'll charge five skilts." Tigdur scowled at Evaleen. "Her, twenty."

"That's robbery!" Evaleen said.

Tigdur slammed his thumb against his chest. "I decide who I do business with and for what price."

Voana counted the money in her purse. "We can both ride mine," she told Evaleen.

"You rent two horses or none," Tigdur said. "Twenty-five is the price. Take it or don't."

Voana pulled the empress aside. "Offer him a pearl."

The audacity. "I cannot give these away!"

"Then tell him who you are. I'm sure he'll lend aid."

"Absolutely not! There are villains everywhere, pulling people from horses, stealing, smuggling. You're the only one I trust with my identity."

Voana went back to Tigdur. "Looks like we'll be walking."

"Wait." Evaleen withdrew one of the pearls from the pouch and offered it to Tigdur. She clenched her jaw but forced out the words. "Will you take this for both horses?"

The man pinched the pearl between this thumb and forefinger and held it up to the sky. "Done," he said. "I'll have my stableman ready the horses."

As they were waiting, a man returned three horses that had been stolen. Tigdur exclaimed with delight over the return of the animals. When he tried to offer a reward, the man refused.

How odd. Who would refuse a reward?

Then, as Voana was helping Evaleen into the saddle, a carriage arrived with a woman and two small children. Tigdur knelt in the dirt and embraced them.

"What's that about?" Evaleen asked.

"His wife left him last year." Voana mounted her horse. "It seems she has returned."

Now on horseback, they made good progress. Evaleen still smarted at having given up one of her pearls. "What if four pearls aren't enough to save me when I reach the pool?"

Voana glanced at her. "Didn't the scroll say they were to help along the way?"

It *had* said something like that. Voana was a little too smart for her own good, but Evaleen needed her, so she would give the impudent woman some leeway with her opinions.

"How old is your brother?" Evaleen asked.

"One and twenty," Voana said.

"And he has lenamia?"

"Yes. I convinced my neighbor to stay with him. It will take most of my wages to pay her and the doctor."

Evaleen looked away. "I will compensate them," she said.

"That's unnecessary."

"Yet I will do it," Evaleen said.

"Thank you."

Hours later, they reached Porsel. Knots of crowded, muddy streets encircled rows of moldering tenements. Voana found an inn and paid with her coins. The room was little more than a closet with two beds. A maid delivered bowls of watery stew. They ate, and Voana fell asleep as soon as she lay down. Evaleen could hear people and music right through the walls. The itchy bedding made her skin crawl. She sighed. My, how far the mighty empress had fallen.

Somehow, time passed. She next opened her eyes to the brightness of three suns. Yet when she tried to move, her limbs were stiff.

She cried out, "Guard!"

"My name is Voana." She appeared at Evaleen's bedside. "If you're so adamant that no one know who you are, you'd best start calling me by name."

"Fine. Just ... I cannot move. Peek down the back of my gown and tell me what you see."

Voana pulled back the covers and lifted the neckline away. Her eyebrows rose. "More of you is gold today," she said.

Her words incited panic. "How much more?"

"Your entire back, the backs of your legs, and the backs of your arms too."

Voana's words turned Evaleen's insides to liquid. She tried to breathe, but there didn't seem to be enough air in this hovel of a room. "Not even the pearls can save me if I die in this bed!"

Voana reached for her hand. "May I?"

Evaleen nodded, her body tense.

Voana pulled her to a sitting position, which felt strange—as if she had a bad sunburn. Not terribly painful.

"You'll have to help me dress," Evaleen said.

Voana reached for Evaleen's gown. "Ready when you are."

So many people, everywhere, rail-thin and haggard. Clusters lined the streets, their belongings strewn like debris beside them.

"I didn't expect so many homeless in a village like Porsel," Evaleen said.

"Few families can afford to own a home," Voana said, "especially with the high taxes."

A twinge of nausea made Evaleen reconsider her recent tax initiative. Was she to blame for the poverty here?

They approached a family seated on the roadside with a basket of fresh bread and a sign that said, "Mending, bread, and song: one kopar each."

Before Voana could advise against it, Evaleen dismounted and approached the family.

"I have a tear in my hem," she said.

"Sit, sit!" said the mother. "Trella, sing. Kolli, bread."

Evaleen dropped in front of the woman, who took up sewing her hem. The boy set a round of bread in Evaleen's hands, and the girl began to sing.

This song of the suns,
For you I sing.
Four suns for Carroz,
Great light they bring.
One eastern sun,
And two in the west.
The fourth one shines bright:
Our great Empress.

Whether it was the subject matter, the child's lovely voice, or both, Evaleen didn't know, but she wept. When the sewing and singing ended, Voana stepped forward to pay the family, but Evaleen held up her hand.

"I will pay them." She pulled out the pouch, revealing gold skin on the back of her hand.

The children gasped, eyes wide as Evaleen placed a pearl on their mother's outstretched palm.

The mother's eyes filled with moisture. "Bless you," she whispered.

As Voana helped Evaleen mount her horse, Evaleen smiled, pondering how she was changing. The gold was hardening her on the outside, but on the inside, she was growing soft.

A wagon stopped behind them. A man climbed out and approached the family.

"Madam," he said. "You are the one who makes such delicious bread?"

"Yes, sir," the mother said. "Would you like some?"

"Indeed," the man said, "and more than that. I run a bakery in town and my cook has quit. Might you like a job?"

The woman's face lit up. "Oh, yes, sir!"

"The previous baker lived in an apartment over the store. You are welcome to it."

"We would like it very much, thank you. Children, get the basket. We are going home."

The family joined the man in the wagon, which he steered away.

"Did you see … ?" Voana stared after them, her voice thoughtful. "As soon as you gave them the pearl, they were blessed with good fortune, just like Tigdur with the return of his family and the stolen horses."

"You think it's because of the pearls?" Evaleen asked.

Voana shrugged. "Don't you?"

Could Voana be right? Had the stable owner and the family both received blessings because of the pearls? If so, why them and not her? She still had three pearls, yet she turned more gold with each passing hour.

They reached the town of Lovat in early evening and used nearly all of Voana's remaining money to rent a room at an inn. When Evaleen mentioned that they were headed to Romont, the young man working the counter brightened.

"My love lives in Romont!" the server said. "I work here to save money so we can marry."

"What is your name?" Evaleen demanded.

"Jakur, ma'am."

The young man hadn't seemed to notice Evaleen's haughtiness, but she softened her tone. "Are there no jobs in Romont?"

"None that I am qualified for."

"Surely it won't take long to save for a wedding," Voana said.

Jakur sighed. "Five years, maybe?"

"Five!" Evaleen couldn't believe it. "Must you have such an expensive ceremony?"

"Oh, the money is not for a ceremony," Jakur said. "It's to build us a house. I've already been working here one year, so only four more to go."

Ridiculous. Evaleen couldn't imagine having to earn enough money to marry. She reached for her pouch.

Voana grabbed her hand. "Are you sure?" she asked.

"Yes." Giving the pearl to the family outside Porsel had been incredibly rewarding. Evaleen wanted to do something for this young man and his betrothed. Besides, it would be a grand experiment. If Jakur received instant blessings, she would know the pearls were the cause.

"Saving for your future is admirable," Evaleen said. "I would like to contribute." She handed him a pearl.

Jakur's eyes widened as he caught sight of the gold on her wrist, but his gaze quickly shifted to the tiny gem. "For me? Why?"

"I just want to help," Evaleen said.

"Thank you for your generosity." Jakur clasped the pearl in both hands and bowed low.

"You're welcome." Evaleen beamed at Voana. "Shall we explore the town?"

"It's not safe out now," Jakur said. "Reports say raiders are headed this way."

"Kupio raiders?" Evaleen asked.

"Yes. They seek the Empress," Jakur said, glancing at Evaleen's wrist. "Word is she is headed to Romont."

"How interesting!" Voana said. "I've always wanted to see the empress." She grabbed Evaleen's arm and tugged her toward the stairs. "We'll stay in our room and have an early dinner. Just to be safe. Thank you for the warning."

"I'll bring your meal right away." Jakur lifted his joined hands, the pearl still inside. "And thank you, again!"

Voana woke Evaleen early. "I thought it best if we left before dawn," she said.

"Anything to avoid the Kupio," Evaleen said, shuddering.

She had turned gold on her front now, but once Voana helped her stand, she was still able to walk. On their way out, they saw Jakur by the stables.

"Friends!" he called. "A man offered me a job in Romont. The innkeeper there is doing a poor job, so I will replace him. Plus, the inn has a house next door for the innkeeper."

Voana eyed Evaleen. "That's a stroke of luck," she said.

"Indeed!" Jakur's grin shone as brightly as the risen suns. "I will travel to Romont today to tell Harpa. Who knows? We could be married tonight!"

"Won't Harpa need some time to plan a wedding?" Evaleen asked.

Jakur laughed. "We need nothing fancy. Only each other."

What an odd notion. Evaleen couldn't imagine being content with so little, yet she longed for a simple joy like Jakur's.

"Congratulations," Voana said.

They bade Jakur farewell and set off for Romont.

"You must not give away any more pearls," Voana said.

Evaleen frowned. "Why not?"

"They're clearly magic. You might need them when you get to the pool."

"But they do nothing for me," Evaleen said. "Why not use them to help others?"

"I simply worry that we will reach the wishing pool and have no pearl to save you."

They arrived in Romont after dark. The wishing pool was another ten miles south of the city, so they decided to eat, then find a place to rest until morning. As it turned out, there was only one inn.

"This must be where Jakur will soon be employed," Voana said. "The inn with the incompetent innkeeper."

"We should still try it," Evaleen said. "I am starving."

A man named Svikari met them at the door. "Welcome!" he said, smiling. "You look weary. Have you traveled far?"

"From Porsel," Voana said.

"I'll get you something to eat while I put up your horses. Will it be one room or two?"

"I'm afraid we cannot afford to stay," Voana said. "We would like to buy some dinner, though."

"I see." Svikari took three kopars from Voana and dished up two bowls of soup. "I cannot send two ladies out into the night," he said. "If you pay to stable the horses, you're welcome to sleep in the cellar for free."

"That's very generous." Voana glanced at Evaleen. "What do you say?"

"Better than sleeping outside," she said.

"Excellent!" Svikari said. "Eat. I will take care of your horses, then make up two pallets in the cellar." He took the last of Voana's money and left.

"He seems kind," Evaleen said.

Voana chuckled. "You've changed a lot on this journey."

"I have, haven't I?" Evaleen said. "With death looming over me, it matters not whether my shoes match my gown or if my toast is burned. The pearls showed me how to bless others."

"Once you're cured," Voana said, "you'll get to do a lot more of that."

"I hope you are right," Evaleen said.

Svikari led them to the cellar. It was dark—lit only by Svikari's candle and dim moonlight coming through a casement window near the ceiling. Evaleen did not see any beds.

"Make yourself comfortable," Svikari said as he climbed back to the top of the stairs. "I've been hoping you might stop by, *Empress*."

Evaleen's heart raced at his use of her title and snide tone. "What do you mean?"

"I am Kupio by birth," he said. "Loyal to my homeland. I sent my son to alert our army in Lovat. They will be here by morning."

Evaleen gasped. "Guard!"

Voana drew her sword and charged, but Svikari slammed the door behind him. Voanna tugged at the handle with her free hand. "He's locked us in."

"I'm sorry!" she wailed. "We should never have come."

Voana put her arm around Evaleen. "Don't blame yourself."

Sniffling, Evaleen leaned into the embrace from her friend.

"Hello?" a small voice said.

Evaleen and Voana startled. A thin boy stepped out from the dark corner. A chain on his ankle jerked him to a stop.

"Gracious!" Voana hurried to his side. "What happened to you?"

"Svikari bought me," the boy said. "I do the laundry and catch rats and—"

"What's your name, child?" Evaleen asked, wiping her eyes.

"Osk."

Voana pushed her sword's tip through the chain link attached to the shackle until she made a gap big enough to unhook the link.

Osk stepped away from the wall. "Thank you," he said, rubbing his ankle. Now that he was out in the open, Evaleen could see bruising on his face. Svikari must beat him. Her jaw tightened. How could anyone beat a child?

"Give him one," Voana said.

"What?" Evaleen asked. Voana couldn't be talking about the pearls, could she?

"You have two left, so give him one."

Evaleen wrung her hands. "But ..."

"You'll still have one for yourself, just in case," Voana said.

What could she do? Ever since Evaleen had realized the pearls were magic, she had planned to save the last two. One for herself, in case she needed it at the pool, and the other for Voana, to give to her brother.

"Why do you hesitate?" Voana asked. "Give it to him!"

Evaleen withdrew one of the last two pearls. "This is a special gift," she said to Osk. She glanced at Voana, who stood on a crate by the window, stabbing her sword at the frame. "I want you to have it." Evaleen set it in the boy's grubby palm.

"Is it food?" he asked.

"No, it's for luck. Put it in your pocket. It will help you."

Just as Osk safely tucked away the pearl, a crash pulled Evaleen's attention to Voana at the window, which now lay on the floor.

"We can't fit out that opening, Osk, but you can." Voana knelt next to Osk. "I'm going to lift you up, and I want you to run fast and far."

"Be careful," Evaleen said to the boy.

"What can go wrong?" Voana said. "He's got a pearl."

Osk patted his pocket. "Good luck pearl right here."

Evaleen laughed. "That's right. It was very nice to meet you, Osk."

Osk grinned. "I'll send help for you."

"Only once you are safe," Evaleen said.

The boy nodded, and Voana hoisted him up to the tiny opening. Osk wriggled out. Crouching at the window, he reached in a waving hand.

"Bye!"

Then he was gone.

Evaleen sat on the floor, exhausted. "I can't believe it's going to end like this."

"It's not over yet," Voana said, sitting beside her. "Give Osk a chance to find his luck."

What if escape had been Osk's luck? What if he never came back?

Hours passed. Evaleen lay on the hard dirt floor. Her limbs were heavy, completely coated in gold now. And the Kupio were coming. All was lost.

She fingered the pearl in her pocket, marveling at its smooth surface. So powerful, yet it couldn't save her from this curse. But maybe it could help someone else.

She sat up straight, shoulders back. Peace washed over her as she pulled the pearl out and extended it toward her guard. "Voana, I want you to take the last pearl."

Voana didn't even look at her. "No."

"Listen before you refuse. Take it for your brother."

Silence stretched out long and heavy. Then, "I appreciate that, but I can't."

"If you do, you'll be blessed. Someone will come to free you, then you can free me."

"It's a good idea, ma'am, but I could never live with myself if I took the last pearl and you needed one. No amount of blessings could erase that sorrow. You are my empress, but you are also my friend. I will wait here with you."

Evaleen blinked hard and pocketed the pearl once more. "You are a good friend," she said.

"As are you, ma'am."

"Call me Evaleen."

Creaking hinges woke Evaleen, who could barely move.

"Friends?" a familiar voice said. "It's Jakur."

"Jakur!" Voana leapt to her feet. "We're here. Svikari locked us in and alerted the Kupio to come for—"

"For the empress. I know," Jakur said. "That's why we must hurry. Svikari has fled, but he will come back with the Kupio."

Brows creased, the pair looked down on Evaleen. "Is it bad?" she asked.

"Your face and clothing are gold," Jakur said. "All but your eyes."

The words didn't shock this time. Evaleen knew the curse had overtaken her. She would die soon, but at least she'd made a difference in a few lives.

"Help me lift her," Voana said.

Voana and Jakur picked up Evaleen and carried her up the stairs and outside the inn.

"Last night I married my betrothed," Jakur said as they loaded Evaleen into the back of a wagon. "It never would have happened without your generosity. Make haste and faith go with you."

"Thank you, Jakur," Evaleen mumbled from the back of the wagon.

Voana drove the wagon away. Evaleen watched the clouds overhead. By the time they reached the wishing pool, the third sun had risen. Voana carried the empress to the pool and helped her sit on the ledge. Her feet, golden and heavy, sank into clear water that sparkled like diamonds under the brightness of three suns.

"It's too deep!" Voana said. "I hoped to carry you in, but we'll drown."

"*I'll* drown." Evaleen said, her voice strange with her lips now stiff. "Take the pearl." She tugged the pouch around her neck.

"No," Voana said.

"It matters not what happens to me." Evaleen gritted out the words. "If it helps you, it's worth it."

Voana shook her head, her eyes filling with tears. "I can't."

Evaleen shifted her gaze toward the water. "The scroll said I must bathe in the waters. Take the pearl home to your brother." She dropped the pouch on the ledge.

Voana picked it up. Before she could argue, Evaleen tipped herself into the pool.

"No!"

The water muffled the sound of Voana's protest and felt cool against Evaleen's skin as she sank slowly to the bottom of the pool.

"I wish for the empress's healing!" Voana yelled.

Moments later, a pearl drifted past Evaleen's face, yet she remained solid. Voana had wasted the wish set aside for her brother.

Voana dove in and swam down to Evaleen. She tugged on her arm, but Evaleen didn't budge. There would be no lifting her.

Voana swam to the surface and climbed out. "I must go for help," she yelled back, "before the Kupio arrive."

She left, and Evaleen saw nothing but water and the sky above. She couldn't breathe, which didn't seem to matter. She was fully gold now, a statue at the bottom of the pool. Her wish for healing had not been granted. Nor had Voana's wish. Evaleen could see the pearl now, shimmering at her feet, useless.

Above, shadows swarmed the poolside. Green and white uniforms. The Kupio.

Evaleen's heart flared, which seemed odd. Shouldn't her heart be solid now too?

A Kupio man dove into the water and tried to lift Evaleen. When he failed, four others joined him, but not even five of their strongest warriors could budge the golden statue. The Kupio swam to the surface and discussed Evaleen's fate. Though their voices were stifled, Evaleen caught the words "wagon" and "winch." They were determined to have their prize, one way or another. It wouldn't be long now before Evaleen was broken to pieces and melted down by her greatest enemy.

The Kupio departed, and Evaleen waited, her hopes dashed. The journey she had made with Voana had been a grand adventure but a failed one.

If only she had been a better empress. Her people deserved better. At least she had gotten to know some of them. Osk, Jakur, the family in Porsel ... She wished she could have done more than hand out a few tiny pearls.

A shadow moved above, drawing her attention back to the surface. It was not the Kupio this time, however, but Jakur.

"Thank you, Empress," he said, dropping something small into the water. It sank fast, hit the bottom of the pool, and drifted a few inches before coming to a stop.

It was a pearl.

By the time Evaleen again heard Voana's voice, a crowd had gathered around the pool's ledge. She could not believe what was happening above the surface. Her people had come, not to steal her, but to thank her and pay tribute.

At her feet were two more pearls to add to those Jakur and Voana had thrown in. Osk had arrived and introduced his parents, and the family from Porsel had come to thank her, as well. Blessings returned in thanksgiving. She had never been so touched.

"I didn't know it was you," a man said, his voice stifled by the water. "I never would have been so rude."

It was Tigdur, the stableman from the capitol. Evaleen wanted to comfort him. She had been rude first, demanding free horses. If only she could apologize.

Tigdur dropped his pearl into the water. Evaleen watched it sink toward her, her own hopes sinking with it. She had come so far—changed so much. It had not been enough. At least she now understood why she deserved this fate. She was grateful, though, to have had a chance to make even a small difference in the world.

Yet when the pearl hit the bottom, Evaleen suddenly felt cold. And wet. A strand of her hair drifted before her face. Her heartbeat throbbed in her ears. Could it be?

Could it?

She suddenly felt light as her skirt floated around her. She bent her knees and pushed, swimming to the surface where Voana and her people were waiting.

The Sun Still Rises

AJ Skelly

Black acrid smoke rose from the village, burning my eyes and choking my lungs. Ash hung at the back of my throat and burned in my belly. Tears streamed down my time-worn face as agony clawed at me, desperate to escape the physical confines of my body. Timbers creaked as fire hungrily ate at them, breaking stone, and cracking mortar.

"Abbess! We must flee now! There is no more time. The city has fallen! The abbey is lost!"

With one more anguished glance around what had once been the grandest chapel in the upper Evergrown Mountains, I lifted the hem of my soot-streaked habit and sprinted as quickly as my old legs would take me through the crumbling building, embers lighting the way like angry spirits in the darkened sky.

No more was the village surrounding the abbey, the peaceful epicenter of the mountains. No more the gentle markets, the cheerful banter of neighbors, the joyful festivals. Our peace had been stolen—ripped from us with devastating force, trampled upon, and usurped by demons from the dark. Demons who had slunk from over the mountains, crept in amid the darkest night, befouled our land, and stolen our future.

Even as my life burned around me, and invaders slaughtered without restraint, two brave souls—my self-appointed protectors—gripped my frail, aged arms to rush me to safety. I clung to the Truth that burned in my heart.

Gray fingers of dawn light stretched across the sky as if to snatch the bodies of the broken and lifeless that littered the blood-soaked earth that had once housed the prosperous Sunstone Abbey—my home. My chest rose and fell heavily with the exertion of our escape as I gazed back upon the destroyed valley. A chill wind blew down from the mountain pass just ahead of us. My journey would take me between those two slabs of mountain where I'd turn my back forever on what had been. There was nothing left. Even if we could rebuild what the invaders had razed, it would never be the same.

But not yet.

Even as pain shattered my heart, I looked out once more over my beloved valley—the valley where I'd found life, peace, and the Truth I still clung to with all the tattered remains of my soul.

Smoke belched black stains across the dawn-lit skies. Beauty marred by pain. Life destroyed by hate. Abundance dashed by loss.

Anguish, defeat, and assurance churned against my breastbone.

Though I did not feel the words that clawed up my throat, I believed them. With every scrap of being that I was, I *believed*.

"*It is well*." I breathed the ragged words with as much conviction as I could. Tears tracked down my weathered cheeks, and I clenched my bony knuckles so hard around the silver cross still hanging from my neck the edges bit into my flesh.

"Mother Abbess, how can you say such a thing?" one of the brave souls asked bitterly from my side. Ash streaked his face black and muddy red where blood mingled with it. His shattered gaze seemed to grope for understanding among the ruins below.

I took a shuddering breath. Everything I once knew had been altered. My life would never be the same. It would never hold the *same* joy, the *same* love, the *same* worship.

Because now I had experienced the pain of loss. Bone-shattering, mind-numbing pain. It would color the rest of my life, however long or short it was.

But I also knew the One who had allowed it. And I clung to what I *knew* to be *true*. I knew Him. And *nothing* happened without His allowing it. Even in my weakness and grief, my faith firmed, leeching resolve into my frozen limbs.

Swallowing back my tears, I pointed at the far edge of the horizon. There the sun peeked over the edge of the world in a blaze of orange glory. I took a shuddering breath and refused to let my emotions better my will. In the midst of pain and ugliness, I could still grant this man who had saved my life something more precious than life itself—hope. Hope and Truth.

"It is well," I repeated. "And I know it is so because the sun still rises. No amount of pain, of agony, of loss—not rain, and not shadow. Not darkness, not evil. Nothing but the hand of the Creator Himself can stop the sun's ascent. So long as the sun rises, even if some days it is covered and I do not see its beauty, I know He still holds it. He still causes it to rise. And so He must still have purpose for me yet. Though I wish it did not come at such a cost, I choose to believe that He has a path laid out for me, and I will walk it gladly. I will grieve, and I will sorrow. I will remember. But I will also believe.

"Because the sun still rises, I know He is with me yet."

The Evenglow

Cassandra Hamm

He doesn't want to see you.

The thought repeats, churning, swirling around my brain like acid. I focus on the warmth of Ronan's hand in mine as he follows me through the forest instead of the clawing anxiety threatening to send me back to the village.

Adriel? I reach out a thought tendril, trying to catch a glimpse of Adriel's mind and let him know I'm on my way. He doesn't like surprises. I know that. But all I find is a wall.

He'll be mad if you drop by unannounced.

"Gwen?" Ronan's voice breaks into my thoughts.

I jerk my mental walls back up, almost on instinct, to find my feet planted firmly in the dark soil. Did I stop walking? Was I that caught up with trying to reach my twin?

This is a bad idea. Just turn around and go home.

Ronan's lips quirk in a smile as he looks down at me. Light filters through the canopy, beaming against the back of his head, marking his face in shadow.

Something prods against my mental walls—a gentle pressure, barely enough to notice, but I drop my defenses immediately. *Adriel?* I transmit.

Not Adriel. Ronan's baritone voice enters my head.

My shoulders droop. I hope he can't sense my disappointment.

I don't have many telepathic connections in the world, those threads that link two souls in friendship and intimacy. Ronan is one of those. Our connection is new and delicate, like a tightrope of vines in the evenglow. But Adriel was my first bond. Twins, connected even in the womb.

Ronan's eyebrows dart toward his hairline. *Why were your walls up?*

I don't know how to answer. *Because I don't want you to know why I asked you to come along with me? Because I don't know what Adriel will do when we get there?*

I want to reestablish my mental barriers and block out everyone and everything, but pushing someone out of my head is a lot harder than letting them in. So I reinforce my shields around my personal thoughts, making sure nothing seeps through.

Gwenny? he prods.

"Um ... just ... why don't we talk normally?" I say aloud. "Not everything has to be in our heads."

He withdraws, leaving cold emptiness. I yank my barriers back up, feeling safe and strange and ...

Oh no. I did something wrong. I know it in the pit of my stomach, the way his lips droop and his eyes go cold. I shouldn't have raised my walls again. I should've just let him speak in my head like he wanted to, but it's too late now. *Fix it,* my brain chants. *Fix it, fix it, fix it.*

"It's just ... um ... I like hearing your voice." I gaze at the vines hanging behind his head instead of into his dark eyes. "Out loud. Not just in our heads. It's nice. It helps me relax."

"Oh." His eyes soften. "Because of the trees."

"What?"

He gestures to the thick, leafy canopy, the creeping vines, the thick moss. "The ... you know. "

I blink up at him. "The evenglow?"

"Yes." His nostrils flare, as though saying the word pains him.

When night falls, the plants shine with a brilliance the daytime could never mimic—and Ronan thinks that's a *problem?* Sure, some of the townsfolk think the luminescence is due to spirits inhabiting the plants, but I never thought Ronan would be one of them. Not strong, sensible Ronan.

"Why would I be afraid of the evenglow?" I say, a little sharper than I intended.

Ronan clenches his jaw.

My heart sinks into the pit of my stomach. *You made him upset. Fix it, Gwen.* "But if you'd rather turn around and go home, we can come back when it's early in the day," I blurt.

Really, I don't need to come here today. I just ... *wanted* to. Because every day that passes is a day I worry Adriel might no longer be in this world.

He's fine. He wouldn't really end his life ... would he?

Ronan smiles, but there is still something hard and strained about him. I didn't fix it. Not well enough. I failed. "No, it's fine, Gwen. You said we're almost there?"

I nod, then pause. At least, I *think* we're almost there. Sometimes these trees play tricks on me.

"You *do* know where you're going, right?"

I stiffen. I shouldn't be offended—my directional knowledge is questionable on the best of days—but I know my brother's walled presence.

Ronan ruffles my hair. I swat his hand away. *I'm your lover, not your little sister.*

"Don't be mad, Gwenny. I just wanted to make sure you weren't lost."

Sighing, I move forward. Ronan's boots crunch the moss next to me, his long legs eating up the distance. "Thanks for agreeing to come," I say. "You didn't have to."

He laughs, features sharp and defined even in laughter. "You think I'd pass up a chance to see the mind whisperer?"

I stiffen. He wouldn't just use me to get to Adriel. He *couldn't.*

Even when we were kids, Adriel's telepathy was incredibly advanced. He could always tell exactly what I was thinking and feeling, not that I was any good at hiding my mind's inner workings. He could also sense the thoughts and feelings of most everyone in the village, no matter how strong their walls. Words, images, feelings, good and bad, all pouring into him all the time.

But there was too much bad.

The hut nearly blends into the trees. If I hadn't been looking directly at it, or if I hadn't been here, once upon a time, I never would've seen it. Vines crawl up the side and snake across the roof. The trees bend their branches so low they brush the wooden siding.

Ronan lets out a low whistle. "You sure anyone lives here?"

"Of course I'm sure!" I snap.

"Calm down, Gwenny." Ronan tweaks my nose.

I flinch away from him. My heart is beating so loudly I'm sure even Adriel hears it. It slams against my ribcage, *poundpoundpound,* and my lungs constrict, tightening, tightening—

Turn around and run before he hurts you any more—

Ronan shakes me, rattling my brain. "What's wrong with you? It's just your brother."

How can he say that to me? It's not *just* my brother. It's my former best friend, my once-confidant, my shattered idol.

But I guess I haven't shared that with Ronan. Not really. Just bits and pieces. Things like, "We used to be close" and "We haven't talked in a while." Not, "He severed our telepathic bond."

I remember how it felt—a sharp tug, an almost-physical slice across my abdomen, then emptiness. Deep, swallowing emptiness. Perhaps not so different from the fog Adriel battles.

"If you're not going to knock, I will." Ronan lets go of me to bang against the door. The pounding syncs with the pounding of my heart.

I shake and shake and shake. What if he slams the door in my face? What if he doesn't even answer because it's me and that's too much for him to handle?

The fog came like a whisper. First, quietness. Reticence. Dwindling conversations. Cutting off a few telepathic bonds here and there. Then, the fog became almost tangible—shrouding him, darkening his mood, skewing his thoughts, blocking his bonds.

My bond was the last to go.

"Hey!" Ronan yells. "Mind whisperer, I know you can sense us—"

"Go away." Adriel's voice is low and jagged. My thirsty heart drinks in the sounds. "This is private property."

"We came a long way to see you." Ronan seems unfazed, even though I want to curl into a ball.

I'm sorry, twin. My words bounce off an invisible, impenetrable wall.

"We should go back," I say in a quavering voice.

"Blazes no! He's your brother. If he doesn't open up—"

The door opens. Ronan loses his balance mid-knock, catching himself on the doorframe. Past him I glimpse a gaunt, hollow face. Dark stubble bristles on an angular chin. Dark circles ring haunted, beautiful eyes, staring into mine.

I open my mouth—

The door slams. It cuts deeper than any word ever could. Tears prick at my eyes, and I sink to the ground, my legs suddenly too weak to hold me up. My hands brace against the moss.

Too loud, too emotional, too much. So much that Adriel had to block me out to keep from exploding.

Ronan bangs harder and harder on the door until it's pounding like my heart, *bangbangbangbangbang*—

"Go away!" Adriel shouts. "I want to be alone."

"It's your *sister,*" Ronan says.

"You're not my sister."

"Yes, but she and I, we go together."

Ronan's words thaw the icy chill that crept into my bones. *Someone wants me.*

The door cracks open. Ronan reaches in and grabs the thin, pale arm, dragging my twin into the open.

Adriel is stick-thin, bones jutting out, hair long and scraggly. He blinks at the dying sunlight, as though he's unused to being in anything but darkness. His eyes refuse to settle on any one thing—not Ronan, and certainly not me.

This isn't my brother. And yet it is. *What happened to you, Adriel?* I almost transmit the words, but I already know the answer.

The fog. It stole everything from him—from us. I can't hate him; I hate what destroyed him. What made him sink in on himself, sucked the joy from his life, transformed every small task into an insurmountable obstacle. If I could burn it from his brain, I would. I would tear it out with my bare hands.

I just want my brother back.

I clamber to my feet, hoping the movement will draw Adriel's attention, but he keeps his gaze on the still-dark forest, not yet lit from inward luminescence. Without thinking, I send a telepathic thought that never reaches him. *I missed you.*

"I told you I wanted to be left alone, Gwen." His voice is flat, nearly emotionless.

"Sorry," I mumble. That's all I ever say—*sorry, sorry, sorry,* echoing in the air, never truly healing anything.

"Your sister came a long way to see you, and you won't even let her in?" Ronan's jaw is set.

I dig my nails into my palms, focusing on the sting instead of the pain pulsing behind my ribs. The trees seem to press in on me, dark and solid, their leaves blotting out the last rays of sun. I want the evenglow to start. I want *light.*

"Why did you bring someone here?" Adriel's tone is still dull and uninterested, even though we literally dragged him from his sanctuary. I *think* he's addressing me, but it's hard to tell when he won't look at me or use my name. Am I so much that just the sight of me would send him into a spiral?

"He's my ..." I start. "Ronan's my ..."

"I'm her lover," Ronan says.

"I don't care who you are." Adriel's stony expression is somehow more chilling than Ronan's red-faced fury. "You need to get out."

"Like blazes I will." Ronan straightens his shoulders. "You can't overpower me. You're barely strong enough to lift a pebble."

A muscle in Adriel's jaw throbs. I hate that Ronan's right—Adriel is a shadow of his former self. Is he eating? Is he getting enough sleep? I want to ask, but he'd just shut down even more.

He's always been sensitive. To sound, to light, to stimulation—to others' emotions. The pressure pushed until all he could do was shut out the world. At least then there would be peace. But shutting out the world meant shutting out ... *me.*

"You need to leave," Adriel says. "Both of you."

"Adriel, please." I nearly choke on the words. My chest feels too tight, my hands clammy, my limbs weak and unsteady. "I just ... I want ..."

I want things to be the way they were, before the world became too much, before I had to walk on eggshells and bend over backward and hope that you would be in a good mood and I wouldn't screw everything up and I—

Adriel's eyes flick toward me, just for a fraction of a second. I know those eyes so well, a mixture of green and brown with a hint of blue, a color you wouldn't dare call hazel. *My* eyes.

My breath catches. *He's looking at me. He's actually looking at me.*

What does he think of me now? Hollow-eyed, sallow-skinned, a few extra pounds hanging off my frame. Not the lively, cheerful sister he once knew. But, maybe someone lovable. Someone he missed.

He turns away. It is a physical blow.

I struggle to form words, finally settling on, "Adriel, please."

He just grunts.

"I just wanted to see you," I say, a too-wide smile frozen on my face. "We won't be here long."

"*He* doesn't just 'want to see me.'" Adriel stabs an accusing finger at Ronan. "Why don't you ask him what he wants?"

"What ... ? " I look up at Ronan, then back at Adriel. "I thought you weren't reading thoughts," I say. "I thought it was ... too much. Besides, Ronan's just here to support me."

"I was unguarded," Adriel says, almost sulkily. "So was he when he rushed the door. I couldn't help overhearing."

Ronan stiffens. Others probably wouldn't notice, but I've spent a year reading Adriel's body language, trying to navigate his moods, trying not to upset him. I have walked on brittle, cracking eggshells far more than I'd ever care for. So I notice.

Doubt trickles into my mind, cold and slick, like freezing water. I prod at Ronan's mind, which has suddenly gone rigid.

"I'm not leaving until you give me what I want, mind whisperer," Ronan says. "Tell me my future, or there will be consequences."

The blood drains from my face. Ronan's mind stays cold and impenetrable, no matter how hard I push. *No, no, no—*

"I can't see the future," Adriel says.

"Liar." Ronan makes himself taller. "I know you do."

All this time, he didn't want *me,* just the connection to my brother? *No one will ever want you. No one ever has.*

"They talk about it all the time back in the village—how you told people what would happen to them, back before you became a hermit." Ronan's lip curls. "Why don't you do it for *me?*"

"People tell all sorts of stories," Adriel says.

I thought Ronan would be different from the other guys. I thought he cared about me, not just what I could give him. I thought I was *enough* for him.

I never want to see him again. I hate that I ever kissed him. Hate *myself* for believing someone could love me.

The sun has almost slipped behind the horizon. The forest seems to hum with anticipation. Ronan peers at the dying sun, his nostrils flaring.

Maybe his superstition will get the best of him. Maybe he'll leave me to my sorrow in the fluorescent forest. *Go away and never come back,* I think, and suddenly I wonder if that's how Adriel feels about me.

"I didn't know he wanted this, Adriel," I say. "I promise. I wouldn't have—I didn't—"

Ronan's voice jabs into my head. *Stupid little Gwenny. No wonder the other guys all talk about you like you're easy. You're so desperate you don't even see the facts when they're right in front of you.*

I gasp, each word stabbing. Pain seeps from each wound like blood. *Desperate. Easy. Gullible.*

"What are you doing to my sister?" Adriel snaps.

Ronan grins. "Wouldn't you like to know."

"Stop *feeling* so much," Adriel told me once. "It's so annoying."

But I can't *stop* feeling. My heart latches onto whoever is around, pouring out my affection, smothering, choking. Each rejection is an amputation. Each slamming door batters me further into myself. Each abandonment steals more of my soul.

I should have remembered how the people you love the most can hurt you the worst.

"I don't read people anymore," Adriel says through gritted teeth. "All right? You're not going to change my mind. And don't bother trying to force your way into my head. It won't work."

"You mean you won't use your power anymore?" Ronan snorts. "Are you serious?"

"You mean Gwen didn't tell you?" Adriel's eyebrows draw together.

"Of course I didn't!" I blink at him, hurt. "I don't tell your secrets."

Adriel's eyes flick to me again. My breath catches.

"You can't just *ignore* something like this," Ronan says. "You can tell the future, and you're just going to hide away in the woods?"

"Yes!" Adriel shouts. "Because it's not a power; it's a *curse.*"

"Coward."

I can't move, mesmerized by the volleying of insults between the two people who meant so much to me—one of whom still does, even though he doesn't deserve it. I need to stop this, but how? Ronan is much too strong for me to drag him away.

"If you don't read my future—" Ronan's hand closes around my wrist, wrenching it behind my back. I yelp. Tears prick at my eyes. "Your sister pays the price."

No. He wouldn't. But the pressure of his fingers and the tone of his voice tell me otherwise.

He never loved me. It was all a lie. No one ever loved me.

"It's not this incredible power you're making it out to be." Adriel's voice pitches high. "They're just flashes! I can't guarantee that they're true. Mostly, they're people's wishes. They're not real."

"Liar!" Ronan pulls harder. I gasp, my shoulder burning. He could break my arm. Despite my height, I'm no match for him.

"You think I *want* this power?" Adriel's eyes are twin coals. "If I could give it up, I would."

He wants to run back through that door and hide from the world. I can see it in his face. He wants to shut himself out from the almost-awakening forest, from his imperiled twin.

"Power is wasted on the likes of you," Ronan sneers. "If I could see the future, I would *use* it."

"When I used the power, it only brought pain!" Adriel cries.

Not just pain upon himself. Pain upon those he read. Dark fortunes, hopes lost. But Ronan wouldn't understand that. All he can see is possibility.

The tears flow freely now. Adriel won't do what Ronan wants. Maybe he would have before the fog, but now, it's just him in his little world, stewing and ruminating and hating. Opening himself up would be too much risk—and if he opened himself up to the pain, he might just give up entirely.

The trees start to come alive around me. Just a faint glow for now, blue and green, violet and gold, but once dusk fully settles into night, they will burst into untamed brilliance. Will I live to see it?

Unthinkingly, I reach for Adriel's mind. It remains hard, an unyielding surface, just as I knew it would. *Please,* I beg. *Why don't you love me? What did I do wrong? How can I fix it?*

Ronan releases my neck to grip my elbow with both hands. One holds my arm in place as the other thrusts my forearm the wrong way. I scream. Pain jolts through my arm, my hands, as my elbow flops numbly.

Something shudders, something outside myself. The walls I am still pushing against. Then they collapse, and I pour into Adriel's mind.

Dark fog shrouds his senses, writhing and twisting, choking the life from me. I gasp at the desolation of it, the deep, immeasurable agony, so much deeper than the physical pain of my elbow.

This is what he lives with. I knew it, and yet, seeing it for myself ...

Adriel's face twists as the weight of the world hits him. Loneliness, desolation, agony—they all pour past his dropped walls. He drops to his knees, his body twitching.

My elbow seems a faint, distant throbbing. *Adriel,* I send, desperate. *Don't listen to all that. Just listen to me. Breathe. Focus on my words.*

"What the blazes?" Ronan stares down at Adriel in horrified amazement. "If you're just trying to get out of telling me my future, it won't work. You saw what I did to Gwen. I'll do it again—"

Ronan keeps going, but I ignore him. *I know how much the world hurts you, Adriel,* I say. *I know why you put up those walls.*

The fog twists and whirls, trying to block me out.

I love you, Adriel. I love you, even though you hurt me. I know it was the fog. Just please, come back to me. I ... I want my brother back.

Something shifts inside his head—a resolve, a strength I didn't know he had. *Get out, Gwen.*

The words slice into me. I yank my mind back and shove up my own walls. I'm trembling, legs weak, skin clammy. The burning in my elbow resumes with full force, so vivid I nearly pass out. *He doesn't want you. He'll never want you. Your love will never be enough.*

Something slams against my walls, which just barely stand. Ronan lets out a cry, releasing his hold on me. I stumble back. He holds his head, screaming, "What are you doing to me?"

Adriel peers up at Ronan through bloodshot eyes, mouth set in a grim line. "Showing you my *power.*" He spits the word like a curse.

He must be sending all the input of the world out on Ronan—showing how that sensitivity to stimuli feels. I didn't know he could do that. Maybe he didn't either. And Ronan can't handle it.

He shoved me out of my head so I wouldn't have to face the pain he's inflicting on Ronan right now. He doesn't hate me. He let the world in and went through that overstimulation to spare me.

Maybe I *did* reach him after all.

All around us, the forest comes alive—bark shimmering an iridescent cerulean, clinging moss glowing phosphorescent violet, leaves an incandescent seafoam green. Vines and flowers and leaves, all lit up in glorious, cleansing light.

Tears fill my eyes, and not from pain. How could anyone consider this unholy? It's beautiful, light pouring from what was once dark and dull.

Ronan scrambles away from the trees, trying to stay away from the blinding undergrowth, but there is no escape. He is inside the Awakening Woods, and they will continue to shine.

Eyes crazed, movements jumbled, Ronan tears through the trees, screaming, "A curse! A curse!" His footsteps recede as he leaves the holy clearing.

Adriel collapses with a muffled moan. I kneel next to him. "Adriel? Are you all right?"

"Give me a moment." Groaning, Adriel squeezes his eyes shut. His face screws up in concentration.

I sit, my arm pulsing with agony, wishing I could help. Maybe my being here is a comfort. Or maybe that's stressing him out like it usually does.

But it *shouldn't* stress him out. I forget that sometimes—that it isn't my fault. It's the fog.

"Do you want me to leave?" I ask, fearing the answer.

"No." It's a grunt of a word, but it makes my heart soar.

He breathes in, out. I can't stand the silence. I have to say something.

"I'm sorry I brought Ronan here. I shouldn't have done that. I should've known he was just using me, and I was invading your space, and ..." I need to stop talking, but *he* isn't talking, and anything is better than the silence.

I stare at the cerulean bark, letting the soft, pure light sweep over my soul. It washes away the stain of Ronan and leaves me with a peace I haven't felt since Adriel shut me out.

Gwen. Adriel's voice whispers into my mind, soft and clear. Does that mean he has his walls down? What about the weight of the world? What about the fog?

You know why I moved out here? he says.

I blink at him, measuring my words. I don't want to break this fragile peace between us. *Because you wanted to be alone.*

Sort of. He pauses for a while. I think he's not going to tell me, but gradually, his words filter into my head. *It's because of this.* He gestures to the luminescent forest.

"Isn't that a lot of stimulation?" I say out loud, forgetting myself.

He shrugs. *Yeah, but it's ... good stimulation, if that makes sense? It keeps the fog away.*

I hesitantly reach for his mind, then realize he's right—the crushing fog isn't so heavy. In fact, his mind is clearer than I've seen it in a long time, despite the recent overstimulation. The light is driving his darkness away, at least for a time. It makes me love the evenglow even more.

Do you think I could visit you again? I ask. *I get it if you want your space, and obviously I won't do anything you don't want me to, and I won't bring anyone here, especially people who want to use you for your—*

"Yes," he interrupts.

My mouth falls open. "You mean it? You won't change your mind when the fog is back?"

Maybe I will, he admits. *But I shouldn't have cut myself off from you.*

I blink away tears. *But ... aren't I too much?*

Silence stretches on too long. My chest tightens. *He's going to spiral, and it will be your fault, and—*

I crush the thought before it can choke me. I'm not responsible for what he does. I can only control what *I* do. And I will choose to love him.

Adriel reaches out to touch a patch of phosphorescent moss with long, thin fingers—a musician's fingers. He always made such beautiful music. I wonder if he still plays his lyre out here in the forest with only the wildlife to hear. Maybe it helps heal his soul.

I love you, Adriel. I don't send the thought. It's just for me. *I will love you through this fog.*

You're a lot, Adriel finally says. *But it's good stimulation. I think I forgot that.*

I let out a choked sob. The words are a balm for my cracked soul.

Will you stay for a while? he asks.

Yes, I say. *But what if you spiral?*

He's silent for another long while. My elbow decides to remind me that it's no longer in its proper place. I can barely look at the awkwardly-bent limb without wanting to throw up.

I won't spiral during the evenglow, Adriel says.

Yes, but what about after? *He'll just hurt you,* my heart warns.

I'm sorry I hurt you, he says.

Blazes, I must have sent the thought on accident. I swallow hard, waiting for him to back away.

I know that's not enough. The fog … it does things to me. But I'll try to make it up to you, Gwen, I swear.

I nod, not trusting myself to speak without bursting into sobs.

Will you sit with me during the evenglow? Adriel asks. *Tonight, and … well, other nights, if you want. Then maybe …*

Maybe the soft light of the forest will cast healing magic on not only my soul but on our bond. I can already feel it reforming, fragile but existent. Even just sitting here in silence is soothing and strengthening. Existing together in the same space, not needing to fill the silence with words.

Yes, I tell him.

He smiles at me, and my whole world is new.

Our communication isn't as open as it used to be, but the channel is there. And maybe it's best we aren't as inseparable as we were. Maybe that wasn't healthy.

I can live without him. I just don't want to.

I'm glad you're here, he tells me.

I'm glad you're back, I say.

He leans his head against my shoulder, and we watch the forest shine.

Rookie Mistake

S.D. Grimm

Thunder rattled my bedroom window. I curled up in the corner of my bed with my unicorn blanket pulled up to my chin and held in a whimper. Lightning brightened my whole room and gave my stuffed animals big, angry shadows.

One Mississippi, two Mississ—

Another crack of thunder boomed. The storm loomed closer. I squeezed my eyes shut, praying it would be over soon.

"Casey?" Dad's gruff voice rose above the pounding rain.

Footsteps in the hall told me he was just outside my bedroom door. I held my breath. Maybe Dad was coming to comfort me ... like Mom always had. Before the monster got her.

My bedroom door slammed against the wall. A flash of light cut through the darkness and revealed my father filling the doorway. "Casey?"

The lightning died, but candlelight still allowed me to see Dad's face.

"Yeah?" My voice sounded so small in my room. Hot tears flooded my eyes. I blinked them away so he wouldn't see evidence of my fear.

He scanned my windows. "Come on. You have to get to the crawl-space."

I froze halfway to my father. If there was anything more terrifying than a thunderstorm, it was being in the crawlspace during one.

In two strides, he crossed my room and stood towering over me. "Are you scared?"

I couldn't even look at him for fear that the tears were still wet on my face. "No, sir."

His eyes narrowed. "Don't lie, Casey."

More tears started to come. He wanted me to be brave, and I was failing.

His thick finger pushed my chin up. "How many times have I told you? Never let fear control you."

"I know." I sniffed.

My father sighed. "Do you know what it means to make sure it doesn't control you?"

"No crying?"

His stern eyes softened. "It means that when you're scared, you better swallow it so you can do what needs to be done. That means, when I tell you to get in the crawlspace, you go. Scared or not, you go. Above all, never let your fear freeze you."

A low moan, like a sorrowful howl, struck up outside my bedroom window. Goosebumps sprouted on my skin, and I flung myself into Dad's arms. Even though I'd heard the sound before, I still asked, "What was that?"

He crouched next to me and looked deep into my eyes. "Something *I'm* afraid of. Now, go to the crawlspace, and no matter what you hear, don't come out till I call for you."

I curled my fingers around the cool metal of the flashlight and tried to choke back my fear.

"Take this." Dad took something off my dresser and gave it to me. "Put it in your pocket."

I held up the thin, jeweled, metal object Mother had given me to hold up my hair like the pretty ballerinas did. Candlelight danced across its silver surface. "My nightgown doesn't have pockets."

My father twisted my hair into a bun. A talent he'd learned after Mom passed. Then he plucked the object from my hand and slipped it into my hair, fastening it tight. "For protection."

I clutched his sleeve as he tried to push me past him. "From what?"

He stared at me while my insides froze.

"It's them, isn't it?" I whispered. "They're back, aren't th—"

He gripped my upper arms. "You get in that crawlspace and shut the door. If something tries to enter, don't you dare open the door. You stab this through any opening in the cracked wood. Do you hear me?" He touched the miniature knitting needle in my hair.

"What if it's you?"

"It won't hurt me. Do as I say, Casey. Don't let your soft heart get the better of you."

Lightning pulsed through the sky and a dark shadow lurked outside the window. The same shadow that had killed my mom. Holding in a scream, I ran to the crawlspace and climbed inside.

Thirteen years later.

"Is that the best you've got, Casey?" Jon's voice betrayed him. He was out of breath.

Strands of my ponytail clung to my sweaty neck. I kicked, heel aimed for his diaphragm, and I struck.

He backed up and shook it off. "You're losing your touch." But his voice was strained. A huge wet triangle took up the whole front of his shirt. Even Jonathan Tate couldn't best me forever.

"We've been sparring for hours."

"So? Monsters don't wait for you to recoup." He lunged at me again.

I ducked and managed a nice uppercut to his torso. "That's why we bring backup."

He shot me a half-smile. "Don't you forget it."

"How could I?" All he'd been talking about for the last two hours was how important it was to trust your partner. To know their strengths and weaknesses. Anticipate their decisions. "I heard you the first dozen times."

"I have to make sure I get through that skull of yours." He tapped my head.

I batted his hand away and laughed. Jon's ribbing always brought out my competitive nature.

"So, rookie." His grin held a challenge. "What are the other two golden rules?"

"Do you even know what time it is?" I grabbed a towel and dried my face. "I think I'm going to go home, fall on my bed, and not get up for two days."

He smirked. "Good. I still need an answer."

I dropped the towel and blocked his punch. He was relentless tonight. It was like he was training me for big-game hunting or something ... wait. Was he going to ask me to be his partner?

My forearm stung as I blocked another of Jon's attempts to get me off balance. I kicked, my shin guard smacking his thigh.

He backed up. "Nice hit."

"Good. You're getting on my nerves."

"Already?" He advanced again, still fast. "If I were a vampire—"

"You'd be a lot faster."

His blue eyes sparkled as he smiled. "Listen, rookie—"

"That's right. I'm a graduate now. Top of my class. That's why *you're* going to pick *me* as your partner." I swung at him.

He blocked my hit, sweaty arm against sweaty arm. "Not unless you can recite the golden rules."

I paused, excitement jittering through my blood. "Are you going to pick me?"

His face drew closer to mine. "Didn't say that."

"I have what you're missing. We balance each other's weaknesses."

He chuckled. "Are you saying you complete me, Case?"

I swung my leg out and tripped him. "Rule one"—I reached my hand down to help him up—"always bring backup. Rule two"—standing, he squared off against me again—"no hunting on full-moon night. And rule three: never look your prey in the eyes." I placed my hands on my hips. "Did I pass?"

He threw my towel back at me. "You nailed it. But will you actually follow those rules?"

I wiped my face and grabbed a water bottle. "Of course. Come on. I'm not reckless enough to look a monster in the eyes."

He regarded me dubiously.

"I'm your best way of getting the big prey, and you know it."

"Big prey, huh?" His arms lowered and his eyes searched my face. The long scar above his eyebrow pulled down as his eyes narrowed. "You really think that's what I'm after? You think I wanted to be your partner so I could make Carlson's team."

My heart stalled. Didn't he? Together we were dynamite. We'd already taken down three redcaps and a skin-walker and aided in a vampire-nest attack, although I didn't get to hunt the vamps for that mission. No rookies allowed on a vamp mission. I thirsted for big game. The soulless. Werewolves especially. Heat spread through my veins. I needed to kill one of those.

For my mother.

A blow made me stumble backward.

"Where'd you go? Head in the game, Case."

I held up my hand to signal that I was done sparring. "Please tell me you're joking."

His gaze settled on me, as if he could read my thoughts. "You're still set on making Carlson's team. Rookies don't—"

"Rookie or not, I'm a Carlson too. Of course I want to make my father's team."

His smile faded and he shook his head. I knew what memory he'd gone to. I went there too. He closed the distance between us, sternness softening. "You know your father wants a specific skillset."

"Yeah. Smart, fast, and cunning." I took a drink. But when he didn't reply, I added, "You don't think I'm those things?"

"You *are* those things. But that's *all* he wants."

My dad's words echoed in my skull like a constant pounding. I spoke them aloud. "But I let my soft heart get the better of my decisions." My shoulders sagged. "He—he still thinks I'm a scared little girl, waiting in a crawlspace." I turned away, stripping off my shin guards.

Jon spoke softly. "You were just a kid."

I had to prove to my father that I wasn't that scared little girl anymore. Maybe I had to prove that to Jon too. He still looked at me with pity in his eyes. Well, he was wrong. I wasn't scared anymore, and I'd prove it.

I'd finally been given silver bullets, and I wasn't waiting for another full moon. I'd rise through the ranks faster than any trainee before. I'd bypass the Rookie title and go right to Hunter status. No. Master Hunter. Then my father would have to accept that I was ready for an elite team. His team. Tonight I'd be the first rookie at Knight Owl Academy to bring down a werewolf.

And I'd do it alone. If that didn't make my father see what I'd become, nothing would.

"Casey, you're crushing the water bottle."

I looked down at the crinkled plastic in my hands. "Sorry." I gave it back to him. "I should really call it a night."

Jon glanced at the mat. "Your father's team is still your dream, huh?'

I crossed my arms. "Yes."

He nodded. "So, you wouldn't want to be partners with anyone who wouldn't get you there?"

I touched his arm. "Jon, we could both make the team. Don't you see? Together, we're unstoppable. We know each other's strengths and weaknesses. And we trust each other completely."

I gained his eye contact then.

"Come take a look at this." He walked over to the double doors leading to the computer lab where all the Knights, rookie through elite, could watch their sparring matches in replay on the screen ... and learn from their mistakes. Like a montage of humiliation.

"Is this so you can show me my weakness?"

"Something like that." Jon pulled up a fight, and it displayed on the big screen.

I should have known he'd choose this one. Most humiliating fight of my life. Me against another rookie—big guy named Travis. "I don't need to see it."

"Yes. You do." He pressed play.

I slumped into the chair and watched.

A cocky smile formed on Travis's lips as he bent his knees and squared off in front of me. "I'll be a werewolf. Remember, they fight dirty."

In the video, I chuckled. "Tell me something I don't—"

His arm came at me fast. I bent over and sprung back onto my hands. My heel definitely made contact with his face as I flipped over and landed on my feet again. Knees bent, I awaited his next advance. There wasn't one. Instead, he crumpled away from me, his hands on his face.

"Travis?"

"I'm fine." His voice was a little shaky, like he was in pain. His knee dropped to the mat. His fingers spread, and red blood gushed between them.

I rushed over to him. "Let me see."

I touched his shoulder. He grabbed my wrists, flipped me on my back and pinned me down.

I pushed back but didn't move him even an inch. "What are you doing?"

He wiped the red away. "I told you I'm a werewolf. They use tricks. You should have seen your f—"

I pushed him off me and stormed out.

Sick of watching how everyone laughed as soon as I'd left the training room, I spun the chair around, turning my back to the computer screen. "You done humiliating me?"

Jon pointed to the monitor. "Watch, Casey."

No thanks.

"She'll never make it." My father's deep voice resounded from the speakers behind me. I whirled around. This was part of the video I hadn't seen—the uncut version. My father had seen the fight?

On the screen, Jon faced my father, his arms crossed. "The test showed her greatest strength. Her ability to keep her heart in the game and still make clear decisions."

"Greatest strength?" My father laughed. "If she can't learn to separate her emotions from the job, she'll end up dead."

Jon squared his shoulders and widened his stance. Classic male posturing. "She thought she'd hurt a *classmate*, Carlson. Not a monster."

"I don't care what your recommendation is; I don't want her on my team."

Jon's fist flexed. "You're here for one of her fights, and you decide just like that? You made Travis play that trick on her, didn't you? Because you knew how she'd react. Well, let me tell you something, Carlson; she's got a clear head *and* a big heart. Some of these monsters are human beings, and you know that we can help them if we—"

"Help?" My father's eyes narrowed as he stared down at Jon.

The screen paused, and I looked up at Jon. "You—you tried to get me on his team?"

"Of course I did, Case. It's what you wanted."

I let my head fall against the back of the chair. "And he doesn't want me. Again."

"He thinks he's keeping you safe."

"Safe." I faced Jon. "That's a joke. He thinks I'm too weak."

"Well, I don't." He pulled something out of his pocket. A small velvet box. He lifted the lid and showed me a pretty necklace on a silver chain. The charm was a silver lightning bolt. It reminded me of a fear I'd conquered. Something I'd shared with Jon.

"It's beautiful."

He took it out of the box for me. "Happy graduation."

As he held up the jewelry, I cupped the bolt in my hand. "Jon—"

"Here." He took the necklace and stood behind me. The silver chain was cool against my neck. His fingers, as they fumbled with the clasp, brushed my skin. They were warm.

Once the necklace was secured, I turned to face him.

He stood there, looking vulnerable—a look I hadn't seen since we were kids. "I was hoping you'd want to be my partner."

Warmth flooded my heart. "And you'll help me make my father see that I am worthy of his team?"

He glanced at the computer screen behind me. "You'll never be happy otherwise, will you?"

Why was he trying to change me? Finally he looked at me but didn't say anything. It was like he was waiting for me to speak. "Does that mean you won't help me?" My voice came out unsure, scratchy. As if the question itself didn't really want to hear the answer.

"I just don't understand why you still care what he thinks," he whispered.

"You wouldn't."

Jon backed away from me and crossed his arms. "You're right. I don't get it. Even after watching the recording—and seeing what he said about you—you know, if he's not impressed with you now, he'll never be."

That stung. My eyes burned. How could he say that? "Are you saying—"

"I'm saying I wish you could see that his opinion of you shouldn't matter. There are plenty of people—your instructors and trainers here at the academy!" He paused, eye contact flicking away from me as another word tumbled out softly. "Me." He looked at me again, closing the distance between us. "I wish you could view yourself through the eyes of those who do see your worth. Instead of fixating on the ones who don't."

But that was the thing he'd never understand: my father's opinion of me would always matter.

He nodded once. "Apparently you never wanted my approval." He walked out.

So many thoughts flew into my head. I wanted to call out and tell him to stop, but if I was going to prove to my father how strong I'd become, I had to stop letting my heart make my decisions for me. I blinked back tears. And that started with breaking my connection to the one man who encouraged me to keep my heart in the game as much as my head—Jonathan Tate.

I sank into the chair at the desk and stared at my father's face. His angry finger pointed at Jon's chest.

I pressed play.

"She told you, didn't she?" My father's recorded words made my heart catch.

Jon stared at him, unflinching. "She told me her mother was killed by a werewolf."

"Then you know why she wants to hunt them?"

Jon nodded.

My father stepped closer to him. "And you know why it's so important that she keep her emotions in check. All they do is give these monsters an opening."

I touched the silver lightning bolt on my chest. Had Jon been trying to keep me away from my father's team all this time? All the encouragement to make decisions with my heart. How could he do that to me? I slammed my palm against the desk. I'd prove him wrong. I'd prove them all wrong.

I grabbed my gym bag and walked out. If my father wanted me to leave my soft heart at home when I went to work, then that's what I would do.

I laid my uniform out onto my bed and nodded to myself. This was it. I was really going to do this. Take down a werewolf. Alone. No rookie ever had. That way Jon—Jon? Who cared about Jon? That way *my father* would have to pick me for his team.

My black form-fitting jacket slid easily over my heavy nylon shirt. Beneath that, tough Kevlar fabric, to prevent claws or teeth from puncturing skin, encased me. I zipped the jacket all the way up to my chin. The turtleneck part always felt so constricting. But if I ran into a vampire, I'd be glad of it. I slipped into the black slacks and knee-high boots. I pulled my hair into a bun to keep it from getting in the way and fastened it with a few bobby pins and the long, silver hairpin my mother had given me—her favorite hidden weapon while she hunted big prey. I'd need the reminder to remain courageous tonight.

I picked up my Smith & Wesson M&P Shield and jammed in the magazine.

Silver bullets.

I tried to keep my teeth from chattering as I crept farther into the forest. My breath made a cloud in front of my face as I walked. Despite trying to avoid them, twigs cracked under my boots. The scent of damp leaves hung in the air. The full moon was bright, so I didn't need a flashlight.

Another snap echoed through the maze of trees. I wasn't alone.

I stopped, hand resting on my Shield strapped to my thigh.

A low, agonizing scream punctured the sounds of quiet life. The change had begun. The soulless were out there, morphing into the hideous beasts. They'd start their killing sprees. Take innocent lives like they'd taken my mother. And one of them would die tonight.

I found a tall spruce with large, sweeping branches and a bed of orange-brown pine needles beneath, and I settled next to it. Spruce masked human scent, and the sap smelled strong here. Time to lure in the beast. I threw back my head and let out a long, low melancholy howl.

Nature seemed to hold its breath as I waited for any answering song. Nothing.

The full moon's silver light spilled through the bare tree branches, lighting my way. I stood up, pushed my way deeper into the forest, and tried again. The howl rumbled in my throat, then dipped into low, minor tones.

Still nothing.

I had it on good authority that my sorrowful call for a mate was near perfect. Any werewolf within a two-mile radius should have come running. It didn't make sense.

Leaves and dry shrubs crunched and cracked as I walked. I sent out one more mournful cry, then sank to the ground with my back to a tree and waited.

Dew covered the ground. My breath puffed visible mists in front of my face. And nothing stirred for a very long time. That's when I realized—everything was too quiet.

Once more I howled the mournful tune.

A sharp crack split the silence. I swallowed hard, rigid. Scanning. Waiting. Afraid to move in case I gave myself away.

A pair of eyes, reflecting moonlight, stared at me from the bushes. With one hand on my gun, I leaned forward. Whatever it was retreated.

Warmth—like a mist of hot breath—melted against my neck at the base of my head. I stifled a shudder. A resounding growl spurred my heart to beat faster, and I turned toward the heat.

The serrated smile was inches from my face. Breath, rank with the stench of blood, warmed the air. Red dotted its muzzle. Goosebumps rippled over my body, starting at my scalp. A scream clamored up my throat, begged to be let out, but fear froze me. I was that little girl again. No. I inwardly screamed at myself to stop being a coward, but it didn't work. All I could do was whimper.

The werewolf cocked its head.

Right. Because I sounded like an animal. Slowly I inhaled. The breath I pushed out fueled the bleakest howl I'd ever mustered. It was perfect. Beautiful. The werewolf threw its morbid head back, stretched its un-naturally long neck, and joined me.

Our voices mingled in bittersweet communion for an eternal moment. So sad. So alone. Did this grotesque creature really mean me harm?

Stop thinking with your heart. Carefully, I pulled my gun from its holster and cocked it. At the sound of the click, the creature's shaggy head jerked toward me. I didn't move. Slowly it leaned in, put its cold, damp nose up to my throat—the exposed skin right below my jaw—and inhaled. It exhaled so forcefully that wisps of loose hair fluttered around my face. For a heartbeat neither of us breathed. Then the beast swiped the gun from my grasp and grabbed me.

I kicked and scratched and screamed, but it threw me over its shoulder and ran.

Razor claws ripped through my Kevlar and penetrated my skin. How was that possible? Hot pain stabbed me as its claws embedded in my flesh and anchored me to itself. I stopped struggling, for fear that any movement would cause the claws to slice right through my insides and leave me gutted on the forest floor.

This was it. It would carry me back to its den and kill me. I'd failed.

The creature stopped running in front of a shack surrounded by leafless trees. They cast shadows over the weathered siding like long, black claws.

The door creaked as it opened, and the stink of wet dog and rotting produce hit me as we crossed the threshold. The beast tossed me onto the bed. Pain stabbed through my side. I curled over and retched onto the wooden floor. It drew closer, towering over me on malformed hind legs.

Was there concern in its eyes?

Oh no.

I'd looked into his eyes.

But suddenly I wondered ... why was that so wrong? Nothing in his eyes spoke of harbored harm for me. In fact, he seemed almost sad to see me in pain. Slowly, and with a whimper, he reached toward my injury. I remained still.

Moonlight spilled through the window, casting shadows on the wall and lighting up the side of his face. His ears twitched. He leaned closer, sniffing my hair. And I pitched away, severing eye contact. That was when my wits returned, like a flood of adrenaline back into my blood. What was I doing? Falling for his—no *its*—spell? I had to get out of here. I cast about, looking for anything that might aid me as a weapon, and a deep growl reverberated through my core—from the monster beside me.

And I found my scream.

I scrambled away and rolled off the mattress, slamming into the floor, my side throbbing. How deep had his claws gone? I dragged myself beneath the bed, leaving a trail of hot, slick blood. My hair fell into my eyes as I pulled the silver hairpin and held it in front of me.

The werewolf dropped onto the floor next to me. On all fours, he crept closer. A deep growl thundered in his gullet, and saliva dripped from his lips. I held out the silver in front of me. It reflected in his eyes. Big, black eyes that looked ... scared. The growl resounded again, but I thought I heard words beneath it: *I won't hurt you.*

Could he be—?

No! It was a trick! Images of Travis on the floor with fake blood gushing through his fingers shot through my mind. I lunged forward, the burn in my side making me stop short. Still I managed to nick the beast's cheek with the silver.

His skin broke open like I'd dragged a blade across his face. He screamed and grabbed my arm with deformed fingers. His claws dug into my skin as he yanked me out from under the bed. I turned the silver spike in my hands and pushed, driving the hairpin into his arm. It sank in easily, and he jumped back. The hairpin snapped in two, leaving the tip embedded in his bicep.

He howled and staggered away from me. I stared at him for a heartbeat. He fell on top of the bed. His whole form shook. Foam dripped from his mouth. The silver poisoned him. But I hadn't pierced his heart. He could still recover. I had to get to him and finish the job. His massive claws dug at the wound in his arm. Slicing through more skin. He was trying to get the tip out.

The mattress shook. Inhuman screams echoed off the walls.

Then everything went still. Quietness enveloped me like a thick fog dulling my senses. He lay still on the bed, skin drenched with sweat. Vulnerable. His wounded arm was shredded but closing fast. He must have gotten the silver tip out. My whole body shook. It was now or never.

I raised my hands above my head and thrust the silver weapon into his chest. The broken edge passed through his skin with ease. But I stopped when I looked at his face.

He was human. Slick with sweat, he shivered, but his eyes remained closed even as crimson leaked out around the silver blade in his skin.

No trace of monster remained now. He was a man. A young man. Weak and cold. I could have finished it there. I could have killed him, but my heart wouldn't allow me to press the spike that so easily penetrated his sternum any farther.

Jon was right.

I should have let my heart guide me all along.

I pulled the makeshift weapon out. His eyes shot open as if the silver leaving his system had awakened him. Eyes wide, he stared at me as he pulled blankets around himself and moved away from me. "Who are you?"

Dizzy, I sat on the edge of bed furthest from where he'd curled in the corner. "I'm—"

His eyes wandered to my bloodstained clothes and ripped and punctured side, still slick with blood, and his mouth dropped open. "I did that?"

Were there tears in his eyes?

"Did—did I bite you?"

"No." My breath left in a rush as realization sank deep. That was the thing. With all that was going on, he'd never once tried to bite me.

His eyes fell on the blood at that dripped so freely off the weapon I held. Then his fingers touched his chest.

"I'm sorry." The words spilled out of my mouth. "You—you were a monster. I—I didn't—But now you're—"

"It's okay."

"I thought I wanted to kill you, but I—I don't. You're a slave to it, aren't you?" I tossed the weapon aside.

"Yes. I am. You—you should kill me." He looked at me. Into me. I swear his gaze reached my soul.

I extended a shaking, bloody hand and touched his. "No. You can't control it. If—if you let me call my partner, we can help you."

"Help?" Darkness covered his eyes, and he lunged at me. I jumped back, but not before his fingers curled around the chain on my neck. It snapped as he pulled. I flailed to stop him, but it was too late. He plunged the silver lightning bolt into his chest.

He slumped back against the headboard, the silver sticking from the hole I had started. A desolate ululating echoed in the distance. Moonlight broke through the clouds, filtering through the window, kissing his face.

His shadow spilled out beside him, the shadow of a wolf.

Trembling, I slid off the bed. I'd seen the shadow before. Outside my bedroom window. My father was hunting these men. Did he know? They weren't the soulless creatures I'd thought. Jon was right; I needed my heart to be able to do this job effectively. And it was too late to tell him. Too late to ask for forgiveness.

Chills rocked my body. I glanced at the floor. So much blood stained the surface. There was no way I'd make it out alive. I pulled my cell phone from my pocket. Slick blood covered all my fingers. The phone was cracked, dead. I sank to the ground and listened to the howls around me. It was like I was locked in the crawlspace again, only this time, I had stuck the stake through a creature's heart. A creature I could have saved.

I opened my eyes to a soft yellow glow. The room smelled familiar, like cinnamon. And my side no longer hurt. My throat constricted. I was dead.

"Hey, look who's up."

My heart jumped as my senses tried to wake up. "Jon?"

He knelt next to me, and I realized I was on my own bed. "How are you feeling, Case?"

I blinked. "How long have I—"

"Couple hours. You lost a lot of blood, but Doc says you'll be fine. Apparently the werewolf didn't bite you." He took my hand in his and squeezed.

Doc. I smiled. Of course Jon called the Knight Owl's medic. "He didn't. He never meant me harm. Jon, you were right about helping them—"

"Save your strength, Case. We'll have plenty of time to catch up."

"Jon, how did you find me? How did you even know I'd gone?"

His thumb brushed the back of my hand. "You really are predictable, Casey."

"Predictable?"

He held up the silver lightning bolt necklace he'd given me and placed it in my hand. "Tracking device."

My jaw dropped. "I can't get away from your protectiveness, can I?"

His eyes softened. "Do you really want to?"

I smiled and lifted my hand to touch his stubbly cheek. "No, partner, I don't think I do."

A smile lit Jon's face. "Partner?" His eyes narrowed. "You're not just using me to make your father's team, are you?" The smirk on his face told me he was going to tease me about this for a long time. But then concern returned to his gaze. "You had me worried, Case."

All this time I'd wanted my father's approval, acceptance. I'd tried to become someone that wasn't me. But it was Jon who knew me best. He didn't see me as a scared girl, but a partner. He always had. "My father? No. He'd never let me utilize my biggest strength."

Jon leaned over and kissed my forehead. "Just promise me one more thing, partner?"

"What?"

"No more solo missions."

I smiled. "Consider this my official request for backup."

Crimson Stain

Jamie Foley

I've been in this frigid prison far longer than my sanity can withstand.

Stifled under the snow, an icy mold encases every inch of me, preventing all movement except the living evil that sludges through my veins. Dormant. Festering.

Perhaps it was an avalanche or a trap set by my prey that caused the endless white to slosh around me and solidify like stone all those years ago. Hundreds? Thousands? I no longer remember.

Maybe I deserved it.

I'd like to believe I wasn't born this way, with these irresistible cravings. This dark appetite from my most gruesome memories. But I can't recall ever being mortal. Human. I don't remember what bit me. Or clawed me. Or somehow infected me with this hunger. Gnawing, writhing, pulsating. It's all I know. All I feel. The hunger of a thousand years of starvation. It consumes me, and yet I am never consumed.

I lost count of how many times sunlight illuminated the compacted snow above my frozen eyes, tempting me with hope, then plunged me into darkness again.

There is no god. If there were, he would either let me die or save me from this frigid hell. So I could have one last indulgence. All I need is one more.

Perhaps it is good that I'm trapped here. For if I am ever set free, I will devour any human foolish enough to cross my path. Or all of them. Anything that might end my suffering.

Thump.

My endless circling thoughts cease. Had I actually heard something, or was it wishful thinking?

Thump ... Thump ... Thump.

No. Not heard. I *felt* it. A heartbeat.

Wildlife!

My own pulse answers, slamming through me with new determination. Hopefully a hungry wolf or bear might detect my scent and dig through the compacted snow, exposing the ancient blue ice to the sun.

A different kind of thumping reaches my ears now, just barely. Footsteps, heavy and intermittent.

I listen closely as they approach. The pattern of the rhythm isn't right. It sounds more like ... two feet. Animals don't walk on two feet.

A human?

My heart kicks faster than it has in years. Should I cry out?

"I see you down there."

I stop breathing. The voice is male, middle-aged.

How can he see me under the snow? What is he doing here? Perhaps he's a monster hunter, and the snow has finally melted thin enough for other immortals to sense me.

Torn between overwhelming relief and staggering fear, I wait and listen. My hunger writhes and scratches at my insides.

"Don't worry. I'll get you out."

Shock lances through me. I hear a *thunk* above my head, then a scraping sound. Then another. He's digging me out!

I can't believe my luck and prayers and begging to the unseen sky are finally realized. Should I respond? Does my voice still work?

"Thank you," I say, my words grating and raw.

He continues to work. The light filtering through the snow brightens with each stroke. I worry for a moment that his shovel will strike my head, then brush the thought away. Freedom would be worth it.

Craving surges through my veins as I feel his heartbeat speed in exertion. His blood will be my first meal in millennia.

No, I tell myself. This man is my savior. I will spare him and hunt for another victim.

But my appetite is so powerful, like a rabid beast. I can barely maintain rational thought as sunshine breaks through.

It's blinding. Pain sears my dark-weary eyes, and yet I can't stop staring upward as shapes appear. And the colors! Blurry, burning smears across my vision.

Trees, like jagged green swords raised toward a breathtaking dawn—or is it dusk?—azure, fiery orange, and brilliant pink slashed by streaking clouds. Mountains firm on the horizon, covered with lazy mist.

Inwardly, my soul admires the god who created such beauty. The foolish god who never should have created me.

His face comes into focus. Lines of determination cross his forehead as he continues to free me, digging compacted snow and ice from around my head and neck. His sculpted muscles flex as he digs, and I notice calluses on his hands. Perhaps he's a blacksmith or carpenter.

My right arm is freed. I stare at it in joyous disbelief as I instruct my fingers to move. The bones ache and stutter with resistance like a door in an old house, but they move. I can move!

I watch the man work on my other arm like a deer unknowingly freeing a wolf. His heartbeat thuds like a drum in my ears, and my hunger roars within me.

No, I shouldn't!

But his blood has the most tantalizing scent. How I can taste it already, I don't know, but I will die without it. He's strong, full of life. Life that must be mine.

I scan the mountain slope and see only evergreen foliage and a glacial river in the valley far below. No witnesses. No one would know.

I resist the thought with all my strength. Well, *most* of my strength. The warmth I feel radiating from him ... I haven't felt anything like it in years. I must have it.

Surely he will satisfy me. Then I will be able to control myself after this one. Just this one.

My left arm is free. I can taste the freedom! Bliss and joy swirl within me.

I will use my freedom to sustain myself. My own desires. Anything I want. What else is freedom for?

No! I should banish the thought from my mind entirely, uproot the temptation. Refuse to think about it. Think about something else. Anything else. I close my eyes and focus instead on the feeling in my own limbs. The frost on my skin creeping away from the sunlight.

But why should I care? What's so wrong with keeping myself alive? Survival of the fittest. That's the law of this world. And I will be the fittest.

My eyes open as he cuts away the compacted snow that clutches my back and hips. Will I have the strength to pull myself out? My body feels like a shriveled husk. Like it's been drained of blood. I need blood.

I want him, so I will take him. I am my own god. I can take whatever
I want.

Why should I deprive myself? No one will stop me.

My fangs grow long and sharp in anticipation. I claw for purchase
against the surface of the snow and wriggle until I know I can break free.
A rush of violent energy floods me.

The man stands back and watches me. His expression is so strange—I
can't decipher it. He doesn't smile or frown or say anything. He just
stands there, like he's waiting for the inevitable swiftly approaching
death.

I lunge, and he doesn't resist as I destroy him.

Blood splatters across the snow. It tastes like life. Like eternity. It is the
most beautiful evil I have ever witnessed. And I cannot stop.

Then he's dead, and I am standing over him, panting and grinning
with elation like the monster I am. I am covered in a crimson stain that
has painted the snow red.

Everything is still except the warm liquid dripping from my chin.

Horror dawns on me, slowly, as I realize I've murdered the man who
saved me. I've been praying to any god that would listen for a millennia,
pleading for anyone to find me and set me free. And as soon as he was
sent, I killed him.

I can't be a god.

I'm a demon.

I fall to my knees and weep. His blood courses through me, searing
new life into my dead and dry tissues. I wish it would incinerate me. Burn
away my curse. My guilt.

"I'm so sorry," I whisper to his ruined body. "Forgive me or let me die.
I don't want to live like this."

I hear only silence and my own sobs as my tears mingle with the scarlet snow. Time elongates and becomes vague. I can't stop crying. I hate myself.

The snow is clean. I blink down at it and rub my eyes, smearing blood across my face.

Except my hand is clean. I look down at myself. I am clean.

I scramble to my feet and glance around, bewildered. The mountainside is pure white except the glistening blue ice within my former grave.

"You are forgiven."

My heart lurches as I whip around to face the voice behind me. The man is standing there. Alive.

I can't breathe. How can this be? Not even immortals can resurrect what was once dead.

Then ... does this man wield the power of a god? No—he was surely dead and couldn't wield any power.

I turn my face to the sky, searching for a sign of that same power to descend and destroy me. The sky has fallen dark, as if in an eclipse.

My bones rattle within me. What have I done?

"Why? I don't ..." I fall to my knees before him. "How did you ... ? And how did you find me? If you knew I was here, did you know what I am?"

"Yes, I knew you. That's why I came," he says. "Do you want to be free?"

I try to puzzle through his words. Hadn't he already freed me? "Free of what?"

"Every chain."

I stare at him. Is he claiming to be able to break *every* chain? What about my cravings? Surely those are not included in his ridiculous offer.

Then again, he broke the chains of death. What bonds are more powerful than that?

"Yes," I say slowly.

"Then follow me." Snowy wind whips around him, but his gaze is steady. "I am the resurrection and the life. The one who believes in me will live, even though they die."

Despite his riddles, I can't meet his gaze any longer. There is something about the countenance of this man ... His eyes are like living fire. I feel like I'm in the presence of a god. A god who could—and should—have destroyed me. But did the unthinkable instead. Why? How?

None of this makes any sense.

My voice falters as I force myself to look back up at him, desperate for some clarity. "If I follow you, where will we go?"

The sky brightens as he smirks. "Did you think you were the only monster who needed saving?"

Psalm 107:1-14

Dark Flames

Ronie Kendig

Haegan Celahar, Prince Regent of the Nine, gazed up at the two Guardians towering over him. Their brows drew in tight disapproval and judgment as they eyed the crown weighting his brow, the scepter occupying his hand, the throne supporting his reign.

"Why do you condemn me?" he asked. "What have I done?" Was this a dream?

The question pitched him back to the Battle of Ironhall. Standing in the blood of both friends and enemies, including those who wielded dark flames as they fought Poired Dyrth—the Dark One—and his Sirdarian Silvers. Howling pulled him around.

Unbelievably, a glimmering tear in the fabric of the world blinked open—and sucked in those around them. The Dark One glowered back at him. And beside him, just as on the battlefield, another form jarred his heart. A rogue marshal he had once called friend. "Princeling!" Eyes shadowed by the dark flames yet blue as the sky locked onto him.

Haegan started forward. "Drracien, no!" With a jolt of both heat and cold, he snapped awake. Found himself staring into the wide brown eyes of his wife, Kiethiel.

Lips parted, she gaped at him. "A dream?" She swallowed. "Again?"

He nodded. "Yeah ..." He lay back against the mattress, arm over his forehead, hating himself for letting her continue to believe the so-called dreams were about his childhood, when he was still paralyzed. But this seemed less dream and more ... like the dreams where he'd heard his long-thought-dead calling him. They'd found him held captive in the underground caves of the enemy. The thought of finding Drracien alive, too, tightened his gut. The accelerant had betrayed the realm, Haegan.

"Yer sure?" Clever, intuitive Thiel bent over him.

He cupped her shoulders. "I'm fine. Do not wo—"

Shouts from outside drew him to the window. By the light of the moon glinting off the Lakes of Fire, which no longer held flames but water, he saw the restless pacing of Chima, his raqine. The enormous winged creature trilled her objection, wakes of heat roiling around her.

Haegan dressed quickly and rushed outside. "What is it?"

His guards did their best to herd Haegan's bonded raqine. "No idea, my lord. She is not happy, that's for sure."

Palm out, Haegan approached slowly.

Obsidian eyes locked on him, Chima trilled at him and thudded closer. Shoved her thoughts at him.

He staggered back, processing the images. "How ... ?" He ran his hand over her broad skull.

"What is it?" Thiel eased to his side.

Haegan frowned. "It's as if she had the same dream I had." He would not recount what—who—he'd seen in that dream. Did not want to find out he was going mad as had his own father, who now sat staring silently into the fireplace for hours on end each day.

"What did ye dream?" Thiel asked.

"Nothing. I—"

"Tell me."

He hesitated. "It's just … a memory. I guess." He shrugged. "The tear—Drracien was being drawn into it. He shouted to me, asked me—"

"To help." Thiel stared at him, her face unusually pale. "I had the same dream."

"*Drrracccieeen.*"

Wind and pain tore at Drracien Khar'val. Howling plugged his ears and forbade him from making sense of the screaming voice. The memory of that place, the moment Dromadric shouted after he'd used dark flames to kill the accelerant high lord, his mentor. But that had been ages ago. Right before he'd died.

So how can I hear him?

And why was there so much haze? Why could he not see? What muddled his hearing? Ahead, the blur that consumed the air cleared. He reached for it.

Fire rushed at him, singeing and searing.

He yanked away, dropping to a knee. At least, he thought it was his knee. Direction seemed to have no compass points, no definition. In truth, he wasn't even sure if he was standing or lying down. Sitting. Floating. The pain and fire roiling over his body made him feel like a pig on a spit … rotating … cooking … burning.

Where am I?

"It's not a dream." Astadia Kath strode toward him with Tili, her future husband, who was also Thiel's brother.

Haegan sniffed. "Of course it is. They're all dead. Poired, Drracien—"

"You don't know that. Can't know that," Astadia said. "If you recall, after Drracien killed Poired, he vanished."

Tili glanced around, brows drawn. "Yer saying Drracien escaped into the void?"

"No, because I *sealed* the void, eradicated it." Hope and dread warred within Haegan. "It's just a dream. There can be no other explanation."

"Actually," Astadia said, "there is. When you sent that wake through the air at Ironhall, it healed the lands, Haegan. Turned death and destruction into fertility and growth. Look around you—Lakes of Fire are now beautiful, the lands once covered in ash are green and lush."

Haegan's heart thundered, thinking of his friend. Daring to hope. "What're you saying?"

"What if that wake *healed* the tear in the void?"

"But I *sealed* the void, no access to it from this world permitted again. It's gone. No accelerant, including yourself, has been able to open the void since the battle."

Astadia hesitated. "True ..."

Surprised at how much he'd hoped for his friend to still be alive, Haegan accepted the reality—Drracien was gone. They needed to move on. "We should—"

"What if it takes two powerful accelerants to open it?" Thiel shifted closer.

"Even if it did and people are captive within," Tili said with more than a little warning in his voice, "are we sure we want what went in coming out? We are better without Silvers and incipients in our world."

"We cut off people, not evil," Haegan said. "Incipients are simply accelerants choosing selfish, dark flames instead of Abiassa's way. Nobody can eradicate evil itself." Haegan slumped. "But Tili is right. After all that was sacrificed to rid the land of the Dark One, the risk is too great. We need to focus on rebuilding Hetaera."

But he could not escape the fear that he was abandoning a friend to a terrible fate.

Drracien faltered in the tearing agony, realizing at once where he was—in the void. Trapped! On the other side of that flickering veil, he recognized the man there. "Haegan, help me!"

The constantly blurring form of the princeling danced beyond the veil.

Though pain and fire crackled along his arms and legs like a lightning storm, it had nothing on realizing the only man who might help him could not hear him. Or he was ignoring him, but that ... that was not like the princeling.

I don't deserve their help anyway.

Not after what he'd done. Killing the Dark One wasn't done to buy mercy. It'd been done to protect the only people worth saving—Haegan, Thiel, and those who'd seen the goodness buried deep beneath his dark embers of anger and vengeance.

Drracien sagged in the haze, the blur of times whipping past him. A visual torment, terrorizing him with near-tangible reminders of what he'd never again have—life. Freedom.

This is my punishment. The price I must pay.

Frustration spun him around, wielding flames sizzling across his fingers. He growled at the psychological torture of being trapped in a place intended as a go-between, not one meant to support life.

This definitely wasn't life.

The crackling haze surrendered in one spot, cruelly revealing Haegan. Again.

"Augh!" Drracien threw a punch.

Through that glimmer, Haegan spun around. Looked over his shoulder. And though Drracien knew it couldn't be, his friend met his gaze. Called his name.

Wait. What?

"Haegan." He tried to move closer, but the more he tried, the farther backward he went. "No." Though he glanced about, Drracien knew his only hope wasn't in here. It was out there. With ... "Haegan, help me!"

"He's in there!" Hagen said. "We have to get him out."

"Lord Regent, we *cannot* open that void again," Tili stated, shoulders taut. "The risk—"

"I will not abandon a friend to a void."

"Friend? He led them against us, sided with the Dark One."

"Whom he killed!" Haegan growled. "Eliminating Poired Dyrth alone is enough justification to help, and in my opinion, it marks Drracien the truest of friends."

"But how are we to help?" Thiel asked, her expression filled with confusion. "The void is *sealed*—none of us can access it."

Haegan thrust a hand to the glimmer in the air. "He is there."

"It is my theory," Astadia said, "that the combined powers of Drracien and yourself are what's keeping it open. He's like a bookmark. Once removed, the place is lost."

"That's an oversimplification." Tili scowled at them and shook his head. "I cannot believe ye are contemplating this. And again, the danger—"

"Haegan, you are the most powerful accelerant in the Nine. Your gift is likely the only one strong enough to free him," Astadia said. "Perhaps my ... gift can hold back the dark embers." That *gift* absorbed the embers of other accelerants. "When we release Drracien, I can draw out the last of the life in there. Force it to collapse in on itself."

"Like a sinkhole." Haegan straightened, his heart alight with the hope of saving his friend. "Will that work?"

"It should," Thiel said softly.

"My sister speaks out of turn," Tili argued. "No one can know if it will or won't work; it's never before been done."

"We cannot fail to try for that reason alone." Conviction dug into Haegan. "Abiassa allowed me to see Drracien trapped there. I will not stop until I have exhausted every possibility to rescue him. Especially since he sacrificed everything to save our world against the Dark One. This is the *least* I can do."

Drracien braced, the haze-like membrane fighting his hope. Fighting him. Had they really said they would try to pull him out? But the void wouldn't open. Few could traverse it. Could Haegan? It took an accelerant with the embers hot enough to wield the Flames and step across time and space. The first time Drracien had done it, he'd puked his guts out. Thought his brains would come out as well.

After Haegan's powerful display at the Battle of Ironhall, Drracien imagined if anyone could, it'd be the princeling. Was he a fool to hope?

No, actually—he was a selfish incipient. The danger—what lurked in the haze around him, pulling at him, tearing at his consciousness—couldn't get out. Even as that epiphany hit him, he saw Haegan aim at the membrane separating them.

You spent your life looking out for yourself. Now fight for them. *For Haegan and the world to have peace.*

The void sizzled and popped, the air lightening, the darkness ... parting.

No.

Drracien shifted around, the void globbing around him as if he sat in a gelatinous orb, every stroke thick and heavy. He angled and used his core to balance as he moved his arms and hands to wield the Flames. Closed his eyes and pushed against the flickering in the fabric of space and time. Wielding strained his muscles, pulled on his embers, challenged his senses. But he could not let it open.

But the push inward, as if the real world forced itself into the void, resisted.

Didn't realize you were this *powerful, princeling.* Drracien gritted his teeth, rotating his arms and tensing his hands to keep the Flames in constant motion to block the moves.

Sorry, friend. I fear we must part ways.

With all he had in him, Drracien pushed outward.

"He's fighting me!"

"Haegan, it's too much. Yer bleeding," Thiel cried from beside him, holding him. "Let him go."

"No," he ground out, leaning in, honing his embers to pin-point accuracy. Reached within the tear. "Drraccciiieen," he growled.

"My lord!" Tili pleaded. "Release him before it kills ye."

Fingertips grazing fabric, Haegan knew he'd found his friend. He surged forward with both his embers and his reach.

The void swirled with chaos, darkness, and heat—and an icy hot that seemed ten times as painful.

"Let me go, princeling. Close the void."

As Drracien's words met his soul, Haegan tensed. Considered them. Tested them. And lunged, seizing his friend by the shirt. He hauled him backward. Felt the ebb of movement, of darkness and chaos rushing at him. In that moment, he saw bloodied hands grasp his friend's arm.

Drracien's eyes widened as he thudded into Haegan and knocked him down. "No!" He stumbled to the ground, turning. Hands out, wakes roiling as he wielded against the two shapes struggling to escape the opening.

"*Miembo Thraeïho!*" Haegan hopped to his feet, fighting beside the rogue marshal. Braced. And thrust with all the embers he had. Watched the void simmer and crackle. Bolts of lightning scissored along his lip as the thing seared shut.

Crack-crack! Boom!

Heaviness thumped Haegan from the rear. He pivoted and saw the silver helm over a bloodied face!

"Fierian!" In a fighting stance, two hands firmly gripping his crimson-stained broadswords, the large Sirdarian sneered at Haegan. He lunged as fast as the lightning that had delivered him through the tear.

His blade sang through the air. Over and over. Slid into one of the guard's sides. Then nicked the cheek of another.

"Back!" Haegan ordered. "Leave it to me."

"Us," Drracien corrected.

Appreciating the assistance, Haegan darted aside and flicked a wake of heat at the steel, sending it along the blade to the hilt and straight into the Silver's hand.

"Augh!" The man shifted backward but—unbelievably—kept his weapon. With a flurry of strikes and parries, he drove at Haegan, who glided backward, sending sparks and volleys in return. In his periphery, he saw Drracien wielding against the man, too.

As Fierian, he had delivered enough death to last a lifetime. He did not want that here, but this Silver left little choice, especially when his attention turned to Thiel, who held her own blade, and beside her, Astadia Kath.

Recognition glinted in the Silver's eyes—most Sirdarians knew Poired's assassin. Deemed her a traitor. And that was evidenced in the way he launched at the women.

Anger shot through Haegan. He drew his right hand back and wielded. Another volley of fire amplified his own as Drracien slid up next to him. Together, they drove the vicious Silver to his knees. Wielding combined, they seared fire through the Silver's chest.

Shielding his wound, the man dropped. He groaned, then lay still.

Expelling a thick breath as guards verified the death, Haegan turned his gaze to Drracien and smirked. "Always were looking for trouble."

Drracien nodded to where the tear had been. "Though it was more like terror than trouble, and not unlike escaping mother's womb." He sobered. "Thank you, princeling."

"He's no longer just a prince." Tili's disapproval hung in the air. "He's now yer lord-ruler."

Eyebrows lifted, Drracien considered Haegan. "I suppose now you'll want me to kiss your feet?"

Haegan grinned and extended a hand. "Kissing my feet, no. But wielding at my side, yes."

"But here." Tili stuck out his hide boot. "Since ye could use some humility."

"We are all friends here," Haegan laughed. "Let us not nurture darkness nor fan dark flames any longer."

Dragon Smoke

Jessica Noelle

The burned branches cracked beneath Hope's feet as she made her way to the iron-wrought castle gates. Her hands twisted the key necklace she always wore, the one that her mother had gifted her. *The king will pay.* Tears stung her eyes, and she brushed them away, swallowing the grief like it was molten lava. *This was for Faith and Mama and Papa.*

"You know we can still turn back now." Conrad's voice sounded behind Hope, hoarse from years of living in a land where dragon smoke constantly billowed.

"We're not turning back." With a grim smile, Hope tightened the band holding her hair. Ash clung to the thick strands, turning them gray. "This is our chance to do something for once in our lives. This is *my* chance."

"By murdering the king?" Conrad looked at the palace before them with its sprawling green lawn and gold inlaid towers. "I don't see how that will help with anything."

Hope ground her teeth together, biting back her frustration. How many times did she have to explain it? "If it wasn't for King Rhydian, Mama and Papa and Faith would still be here. Instead, my family is gone." She should feel something saying the words instead of this numbness. This cold, hollow ache. Shaking the thought away, she continued.

"Because he made a deal with the dragons and has done *nothing* as they have razed our kingdom."

"Hope, that's not—"

"We haven't been able to see the sun in eight years, Conrad. *Eight years*." Hope gestured to the sky, studying it for some shred of sunlight, but all she saw was the thick, billowing soot that blocked out both sun and moon, the cinders that clung to every surface and turned the world into a myriad of grays.

"He made a deal—"

"There's always a chink in the armor, a way out." Hope cut Conrad off. "And if killing the king is the answer, I'll do it."

"And if it isn't?" he shot back.

"I didn't let you come with me just so you could try to talk me out of this!"

Conrad sighed, moving toward the gate and picking the lock with nimble fingers. "What if in condemning the king, you condemn yourself, too?" His voice trembled. "And what if that still changes nothing?"

"Then I'll slay every last dragon there is." Black anger blazed through Hope's veins, a welcome heat compared to the ice that grief wrought in her heart.

Conrad gave her a disbelieving look but handed her the lock. Somehow, his silence stung more than his protests.

"Not all of us can be of noble birth," she said icily. "You lords get to live in the one part of the kingdom that hasn't been ravaged by the dragons. I have always just been the royal gardener's daughter, and I'm not even that anymore."

A lump welled in Hope's throat, pain shredding her insides as she thought of her father and the days he had spent in the garden, but she shoved the pain down, clenching her hands until the lock bit into her hands.

"You were never just the royal gardener's daughter, Hope," he said quietly.

The wall Hope had built between herself and the world cracked with the way Conrad looked at her, his pine green eyes glimmering with tears, but she focused on her surroundings, desperate for something—anything—to distract her. The arid air and smoke stung her nose and eyes, but her fingers traced the lock, finding the keyhole, a sharp reminder of everything her family had stood for, everything she had once stood for.

No. Hope gritted her teeth, staring down Conrad in front of the unlocked gate. She forced herself to fortify her emotions, to cling to the rage simmering just beneath her skin.

"What else would you have me do, Conrad? Give the king my love and loyalty? I *can't.*" Her voice cracked.

"I—" Conrad hesitated, his brows furrowed. "What about *dochas?*"

Pain shot through Hope, stilling her. "Where did you hear that term?"

"Faith told me." Conrad began moving, guiding Hope toward the servants' entrance of the palace as he talked. "She said that it was what inspired your name."

A wave of memories slammed into Hope, each one more painful than the last. Faith and her picking flowers. Faith reading. Faith writing late into the night and spilling ink on the bed sheets.

Hands shaking, she forced herself to speak. "*Dochas* is nothing when compared to what I feel, Conrad. My *dochas* was crushed when I buried my family." When she had choked on the destruction left in the dragon's wake.

Flame. Ruin. Ash. So much ash, filling her mouth and hair and lungs.

The memories threatened to overwhelm her, to gut her all over again, but Hope shook herself, suddenly aware of the fact that she and Conrad were alone in the narrow corridor of the servants' quarters and that he was looking at her like he actually *saw* her, rage and all ... and he wasn't running away.

"Faith used to say that *dochas*, true hope, couldn't be crushed easily," Conrad said.

Hope blinked hard, hating the words as they came out. "She was wrong."

"She said that it could last through the darkest of times. That no matter how much it bled or broke, it would never surrender. She said it was a torch against the darkest night."

A torch? She was tired of flame, tired of the destruction and ash it left behind.

Hope whirled to face Conrad, stopping him in his tracks. "I am *not* my sister, Conrad, no matter how much I wish I were her. I have never been the perfect daughter and have never been the one to have *dochas*, not like she had." She drew her dagger, pointing it at Conrad.

His throat bobbed as he swallowed, his eyes on the blade.

Lowering her voice, she said, "Now, I am going to kill the king and *anyone* who stands in my way. So either get out of my way or stop preaching at me and help me already."

His shoulders slumped. "I can't, Hope. I can't condone murder."

"It's not murder, it's justice. Eye for an eye, life for a life."

Conrad shook his head, pity filling his gaze. Hope *hated* that look.

"Fine." She spat out the word like acid. "Then you might as well leave."

"If that's what you want," he said after a long moment. Then he disappeared down the hallway with barely a glance in her direction.

She felt like she had just stabbed herself. Hot tears spilled onto her cheeks, but she scrubbed them off her face. The pressure reopened the jagged cut on her cheekbone that she had gained courtesy of a palace guard last week, the time she had first attempted to kill King Rhydian.

What if Conrad was right? What if killing the king wasn't the answer to her pain?

Shaking away the thought, Hope pushed herself to move through the maze of hallways and away from Conrad, getting more and more lost in both the memories and the castle itself.

My family is dead because of my carelessness.

Three left turns later, she hit a dead end and had to backtrack.

If I had just done what Mama had asked.

Two hallways opened before her. She turned right, fingering the key that hung around her neck, the one Mama had given her when she was seven.

"Only our family has this key." Mama fastened the necklace around Hope's neck with gentle fingers. "Guard it well."

"But what is it, Mama?"

"It opens the doors to the Well." Her mother brushed a lock of Hope's hair out of her face. "The Well is what the dragons fear most, for that alone can put out their flames, but the Well has run dry."

"Why?"

"I do not know, sweet child." Mama couldn't raise her dark eyes to meet Hope's. She was the picture of defeat with her slumped shoulders and shadowed face. "But we check it every day just in case the Well finally decides to give again."

"The Well opens with this key?"

"The entrance does. But the Well itself requires a pure heart to open it. That is why we must always remember the light."

"Even in the darkness?"

"And even in the midst of false light, like the dragon fires."

Hope nodded, clutching the necklace, as she promised her mother to protect the Well.

What good was light when her family was dead?

Hope stumbled, turning into a new hallway full of armor, but she hid as voices approached.

"She means your father harm, Your Majesty, and you still wish to keep her alive?"

"She's angry and hurt, that's all, Fen. Really."

A chill ran down Hope's spine. She *knew* that voice.

"As you wish, Prince Conrad."

Hope bit back her gasp, sinking to the floor as a guard and the person she thought she knew so well passed by.

Prince.

The crown prince.

The realization hit Hope in the stomach like a sack of flour. Conrad had been lying to her all this time? They'd known each other for three years! He'd said he was a nobleman's son, that he just wanted the good of the kingdom, but he just wanted what was best for himself. No wonder he'd tried to stop her from killing the king—his father.

She brushed her hand against the pouch on her hip, feeling the familiar weight of the nightshade vial. If she went through with her plan, she would be robbing him of his father ... but she would also be ending the reign of a vicious, cruel tyrant. She would be killing the man responsible for her family's death.

She headed in the direction Conrad and the guard, Fen, had gone. At the sound of voices, she ducked behind a suit of armor.

"Father, please eat."

Conrad.

The hall opened into a ballroom. Conrad sat at the lone table with an old man, a bowl of soup between them. One lone guard flanked the doorway, but his interest was directed toward where the piano would have gone. Instead, a cage with a huddled, barely moving shape rested there. A person.

Hope flinched. More cages bordered the room, some filled with gold and others filled with exotic animals. But a person ...

Her stomach churned, her eyes trailing back to the huddled shape. The figure moved, coming into focus. A woman, pale and gaunt with stringy brunette hair reaching just past her shoulders. Her face seemed familiar, somehow.

"He won't eat, Conrad." Her voice was just a rasp. "If you keep trying, you'll end up like me."

"He has to." Conrad didn't turn to face the prisoner, but his voice was tight. "I'll be careful, Mother."

That woman was his mother? The queen was in a cage? Hope nearly gasped aloud.

The old man let out a wheezing laugh and held up a gold spoon, letting soup drip onto the table. "We need more gold, Connor."

"Conrad," Conrad gently corrected.

"Gold," the king proclaimed. "Write up a decree. Send out the collectors. The people must be taxed more."

Hope took a half step out of her hiding place to better take in the scene. How could Conrad defend this frail, despicable man? A man who had everything and still demanded more? Who'd caged his wife?

"Bring me more riches by sundown or your mother will face the guillotine."

Conrad tensed. The queen merely sighed before speaking, but her voice was drowned out by the sound of wheels rattling. Hope jumped back into her hiding place, taking in the tea cart and the jovial servant woman pushing it. The servant left the cart before entering the room, curtsying. The guard searched her while she talked.

"Tea, Prince Conrad?"

Hope moved to the cart, listening.

"Please make my father his usual, Miriam."

Hope fiddled with the pouch and drew out the poison, its purple label bent.

"Of course, Prince Conrad," Miriam said.

With one swift motion, Hope uncapped the poison.

"Any for you?"

Hope hesitated, the bottle in her hand half-tipped, the poison only a centimeter away from sloshing out into the scalding water. That moment cost her, and she didn't hear Conrad's answer as strong fingers grasped her wrist. She gasped. The guard yanked Hope up, knocking the bottle to the floor and shattering it. Violet liquid splattered across the stone floor, seeping into its cracks, and with it, every dream Hope had of avenging her family melted away too. She fought and bucked the guard, pounding against his armor, but the guard was stronger than she was.

She had failed her quest. Hot anger sloshed inside, scalding her, and Hope slumped, the fight inside her ebbing as tears of anger pricked her eyes.

"Prince Conrad, what would you like to do with her?" the guard asked.

Her breathing suddenly shallow, Hope gazed up at Conrad, but he wouldn't meet her eyes. Coward! The queen was talking to the king about gold now—distracting him, Hope realized. *I could have saved her.*

If only she hadn't hesitated. Hadn't let her concern for Conrad keep her from doing what needed to be done.

"Just take her to the dining hall my father never uses. I'll handle her from there." Conrad's words were tight, strained.

"Are you sure?" the guard asked, raising an eyebrow.

Conrad nodded. "She won't hurt me, Fen."

Hope tried to lunge at Conrad, but Fen caught her. Hope struggled against Fen's iron-hard grip to no avail. "You sure, sir?" Fen repeated, concern coating his eyes.

Conrad gave Hope a sad smile. "She's just being stubborn. Have Sylva bring us a meal, all right?"

Fen nodded, and Hope was yanked away. As she took in each step of the palace, she forced herself to see the opulence of it and remind herself what it had cost—her people's blood. Each hall was inlaid with gold, and the columns seemed as if they were hewn of the precious metal. The light of the candelabras glinted off the precious gemstones chipped into the wall, creating an illusion of a rainbow-covered fire. How could the royals live like this? How could *Conrad* live like this knowing how his people suffered?

Fen shoved her into a dining hall, the soft carpet caving under Hope's ash-stained boots. "I don't know what Conrad wants with you, but don't hurt him, miss. That man is the kingdom's only hope."

Hope snorted and collapsed onto a seat, propping her feet onto the table. She crossed her arms and stared sullenly at the wall as Conrad entered.

"Hope, you need to get out of here before my father realizes what just happened. Just because he's slower now doesn't mean his mind is completely gone yet."

"Why should I believe anything you tell me? You're a liar. A dirty, good-for-nothing liar." Her voice broke. "I trusted you—"

"Hope, please," Conrad interrupted.

"No!" She stood, anger flowing through her veins and burning her cheeks. "My family is dead because of a deal your father made with dragons. That deal killed my family. *My sister.* They're all gone because of him. Because of *your* father."

"Please," Conrad choked out. "Just hear me out. If you have ever trusted me, listen."

Hope hesitated, running a hand over the tablecloth as if she were bored. What choice did she have, really? She was at his mercy. "Fine."

"My father asked the dragons for gold to save the kingdom from war, but then he got greedy and asked for more and more gold," Conrad said. "A dragon's hoard is cursed, you know. If one piece you keep, a dragon's heart you'll reap."

Hope nodded, familiar with the old adage. "What then? Why did no one stop him? Why did *you* not try to stop him?"

"A dragon's curse is a powerful thing, Hope. It grants one protection, but at a cost. Nothing can dethrone my father, and I will not kill him, no matter his crimes." Conrad's eyes darkened, giving him a pensive, far-off look. After a moment, he shook himself. "But I have not been doing nothing. Since I returned from boarding school three years ago, I've been trying to stop the dragons."

"I have no reason to believe you, Conrad," Hope spat, her heart fracturing more than she thought possible. "You kept so much from me, and even now, you refuse to meet my eyes!"

A muscle in his jaw tensed. "What reason do I have to lie to you?"

"To keep me from running you through with my knife as I almost did earlier." But she knew she could never do that. She could not take another loss.

A knock sounded at the door and Fen entered, bowing. "The king wishes to see her."

Conrad stiffened. "Why?"

"You seek to keep her hidden. Therefore, she must have value."

"So he wants her." Conrad sighed, collapsing in a worn upholstered chair.

"I can stall for a few more minutes, my prince."

"Yes, please." Conrad rubbed his brow, exhaustion seeping into his features. Fen bowed and left.

"I won't go into a cage like your mother." A sudden burst of fear flooded though Hope, making her breaths jagged and sharp. She backed away from Conrad. "I won't lose my freedom."

Conrad spoke quietly, his voice calm. "I would never dream of letting him cage you, Hope. I would never let him keep you as a trophy on a pedestal."

She stared up at his earnest eyes and found that, liar that he was, she believed him. Her breathing eased.

"We need to flee while we still can," he continued.

"So we're running?" Hope couldn't keep the scorn from her voice. Of course she had been planning on running, but all she wanted was to keep challenging Conrad, if only to distract from the ache in her chest. "Because that's what you do best?"

Conrad shot out of his seat, anger flashing in his eyes. "I am no coward, Hope, whatever you might think. There is one path that might lead to washing away the dragon flame scorching and razing our land, and that is but a myth, but if you will give up your desire for vengeance, I would gladly take your help."

"You expect me to roll over and surrender just because I know you?" Hope folded her arms over her chest. "Are you insane? Oh wait, don't answer that."

"I seek the Well of Light." Conrad's words silenced Hope.

After a moment, she let out a brittle laugh. "The Well is dried."

"How do you know?"

"My family guarded it for centuries. Why do you think we stayed in our house even though we could live inside the palace grounds if we had chosen to? Every day, my parents sought to see if the Well had regained any of its might, and it never did. You cling to dead hopes and dreams."

Conrad let out a soft, broken, sob—just one—before composing himself. "Then are things truly so hopeless?"

Hope thought of Faith's words. About how *dochas* was so powerful that it could never be dethroned. A beautiful, terrible lie. But she didn't want it to be a lie. She wanted to believe in something like that again.

"Take me there, please," Conrad begged. "I need to see this with my own eyes."

Hope managed a nod, if only because Conrad looked so broken and she herself wanted to walk where her sister had last walked, breathe where her mother had breathed last, and rest where her father had last rested. Pain twisted in her heart as she remembered the awful truth of the day her family died.

She had been supposed to check the Well that day, but she had begged to be released so she could train with the village healer. Her sister had agreed, and her parents had wanted to check on some secret project anyway, so everyone but Hope herself had gone.

I should've died instead.

And if Hope let herself think like that for a moment, the guilt would overwhelm her. It was far easier to blame it on the man who had brought the dragon flames to her homeland, far easier to blame it on the king and his family.

Yet now his family was standing in front of her, and she was taking him to her family's greatest secret, taking him not out of fear, but out of some other tangled knot of emotions that she refused to unravel.

She huffed in exasperation.

"Hope?" By the worry in Conrad's voice, Hope realized she had been lost in her own mind for a while. "We have to go."

She nodded. "You know where my house is, but the Well is not in those charred ruins." Her voice caught. "It's where my family's garden was."

"But I've been there a thousand times," Conrad protested as he led her through the maze of halls.

"We've been protecting it for centuries. Do you really think we could do that if it was in plain view? Where anyone could access it?"

"But you can access it?"

Hope hesitated.

Conrad frowned at her. "Right?"

"The Well of Light can only be accessed by those who have light in their hearts."

"But you've accessed it before?"

Hope flicked her eyes up, meeting Conrad's. "That was before my family was slaughtered. Before I decided to kill the king."

The admission seemed to unlock something inside her. A gate long shut, swinging open to reveal only darkness. When Conrad saw, he would undoubtedly leave. But she couldn't stop speaking now that she'd opened the door.

"I used to feel the light in my heart, but now ... now, all I feel is dark, roiling anger." She swallowed thickly. "I feel *broken*, Conrad. When I reach inside my heart, Conrad, all I feel is darkness. I've lost myself." Before she knew it, her chest was heaving, and tears were streaming down her face.

Conrad caught her as she fell, holding her to his chest.

"It's going to be okay, Hope. Let it all out."

It had been coiled so tightly in her chest, the pain, the guilt, choking her, strangling her. But he'd seen her darkness and hadn't run away, hadn't abandoned her. Instead, he held her. He stroked her hair, each touch and each word helping cut through the bitter knife of grief lodged in her chest.

After a few moments, Conrad helped her to her feet and led them outside into the gray air. Her eyes were puffy and swollen in a way they hadn't been since the day she'd discovered the ruins, but it made her feel alive, somehow, like she'd faced the pain head on and survived.

In the woods she had roamed all her life, Hope's feet found the familiar path to her house. Each step weighed heavier and heavier on her heart.

What if she wasn't worthy anymore? What did that make her? Was she truly no better than the tyrant she had set out to kill? The tyrant who, according to Conrad, was cursed by the greed of the dragon hoard? Was she then worse than him?

Fear clutched at Hope as the smell of smoke and ash, the smell that always lingered in the air, grew stronger. The fire that had stolen everything Hope loved had never been put out. So long as the dragons raged and the Well remained dry, no dragon flame could ever be put out truly. Always embers would remain, smoldering constantly.

Hope stopped, her eyes trailing over the ruins of what had once been her home. She drifted over to the scorched hearth, centering herself. Her family's kitchen would have been in front of her, their table where they had shared so many meals and memories. Her parents had always sat at that table when they worked on their books and balanced their wages. It was where her parents had taught Hope how to read, where her sister said they had picked out Hope's name when she was but a day old.

A lump had built in Hope's throat as she sifted the burning rubble with her thick-soled boots, searching for some remnant of her family.

None remained.

Conrad's gentle touch broke Hope. She leaned into his embrace, silent tears streaming down her face. "I don't know who I am without them."

"You are who you've always been, Hope. The only difference is you now carry your parents and sister in your heart."

Hope let out a harsh laugh laced with pain. "The Well is this way."

She led Conrad around piles of burning ashes, avoiding the small fires that still burned. When she was in the wasteland that had once been her family's garden, she paused, glancing at Conrad.

"The Well can only be shown by my family's blood as long as we still live." She pricked her finger with the tip of her blade. A crimson droplet welled up and she leaned down, brushing the one flower untouched by flames, the one flower that had never died or wavered. Its pale petals bloomed bright red, and Conrad stepped forward to examine it only to have Hope pull him back.

The ground erupted as the Well emerged right where Conrad had been standing. Its onyx stones gleamed even in the fading light, and the oak-hewn lid was lined with diamonds, making it impenetrable. With well-practiced movements, Hope unlocked the clasp with the key that had hung around her neck for as long as she could remember before flinging open the latch.

"That wasn't so hard," Conrad said, peering over, but she stopped him.

"That was the easy part." Hope steeled herself as she spoke. "The next part is where someone's heart is weighed."

"How?" Conrad asked.

Hope bit her lower lip. "It's just as simple as reaching for the second hatch, but Conrad, if I'm not worthy ... if someone is not worthy, they could die."

Conrad gazed at the Well's second door, its ash wood plain and unassuming, but Hope kept her eyes on him.

"Aren't you going to say anything?" Her voice cracked.

He wouldn't look at her as he bit the inside of his cheek. "I—you—"

"Is that how little you think of me?" Hope had thought her heart couldn't hurt any more than it already did, but she had been wrong. So, so wrong. She let out a shuddery breath and stretched her hand into the Well, brushing her fingers against the final lock.

The world went white, and when Hope opened her eyes, she was in a field of flowers like the ones of legends, for that is all they were to her now. The emptiness pressed against her spine, and she knew the true Guardian of the Well was weighing her.

"Please." Hope felt as if she might cleave in two. "All the Keepers are dead except me."

A blast of hot wind gusted past her.

"I miss my family." The words caught in her throat as she found tears pricking her eyes. "I miss them, and I tried to kill the king of Isador. And I'm so, so broken."

This time, a gentle breeze caressed her cheeks, and she leaned into it, no longer trying to cage away her emotions. "I feel so lost and confused."

She squeezed her eyes shut, suddenly acutely aware of a calloused and familiar hand squeezing her own. *Conrad.*

When Hope opened her eyes, she was no longer in that meadow but above the Well, one hand clutching Conrad's as if he were her lifeline and the other hand on the latch. The cut on her cheek stung with each salty tear that traced it, but she tugged and the Well gave way. With a creak, Hope opened the final doorway, her breathing easier despite the tears that wrenched at her lungs.

Somehow, the true Guardian had still allowed her passage, still seen some spark of light in her when all she felt was darkness. She still carried her family's legacy, and with each tear, more of her anger at the king seeped away.

Instead, Hope only felt sadness for the kingdom and her people.

"You opened it, as I knew you would." Conrad's soft voice tickled her ear.

"But you stumbled?" Hope said, for a moment forgetting why they had come.

"I sought to find some way to reassure you, but I failed. Hope, you fight for the good of others, whether or not you see it. That alone should gain you access to what you seek. And despite what has transpired between you and me, you have still chosen to trust me. I could ask for no better friend." Conrad paused. "Now, shouldn't we at least take a look into the Well?"

Hope nodded, and with a trembling breath, she peered into the Well. It was bone dry.

A silent tear traced down Hope's cheek as the wind swirled around them. Conrad clutched her hand tighter. The wind was soft yet fierce, reminding Hope of the same wind the Guardian always seemed to be associated with.

It rose around Conrad and Hope, and Hope watched as the tear she had shed hung in the air for a moment, suspended by wind.

A shaft of sunlight, the first she had seen in eight long years, broke through the clouds, reflecting a prism of colors.

The frozen droplet hovered for what seemed like ages before exploding, releasing more water.

The fires sizzled and hissed, and around her, Hope heard the wind *speak.*

"Light always defeats darkness."

The wind faded and the spell broke, the water droplets extinguishing the dragon flames with a soft hiss.

"Did you hear that?" Conrad asked, turning to face her.

"It was the Guardian of the Well," Hope gasped. She peered into the Well again, and the sight of water bubbling up from its depths stole her breath away.

The sun had once more been hidden behind clouds, but Hope felt a familiar spark in her heart. *Dochas.*

Even now, there was still that eternal hope.

Faith had been right.

"We can stop the dragon flames," Conrad cried, joy lighting up his face.

"We can indeed." Hope smiled, looking at the sky just as a swarm of butterflies burst through the trees, their wings painted with every color imaginable. "We can save our kingdom."

Hope entwined her fingers with Conrad's, her heart full as she remembered the deep love she bore for her family, her kingdom, and her friends. As she remembered *dochas* and her sister's words. She could do this, could beat the darkness because she had something far more powerful than darkness ... love.

After Stars Fall

Nicole Wheeler

Lyra would have another chance that night.

She feigned disinterest, discreetly watching Gran assemble a basket of food at the other end of the taproom counter. The message had come less than an hour before, asking for Papa's help at the lighthouse.

"Dinner for your father," Gran announced, though Lyra clearly understood who it was for. "He'll be gone the whole night, and then fall right into bed and sleep most of the morning away," she coaxed.

Lyra nodded and smiled pleasantly, pretending to miss what Gran was implying: that Lyra could slip out after dark, unmissed. She felt Gran's eyes on her as she prepared a tray of hot cider and biscuits, keeping her head down as her thoughts spun out.

The lightkeeper—a gnarled, ancient seaman with no family of his own—had called for assistance at least half a dozen times that spring. Papa was one of the few men with the knowledge and freedom to come at short notice when the coughing fits overtook him and sent him back to his bed.

Well, she didn't need to wonder any longer if Gran knew about her late-night outings. And, if she knew that Lyra snuck out every time Papa went to the lighthouse, then Gran would know there were only two possible explanations.

She exited from behind the counter carrying the tray. *Hopefully, Gran thinks I'm sneaking off to meet a boy.*

The thought nearly tripped her as she walked to the group of young men sitting in the corner, efficiently neglecting the textbooks they'd come to the taproom to study. Their good-natured laughter made the room seem brighter somehow. Dean and his friends had gotten into a routine of studying for the university entrance exams together in the cozy taproom of the Noble Inn. Lyra couldn't decide how she felt about the development.

On one hand, she had to stifle her annoyance that the boys were flaunting the likelihood they'd move to the university in a few short months. Attending university would take a miracle she didn't have on hand.

All right, maybe flaunting wasn't fair; they couldn't know that she wouldn't be able to attend. Lyra wouldn't bother taking the entrance exam, so there was no need to study. No need to be envious, and certainly no need to be annoyed that they were squandering their study time.

Lyra was top of their class, and it only irked her a little that she wasn't first in line to go. Just the same, it thrilled her a little each time he came in with his friends. Lyra was unquestionably the smartest in class, but Dean was probably second smartest—and the most handsome.

She shook her head as she deposited the tray at their table, annoyed with herself. It was a perfectly reasonable place for them to meet to study. It had nothing to do with the fact that her family owned the inn or the likelihood she'd be working the taproom when it was busy. That thought led in a direction best not to open herself up to.

"Thank you, Lyra." Dean beamed a glorious smile up at her. He seemed to want to say more, but Lyra bobbed a polite nod and quickly turned on her heel, retreating to the counter. She didn't want to explore the reason behind the flush she felt burn her cheeks when he said her name. She certainly didn't want anyone to notice it.

Nonetheless, she felt Gran watch her escape, a knowing smile on her face. Lyra silently prayed that Gran would keep her observations to herself. Maybe she'd rather talk about the stars after all instead of the young man sitting in the corner with his friends. Him, or the hopes and disappointments that lingered in the corner with him that she preferred to ignore.

The sound of Papa stomping down the stairs saved her from whatever Gran was poised to say. He smiled warmly at them each in turn, taking the basket. "I'll be back after sunrise. Go ahead and close the taproom early; no need to take chances with a full—"

"Get out with your ridiculous suggestions, boy." Gran swatted his arm. "I've run this inn longer than you've been alive. And I expect you to go straight to bed when you come home and stay there until noon tomorrow at least, if we're handing out unnecessary orders to grown adults. You'll turn useless without enough sleep. I've got a few strapping lads over in the corner to call on if we need assistance." She nodded over her shoulder, smiling mischievously. "And if it comes to it, I've got my loaded pistol under the bar. Same as I do every time you go to the lighthouse." She winked at Lyra.

Papa yielded with a smile and kissed them both goodnight before he hefted the over-packed basket out the door. This little argument was becoming something of a ritual on nights he went to the lighthouse. Lyra didn't miss the assessing look Papa shot the group in the corner on his way out.

Gran waited two full hours before she began prodding Lyra again between tending patrons, dropping not-so-sly comments. "It's a perfect night for a go at it," over a frothy tankard to a burly fisherman. "You'll regret it if you don't try," as Lyra passed payment from a table for Gran to deposit in the drawer.

"The stars aren't going to fall too many more times this season, I'd reckon." This time Gran cornered her in the crook of the counter where there was no escape to a table or patron waiting for a mug.

Lyra's heart sank to her feet. Gran *did* know.

It took a moment too long for Lyra to shake off her surprise, to be convincing when she said, "I don't know what you're talking about."

She tried to look Gran in the eye, tried to give substance to the lie, but she couldn't measure up to the steely wisdom she saw in the older woman's unfaltering gaze. It held no judgment, only a challenge.

"Well, I have gone to watch once or twice ..."

Gran's intense stare did not falter. "Only to watch?"

Lyra relented, dropping her eyes to her hands, her voice low. "Might as well be. I've tried every night Papa's gone to the lighthouse, and I've got nothing to show for it. Maybe Mama didn't *really* have the gift; that it was something she just made up for my bedtime stories? Or maybe it simply didn't pass on to me?" Lyra sighed and began wiping down the counter, chin to chest, trying to erase the disappointment gnawing in her stomach.

She felt Gran step close, voice low despite the din of the taproom. "She did."

Lyra's breath hitched at Gran's confession. No one had ever acknowledged her mother's gift to her before.

"I saw it with my own eyes. The Gathering talent—call it magic, maybe—is so rare that most believe it's just an old fairy tale. But why else would people think they could wish on a star and get anything for their trouble? I witnessed her bring them home more than once. It's because of her gift we have you. I believe you have it too."

As a little girl, Lyra believed Mama's stories about the clever women of their family line who knew how to find the pieces of broken stars fallen from the sky. Shards that held enough magic to meet one simple need—an earnest, sincere wish that wasn't rooted in greed or malice. The stars knew better, Mama had said. She'd spun beautiful tales about the majestic star-falls that came in the spring and had promised to teach Lyra the family secret when she was older.

But the stories stopped when her mother died. She'd never dared ask Gran or Papa any of her questions and risk opening old wounds. She didn't know precisely when her belief in mother's stories wilted, but when the star-falls began again at the first thaw that year, they revealed an ember of hope still alive in Lyra.

Gran's strong arm on her shoulder brought her out of her thoughts. "The counter is clean, my dear."

Thirty minutes after they closed the taproom for the night, Lyra stepped out from the front porch of the inn, Prince Rollo at her heels. She'd spent the time watching the sky and scratching the pup's belly. When the intermittent streaks started across the horizon, all she'd said was "Let's go," and he joyfully bounded in her wake, tongue lolling out the side of his smiling mouth.

The cute little mutt didn't understand the nighttime outings she took him on, but he clearly didn't mind. His presence comforted her, encouraged her. Rollo practically pranced as he kept pace with her, his tail curled all the way up to his back.

They'd made it to the edge of town when Rollo stopped, alerting her to something behind. Lyra tensed and reached for her dagger. "Who's there?"

She didn't carry much with her on these outings, just a small lantern, a bag tucked in her belt, and a dagger in her boot—just in case. Their little hamlet was usually quite safe, even with the traveling merchants who frequented the cove. Still, she knew it wasn't the smartest idea for her to be out in the dark, alone.

"Stay back," she warned, holding her knife out at an angle in the hope it would reflect the moonlight and look menacing. Rollo bounded over to the figure emerging from the shadows, little traitor.

Dean stepped around the corner she'd just turned. "Whoa, Lyra, it's just me." He kept his distance, his hands raised.

Relieved, Lyra lowered her dagger.

"I called your name a block back, but you didn't hear me. I guess I didn't call loud enough, I'm sorry. I was trying not to wake the whole town." Dean knelt down to pet Prince Rollo.

"Why are you following me?"

"I'm not."

She huffed and raised an eyebrow at them both.

"Well, I guess I did, after you didn't answer me. The fellas and I had stood out by my family's shop talking for a while after you closed the taproom. I'd said goodnight to the others not long before I noticed you go by. What are you doing out so late?"

"I—" Lyra looked up to the cliffs beyond the edge of town, unsure how to explain herself.

"Oh, are you going to watch the stars fall?"

"Yeah, I guess."

"Can I walk with you for a bit?"

Lyra nodded, not sure what she wanted to say. She'd imagined walking home from school with this boy countless times. But tonight, she was on an errand, and it wouldn't do to have an audience. He might think she was crazy. Or laugh at her. Or worse.

Still, a traitorous part of her heart sped up in excitement at the thought of watching the stars with him. "All right." She smiled in the semi-dark as she put away her knife.

The trio made their way up to the bluffs above the cove where the little village was nestled. Far in the distance at the other side of the inlet, the lighthouse beam swept across over the rocky shoals and out to sea. Lyra was comforted by the knowledge that her father was up in that tower, manning a beacon that could guide her home.

Dean broke the silence after they'd gone some distance across the open land that stretched from the sea-cliffs to the edge of the forest. "Do you come up here often for a better view of the star-showers?"

"Yeah, sometimes," Lyra conceded. "My mother used to tell me stories about them."

Dean let out a small laugh.

"How is that funny?"

"Oh, it isn't. I—" He ran his hand through his hair, as if to loosen his thoughts or master his words. "I apologize, I wasn't laughing at you ... It's just ..." He faltered again. "I laughed because my father sometimes tells me stories about the stars too—and about your mother."

Lyra snapped to attention at the mention of her mother. She stopped walking to look at him.

"My father used to tell me stories of magicians who could charm the stars from the skies and use them to cast magic spells on people. Once, when I was caught sneaking cookies as a little boy, he said he would fetch one and have them turn me into a pocketknife or a new hat. Something useful." He let out a little huff of a laugh, as though embarrassed.

Lyra's stomach clenched, morphing into something cold and hollow. "That's appalling. And what does that have to do with my mother?" She did not like where the conversation was headed. She frowned, letting her attention follow Rollo as the pup stalked an insect through the grass.

There was no telling what a person thought of magic. It was so rare that most people were unfamiliar with it. Some were ready for awe and wonder ... Others, well, others were too quick to fear and too ready to strike out before they understood. The magic didn't even have to be real for fear to overtake someone. It was dangerous for people to even suspect a tie to magic unless they were capable of enough wonder to outweigh their apprehensions.

Even if Mama's stories had been only that—just stories—Lyra had learned some of the lessons Mama had tucked in them. Lyra knew magic didn't have to be real to make monsters out of men. There were good reasons to keep it secret—if it were real at all.

"He was just teasing me." Dean smiled at the memory. "Then he handed me another cookie and mussed my hair and said that he'd rather have his son over a new hat anyway. And as for your mom ... apparently he fancied her when they were in school. He used the word 'enchanting' to describe her. He said that he'd wished that one of those sorcerers"—*Gatherers*, Lyra mentally corrected him—"were real and in our town so he could've asked them to cast a spell to get her to notice him."

"I don't understand." She desperately wanted to move Dean's thoughts away from stories of magic or her mother. He couldn't know the truth, but he was too close for comfort, all the same.

She also wanted to get to the point of his story and understand if she should be offended on her mother's behalf.

Or afraid.

"You haven't explained what that has to do with my mother, really, or why it made you laugh."

"Well ... my father ... He—" Dean sighed as though he were about to make a grave confession. "He was teasing me about how often I find an excuse to come to the taproom." He studied her face in the moonlight, searching her eyes. After a moment, he went on. "The lads and I could easily study at one of our houses ..."

"But the taproom has cookies and cider and fewer chores," Lyra suggested, a peace offering.

"And you." He swallowed.

Lyra suddenly found it difficult to breathe.

"My father couldn't resist teasing me this afternoon when I told him I would be studying at the taproom again tonight. He speculated that I'd fallen under a magic spell, just as he'd been enchanted with your mother." He huffed an almost laugh, a crooked smile teasing his face. "But your parents were already in love, he said, and she didn't take notice of any of the other boys in town. Neither do you, it seems. You don't pay attention to any of the boys in our class ..."

"I don't?" Her voice was barely above a whisper.

He shook his head, almost imperceptibly. "Then, here you are, walking out in the dark toward the stars ..."

Lyra suddenly became aware of how hard her heart was pounding in her chest. How close Dean was standing. Her mind was racing, looking for purchase. She noticed how his eyes flicked down to her mouth; in reflex, she returned the gesture.

"He doesn't honestly think you are under some kind of spell?"

"No." His voice had become soft, close. "But I think he likes believing in the possibility of magic. That's just like my pa; he loves to imagine wonderful, hopeful things like that."

Lyra felt herself relax a little as the hollowness in her stomach flooded with warmth. "And your ma? Did it bother her that he said such things about someone else?"

"I asked her." Dean smiled again. Lyra felt his fingers brush hers, as though asking a question of their own. She twined her fingers with his in answer. A new tension sprang to life inside her.

"She said that she knows that Pa loves her with all that he has, and she can't begrudge the memory of a woman who borrowed his eye before she met him. Nor will she speak ill of the dead." He registered Lyra's response, even in the dark. "I'm sorry."

Lyra shook her head and looked to the cliff for a reprieve but did not let go of his hand. "What for?" She didn't know why she asked. She knew she'd flinched.

"For mentioning her. You probably still miss her, and I might've hurt you by speaking of your loss."

She studied the contours of his face visible in the moonlight. "That's kind of you to say."

He seemed closer now, and she wasn't sure if he had stepped nearer or if she had done it when she turned back to him. She could feel the warmth radiating from his tall, broad figure. It was nice in the chill of the night.

Her eyes dipped again to his lips, and somewhere in the back of her mind, she wondered if the faint stubble on his chin would feel—

Dean closed the last breath of distance between them, brushing his mouth gently against hers before she could finish the thought. She didn't notice anything scratchy in the contact. On the contrary, it felt dazzling.

Sparkling bolts shot through her; down to her fingers, her toes, weakening her knees, shorting her breath.

This must be what it felt like to be a falling star. Bright, and effervescent and joyous and out of control.

His other hand cupped her face, just under her ear, sending another thrilling charge through her as he brought his lips to hers again.

Light showered around them as she kissed him back.

Lyra had never been kissed before. For her first kiss to be under the star-fall ... with Dean ... was more than she'd imagined. It was enough to convince her that all the stories of magic were true.

When they parted, Lyra saw a streak of light reflected in his eyes. They took a small step apart, his hand reluctantly falling from her neck, as they looked over the cliff out to sea. The stars were falling in earnest now, the heaviest fall Lyra had ever seen.

"You could join us, you know. If your gran would let you when the taproom isn't too busy."

"What?" Lyra almost shook her head to clear it, but she didn't want to dispel the magic she felt surrounding them.

"To study for the entrance exam. You're planning to apply to university, aren't you?"

It was Lyra's turn to let out a small laugh, surprised that he could think of university at that moment. "I would love to, but ..."

"You have responsibilities at home?" he guessed.

"Nothing is for sure yet," Lyra hedged. Unless her luck changed one of these nights, it was certain she would have to stay home. Her family lacked the finances to send her—not just the cost of tuition, room and board, but also the wages to hire someone to cover the work she'd leave behind. She didn't want to admit any of that to him.

She turned back toward the view beyond the cliffs. She wanted to keep her focus on that moment, not the future. Not the inevitable disappointments. "Let's sit and watch the stars a little while."

They found a relatively flat spot, and Dean sat close, his arm braced behind them in a way that felt like a kind of respectful invitation. Rollo wasted no time curling up on her other side, placing his head on her lap. Lyra spent the rest of the star-shower in tense excitement, hyper aware of Dean next to her, hoping he would lean in and kiss her again.

He did.

Twice.

For the third time that night, Lyra crossed the sleepy hamlet in the dark. She should have been tired, exhausted, really. But the excitement of sitting with Dean through the star-fall and then allowing him to hold her hand as he walked her home had energized her.

When the stars stopped, she couldn't think of an excuse to stay behind alone. What could she say? *Excuse me while I scour the ground between the cliffs-edge and the forest to see if I can find the broken pieces of a fallen star?* No. She couldn't send him away, and she wasn't ready to reveal to him she'd been there to do more than just watch the stars. Instead, she let him walk her home.

The exhaustion from a full day of school, work at the inn, then her late-night escapade only hit her as she made it back to finally begin searching. It didn't take long for frustration to overtake her.

"There has to be more to it than just wandering and looking in the dark, don't you agree, Rollo?" The pup yawned and smiled up at her. "Otherwise any fool could be up here having better luck."

He sat patiently next to her, waiting for her next move. Lyra didn't have one, so she joined him on the ground and stroked his head, considering.

As fatigue rolled over her, she became aware of a new ache in her chest. No, not new, different. It had morphed during the night into something more acute than it had been before.

On previous nights, Lyra had wandered back and forth with a confident expectation that she would simply find what she was looking for. All the while, the shadow of a pain had been in the dark with her. An ache for something she was missing or waiting to fall into place.

This night, it felt sharpened to a keener edge. Not desperation, exactly, but a more earnest want, a need. It was the blade hidden within hope that could prune a heart—or maim it. Finding a shard would be the only means to make it possible for her to go to university. It could help a lot of things, really.

And if her mother had brought home shards in the past—and she believed Mama had, no matter what she'd said to Gran—then maybe Lyra could too.

She also knew what Gran meant when she said that the shards were the reason Lyra was with them. She'd learned over the years of her mother's difficulty carrying a baby. How her parents had tried for years to start a family. She'd realized Mama must've used the magic of wishing on a shard to carry Lyra safely to term.

The thought made her almost double over. Why hadn't Mama done the same for her baby brother? Maybe they'd both be alive now.

Should Lyra have tried to find a shard back then? She'd been only ten, but perhaps she could have done it. If only she had done more, known more, perhaps she could've saved them both.

Rollo made a soft noise, pulling her from her spiraling thoughts. She looked down at the sweet little pup, who licked her hand in response. She realized that at some point she'd started crying. "It's all right, boy. I'm all right." She stroked his head until he fell asleep.

But the dark turn of her thoughts had done its work, and another melancholy wave washed over her. Lingering grief over the mother she still missed, the little brother she never had the chance to know. The desire to go to university, so strong that it hurt. And now, the idea that something could begin with Dean only for it to be cut short when he inevitably left for school.

She was so tired, and really, a little embarrassed with herself. She would have to return home, empty handed once again, and pay the cost of a sleepless night with no reward to show for it. It was easier when she believed no one knew she'd been failing.

She closed her eyes and pictured the broken shards of a fallen star, like small pieces of broken glass. Lyra imagined holding them in her hands, feeling them dissolve into nothing as the tears overtook her in earnest.

She had been a fool to waste her time on a dream. A fool to get her hopes up. She needed to get her head out of the stars and on to practical matters. To stop wasting her time on something that would never materialize.

Lyra stood, letting the melancholy pull her weary feet closer to the cliff's edge. When she was as far as she dared go, she stared at the dark horizon, unable to determine where the sky and sea met. The stars that remained above were still enchanting, even if they were unreachable.

"I'm sorry, Mama," she whispered to the silent confessional of the darkness and the sea.

Unbidden, Mama's face came to mind, so strongly that Lyra thought she might be hallucinating. Mama smiled at her, the warmth of her mother's love washing over her so powerfully it nearly knocked her down, and for a moment she feared she would topple over the cliff.

She wanted to step back, frightened by the sudden vertigo. But the sensation of love washed over her like a powerful ocean wave, and like a wave, it pulled her closer to the edge. Like a swimmer too far from the shallows, it would mercilessly wrench her out to sea.

Lyra took one trembling step forward. Another. With each inch the tug on her heart became stronger. Lyra didn't want to fight the pull, but she was getting too close to the edge. Yet, to fight it felt as treacherous as letting her dreams go.

She didn't want to let her dreams wither in the inky darkness and die. She wanted them to pull her past the edge of her fears and give her flight.

Adrenaline coursed through her body. This was too close. *She* was too close. But the pull seemed physical somehow. Dragging, pulling, urging her to look down, climb down, reach down. To discover what waited in the darkness beyond.

Lyra carefully slid one foot back, lowered herself to a knee, and dared look over the edge ...

There, resting on a small ledge just within reach, lay three beautiful, perfect shards of fallen star, gently pulsing a faint glow that Lyra would never have been able to see if she had not come close enough to the edge to look into the darkness beyond.

On the way home, Rollo bounded along next to Lyra as though he'd captured an endless supply of energy from his nap. Or, perhaps, he instinctively understood the elation coming from her and could not help but share her joy.

The joy of a Gatherer after stars fall.

Beyond the Waves

Laura L. Zimmerman

There's no place like home, right?

My knuckles turn white as I grip the handle of the suitcase. I stand in the doorway of my new summer home—the one which clearly needs updating—in the town my mom once called *her* home. There's no way I could ever call it mine.

I scratch a hand through my thick, dark curls as I crinkle my nose. It even smells old. Like mothballs.

"Move it, Maren." My mom bumps my butt with the box she's holding, forcing me indoors.

Even inside I can hear the crash of waves that tumble a few yards from the back door.

An entire summer at the beach? You're so lucky!

Can't wait to see your tan!

Bring a handsome surfer back with you!

I groan. My friends' enthusiasm for the impending eight weeks is far too optimistic compared to reality.

This place is a prison. I'm trapped with my mom for the summer.

Not that she *doesn't* control me no matter where we live—a past trauma has made this our lifelong vibe. But now we're four hundred miles from home. No friends. No fun.

"Stop sulking and unpack the car, please!" Mom's voice cuts through my melancholy like a surfboard slicing the sea.

"Why did we come here when you hate the ocean?"

She ignores me.

After another trip to the car, I wander to the back of the rancher and find my bedroom. More mothballs. I drop my suitcase next to the bed and flop on it. Ouch. Not soft.

With a sigh, I drag myself up and finish helping my mom.

Lana—my mom—grew up here. Well, not *here* here. Just in town. Which is surprising, considering how very white her skin is, not to mention the way she burns to a crisp just looking at the sun. With my creamy brown skin—which will undoubtedly be considerably darker by the end of the summer—and my deep brown eyes, no one ever believes we're related.

Seaville (yes, it's literally called *Seaville*) has a population of way-too-small-for-my-taste. My mom never explained her departure from her childhood home. I just know we left when I was a baby and never returned. *The End.*

"Do me a favor and unpack the box marked *cookware*? I need to get lunch started." My mom nods toward a box.

"Aye, aye. Captain." I give her a salute. "Should I swab the decks while I'm at it?"

"Ha ha." Lana gives me the mom-look with her light blue eyes. "Drop the attitude. You'll be fine without your friends for a few weeks."

"*Eight*," I reminded her. "Are you sure there're no long lost cousins you have here? Possibly a cute step-cousin-four-times-removed that I could meet?"

She raises her brows at me and twirls the pan I just handed her. "No boys."

"Mom, I turned eighteen last week. I'm old enough—"

"End of discussion." Her tone is sing-songy to lighten the mood. But it doesn't. This discussion is as old as time.

Except I'm not Belle about to be saved by the Beast.

"In answer to your other question ..." Her straight blonde hair falls across her eyes. She tucks it behind her ear. "No. No family here. One of the reasons I left this hole-in-the-wall town."

My brows pull together. "This isn't where Grandma raised you? You never told me that."

"She moved away just after Pop Pop died, the fall after my graduation. I remained here alone."

I blink. Why would she stay near the water when she hates it so much?

The pan sizzles as she tosses in butter. A scent of toasted caramel fills the air and makes my mouth water. I poke around in the grocery bags for some fruit to make a salad to go along with the scrambled eggs.

"Drat." My mom mutters as she rummages through the empty cabinets. "I forgot salt and pepper."

"Am I heading back to the store?"

"Would you?" Her eyes are pleading as she holds up the car keys.

I roll my eyes and turn to leave, the same pushover I've always been.

Later that night, the place is almost unpacked. My mom locks the sliding glass door that leads to the beach, slipping a dowel rod for double security, before watching the sea in the darkness.

"I'm headed to bed."

My mom doesn't turn around, but I can see the tension in her shoulders. "Goodnight, hon. Be sure your windows are locked."

I frown. She's been nothing but nerves ever since she announced this surprise trip to the beach. Again, why did she bring me here when she's terrified of water?

I sigh, head to my room, change quickly. Then flop onto the bed in relief. *Ouch.*

Humid air sneaks past the window unit. Sweat pops along my back.

With a huff, I turn over and snuggle into my pillow. Then I kick my sheets to the floor and roll over again. Close my eyes. Force myself to relax.

And I hear it. A song.

I lift my head. It stops.

Okay, never mind.

But when I lay my head back down it starts again. Only two notes. Over and over. I close my eyes and concentrate on the interval. My music teacher said I was gifted and urged me to focus on an instrument.

I never did, though.

It's an interval of a fourth. I listen again. No, wait. It's a *diminished* fourth. Like a C sharp to an F. A sad sound.

Yet, still enticing.

When I lift my head once more, the sound disappears.

Before I know it, I'm asleep—and a little bit closer to going home.

I awake to the sound of waves arguing with the shore. *The beach!*

Despite my hesitation to move to this town, I'm all for catching some rays.

I'm out of bed and dressed in my bathing suit before my mom wakes. I snag a towel on the way through the sliding glass door. My breath hitches when my gaze finds the water.

Forcing an exhale, I move, finding a flat-ish spot far enough from the waves to stay dry, but also far enough from the house that I won't hear my mom if she calls my name.

Because she will *inevitably* call my name once she finds me gone.

Better to ask forgiveness than permission, right? I *am* officially an adult now.

I've only been soaking the sun for ten minutes when a shadow dims across my eyelids.

"Are you the new folks next door?" The voice is feminine.

I sit up to find a girl wearing a fuchsia-colored bikini standing over me. She's about my age. She smiles and her entire face brightens like the sun. Her mahogany skin is glossy from lotion, her mass of tight curly hair tied in a bun on top of her head. Her nails are manicured, her flip flops clearly from a top-of-the-line shop.

"Hey." I stand so we're eye to eye. "Uh, yeah. We got here yesterday."

"Cool." She turns to look at the beach house. "Is the rest of your family coming out?"

I shake my head. "It's just my mom and me. She's asleep. Thank God." I mumble the last part and she laughs.

"She not a fan of the water?"

I fake cough. "That's an understatement. She's downright terrified of it. Something that happened when she was a kid, I think? She doesn't like me anywhere near it."

The girl tilts her head. "And yet she brought you to the beach?"

I laugh. "I know, right? Actually, she wasn't thrilled about this trip. She said she didn't really want to come, but she felt like she had to or something?" I shrug. "I don't know. Maybe it was a graduation present for me or something."

The girl smiles bright again. "You just graduated? So did I!"

"Cool." I lift my long hair from my neck to let the sweat dry. "I'm Maren, by the way. Ren for short."

"Nancy." She bounces on her toes. "How long you here for?"

"Two months." I sigh. "To be honest, I'm not super excited about spending the summer away from my friends."

"I get that." She gives me a wink. "But no worries. I know all the hot spots in town."

I hide my cringe. What would Lana say about that?

No. That's what she would say. Because when have I ever been allowed to leave the house for very long? Or spent time with people she didn't approve of?

And yet ... I'm eighteen. Can't I make my own decisions now?

"That sounds fun." I glance at the house. No sign of movement. Turn back to Nancy. "What did you have in mind?"

An hour later, we've wandered as far down the beach as I feel comfortable—I don't need my mom calling the cops on me.

I meet two girls and four guys, classmates of Nancy's. All of them live along the beachfront.

Maybe this summer *will* be fun.

"Tell me again why we can't go in the water?" Nancy asks as we walk back toward my temporary house. She uses her fingers to fluff her bun.

I avoid her gaze, my chest tightening. "I mean, it's more than just my mom's fear of water. It's sort of mine, too."

"Yeah, but you'll never get over the fear if you don't face it, right?"

I nod. "I guess. I just—" I suck in a breath and watch the waves snake their way along the sand. "I'm just not ready yet."

Nancy nudges me with her elbow. "Well, you better get ready. I've got plans for you, girl."

We both laugh as we cross a dune, our rental in sight. The sound of my name cuts through our mirth.

"Maren Grace!"

Oh shoot.

I turn to Nancy, who already has her brows raised. "Gotta go."

Her gaze cuts to my mom and back. "Think you can hang tomorrow?"

"Sure." *I hope.*

"Cool. See you 'round," she says and runs off.

I steel myself as I approach my mom.

She stands with her arms crossed, leaning against the frame of the sliding door. "Where have you been?"

"I met our neighbors." This comes as more of a question.

"You need to tell me when you leave the house. You don't know the area. What if you got lost or kidnapped?"

I shake my head and push past her. "Chill, Mom. I was fine. Nancy was just showing me around."

"Nancy?" She fumbles with the lock on the door, her eyes falling on the water beyond the glass.

"Our neighbor. The girl I was standing with?" I need to pull back my attitude or I'll get grounded. But it's hard when she gets like this.

She whirls on me. "You could've left a note."

"Yes, I get it. I'll do that next time. But really, I was just sunbathing. I hadn't anticipated going anywhere." I pause. "Besides, I wanted to let you sleep. After our move and all."

That's it. Tugging at those heartstrings should do the trick.

She glares at me. "Uh-huh." She glances out the door once more and wanders away, clearly sensing my manipulation.

"By the way," I call after her. "I think there's something wrong with the air conditioner in my room. It was making a weird noise last night."

She gives no response.

The next week passes with a little less drama. Lana allows me to lounge on the beach with Nancy. In turn, Nancy convinces a few of her friends to come hang with us. My mom watches us almost constantly, as if I'm a precious gem in danger from a jewel thief.

I often find her standing at the sliding glass door, just staring at the ocean. At night, she locks the place up like it's a bank vault.

By the following Saturday I've earned my freedom.

"Guess what?" I bounce up to Nancy with more energy than necessary.

She looks up from her spot on her towel where she sunbathes behind her house. "You won the lottery and you're taking me on an all-expenses-paid trip to Europe?"

"Ha!" I plop down beside her. "Nope. Better."

She slides her sunglasses down her nose to look at me. "Better than Europe? I've gotta hear this."

"I get to spend the day with you. Like, *away* from here."

Her jaw drops. "*No*. Your mom is letting you out of jail?"

We laugh, and I help her pack up her stuff to drop at her house. Then we hit the sand to find some fun.

"Where are we headed?" I pull on a thin oversized shirt. Although I haven't been in the sun very much, my skin is begging to have a break from the never-ending UV rays.

"Brandon's!" Nancy fans her face and wags her brows.

"Oooh." I giggle along with her and kick a sandcrab to the side. *Ew.*

"He's having a small party. I was just going to hit it later, but since you're here ..." She winks at me.

"Shhh." I glance over my shoulder with a snort. "Don't let my mom hear you say *party*."

The two of us cross several sand dunes, farther than I've ever walked on this beach before. We hear the commotion long before the group comes into sight.

There's ten or eleven of them, mostly girls. One girl has been draped in a black robe, a squared off black hat on top of her head. Two of the guys pick her up and balance her on their shoulders while the rest of the group cheers them on.

A girl in the back picks up a large cardboard cutout that looks suspiciously like a tombstone. Another girl holds her phone, the song "If I Die Young" blaring from an external speaker she holds in the other hand.

"What is that?"

Nancy laughs. "It's a funeral."

"Huh?" I stop a few dozen feet away, so the group can't hear us.

She rolls her eyes. "It's just a thing the locals do when a girl turns eighteen. Well, I mean, not every year. Just this one."

I shake my head. "Okay, whoa. Back up. Why just this year? And why a funeral?"

"So, there's this legend ..." She cringes.

"A legend?" I smack my head dramatically. "Small beach town. Lots of history. Of course there's a legend."

Nancy runs a hand along her braids. "It's called *The Curse of the Sea*. Very original, I know. It starts way back at the start of the town. Like, early 1700s or something."

I nod. "Super long time ago. Got it."

"I guess a girl went missing on the beach, around her eighteenth birthday. Then exactly twenty years later it happened again to a girl who also turned eighteen. This pattern has continued ever since. Always a girl turning eighteen, always on the beach."

"Wait." I huff a breath. "You're saying that girls disappear from here every twenty years and no one has ever done anything about it?"

Nancy waves me off. "Don't worry about it. It's literally a legend. Like, I'm pretty sure it was hearsay until the twentieth century. There've only been a handful of documented cases."

"Still ..." I furrow my brow at her. How is she so chill about this?

"Seriously. It's probably just coincidence. Teenage girls go missing all the time. Probably most of them were girls fed up with small town life. My guess is they ran away of their own accord after graduation."

"Dramatic."

She snorts. "Tell me about it."

The girl with the tombstone sign finally turns around so I can read it.

R.I.P. Here lies Samantha Reinhardt. 2004-2022. Destined to live at the bottom of the ocean.

I frown. Morbid.

We end up joining the funeral-party, which is actually far more fun than it sounds. By the time the sun has set, my gut tells me to jet home before Lana realizes what time it is.

As I race back, something niggles at the back of my mind.

The fact that I just had *my* eighteenth birthday. And how my mom felt the need to bring me to a cursed town when I fit the profile perfectly.

It's almost lunchtime by the time I roll out of bed the next day. Nancy is already at my back door, asking Lana if I can head to town to go thrift shopping with her.

I'm shocked when my mother actually agrees.

I slip a pair of shorts and tank over my bikini—assuming the beach will be next on the agenda—brush my teeth and run my fingers through my hair. "Bye, Mom. Back by supper?"

Her brows furrow and lips pinch, but she nods from her spot on the sofa.

Thirty minutes later, Nancy and I duck into a hole-in-the-wall secondhand shop. The sign out front declares *Under the Sea, Seaville's Finest Shop of Treasures.*

"Check out these vintage rings," Nancy says, twirling a display case sitting on a glass counter.

"Cool." I eye the antique items sprawled throughout the glass case, then walk away.

Several bookcases line the back wall. *Score.*

I beeline it for the books. The display is disappointing—mostly nonfiction. Not my thing. I'm about to turn back to Nancy when a line of identical books along the bottom shelf catches my eye. I tilt my head to read the binding.

Seaville High School Yearbook Class of 2002. My interest piques.

Could this be? A literal piece of Lana's past? A past she's never shared with me, no matter how many times I've asked.

I snatch up the book and immediately flip to the senior photos. It takes me all of ten seconds to find a younger version of my mom smiling back at me.

"Dude!" I can't hide my excitement.

Nancy trots over. "What'd you find?"

I beam at her. "My mother's high school yearbook."

Her jaw drops. "Are you serious?" She grabs the book from me, scanning each face. "Oh. Em. Gee!" She squeals this when she finds my mom.

"Cool, right?"

She hands it back. "Which one is your dad?"

"Oh." I flip another page and scan for his name.

Nothing.

"Huh." I frown. "He's not here."

"But you said they met in high school, right? Like, they were high school sweethearts?"

She leaves off the obvious statement, *before he left you and your mom when you were an infant?*

I brush off the stab of melancholy that comes when I think of the dad I've never met.

"Yeah, but maybe he was in a different class?"

She nods and grabs a few more books in the years prior. But he's not there, either.

"Weird." I blink. "Was he younger than her, maybe?"

Nancy shrugs and grabs more books.

Nothing.

I huff. "This is so weird. I know they were in high school together. She's told me like a billion times." My cheeks heat at the fact that I know so little about my own father.

"Did he go to a different high school maybe?"

"Dunno."

She shakes her head and gets back to treasure hunting.

A bout of dizziness clouds my vision. Why does my dad appear to be a ghost?

I wait until Nancy leaves my house to confront my mom. The massive rock that's taken residence in my belly warns me of danger ahead.

"Have fun shopping today?" Lana asks as she twirls her spaghetti against a spoon.

I swallow and sit at the dining table across from her. "Uh, yeah." I pause and gather my words. "I found something exciting, actually."

"You did?" She keeps her focus on her food.

I clear my throat. "Yeah. Quick question, though. You said you and Dad graduated together?"

Her eyes meet mine. "Yes, of course."

"The same year? From the same school?"

Her gaze drops as she picks up her glass to take a sip of water. "Uh-huh."

"That's weird."

She locks eyes with me once more. "Why?"

"I found your old yearbook. At the thrift shop. I found you, but there was no sign of Dad. Not even in the years before or after you graduated. Why is that?"

Her laugh is strained as she twirls her fork absently. "Oh, well, that's probably because ..." She blows out a breath. "Because ..."

The struggle behind her gaze is agonizing. That pit in my stomach grows to the size of a volcano.

"Mom?" She freezes so I go on. "I'm eighteen, Mom. What aren't you telling me?"

She sighs. Her shoulders slump. "I didn't meet your father in high school."

"Yeah, figured that."

She nods. "We met while I was waitressing at the *Silver Fish Cafe*, in town. We dated a few times. Then I never saw him again." Lana won't look at me.

"What?"

"I'm sorry, look—"

"You lied to me? My entire life, you've been lying to me?"

"Ren, please—"

"No!" I step away from the table. "All these years you made me think I had a dad that just didn't want me. When he really doesn't even know I exist! I've felt rejected and worthless my whole life. But the truth is, I really just had a mother who lied to me."

"Maren, enough!"

"Who was he, Mom? Who was the man in the pictures you showed me?"

She blinks a few times. "He was a close friend in high school. He had a similar complexion and features as you. I thought it would be believable."

I cross my arms. "Did you get permission from him? Does he even know you made him a *father*?"

"Maren, this isn't fair—"

"Don't tell me what's fair, *Lana*. I'm not the one who's been lying for eighteen years! Why did you even bring me here? You clearly aren't comfortable with the ocean."

Her lips flatten. "I can't tell you. It's ... complicated—"

"Of *course* it is."

More lies.

I stomp to my bedroom. Fury pounds inside my chest as I crash onto my bed. It doesn't take long for my tears to flow.

Once again, I hear the strange song calling to me as I drift off to sleep.

Lana has been perched on the sofa all day long, her gaze constantly on the ocean.

So naturally I can't leave my room.

At dusk, a knock at my window startles me from the book I'm reading. Nancy laughs at me from outside.

I roll my eyes and open it. "What are you doing?"

"I knocked on your door, but your mom says you're grounded."

Rage explodes inside me. "What? That's so not true."

"Well, you're not going out according to her."

I smack the wall with my fist. "Just great. Now I've got no social life along with no dad."

"Wait, what?"

I shake my head. "I'll tell you later."

"Later? As in, you're good for coming to the bonfire tonight?"

I huff. "No."

"No?" Nancy balks.

I scrub a hand through my hair. "As much as I'd like to blow my mom off for what she did—and yes, I promise I *will* tell you—I can't. It would kill her. She's seriously paranoid."

"Dude."

"Tell me about it. But have fun, okay?"

"I'll try. It won't be the same without you, though."

"I know." I give her a weak smile. "Eat a s'more for me?"

She nods and disappears.

I go back to bed and think of all the ways I could disobey Lana. And all the reasons I shouldn't.

My insides twist and my head fogs with anxious thoughts until I finally drift off to sleep.

It's hours later when I wake.

My room is pitch black, the sky outside my windows just as dark. The ocean roars with attitude. But there's something more.

I rub my eyes as I sit up and listen.

The song. It's back.

I hold my breath as I listen for my mom. Silence. She must've gone to bed.

The sad song plays over and over as I sit still.

I glance at my door. Can I sneak out without sending my mom into cardiac arrest?

The two notes echo deep in my ears.

That's it. I hop up and slide my window open, the only sound the increased echo of the waves as the vibration tumbles around my room.

Once outside, the song calls to me.

My mind goes numb as I walk across the sand, my feet carrying me toward the water. I breathe in, then out. In, then—

"Ren?"

Nancy's voice shakes me from my trance. My heart rattles inside my chest. Water splashes across my bare feet. I jump back.

"Whoa!" Nancy catches me as I stumble. "You okay?"

I blink at her, then look at the water. I'm ankle-deep in the ocean.

The breath leaves my lungs and I freeze. My heart pounds between my ribs like that never-ending tide. How did I get this far out?

"Are you all right, Ren?"

I hold Nancy's hand as I steady myself. "I ... yeah, I think so."

"Are you coming to the party?"

"Huh?"

"The party. Is that why you're standing here?"

"Uh, yeah." I swallow and glance at the house. "Yeah, that's it. I can go."

"You can?" She jumps. "Lana actually let you leave the house?"

"Yeah." Guilt pierces my chest, but whatever. If Lana can lie, then I can too.

"Cool. Let's go!"

It takes us twenty minutes to get there, but that's only because Nancy insists on hunting for a pair of flip flops she swore she'd left by a certain lifeguard chair earlier in the week.

We plop down in the sand just as one of the guys pulls out a guitar and strums a song. The fire blazes strong, and we spend the next hour singing classic rock.

I'm on my third s'more when a pair of guys sit to my right. They're deep in conversation already.

" ... the curse. I mean, it hasn't happened yet, but how many girls are turning eighteen this summer?"

I turn to them. "Excuse me, what did you say?"

The one with the dark hair shifts in my direction. "We're talking about the curse. You know, the one where the girls disappear? This is the year it's supposed to happen, you know."

"Yes, I heard. But, it's just a legend, right? I mean, you don't actually believe all that, do you?"

The blond guy leans forward. "Oh yeah, totally. My mom's great-aunt was one of the girls that went missing. Like, a long time ago, but still ..." He shrugs.

"You know one of the missing girls?" My blood runs cold.

"Cool." Nancy says this from beside me. "I'm Nancy, by the way." She flashes the guys a smile.

I cut off her attempt at flirting. "Still, the summer is halfway over and it hasn't happened. I mean, it is possible it won't, right? Like, I'm sure if we dig deep enough we'll find it hasn't happened exactly every twenty years. That's just part of the myth."

Dark-hair guy drops his smile. "Naw, bro. I did a project on it in middle school. The curse is real. No lie."

"Don't worry, Ren." Nancy pats my back. "I'm sure you're safe. Your birthday was a month ago. It's too late for the curse to get you."

The guy shakes his head. "Actually, the birth date doesn't matter. A few girls that went missing were born in the fall, and one in early spring."

"Yeah but ..." I huff a tense laugh.

"But what?" Blond guy lifts a brow.

These two are serious.

"Uh, nothing. It's fine. I'm fine." I turn to Nancy. "I think I'm going to head home now."

She frowns. "You sure? There's still plenty of night left to party."

I stand and brush sand from my butt. "Yeah. I need to get back. Have fun." I nod toward Mr. Dark-hair and give her a wink.

She laughs and waves goodbye.

I sprint home. I don't know why. I'm not really scared my mom has discovered my absence. And I'm not afraid of walking home alone.

But something tells me to run. That I can't waste another minute. That my life depends on it.

And then I hear it. The song. Those two sad notes.

My house is in sight, but instead of walking toward my bedroom window, my feet turn toward the sea. I hear nothing but the rush of waves. The heavy beat of their crash echoes within my bones. The sand is gritty between my toes. A briny scent dances on my tongue.

"Maren!" Lana's voice is behind me.

I twist around to face her. Water splashes my legs, and I gasp.

I'm knee deep in the ocean. For the second time tonight, I've walked right into danger without realizing it.

What is happening?

"Maren, please. Don't go, honey."

Don't go where? The wind whips hair across my face. "I was going home."

This is the truth. It doesn't explain why I'm standing in the ocean though.

"Please, Maren. Stay with me. I can't do this without you."

"Mom?" I frown. "What do you mean? What can't you do?"

I see tears in her eyes. She laughs, despite her obvious anguish. "Life. I can't do life without you."

"I'm confused—"

"Maren. I should've been honest with you. Not just about your father, but everything. I was just too afraid of losing you. I've spent my entire life assuring you were safe. I'm sorry I never trusted you to make your own decisions."

An invisible vice grips my chest. "Mom, you've lost me. I have no clue what you're talking about."

She nods. "Listen. A couple years after graduating high school I was surfing one night ..."

"Surfing?" My eyes go wide.

She waves me off. "Yeah, yeah. I know it's a shock. But listen ... that night, an infant washed ashore, crying."

"What?"

"I couldn't just leave it there, so I took it home and cared for it, assuming I would hear of a missing child. But no word ever came. I watched the news, asked around, but there was nothing.

"I could've gone to Social Services, but secretly, I wanted to keep it. I had no life, other than serving tables at the restaurant. I had no family nearby and no prospects of love. I wanted a companion. Over time, I grew accustomed to caring for the baby and just sort of kept it."

"Mom. You stole a baby?"

Once more she holds up a hand. "Soon after accepting my role as mother, I took her to the beach. A sound from deep within the ocean startled us both. A song of two notes. She began to cry.

"Then, a voice echoed from the water, as if the ocean itself was speaking. It said that the baby was a *Daughter of the Sea* and had been chosen as the *tithe*, as part of an ancient ritual performed every twenty years. The *tithe* is given to secure provision and protection for the people who live below.

"The child was to remain in my possession until her eighteenth birthday, at which time she must return to make her choice. To either remain human or return to her people. If I neglected to bring her back, the child would *die*."

A tear slips from her eye. "The child is you, Maren. *You* are the *Daughter of the Sea*. I *had* to bring you back here. So you can choose."

I'm sucker-punched by her words.

The *Daughter of the Sea* is me?

"It's my choice?" My voice shakes.

Her tears flow freely. "I tried to take that choice from you, sweetheart. For that, I'm sorry. I didn't think I could do it without you ... survive. But I see now that this decision must belong to you alone. You're free to go, Maren. It's time I let go. It's time you go home."

Home.

Blood rushes through my veins with a pounding as strong as the tide. I look to the sea.

This is it. I've always felt like there was something missing in my life. Like I wasn't where I was meant to be.

I watch the cresting water. *Home.*

With a deep breath, I take a step toward the ocean. Then another.

It's time I go home.

My throat tightens as my feet touch the cold water. As it splashes up my calves, then my thighs.

Home.

I stop. The water beckons me, begs me to dive below. To reclaim what is mine.

The song rings louder. The song of my people.

No. The song of the *ocean* people.

But they're not *mine*. They've never been mine.

Home.

All this time I thought I wanted something more. But what I wanted was what I already have.

Home has always been right here. For the first time in my life, I understand why my mom made the decisions she made, why she tried so hard to protect me.

I carefully step backward, watching the water recede. Wash away to a land I'll never know.

I turn and reach a hand out to her.

She smiles.

"You're right, Mom. It's time we go home."

Falling Scales

C.M. Banschbach

Tendrils of heat reach out to tease my limbs, tucked up close to the hearth. My arms, ensconced in my well-worn sweater, wrap around my knees as I stare into the flickering light. It's been restless days and restless nights with Devin gone. He'll be back in the morning, but each beat of my heart feeds the lurking thought that this is the time my brother won't come back.

Please come back, please come back. I rock back and forth. My legs—one covered in scales, the other slender and taloned from the knee down—tap against the floor stones. I try to draw a calm breath in and out, but the prick of fangs against my bottom lip mocks the attempt.

The restlessness rises up, feeding into the something always curling in my gut. With the full moon rising to its peak, I might not have much of a chance. I pull the sweater off, not about to risk this long-ago gift from Devin.

A tendril of moonlight sneaks through the shutters, and instinct takes over.

Cold presses against my face. I draw back, peeling eyes open, focusing on the damp nose of our dog. It pants happily as it gains my attention. I jolt up, recoiling a little from broad daylight. The walls of the cottage have become a forest clearing filled with feathers and bits of ... I shiver.

"You're awake." Devin's voice draws my gaze up. He offers his crooked smile and extends the sweater. I grab it and pull it over my nightdress, left ragged by the night in the woods and the curse which drove me to abandon what humanity I have left.

"You're back." I curl into the sweater, trying to tuck my mismatched legs under the ragged skirt like my brother hasn't seen them before.

"And I brought pastries."

I smile. My tongue might be bordering on forked, but it still likes sweets.

"Come on." Devin wiggles a hand down at me. Mine, still human-shaped but covered in scales and the tips of claws, closes around his. He doesn't flinch anymore, but some days I wonder if he does inside.

We walk side by side, back to the small cottage we'd claimed in the middle of the woods when I'd been cursed four years ago. For some reason he stuck with his monster of a sister after our father turned me out without a second thought, Devin claiming he rather likes the "eccentric hermit in the woods" reputation. Perhaps it's the way he's also learned to think about others besides himself.

But he's seemed restless the last five times he's come back from the village at the end of the dusty road running through the lonely woods.

"How was town?" I fold my arms tight across my stomach.

"Fine." A distant yet soft smile touches his face.

"Devin?"

"Sylvie," he returns when I hesitate moments longer than normal. I try to think back to the time before, when I was a normal girl and he was a normal boy, both with normal lives, to remember if he'd ever acted this way. But my memories seem lost with any sense of normalcy, my body now a mishmash of animals and scales.

"Did you make any new friends?" I finally ask.

"Maybe." The slight smile plays again, and my heart falls. It is still human, and I remember what that sort of smile means.

He's found someone and she'll pull him away from me and I'll be left alone. Not that I'd blame him for finally leaving.

"Sylvie?" He turns back to where I've stopped, stomach feeling like it's tumbling and falling. "What's wrong?"

My gaze falls to my feet—one lizard, the other a rooster, both nothing anyone would want a thing to do with. Especially when something monstrous awakes under the full moon or with intense emotions, stealing my remaining humanity in a voracious rampage.

"What's her name?" I look back up and try to muster something brighter.

He tilts his head, shoulders rising and falling with a breath, but replies, maybe happy to have this secret out. "Anne. She's wonderful, Syl, better than anyone I ever met before." He chatters on as we return to the cottage. Her father is a woodcarver. It's just the two of them. She has the voice of an angel.

They have a horse that reminds him of the steeds that filled a stable behind a manor house we both loved once upon a time. I try to listen, to not let every breath add to the dryness of my mouth.

He sounds carefree, happy, nothing like the twenty-two-year-old who's been so serious for the last four years. Like he was before my curse. I want to listen, to see what this woman in the outside world might be like, but all I can think is that she will steal him from me.

"Hey." He pivots again, stopping abruptly on the cobbled path leading to the house. "We're in this together, remember?"

I nod, unable to muster words, and dart around him, mumbling something about getting dressed.

In my small room, I sink onto the bed, running hands over my face and carding through the ends of my ragged green hair. It was brown once. *Be happy for him.*

Jealous thoughts and hours spent before a mirror had fed into my curse. I'd wanted to be noticed, to have all eyes drawn to me, to fill up the empty way I felt inside. Be accepted in a way I never was at home. Be like ... Devin.

Part of me still craves attention, but no sane person would have anything to do with me now.

I change into one of the simple dresses I'd made years ago with the cloth he'd bartered for. We are still merchant's children after all, and some skills can't be dulled by curses.

Out in the large common room with kitchen in one corner and sturdy chairs about a cheery hearth opposite, Devin unpacks the two sacks he brought back to this tiny new home we've tried to make.

"Got you something." He sets a wrapped object on the table.

It draws me over. I raise an eyebrow at him as I pull the canvas away. A gasp breaks at the carved rolling pin, tiny flowers etched into the surface to imprint into pastry dough. I've been carving designs in the dough by hand when I bake fruit-filled turnovers, but claws and knives make for clumsy designs.

"How?" We don't have the extra money or supplies to barter for something like this.

"Anne's father made it."

I can't even sour at the name, deciding I like the unknown father better than this mystery woman.

"Thank you." I throw arms around him, and he stiffens at first, unused to this display of affection from me. But I want to get as much in before he leaves.

"You're welcome." He taps my shoulder. "And happy birthday."

The low words sting my eyes. I'd forgotten. Nineteen years today, monster for four, with many more ahead. For who would want to love a selfish monster like me?

Rain sheets down, and a crack of thunder sends me jolting away from the window. Storms always make me uneasy, even with Devin keeping the fire fed and familiar pastry dough under my finger pads. But there is something dangerous about this storm, the way the forest bends before the keening wind, the sharp arguments of lightning and thunder.

The dog keeps close to Devin, tail tucked low. I did not help name it because I'd eaten part of our first one in an episode shortly after we took up residence in the cottage.

A different sound breaks through the tumult—high, sharp, piercing—and I lean closer to the window. Devin looks up from his crouched position by the fire. We share a questioning look. Nothing but rain.

It comes again, wild and desperate and nearly drowned out by thunder. Devin's forehead creases.

"That sounds like someone."

My hands fall to apron strings tied in front of me, worrying the edges. The intent to go look is clear. He's learned to be more selfless, but perhaps I have not. Devin's already moving by the time I manage to say, "Take your coat."

His smile flashes, and he signals Dog to stay. It's happy to obey, hunkering by the door as he steps out. I pace back and forth, ignoring the half-finished pie on the counter.

Minutes later, Dog rises to its paws, alerting to the door. A shout sounds, and I throw open the door to welcome Devin from the pounding rain. A body slumps against him, legs dragging. Devin's strained voice sends me spinning, grabbing blankets and laying them by the fire.

A weather-beaten man is deposited on the rough pallet, rain clinging to the deep lines around his mouth and eyes. Gray-and-black beard covers most of his face. The angle of his leg sends me turning away. Broken, and I am no surgeon.

"We'll have to make him comfortable for now." Devin tries not to drip all over the floor.

I shoo him away to change and bring back more clothes, and crouch by the man, gathering the courage to start dabbing a dry blanket at his face and hands. His eyes fly open, and he jolts. I scramble backward, bracing myself under the glazed stare. But it doesn't linger long as his eyes fall shut and stay that way.

Devin curses softly.

"It's Anne's father."

"Are you going to stand there, then?" I ask when he doesn't move.

His lips purse, but he kneels beside me. I help peel off soaked clothes and change to dry, and learn that a face full of scales can still radiate embarrassment. We both apologize in murmurs as we maneuver around the broken leg. Devin mixes willow bark for pain and my hands fall back to twisting apron strings.

"What are we going to do?" I ask.

"Help with the pain. The storm should pass by morning. I'll head to town for the surgeon when it clears."

Talons scrape the floor. "Bring him *here?*"

"Are you going to help me carry him all the way to town?" Devin crouches again and lifts the man's head to dribble tea between parched lips.

I scowl even if he can't see me. We don't bring anyone here. It's the unspoken rule. We've been driven out of towns three times because strangers immediately turned on me. It's safer in the woods where it's just the animals who think I'm one of them.

The man groans, head twisting and arms straining for a moment before the willow bark helps and he quiets.

We can't leave him like this.

I'll stay with him until Devin gets back and then I'll hide in my room until the surgeon leaves. Then ignore my brother's attempts to convince me to try town again and find someone to break my curse.

I have my small routine, my oven, and my brother for now. There's nothing for me out there.

Morning peeks out between parting clouds, rain still dripping from the eaves and slender pine needles, but not enough to deter Devin. He sets off down the road and I'm left alone again.

Sharp incisors worry my bottom lip until I finally close the door and brew more tea. The man is sleeping, the lines on his face edged with pain, but we've kept him warm. I sneak over, wanting to see if I can tell in any way if he would be a good father to Devin. But there's nothing.

He stirs but doesn't wake. It is past lunch when the creaking of cart-wheels sends me fleeing into my bedroom. There is a tiny sliver between door and frame, and I cannot help myself.

Devin stomps in, followed by a whir of color and a feminine voice exclaiming, "Father!"

I scowl. *Of course he brought her.*

Then comes the surgeon with even tread and deep voice and praise of the work we did to care for the man until now. I set my back to the door, covering my ears for the setting of the bone. I still hear the cry. Then the surgeon is explaining the care of splints and bandages and how the man should not move for three weeks at least.

My heart sinks all the way down my lizard leg. Weeks. Devin pauses but accepts the responsibility. In my narrowed slit of vision, I see him step out, and then the woman—*Anne*—steps in front of Devin.

"You should ride back with the surgeon."

"I don't want to leave him." Her voice is laden with tears, and I feel guilty for wishing her away. But I refuse to suffer her sure reaction to seeing me. And I'd be responsible again for Devin losing a life he is trying to build.

"My sister and I will look after him," Devin promises, and my displeasure at being mentioned vibrates in my chest.

"Your sister?" Anne looks around, wiping her eyes. "Is she here? Can I meet her?"

Devin hesitates. "It's complicated."

Part of me wants to jump out, howl wildly, and drive her away from my brother. But another small part wants to see if she could make him happier, could give him a life away from the cottage in the woods. If it would be easier to just disappear.

His eyes lift to my door and, as if he can see me, he says, "Maybe some other time."

Anne's head tilts in confusion, but she doesn't argue. Instead she goes back to her father, presses a kiss to his forehead, and promises to return. Devin escorts her out, and when he returns, I emerge.

He leans against the closed door, one eyebrow lifted. I try to muster something gentle, but it still comes out strangled.

"She seems nice."

"Would you actually meet her?" Challenge lurks there.

"Perhaps I'll have to since she'll be back." It is maybe a compromise, but the small grin it brings to his face makes me more willing to try.

We take turns watching the man—Liam, I learn his name is—through the day. Devin is out splitting more wood, and I am alone with the man when he wakes.

I am finishing a patch job on a trouser knee when Liam's sharp intake of breath jerks my head up. I freeze in his sights, ready for the inevitable panic at my monstrous form. Neither of us say anything, and finally he breaks the stare to look around the room.

"Who are you?" His voice is gruff.

"I'm ..." My voice squeaks. "I'm Sylvie. Devin's sister."

"Devin?" The confusion only mounts higher.

I nod, not sure what else to say.

"Where are we?"

"Our cottage. He found you last night in the storm. Your leg is broken."

Liam cranes his head to look down at his splinted leg. "Ah." He settles back. My hands are clenching the trousers, the needle about to stab my finger.

"He's mentioned being familiar with curses. I take it you've got one?"

I blink. Devin has been so free with our story?

"What gave it away?" I snap, discomfort prickling under my scales as Liam watches with me an expression I'm too scared to study. This is wrong. He should be angry, cruel ... afraid.

He doesn't flinch. "The green hair."

I stare at him, but there is no laughter or horror in his eyes. And I suddenly cannot stand being in the room. I sweep to my feet and slam out the door.

Devin looks up from stacking split logs.

"He's awake," I say shortly. Devin picks up the axe, propping a log up to cut.

"What's wrong?"

I scoff. What was wrong? I'd expected him to scream in terror, and it is almost more uncomfortable not seeing or hearing it.

"Do you always bandy our story about? Does it help gather sympathy for you to worm your way into a woman's bed?"

It is unfair of me to bring up past faults he has put to rest. Or so I thought. He sets the axe down.

"Sylvie."

I shake my head, stepping away. "He's awake. Go take care of your new father." And I stride off into the woods. I need to calm down or I'll waken the actual monster inside.

He lets me be for a few hours. Dog appears first, weaving through the trees which hide the cottage but not the smell of smoke. Late afternoon sunlight drifts down to tinge Dog's fur a more vibrant gold. It grins up at me, unaware of what fate might befall it one day when I'm not myself.

I drag my gaze up to Devin, ready to not apologize.

"Are you coming in for dinner?" he asks.

"Did you burn it?" I retort mulishly.

A smirk flickers. "No."

When I don't move, he sits beside me.

"They're the first people I've really trusted," he begins softly. "They're good people. Anne ... she makes me keep wanting to be a better person. I told them a curse is what sent me from home, but only because I thought they might understand more about you. If you'd meet them, they might be able to help you."

"Me?"

"Maybe know someone who would be willing to try." He shrugs, feeling as awkward about it as I do. Someone not of my own blood has to accept me, love me, in this form. And there has been plenty of evidence that the world at large will never do that.

"Since no poor young man has come waltzing down the path, I'm assuming no."

"Well, technically, I haven't actually told them about ... you."

I scoff again, ignoring the way his pause stings. Like he really is ashamed of me and my monstrous form no matter what he says.

"At least come meet him properly." He uses his older brother voice, and I growl as I stand.

"Charming."

My forked tongue flicks out, but we walk alongside each other to the cottage.

"Sylvie ... just don't give up." Devin somehow is still hopeful someone could love me. I twist away from it.

Even before our father had made a bad trade and come home with a djinn bottle, I'd not had much hope for things like love. I tried to command the djinn, desperate for something to soothe aches inside, but it was not one to be governed. It cursed me, and our father immediately shoved me out. But for some reason, Devin had followed.

"It's years too late for that."

Liam is sitting in a chair, leg propped on a stool and pillow when I step inside. He doesn't react as I send a ferocious glare his way.

Devin makes me stay long enough to force a proper introduction. Liam bobs his head and thanks me for my care last night. I scowl again, wanting to be left alone. Dinner is not burned, even though I never trust Devin around the stove. He takes Liam food and sits in the armchair opposite, falling into easy conversation. I keep to the table, picking at a bread slice.

The next two days follow the same pattern. Devin and Liam chatting comfortably, even as Devin helps me with some of the washing and chores around the house. It is a routine that has never been disrupted until now.

On the third, Devin announces he will spend the day hunting. I glare, not wanting to be left with Liam. I feel the cautious looks he gives me every time I'm in the room.

There is some amusement in Devin's face as he leaves, refusing to take me with him. Deep down I know we cannot leave Liam alone, and my presence might scare animals off, but I still don't want to be *here*.

"Sylvie."

I jump. It's been so long since my name has come from anyone other than Devin. Liam leans forward in the chair he has spent the last days in.

"I wondered if you might help me outside."

I stare back. He offers a slight smile. It's false. It has to be.

"I was not made to be cooped inside for three weeks. I thought I might start on some crutches for myself."

Maybe I can leave him *outside* and reclaim a bit of sanctuary in my own home. We manage, with some grunts of pain from him, before I deposit him on the low bench by the back door. He sighs and leans against the cobblestone wall.

"Beautiful roses."

"Wild." My voice comes a bit rusty since I haven't used it past necessary the last few days. But the roses twining the cottage corner are some of my favorites—bright yellow, tinted orange at the edges, and filled with a sweet fragrance that reminds me of before.

Two longer pieces of branch already lay against the side of the house. Liam sends me back inside for the small pack he had with him. I grumble a little, feeling more like a servant.

But he starts working in silence. I hesitate, then begin weeding the small garden we've managed to keep alive. The day is too pretty to waste.

Eventually the whisk of his knife against wood stops making me tense, and I settle into my own task, humming a little under my breath. I have no great singing voice but humming fills my chest with calm. And I help Liam back inside an hour later in a much more agreeable mood.

I eat at the table alone that night but bring Liam his food. Perhaps a thanks for not stabbing me once we were alone. Devin glances between us, but Liam just nods and thanks me.

The next morning, Devin has more traps to set. I help Liam outside before hauling up water from the small nearby stream to wash and hang clothes to dry while he works.

I work up the courage to ask if he wants his old clothes washed now that he's in some of Devin's. He smiles and thanks me gently for it. He hasn't changed his demeanor toward me at all, so maybe I'll mend the torn pants for him as well.

The third day, the bread is just stale enough. I make more and leave the uneaten slices in chunks out on a low fence keeping the forest away. The animals will not care if it's fresh or not.

Rain returns on the fourth, and we are all stuck inside. Liam works on something new by the fire, chattering with Devin who cleans a fox hide. He will trade it in town. I make pastries, smiling slightly at how well the new rolling pin prints flowers on the dough. It makes me not mind the fact that Devin sounds happier than he ever did in our first home. Or in this one.

Devin cooks dinner, and I concentrate on mending Liam's shirt to avoid hopping up and making him do it my way—which is much cleaner and uses fewer dishes.

Liam polishes one of the crutches he has finished, offering a few words of conversation that I return in stilted sentences. When Devin calls us, Liam uses it to lever up and hobble over to the table. He sinks into a chair, and I freeze. Devin looks almost challengingly at me, and I take my chair in stubbornness.

It is simple. Rabbit meat, root tubers, some wild asparagus, finished with my pastries.

"It's good," Liam grunts. Devin grins.

"It took me a while to get here. Sylvie was raised knowing how to cook, but we used to have servants. Now she's got my poor excuse for help."

I scowl at the mention of our old life.

Liam nods. "Must be quite a change."

"What? From wealthy merchant's children to hermits in the woods?" Devin asks lightly. "None at all."

A smile smooths Liam's features. But I shove my chair back, its abrupt scrape competing with the angry growl in my chest, and head to my room. I've had no freedom to look back on my curse as anything but that.

I wake with the dawn, stomach grumbling since I never finished dinner. The kitchen is spotless, and regret sparks. Usually, we trade who cleans with who cooks. He must have done it last night.

I tiptoe out. Perhaps I'll make flatcakes in apology. I quietly gather ingredients, careful of Liam asleep on the pallet we've made him on the ground by the fire, when a soft tap has me turning. Liam stands there, crutches under his arms.

"I'm sorry. My words about change were more careless than I realized."

I blink, clawed fingers pinching my skirt. I had almost forgotten my appearance, but now alone and under his quiet scrutiny, I remember how ungainly I am.

"It's just ..." My voice slides out. He's being kind. "Devin is ..." I don't know what to say.

"How do you know he doesn't want to be here?"

The thoughtful words bring my head up. It's like he's read my mind. I scoff.

"Who would want to be here with me? He could be with Anne and you, making friends again, reclaiming a life. He only feels obligated." Maybe even long-lasting pity.

"Has he said that?"

Irritation bubbles, but I am forced to admit, "No."

Liam nods as if it is settled. "I can tell he loves you very much."

I stare at my fingers twisting and twining the skirt.

"Here." He points to something draped in cloth. "An apology is just as good a time as any to give this to you."

I hesitate, slowly pulling the cover off to reveal a serving platter carved in roses and stylized letters with my name. I blink.

"Thank you." My voice, already husky, drops again.

"You need something proper to serve your pastries on. You could put the town baker out of business."

A smile twitches before I can stop it. "And call it what? 'Monster's Eats'?"

He half-smiles. "You've already thought about it, then?"

My head tucks. Perhaps. "Enough to know that'll never happen. I haven't gotten within a hundred yards of a town in years. Not for lack of trying on Devin's part."

There's a soft look on Liam's face, almost paternal, and I look away from it.

"How do you break your curse?" he asks.

"A man, not of my own blood, must love me." Bitterness taints my smile. I must also accept that true love, believing in myself for once. But that never seemed to matter much since the first part would never happen.

"I was perhaps not very lovable when I looked human, and certainly not now."

He grunts. "Perhaps you need to look deeper then. You are kind, talented, and love your brother despite how much he talks."

My mouth tips up. I'd wondered if Liam preferred the quiet. "Send him out for errands if you need to."

A brief chuckle breaks from Liam. My fingers twist again.

"He cares about you and Anne very much. And ... and I am glad he has found someone."

"You're welcome to come with him any time, you know. Maybe then I'll have someone to commiserate with as they make doe eyes at each other," he says in wry amusement.

A laugh bursts from me, startling me so much I clap a hand over my mouth. The brush of fangs kills it, reminding me that I shouldn't go. But something loosens inside me at the sight of Liam's smile. And we laugh again as Devin stumbles out and groggily asks what is happening.

We are both outside that afternoon, me weeding and him carving, when a light "Father!" sends me tensing.

Anne bounces around the corner, fixing immediately on Liam. He smiles and levers up to receive her hug. I slowly stand, dirt and some weeds falling from my nerveless hands. The motion draws Anne's attention.

A gasp catches in her throat, and her face blanches as she scans me up and down. I back away, bracing.

"This is Sylvie," Liam says.

Anne's head tips, then she musters a smile, lifting her chin, and marches over to me. I want to run away, but I am flummoxed by this response.

"I'm Anne." She thrusts out a hand.

I stare in bemusement, taking her hand only because I don't know what to do. She doesn't flinch.

"Thank you for helping my father."

I whisper, "You're welcome."

Her glance snags on my fangs, but then she fixes back on my eyes with an effort.

"Where is my patient?" another cheery voice sounds.

My heart falls as the surgeon strides into view. He sees me first, mouth dropping in horror before emitting a scream.

"Monster! Get away from that woman!"

I curl into myself as he curses at me. Devin tries to grab his arm, Liam is hop-skipping over between us, and Anne doesn't know what to do. The surgeon struggles free and sweeps a stone from the ground, hurling it at me.

I push Anne clear as I twist away, but it hits my temple, sending a burst of pain through my head. I tumble to my hands and knees with a cry. One trembling hand touches a bleeding wound. The scent of iron fills my nose, and a feral growl fills my chest. My gaze sharpens and the thing inside awakens.

Dog finds me first as always, Devin close behind. He doesn't flinch at the mauled deer carcass, the blood covering me, tears dripping down my face.

"Sylvie."

I shake my head, tucking knees closer to my chest. I can't go back to the cottage like this, not where Liam and Anne will see. He'll take back all his words and kindness and drag Devin away.

"The three of us sent the surgeon packing. It's safe to come back."

A sound catches in my throat. *The three of us ...*

"Come on." His hand stays extended for the heartbeats it takes me to decide to take it, stand, and begin the trek back.

Twilight turns the cottage windows into warm golden squares. Smoke curls lazily from the chimney and Dog trots ahead. Devin ushers me inside. I keep arms wrapped around myself, eyes down, not daring to look up and see the others. But ...

"Are you all right?" Anne rests a hand on my arm, and there's nothing but concern there.

She and Devin guide me over to the table where Liam sits. He touches my shoulder and takes the damp cloth Devin wrings out.

Liam dabs at my face, brow wrinkled in focus, not flinching at the touch of scales. He rinses in the bowl of water Devin sets down and continues.

Our kettle whistles and Anne pours tea, leaving the mug to steep in front of me. I look up from the steaming liquid, daring to take in the sight of the three of them moving about like a little family around me.

Liam meets my quick glance and pats my hand. "I'm glad you're all right. And whenever he decides to propose to my daughter, I hope you'll come along. It'd be nice to have another daughter around."

I blink back more tears, taking a shaky inhale at the way the word comforts me. "I'd like that."

A pang lances through me, bright and sharp. I fall forward, gasping in surprise. Hands grab my shoulders, but they sting and I twist away. Bolts shoot down my legs and burning rushes over my skin.

It passes, and I am left half-draped over the kitchen table, panting as tea ebbs from the overturned mug.

A soft, "Sylvie?" draws my gaze up. Tears trickle down Devin's face, and I do not understand until the touch of his hand against mine tells me.

My trembling fingers trace my lips, brushing my teeth. No more fangs. Bare feet touch the ground; dark hair tumbles over my shoulder.

I look to the man who accepted me, scales and all. At his daughter who wraps arms around my brother, still smiling through his tears.

A laughing sob breaks from me and I throw my arms around Liam's neck. He hugs me back, letting me stay there, showing me what Devin might have already learned. Some fathers loved and accepted. And it might not be such a bad thing to have one again.

To Share the Sky

A.C. Williams

Another belligerent samurai postures at the mouth of my cave, screaming at the top of his foolish human lungs.

If these smelly creatures are going to continue to invade my privacy, I'm going to have to learn their ridiculous language.

Perhaps this one won't attack. Bits of the one from last week are still jammed between my molars.

Humans. Disgusting, flabby creatures. If they had any substance to them, they wouldn't need armor. That's the worst part of eating them.

The young samurai brandishes his sword, shouting and going on as though I care what he's saying.

I don't have to understand his words to know why he's here. It's the same as all the others: He's staked his family's honor on my hide.

Maybe I won't eat this one. My digestion is still off from last week's samurai.

Is he still talking? Stars bless him. He's trying so hard.

Blah blah blah. More sword waving. Yammer yammer—threaten threaten—stomp stomp.

Forget eating. I think I'll burn him alive.

I huff black smoke out of my nostrils and taste the citrusy scent of burning saliva pooling beneath my tongue. Setting them on fire never really gets old. Something about their panic-stricken, disjointed flailing makes me chuckle every time.

"For the ancestors!"

Oh, good. Charging now. Because that works every time.

The liquid in my mouth churns, bubbling like acid. Heat ignites at the back of my throat as I inhale, and I spew fire from my lips in a narrow stream that erupts on contact with the air.

The purity of fire is soothing.

Really cleans the sinuses out too.

I cut the fiery stream off and snarl in irritation. Foolish boy. Nothing left of him but charred rocks.

Why do they keep coming? How many more of their young men must I turn to ash before they leave me alone? Warriors far greater than they have sought to slay me, yet I remain.

Unlike the other nestlings from my aerie. All either bonded or dead.

Not me.

Never me.

Rocks skitter down the wall of the cave. A flash of blue-lacquered iron, the dim light blazing on the edge of sharpened steel. A man's high-pitched scream is the only warning I have before the young samurai flings himself at me and stabs his cursed sword all the way through my left talon.

The icy burn of hide and flesh and sinew being slashed rips a roar of pain from my throat, sending thick ribbons of crimson blood seeping out of the wound. I rock back on my haunches and pluck the katana out of my bleeding talon, flexing my claws.

The little insect actually wounded me.

Bravo.

I gather more acid under my tongue and glance to where he should be standing, shivering in terror at my size and the horrifying knowledge that he hasn't hurt me at all.

But he's gone.

More rocks skittering. The fool boy is scrambling up the steep wall to the mouth of the cave, and in his hand he clutches a clay jar dripping with blood.

My blood.

Oh, clever boy.

But not clever enough.

He hadn't come for his ancestors. He'd come for my soul.

I flick his useless sword away and stand, stretching my wings as far as they'll go. They brush the walls of my cave. Two steps puts me in reach of my attacker, and I pluck him off the wall by the back of his gleaming blue armor.

He screams and kicks his legs—and drops the clay pot. It shatters on the stone below, splattering my blood on the rocks.

My mouth fills with fire, and I pour flames on the rocks beneath us until every drop of my blood has been consumed in the inferno. With the final bit of fire, I cauterize the seeping wound in my talon.

The little samurai still screams, flailing and struggling in my grip.

I show him my teeth, some of them longer than his forearms. He silences, his breath coming in great gasping heaves. He smells even worse up close.

Pity. Burning him alive would have made less of a mess. But he didn't come here to fight me. He came to enslave me—to bond me through blood magic—and that's just not something I can forgive.

I drop him.

He tumbles through the fire-scorched air and collides with the still-burning rocks under me. He shrieks and tries to scurry off the blazing embers, but I pin him down with my good talon.

He's really screaming now.

I lower my smoldering snout to him. Ugh, this one smells particularly bad. What did he do? Bathe in fermented fruit? He swings a fist at me with his one free arm.

He's got spirit, at least.

But as he spits and curses and sobs, the darkness—the hate—in his eyes doesn't waver.

The little insect had known precisely what he was doing when he came for my blood. Good. I can treat him like the bug he is.

I step down on him.

His obnoxious screaming stops.

Humans. Why won't they just leave me alone?

I lift my nose toward the mouth of my cave and scent the wind. I can't stay here. If one of them knows where I am, others will inevitably follow. I'd fled to these mountains in the western American province to hide. So much for that strategy.

I scrape the remains of the young samurai off my talon and ascend the boulders to the world outside my cave. The air at the top of the mountain ridge is clear and cold, brushing gently over my horns and scarred hide, tingling in my sensitive wing folds.

I shake my wings and stretch them to their fullest width, each wing longer than three men. The power in their unfurling loosens rocks and bends grasses as I launch into the sky.

This high, the world smells sweet and fresh, like it did before the invaders crossed the sea in their flying machines. I was but a hatchling then, but I remember.

Then, my clan lived with the Raven's Children of these high plains. When the samurai came, we forged an uneasy peace, but it wasn't meant to last. The invader's emperor—their terrifying deity across the great sea—wasn't satisfied with his awkward, ugly flying machines. He wanted an army of dragons. So he sent sorcerers with blood magic.

Now I am the only dragon left with a will of my own.

I catch the warmth of a thermal a few hundred feet into the drop. The cold air shivers beneath my scales and burns in the still-tender wound in my talon as I twist into the clouds.

Puffs of white scatter away from the power of my beating wings, vaporizing in the heat of my passing. Far below, the shimmering blue veins of the rivers pump life into the desolate plains, and the scattered forests clump together like the wrinkled hide of an elder's underbelly.

Perhaps if humans could see the world like this, they wouldn't value titles as much.

I scoff.

Perhaps they hunt us so they *can* see the world like this.

I burst through a bank of rain clouds and let the droplets evaporate with a sizzling hiss as they bead and bubble on my scales. Mid-spin, my gaze falters on the world below. I pause.

Choking black smoke pours from a canyon. Rare for something in the heart of the earth to catch fire.

I tilt my wings and dive, my shadow darkening the bronze grasslands in my wake. The striated canyon stretches for miles in bright bands of red and orange rock, nestled at the base of the large mountain range that divides the prefecture nearly in half.

The smoke concentrates at the far end of the ravine, and I touch down on a cliff overlooking it.

Ah.

So that explains it.

Tucked away at the base of the ravine, a human village had sprouted up. Industrious little ants. They'd carved homes into the face of the rock walls.

For all the good it did them.

The smoke billows from the doors and windows of the cave-homes. The walls are singed and scorched. Swords and arrows lay scattered and broken amid the rocks, and a pile of burned corpses decorates the central gathering place.

Humans. No wonder they've made a life of killing my kind. They can't even stop killing themselves.

I turn sharply, my tail carving a line in the dry dirt and grass on the cliff, when motion in the canyon draws my attention. One of the attackers, perhaps? Or a survivor?

My sight narrows to the figure—human-shaped but tiny. A child, perhaps the age of two harvests.

I glide toward the tiny creature struggling through the dirt and scrub at the bottom of the canyon. I hit the dirt in a skittering rain of rocks and dust, and the human topples over sideways, pudgy arms and legs flapping.

It lays still beneath my snout, blinking eyes up at me in surprise.

Then, it reaches for me.

Not with closed fist or striking hand but with gentle fingers, small and mouse-like stroking the rough skin of my lips. The creature's mouth forms a round O-shape and joins its other hand with first, softly brushing its tiny hands over my leathery hide.

And then it does the strangest thing.

It giggles.

I huff smoke at it, and the creature laughs louder still. It wraps its fingers around one of my teeth and levers itself to its bare feet.

Absurd. What is it doing?

It lifts its little head high enough to find one of my eyes and beams at me. Chubby cheeks split wide in a goofy, gummy grin that turns its face to pure sunlight.

It babbles and coos and brushes its hands against the harsh texture of my snout, laying its head of dark curls against my lips.

I have lived for centuries. I ruled the skies of this land before the invaders arrived—both the samurai from the West and the English from the East. I have watered the dust of the earth with the blood of the hundreds who have tried to slay me. No human has ever touched me like this, trusted itself so close to my lips where my fire could easily consume them.

The child meets my eye again and blinks at me like an owl—a bald, smelly owl. It pats my nose and turns, waddling up the path with its stiff legs and wobbling arms.

The human child is fearless and full of light. Not a speck of darkness lurks in the child's gaze. Only wonder.

I should leave it. It will not long survive on its own without its village.

Ahead, the child stumbles sideways and falls to its hands and knees. It grunts and stands again and continues forward.

Strong.

But not strong enough. The child will draw predators like a flame lures the moth.

What am I thinking? It's a human. They're all the same. They all embrace the darkness that condemns my kind to servitude.

But perhaps this child is different.

I heave a sigh that scorches the rocks around me.

Stars above, what is wrong with me? Feeling sorry for a human child? Choosing to help it find its own people rather than leaving it to be eaten? Yes. Stars help me, I am.

In two steps, I'm directly behind the child. It stops and turns halfway around to grin up at me, waving and giggling, and then it continues forward with halting steps.

If the stars are kind, I'll get it to a village, and they'll take it with no questions asked. If I am fortunate, no other humans will even see me. I will simply leave the child and disappear.

Except the stars are rarely kind, and I have no luck at all.

The child tips backward, and I bend my head to steady it with my snout. The child pets my nose and pushes off to continue on its way.

Very well, small one. I vow to take you to your people.

As though the creature could hear me, it turns and waves at me with a shining grin.

Great Stars, do all humans begin like this? It would have been far preferable to go on believing they are hatched from the shadow and remain in darkness all their lives.

The canyon village burns behind us, the stench of burning flesh and scorched earth overwhelming any other smells. If I am to find a village for this orphan child, I must get higher and further away from this slaughter.

Hopefully the child doesn't mind heights.

Oh Stars. What if it does? I killed a samurai once that hated high places. He went all rigid with terror, which only made it easier to kill him. Admittedly, that was quite funny. But if this child reacts the same way?

Ugh. I've already vowed to take it to its people, and I cannot go back on my word. Well, we shall have to hope the child is braver than a samurai. Otherwise, it will be a very long walk.

I scoop the child up in my uninjured talon, and it wraps its pudgy arms and legs around one claw, squealing with happy laughter.

A positive sign.

I think.

I bound into the air, catching a hearty wind as it races through the canyon. I spiral up-up-up away from the terror of the world below, the chill of the air cooling the fire in my blood.

And the child shrieks, kicking its little legs and wiggling in my grasp, until it runs out of air and collapses against my claws in a fit of giggles. Full-body laughter, bubbling with delight and pure, blinding joy.

Stars above, the child fears nothing.

It twists in my talon and flaps its arms at me, nodding and bouncing and babbling.

Yes, little one. We are flying.

Warmth surges under my heart-scales. Perhaps this was what it was like for my ancestors, who bonded their riders by choice. To share the wind with a DragonFriend was said to be glorious, but all the DragonFriends were gone, just like my clan.

I have seen only the dark sorcery of the samurai magic and what it does to us. Yet, to see the child bear witness to the smallness of the world far below, to breathe in the beauty of the vast azure firmament above—perhaps I can imagine how my ancestors felt.

Perhaps the sky was too great a gift to keep to ourselves.

I toss my horns against the clouds and draw deeply of the wind. Nothing. No human scent for miles and miles and miles. We shall have to fly until we find them.

But we are in the wilds, after all. There may be few humans to find. Ironic. A few hours ago, I would have rejoiced at such a fact.

The child shivers against my talon.

Ah, yes. Its flabby human flesh will not protect it from the cold bite of the sky.

Fear not, small one.

I clutch the creature to my heart-scales, and instantly the child stops shivering. It curls against my chest, one of its tiny little hands stroking my scales gently.

As we sail through the sky, an odd sound reaches my ears. A small sound, tuneless and wandering. A song?

I glance at my chest where the child has snuggled against the warmth of the scales that shield my heart. The child babbles a tuneless melody. Quiet and gentle and serene. Soothing.

How can anything human be soothing?

I scoff and turn my attention back to flying and scanning the ground for any sign of a human village. Moments later, the child grows silent and still, dropping deeply into happy sleep.

Good. No self-respecting dragon enjoys ridiculous human babble.

After a while, the air thickens with the scent of humanity as I soar out of the wilds. The stench is nearly enough to gag me.

Peering through the lazy evening clouds, I spot a human village below us. Nestled between two tributaries, the village isn't large, but it seems to be composed of solid structures. Well-kept. Pleasant, by human standards.

The village center is circular, wood and stone homes all similar in shape and size. Perhaps fifty homes all told, with one at the heart larger than the others. Farmland surrounds the village, and the scent of grains, vegetables, and smelly livestock is strong.

After the long flight, I'm feeling rather peckish. Perhaps I'll nab a cow for a snack.

What the village doesn't have, to my relief, is a watchtower. Most villages on the edge of the wilds always have watchtowers armed with ballista and their poisonous jade bolts. I've seen more than one dragon fall from the sky with one of those hell-wrought darts stabbed through their heart-scales.

I circle in the night sky and fly back toward the village.

Yes, it seems quiet. And calm. Surely I can leave the child in this place. Undoubtedly they would claim it for their own and care for it.

I scan the village for any sign of slayers, any evidence of violence, any indication that the village is a secret haven of samurai or sorcerers. Not because I fear for the child. Not at all. I made a vow, and it would be reckless to simply drop the creature off at the first village I find.

If it is not a good village, I will find another one that will care for the child properly.

Not because the child matters.

It is a matter of honor.

I start to make another round. So far, I see no reason why this village would not suit the child.

A flare on the far east horizon draws my gaze, and the instinct to flee rises with the spikes along my spine. In the distance, a solid thumb of rock spears the starry sky like a blemish. The only landmark for hundreds of miles: the Dragon King's Horn.

The Dragon King, he calls himself, the title inherited from generation to generation. A legacy of slavery and violence and the ruination of my kin.

I saw the Horn once as a nestling. A massive flat-topped butte, jutting from the plains into the heavens, its sides smooth except for the palace clinging against its rocky skin like an ill-formed scale. I remember my enslaved clan-mates kneeling on the monstrous butte, mindlessly obeying their human masters with no will of their own.

My nostrils flare, and I clutch the child closer to my heart-scales. I cannot leave it this close to the Horn. If the child is raised within sight of it, surely it will grow to ask what the Horn is. Surely it will learn of its own peoples' cruel enslavement of my kin. Young as it is now, it will not remember me as a friend at all.

Surprising. The thought of this bothers me.

Not far from the village is a thick patch of forest. Perhaps this will be a safe place to gather myself, although this close to the Horn I must be wary. No place is safe where the Sky Knights of the Dragon King patrol the stars.

I land as quietly as the branches and roots and underbrush allow. I am not built for forests, but it will make a fine enough place to hide.

Cupping the child closer than before, I scratch a hollow in the undergrowth and settle down in the freshly turned earth, breathing in the scent of pine and spruce and dust.

The child hasn't budged since long before Father Sun sought his rest behind the curve of the world. In the forest-scented refuge between the earth and my wings, I tuck my face against my chest, close to where the child slumbers.

In its sleep, it peels away from the warmth of my heart and snuggles against my face, ebony curls tickling the tender skin around my eyelids. It's singing again.

If I'm smiling, no one else is around to see it.

A solid thunk between my eyes stirs me awake, and I blink sleepily. Shafts of morning light spill into the forest around me, and my eyes cross at the sight of the child balancing on my snout.

Stars, the creature has a death wish.

I snatch the child off my nose before it takes a dive to the hard earth below, and the child squeals in delight.

Yes, little one. I have found your people.

The child wraps around my talon again and coos happily, rubbing its cheek against the rough hardness of bone and scale.

I shall be glad to be rid of this creature. I shall. With its constant babbling, so endearing in its cheeriness. With its giant dark eyes so brilliant with the spark of light and life and joy and awe. Keeping this creature alive is a trial I shall be happy to leave behind.

Yes. The creature has caused me trauma.

The child peels itself off my claw to flop at the center of my talon. It strokes the still-tender wound from the samurai sword with its soft fingers, cooing and trilling and beaming at me.

Snorting hot steam from my nostrils, I pluck the child up by the back of its soiled garment as I stand and crawl out of our overnight nesting place. Four strides brings us to the edge of the forest, and I stretch out my arm to set the child on the ground outside the shadow of the trees.

The child rights itself and wobbles, blinking and turning in a circle. With an indignant squawk, the child kicks its unbending, chubby legs and waddles back into the forest, directly to my front foreleg. It hugs my talon again, chattering irritably as though I had offended it in some great way.

Stubborn human child.

I peel it off and set it down outside the forest. This time, I hold it in place until I am certain it can see the village where full-grown humans mill about in plain sight.

Behold, small one. Your own kind. Go forth and leave me be.

The child squeals loudly, clapping its hands and turning in an awkward circle. And then it flails and follows me into the forest, laughing and giggling as though we are playing a game.

Extraordinary.

The one time I truly need a human to flee from me, and it refuses. Not because it hunts me, but because it—what? Enjoys my company?

The child poses below me, little hands poised in the air and waving to some imaginary song. It sways on unbending legs, bouncing with a series of emphatic *bah-bah-bahs* that echo among the trees.

It spins and laughs and holds its hands up to me. I will not indulge this. For its own good, it must learn the natural order. We cannot be friends. The last DragonFriend fell to the self-appointed king long ago.

I lower my face into the child and flash my teeth with a dark, rumbling snarl. The child laughs.

I growl again, showing more teeth. It toddles closer and presses its face against my mouth like it did before, gentle hands patting the leather of my lips.

Stars above, we cannot be friends, no matter how I wish it.

A fierce shout echoes in the forest, and a rain of arrows splinters against the scales of my hind leg.

Fools! Can't they see there's a child here?

I shield the child with my talon and claws as another round of arrows hails upon me uselessly. What pitiful warriors. Their arrows aren't even solid enough to scratch the membrane of my wings.

More shouting. Another storm of arrows. What are these idiots trying to do? Irritate me? If that is their goal, they are most assuredly succeeding.

I breathe in deeply, feeling the acid boiling in my mouth, but I pause. I cannot set them on fire. I need them all alive. I need them to take the child.

Something heavy and sharp slams into my side, and my left wing goes numb. Stunned, I gape at the thick bolt buried between my ribs. I've only got a moment before the pain hits—tingling like lightning through my muscles and joints and organs.

It's a jade bolt. From a ballista. Where were they keeping it? Had they hidden it?

I start to spill fire at them anyway, but my throat and jaw aren't working. My left leg collapses, and all that comes out of me is a roar of agony.

The dull ache of hemorrhaging drives blunt fingers into my spine, and my right leg falls.

The child!

Where is the child?

It cannot be near me!

The child clings to my wounded talon again. Have the samurai even seen it? Do they even know it's there?

The jade poison spreads like fire in dry grass, consuming the veins and arteries of my body and wrapping my chest in a vice. My lungs constrict. My throat is closed. My breath heaves.

I lose power over my right foreleg and close the child in my left talon as I fall. The ground shakes as my body betrays me.

My head pillowed against fallen spruce boughs, my vision blurs and darkens. The jade poison paralyzes me. All they need is a sorcerer, and I'll never be free again.

A line of samurai approach me with swords drawn over their heads. I should have learned to speak their language. Then I could tell them—

Take the child.

My child, you fools!

Don't you see it?

Its light is all I can see.

My child babbles the strange tuneless song, a meandering melody I'm sure I've heard before but can't place. Perhaps it's not the song I know. Perhaps it's just the child.

A gentle hand presses against my snout, a cool pressure between my nostrils. A hand too large to be the child's. I open an eye.

Before me kneels an aged woman. Wrinkled. Fragile. With arms like twigs and hair like cobwebs and eyes as brilliant as Mother Moon's full face.

Soft, tiny fingers brush the scales over my heart, and the child continues her song.

Why is she still here? Who is this dusty old woman? And why do I yet breathe free?

The ancient woman nods toward my side. I lift my chin to see that the shaft of the jade bolt is gone, and the wound has been cauterized and bound with herbs and makeshift strips of canvas. Stars only know where they found that much fabric to wrap around my ribs.

Carefully I lift a wing and straighten it.

It moves with no pain.

I narrow my eyes at the woman, and she only smiles at me. She calls quietly in her language, and the child toddles out from the space between my arms to take the old woman's bony hand.

I peer through the trees. The samurai still stand around the perimeter, and while they have their swords, they aren't raised in challenge. In the shadows, I can see their armors, crimson and black lacquer-work like scales. The twisting sigil of a dragon is emblazoned over their hearts.

The sigil of the DragonFriends.

My nostrils flare, and the old woman laughs.

She bends to press her brow against my nose, and a blinding light overwhelms my senses. The forest fades in the force of the old woman's power, surrounding us both in a curtain of white and silver.

Forgive us, Honored One. We thought you a rogue from the Horn, sent to destroy us.

It's not a voice. Not really. It's more a sense of the old woman's heart, resonating inside mine.

Ah.

The woman is a DragonFriend. No wonder she is full of light.

She must be the last, as I am.

I've only heard stories of how DragonFriends can connect with our minds. How do I do this? Growling, I form the image of the child in my mind.

The woman's heart-voice warms me, as though she is smiling. *We will care for the girl. She has a home among us.*

I cannot show my teeth in whatever state this woman has trapped me, so I think of what I must look like at my most fierce.

The woman chuckles.

Either I am not fierce at all or the woman has the self-preservation instincts of my little one.

We know you now as a friend. A mental image of the Horn forms between us. *We will keep your secret. I vow it. Go in peace, Honored One.*

The woman's presence in my mind withdraws, and my vision shifts back to the dim forest with the samurai standing guard and the child patting my scales.

Slowly, carefully, I gather my talons beneath me. The old Dragon-Friend lifts my child into her aged arms, and the girl waves at me.

Her very presence is pure light. Just like the old woman.

Perhaps my child—the girl—is a DragonFriend too.

I snarl at the line of samurai simply because I can. They were protecting their village, yes, but I am the one with a new hole in my side. I've half a mind to set them on fire just to see them squirm.

The child babbles at me, still waving, the shafts of sun spilling through the leaves shining on her black curls.

I step back two paces and open my wings. The child reaches her arms out and flaps, and for the briefest second, I can feel the stroke of her tiny hands over the scales shielding my heart.

DragonFriend, indeed.

I snap my wings hard enough to bend the trees with the force of my strength and climb into the heavens, spiraling into the vast blue skies. The distant Dragon King's Horn holds no sway over me, nor shall it ever. I am free and will remain free.

Now I shall find a new cave.

And if it happens to be near the child's new village, well, what a delightful coincidence.

A companion story to "The Weaver and the Dragon" by Lauren Hildebrand

A Piece of Sky

Tanager Haemmerle

I don't usually break the law, but tonight is a special occasion.

Dropping to my knees, I lean against the outside of the bakery and peer out from the alleyway. The city's rough stone wall is on the other side of the road, near a set of merchant stalls that are covered in canvas for the night. Cal crouches beside me in the shadows, scouting our target. The gate is well-lit but otherwise poorly maintained. It's small and hangs sideways on a hinge that stains the surrounding rock with rusty shade.

"Told you it would be easy," I whisper, brushing a stray curl behind one ear. I tried to wrestle my short mess of hair into a ladylike ribbon before meeting Cal, but it's not behaving the way I'd hoped. "The gate doesn't latch and the whole thing's basically unguarded."

"Yeah ... *basically*," Cal says, his Northern Islander accent thick. The wall's parapet and twin towers stand empty, but he raises a skeptical brow toward a guards' hut that sags under a roof of moldering wooden shingles. One of the fairy lights along the road catches his cautious grin.

There's a big gap between his front teeth. I find it endearing, but I try not to stare since Cal is self-conscious about it.

"Oh, come on. The soldiers aren't paying any attention to the gate," I say. "No one goes to the Glass Flats. The lake that used to be there sank into the mines ages ago. Without it, there's not much to see."

"Not much to see but the *stars*, you mean?" Cal asks. "Right, Lyla?"

I bite down on my lower lip, choosing my words carefully. I don't want to lie to him. But I also don't want our night to end before it even starts. Tomorrow he's moving back to his family's farmlands in the kingdom's Northern Islands. And I am greedy to hold on to every last second of our time together. "Like I said earlier ... I don't *know* if you can see any stars from the Glass Flats. I've never seen one in my entire life. But there's a *chance* we can see a piece of sky once we're far enough outside the city and its fairy mist. A very *small* chance. Do ... do you still want to go?"

He shrugs his narrow shoulders. "Any chance is good enough for me. But ... why are soldiers guarding a dried-up lake?"

"Because every once in a while an idiot or two disappears into the mines underneath it. But don't worry." I nudge him with my elbow. "We'll be fine as long as we can resist the temptation to jump into any scary caves we see."

"Don't jump into any scary caves. Got it."

A rail-trolley trundles by on the street, its vents sucking in some of the fairy mist that covers the capital, using it as fuel to keep it moving. I grab Cal by one of his suspenders, pulling him back. At this time of night, there aren't many travelers in the horseless carriage, but we still sit back on our heels to remain hidden. I make sure my wisp-lantern's vent is closed. Everything runs on the power from the fairy mist, even this simple tool. And I don't want the crystal inside exposed to it and igniting until we're outside the wall.

We're not in any danger from a rail-trolley operator, of course. But it's more fun to pretend we are. It makes tonight feel like a secret.

"And what happens if the soldiers catch us sneaking out to the Glass Flats?" Cal asks.

"Well," I say, dragging my words out, "they probably won't run us through with their swords. But they probably will make us muck their stables for a week after school. It's a risk."

"Hmm, that is a risk," Cal says. "But the last ship of the summer leaves tomorrow, so you'll be the only one mucking stables, City Girl."

I bite my lip again. I don't want the mood to turn somber. I don't want to be reminded how much tomorrow is going to hurt. "And you think a few specks of starlight are worth me suffering alone, Farm Boy?"

"Not just stars. Constellations too. They're worth it." His deep brown eyes are more soft than teasing when they fall to mine. He gets to his feet and offers me a hand. "I promise."

The reverent way he says this makes my heart give a strange flutter.

Most of the stars vanished behind the fairy mist before I was even born. When I look up, I don't feel the loss of the night sky that Cal and others from the smaller villages feel. To me, the smoke that covers the capital is *itself* beautiful. During the day, the ground mist is thin, but it shimmers with a thousand hues that billow and blur as it thickens to join the clouds above. Magic and faint electrical pulses move through it, making the air feel alive as it powers everything it touches. But Cal isn't used to the fairy mist. He didn't grow up with it. He doesn't love it the way I do.

His hand is soft and warm when I take it. And the strange feeling in my chest expands to fill me. He's given me so much this summer. But I want more. And maybe if I give something back and find him a piece of the sky he remembers, he won't hate it here so much.

Maybe he won't decide to leave.

I let Cal pull me to my feet as the rail-trolley's clacking machinery carries it up the street and out of view. "Okay, let's go see your stars then."

The fairy mist swirls around my skirts as we scurry behind the guards' hut. Cal's nerves show in his tight jaw and the way he rubs his hands on his slacks.

But his fears are unfounded.

We crawl under the window overlooking the road to the Glass Flats and I peek inside. Raucous laughter and warm light spills from the building. One of the soldiers dumps a cup of dice out over a worn table. When the dice skitter to a stop, half the soldiers whoop at the results, while the others groan. A few moth-like fairy creatures flit about their game, attracted by a savory smell wafting from a stew-pot that steams over a small fireplace in the corner.

Cal anxiously prods me to keep moving. Crawling in a dress isn't easy. But the only truly hard part of the plan is containing my giggles until we reach the gate, push through it and its reluctant hinge, and run far enough down the path that the soldiers won't hear me.

"I told you it was no big deal," I say, wiping a bit of the gate's gritty rust onto my skirts. "Every teen from the capital sneaks out here at least once. You're one of us now."

Cal's gap-toothed grin returns. "So this was a last-minute rite of passage, Lyla?"

"Something like that."

"And here I thought you just wanted to spend time with me."

Blood rushes my face, heating my cheeks. "Well, I couldn't let you go back to your island without seeing everything the city has to offer." I fall a step behind so he can't see my fluster.

Cal laughs. "Is it really a *city* offering though, if we're outside it?"

I shove him hard. "You know what? Shut up."

We leave the wall at our backs. Passing between the abandoned structures of the port, we scramble down the bank of the former lake. Soon the old docks stand surreally above our heads on posts as big as trees, and the dry lakebed stretches before us like a strange, flat desert. The ground is patchwork, alternating between sandy silt with the occasional scant scrubby brush, and a strange smooth glass left behind after the lake drained.

The tension Cal always carries in his stiff shoulders melts away. Leaving the city, it's like he feels it's finally safe for him to stretch out and take up space.

I love crowded shopping districts and the excitement of the rotating markets and fairs that spring up in parks. I love the city's sights and sweet smells and feeling like I could talk to every stranger on the street and in minutes call them a friend. I love riding the rail-trolleys and the gondolas that go up to the palace's public grounds where music never stops. I love *everything* about the capital.

But the only place I've ever seen Cal this comfortable before is the library. The massive stone building could seat hundreds of scholars, but there's hardly anyone ever there. Its spires are filled with tall shelves and ladders ambitious enough to reach them. It's all windows and soft chairs and reading nooks with tables worn smooth from hundreds of years and thousands of hands. It's where we've spent most of our free time this summer.

He could spend hours reading to me.

And I could spend lifetimes listening to him.

I wonder if the library is the only thing he'll miss when he's gone.

I'll miss it, too.

There's no point going back without him. I can't read. I've never been able to.

The words shift on their pages, the letters and runes changing their shapes even as I look at them. Losing Cal is unbearable enough on its own. But when he leaves, he won't just be taking his gentle laugh and quiet jokes back to the Northern Islands. He'll be taking a thousand worlds away with him. All those books—all those adventures and far-off places—will be out of my reach again.

A lump forms in my throat. After everything he's done for me, I owe him more than I could ever pay back. I *have* to find a piece of sky to give him.

I look up, hoping there will be something to see soon. The fairy mist extends out from the kingdom in a blanket of haze made gray by the night. Even if I love it, it scares me that I don't know how far it goes.

We keep walking. The wooden heels of our shoes clack as we cross over one of the giant mirrors of glass. And Cal becomes more of his true self. He merrily taps a rhythm with his heel as he hums an old song of his homeland. Away from the noise and the anxiety and the bustle of people and machines, he looks truly happy. When he goes back home, he'll be like this all the time. And that's why I can't tell him how I feel.

I can't tell him I don't want him to go. I can't ask him to stay.

It wouldn't just be selfish. It would be cruel.

And besides, even if he says he'll miss reading to me, or dancing with me at the solstice, or shopping at the markets together, he hasn't told me he's going to miss *me*.

Cal finishes his song and slows down so we walk side by side again. "Lyla? Are you okay?"

"Of course." I force my lips back into a smile.

I'm grateful that more of my hair has slipped from my ribbon, helping my bangs to conceal my face. Cal and I have gone on so many adventures through the books he's read to me. This is my only chance to take him on one of our own. I won't mess it up by getting emotional.

I take out my wisp-lantern and open its hatch. As the machine inhales the thin fairy mist, it turns on, burning a bright shimmering blue that reflects on the glassy parts of the lakebed's surface. It isn't that difficult to see without it. But if the light ever starts to dim, I'll know we're finally leaving the smoky fairy clouds behind. Maybe then we can see what's beyond them.

We've been walking for two hours. My feet hurt, and we've drunk half the water from the canteen Cal brought with him. Cal cranes his skinny neck so he can look upward. The night isn't getting darker or clearer. And as the city falls farther and farther behind, I start to feel more and more like an idiot for bringing him all the way out here. The sky is just as thick with fairy smoke as it is by the refineries that burn it. My wisp-lantern is bright as ever.

But there is a shadow that breaks the monotony of the Flats up ahead. I adjust our course toward it. In case I can't find Cal's sky for him, at least I can still show him something worth seeing.

"Wait ... is that a ... ?"

I grin. Without letting Cal finish his thought, I forget the soreness in my feet and break into a run. Cal sprints after me. Kicking up sand and scaring brush-mice into frenzied squeaks, we race. Soon the thing looms above us, its shadow solidifying into a great ship. Partially buried in a sea of sand, it's frozen by a wave of half-formed crystals of glass that creep up its side.

Cal catches his breath. He looks up in awe at the prow as my wisp-lantern highlights its figurehead guardian in blue. She has wings, with carved feathers that cradle the vessel.

"There's still a ship out here?"

I place a gentle hand on the rough wooden hull. "It's the only one. Most were broken apart and reused in one way or another."

"Seeing it does explain the names of so many inns and taverns around town." He rewards me with a grin when I laugh. "Seriously, there's so many '*The Last Ship*' this and '*The Lonely Ship*' that. But why is it still out here?"

I lift the lantern higher, so we can see the railings above us and the skeletal mast that still proudly points skyward. "I think because it still has a purpose."

"As a ship?"

"No." I run my fingers along the hull as we examine it from another angle. The planks have separated in places. The body hasn't been resealed with tar since it was stranded, and the timber has warped. Even if the craft found itself in water again, it would take a miracle for it to float. "I don't think it's still a ship. I think it's a grave marker now."

"Honoring the lake it used to call home. I can't decide if that's beautiful or tragic."

I turn and lean my back against boards that creak under my weight. "Can't it be both?"

He leans next to me. "It can. But I don't think this thing is a boat or a marker." He raps his knuckles against the wood.

I quirk a smile at him. "What is it then?"

He shrugs. "Maybe it's just feelings."

I cross my arms in front of my chest. "And here I thought what I was saying was weird."

Cal laughs. "No, no, hear me out." He looks up at the figurehead, his voice turning serious. "I think it isn't really an object at all anymore. It's like a container for emotions that are put into it by others. Don't you feel them pouring back out when you look at it—when you touch it?"

I look at the ship and its enfolding wings and I do feel a power over me. Maybe people in generations before us sensed something too, and there is a reason it has been left alone all these years.

The ship is so many things at once. It's awe. It's wonder. It's honoring the past. But it's giving hope for things that can still be. It's memory. It's perseverance.

It's loss and sadness.

"I know exactly what you mean," I say. And a part of me wishes I could pour my own feelings into it, so I couldn't be hurt by them.

"I'm ... I'm glad I got to see it with you before I leave," Cal says. "It seems like it could've fallen out of one of the books we've read together, doesn't it?"

My throat constricts. I don't trust myself to speak, so I nod.

Cal almost seems to be waiting for me to say something. When I don't, he lets out a breath. "The stars are like this too, you know. They're beautiful. But it's not really about what they are. It's more about how they make you feel."

I take a few steps away from the Last Ship and scan the horizon. The Glass Flats continue on for miles before reaching the forest on the other side. Even if we walked that far, would we see anything? My eyes search the sky, desperately hoping for one pinprick of light—a reason to keep going. There aren't any. Even the sliver of moon barely burns its way through the gray clouds. So how could anything else have a chance?

Disappointment settles over me. For the first time I realize I didn't just want to find the stars for Cal. I wanted to see them too.

"They sound really wonderful." My fingers tighten into fists around the fabric of my dress. "But I don't think we're going to see them tonight."

Cal shifts his weight from one skinny leg to the other. For once he's looking at his scuffed-up shoes instead of the sky. "Be honest, were you really expecting to?"

"No, but I wanted to be wrong."

Cal's teasing smile returns, but it seems forced. "Are you ever wrong?"

"All the time. Just not when you're looking."

Without discussing it we both silently say our goodbyes to the Last Ship and turn our feet toward the capital. I don't want the night to end in failure. I don't want the night to end at all. But the time we have left is slipping away fast. It's late. Cal has to be up early. And I can't keep him to myself, as much as I want to.

A globe of light surrounds the capital. It feels welcoming, like a beacon in the far distance, calling me home. Is that what the stars are doing, calling Cal back to his island?

My embroidered corset feels tight. Loss presses in on my chest. It's getting harder to push the pain away, to pretend everything is all right. And it's getting more impossible to fight against saying all the things I want to say.

It's so hard.

But I can do this. I can let him go, even if it feels like the world will collapse when I do.

There's a faint vibration beneath my feet. I almost think I'm imagining it. I'm—

A soft rumbling quakes through the air. I lose my balance, falling into Cal.

He grabs my shoulder. "Lyla?"

He's swaying alongside me. All around us, sand skips over the mirrors like fleas. There's a cracking sound. Faltering over one another, we turn. At the far bank of the dry lake, the shadowy forms of trees move with an unnatural rhythm.

And then the earth itself roars.

We're still close enough to see the Last Ship. For the first time in years it moves, prow thrusting into the air as earth fractures beneath it. Its boards split and splinter. A surging wave of glass forms from the sand, lifting the ship into the sky before dropping straight into the ground.

It's gone.

"Come on! We have to go!" Cal grabs my hand and yanks me along as we stumble in a tilting world toward home.

The city looks small from here. It's so far away. We make it only heartbeats before the sand around us is sucked into the mines. A sheet of glass under my feet cracks. There's nothing beneath it. I scream. Cal's grip on me tightens as a cavern mouth opens to swallow me.

"Lyla!"

Cal won't let me go. All my weight hits my arm, and his strength is security for a second. Then more of the ground collapses and he's falling too. Another shriek tears from my lungs. The wisp-lantern slips from my fingers. Wind rushes over us.

I'm weightless. Then I'm not. My body slams into something solid. Rough stones and shards of crystal glass rip at my dress and skin. I'm sliding. We're sliding. The opening we fell through disappears as we're pulled down a tunnel. I try to grab onto something—anything—but my hands only find Cal.

We tumble dizzyingly through the dark, but eventually we stop. My torn dress and Cal's long limbs leave us in a tangled heap. Scraping, crashing sounds continue above before eerie quiet settles over us.

Cal pushes my mess of hair out of my face and helps me sit up. "Are you okay?"

My heart is beating furiously. One of my hands is cut, and it throbs in time to my pulse.

"I ... I don't know."

He yanks a handkerchief out of his pocket and wraps it around my hand. An aftershock rains sand on our heads. Cal chokes on the dust as he tries to protect me from it.

My wisp-lantern thankfully isn't broken or buried, but the cave is so dark that the light doesn't show more than a few feet around it. I crawl over to it. The glow is much fainter now that the wisp-lantern is cut off from the fairy mist.

I bring it to Cal, and we examine the place we fell from. The hole is sealed with chunks of glass and rock. Fear prickles the back of my neck. We can't escape that way.

As I move my lantern, things creep in the shadows of the cavern ceiling. When the blue light touches them, fairies dart by and vanish into the black, leaving dust shimmering behind. Unrefined, their dust won't keep my lantern lit, but the strange humming of their voices and wings does calm me down before the harmony evaporates and the fairies are gone.

"We're going to be fine," Cal says.

I nod. "Yeah. If fairies are down here, there has to be a way out."

Together we steal along, sweeping the wisp-lantern before each step. Every movement is dangerous. There are unexpected drops in the floor that send rocks bounding and clattering down into unknown depths when we disturb them.

I can't tell how much time passes.

It must be hours.

For a while, the air starts to smell fresher, and the lantern brightens. Then it's stuffy again.

The dark slinks closer, and the wisp-lantern begins burning the last of the fairy mist trapped with us. Then I recognize it. It's the same slide of sand and glass that brought us down here.

We've been going in circles.

"It's okay," Cal says, and I can't tell if he's comforting me or trying to convince himself. "We know which way didn't work, so we choose different this time."

I'm so afraid to choose. I've already messed up so many things. But we find a tunnel that looks less natural and more like a mine shaft. And its upward incline is encouraging ... until we hear drips of water up ahead. The lantern light touches the walls around us, and then vanishes. But I feel it more than see it when the path we've chosen opens up into a massive cavern. There is no way to tell how big it is, but the air feels very different here.

I take a step and freezing water soaks through my shoe. I yelp. Cal pulls me back and we reposition the lantern. The floor doesn't exist anymore. It's all water.

"Well, I think I found the missing lake," Cal says. "Or, I guess, *you* did."

The lake's surface is as smooth and polished as obsidian glass. It's impossible to tell how deep it is or how far it goes, but summer hasn't touched it in a long time. The chill drops the temperature in the air around us.

It feels like a dead end.

I'm too tired to keep walking. I don't even know if there is anywhere to go, and the light is growing dim. Why did I have to bring Cal out here? Will our parents ever know what happened to us?

My throat feels raw. But I finally squeeze words out. "I'm so sorry."

"For what?"

The incredulousness of the question makes me want to scream. "For bringing you out tonight for no reason. For *this*." I swing the lantern around, gesturing at the nothingness pressing close.

"Lyla ... this isn't your fault. I'm the one who wanted to go."

"And I'm the one who knew better. It's impossible to see stars through the mist."

"If it was impossible, why did you come with me?"

I stare hard into the darkness, to give myself an excuse not to look at Cal. "Because I wanted you to think there was something worth staying in the city for. I wanted you to have fun. But tonight's been a disaster." I kick one of the loose rocks around my feet, and there's a loud splash as the water drinks it in. "All of it."

"Really? Before the earth swallowed us, I thought we were having fun." His tone is light, but I think he's afraid of what I might say next.

I don't care.

I can't hold it back anymore.

A tear slides down my cheek. "Fun? How could *any*thing be fun when you're leaving tomorrow? I don't want you to go."

"You ... you don't?" he stammers.

I turn to face him. He looks genuinely surprised. And this surprise makes me furious.

"Of course, I don't, you idiot!"

"But ... I thought ... When I told you I might leave, you didn't say anything. Why didn't you say anything?"

"Because I love you!" The words echo. My heart pounds furiously. He's looking at me with a slack jaw, but I'm too angry to feel embarrassed.

"Why didn't you tell me?" he asks.

With my own echoing voice encouraging me, I keep going before I can stop myself. "Because I know you don't like the city. I wanted you to leave so you could be happy."

I look up long enough to see a crooked smile work over the confusion on Cal's face. He doesn't say anything. When he's not joking, Cal is always a slow and thoughtful speaker, but he's never *this* slow. He must be overwhelmed with trying to decide how to respond. How to keep from nervous-laughing from anxiety. How to let me down easy.

I wish another earthquake would open up the ground and swallow me for real this time. Tears are no longer timid. They're streaking down my cheeks. I can't stop them.

"You're always so kind to everyone," Cal says at last. He takes a step toward me. "I didn't know I was special to you. But—all this time—I wanted to be."

My whole body freezes.

"Why do you think I wanted to see the stars *tonight*, when tomorrow I'd be far enough away to see them for myself? I wanted you to see them, Lyla. I wanted to share them with *you*."

As I meet his eyes, the wisp-lantern slips from my injured hand. It clatters into the center of a glass crystal formation. And one small light becomes many. The glass reflects in a thousand fiery facets. Pinpricks of light shoot into the darkness, igniting other crystals and turning the cave into the starry night we'd searched for.

Cal sweeps me into his arms.

I gasp in a breath. And then I'm kissing him. I stand on my toes, heart hammering as he pulls me closer. I tangle my fingers in his hair. The world slows and stops and I am no longer afraid. Everything is this moment.

And when the rest of the world comes back into focus at last, we're standing at the center of a galaxy. Our bodies still. Across the vast cavern, more and more lights ignite. The walls are covered in a sea of constellations. The lake is an ocean of stars.

And then shafts of a brighter light pour in from above.

There's an actual piece of sky, with a pathway to exit the cavern. We can get out. Through the opening, morning sun scatters across the lake in ripples. I entwine my fingers with Cal's, his warmth and pressure the only things convincing me that any of this is real.

Serene in the center of the missing lake, the Last Ship rocks high and proud in the water. Crystals of stars cling to the figurehead and its edges glow where they are brushed with new sun.

"It … it returned home," I say.

"Guess we were wrong all along. It never stopped being a ship." Cal gives me the gap-toothed smile I like so much.

I laugh softly and lean against his chest. "And what about you? Are you going home?"

"I'm already there." His lips gently press my forehead. "Not this cave, exactly. Not the city either. I think home is wherever you are."

"That's very sappy," I tease as my heart fills with all the joy I've ever wished for.

"I know. But I have a right to be sappy. I'm in love."

The wisp-lantern is wedged solidly in glass, so Cal and I leave it behind to forever make its night sky. Holding hands, we walk along the starry lake. The exit above us is filled with the city's fairy mist and stacks of clouds turned golden by sunrise. We climb the path toward them.

Together we pass through our own small piece of sky and out into the rest of our lives.

Afterword

As any new parent will tell you, having a baby is one of the most exciting and exhausting things you will ever get to experience. But not many new parents walk into the hospital to give birth and walk out with not only a new baby ... but a diagnosis of stage IV metastatic cancer.

The birth of our third child went so smoothly that it felt like a dream. They placed him on my chest and I heard his little cries of life, feeling so satisfied, so joyful that all the hardship our family had been through in the last few years had finally culminated in this one beautiful moment of redemption. After years of suffering from the fallout of others' addictions, job losses, court battles, mental health crises, health scares for our children—it felt like God was finally keeping His promise to me that "it was going to be okay." The story wasn't over. There would be a happy ending after all.

And then my doctor walked into my postpartum recovery room with the last news in the world I expected to hear. I held my newborn baby in my arms as my husband held me, and we cried as she told us about the tumors in my lung, my liver, and my spine. This wasn't what was supposed to happen. Not right after giving birth. Not to a young mom with three children. Not to me. To anyone.

I'd be lying if I said I wasn't still struggling with disappointment. There are many days I wake up in the morning and see the bald patches on my scalp, struggle through pain and side effects of treatment, and think this can't be my life. I hold my baby or watch my two older children play and beg God for as many days as I can to watch them grow up. It's easy to give in to the despair, the feeling of injustice that life shouldn't be this way.

And the reality is ... it isn't supposed to be this way. The lesson I've slowly been learning is that we as humans have this gut instinct that there is a wrongness to suffering and pain because there is a wrongness to it. This was never God's intent for us. That feeling reminds us that we are still longing for the ultimate redemption, that as perfect as our lives may seem in the moment, we cannot escape our desperate longing and need for Christ. We cannot outrun the cost of sin. We cannot outrun death. The pain will always catch up to us and it never feels "fair."

Romans tells us that "what we suffer now is nothing compared to the glory he will reveal to us later. For all creation is waiting eagerly for that future day when God will reveal who his children really are. Against its will, all creation was subjected to God's curse. But with eager hope, the creation looks forward to the day when it will join God's children in glorious freedom from death and decay. For we know that all creation has been groaning as in the pains of childbirth right up to the present time" (8:18-22 [New Living Translation]). Like a woman in labor, we groan and cry out for the moment when this pain will be relieved, when the wrongness of sin and suffering will finally be righted. It's a hope for the future that this pain will one day be fruitful into glorious joy.

But how do we make it until then?

I wish I had an answer to that too. God is showing me every single day that there is the ultimate destination where my disappointment and pain will be no more, where I will find a feast of redemption for my starving soul. But what about here and now in these agonizing moments until that day comes? All I can say is that I have personally seen that

He hides little mercies and blessings laid out for me like breadcrumbs leading me home. They are the small loaves of daily bread we pray for, the gifts hidden along the path to remind me He still loves me. A meal brought to our home. A gift card in the mail. A warm hug and whispered encouragement when I feel like I cannot take another step. All reminders He hasn't forgotten me. He sees my pain. He holds each of my tears in his hands and works through the hands and feet of others to show me that love each and every day. He does not promise to take away our pain on this side of heaven, but He does promise to be with us and love us through the suffering. I have been keeping a list of those little mercies to encourage myself to keep looking for them, to remind myself of how close He still is.

For now, until we all reach the place where the wrongness of sin is finally righted, we can hold onto the glimpses of glory shining bright in the darkness lighting our way home.

~ Lani Forbes (1987 – 2022)

Acknowledgments

The Sun Still Rises exists because of the donations of generous people, both of creative and practical work, and of time and energy. I (Cassandra) am incredibly grateful.

Thank you to my fellow leadership team, AJ Skelly, Jill Williamson, Emily Hayse, Elizabeth Van Tassel, Nicky Wheeler, Katie Phillips, Becky Dean, and Hana Danielson, for helping and supporting me in this endeavor. To the incredible volunteer editors, Ellen McGinty, Andi L. Gregory, Jessica Gwyn, Meghan Kleinschmidt, Sophia Hansen, Sarah Harmon, Mariella Taylor, and Jessica Noelle for making the stories shine. To Emilie Hendryx Haney for the gorgeous cover reminiscent of Lani's own books. To AJ Skelly and Jill Williamson for being a great submissions team. To AJ Skelly for formatting the book. To Tanager Haemmerle and H.S.J. Williams for the stunning promotional artwork. To Emily Hayse and AJ Skelly for helping me with all the practical things I didn't know I needed to know, like uploading files to Amazon and writing copyright pages and setting up ISBN numbers. To Ellen McGinty for answering all my random editing-related questions and generally being supportive. To Elizabeth Van Tassel for the marketing expertise and many, many promotional ideas. To Katie Hanna for the extensive blurb help. To everyone who shared about the anthology and prayed for its impact and execution and offered support in all their own ways.

I want to give a special thank you to the authors, who generously donated their stories to help remember Lani's legacy. I know Lani would have loved these stories. She would be so proud of you all. And, of course, to Kevin Forbes, Lani's husband, and my dear friend. Thank you for supporting our efforts to remember and celebrate her. Your wife was so very loved.

To anyone else I may have forgotten to thank here. We love and appreciate you.

Finally, to God. This project would not exist without Him. He is the light that shone through Lani during her brief, beautiful life. He shines through us now as we celebrate a truly incredible woman of faith. I know she is with Him now. I can't wait to see her again.

~ Cassandra Hamm, Editor-in-Chief

Author Bios

C.M. Banschbach is an overly tall hobbit who's entirely too fond of stabbing and adventure in her fantasy, cares too much about humans even if she pretends not to, and loves to gaze up at the stars in wonder. More at www.clairembanschbach.com

Award-winning sci/fi-fantasy author Jamie Foley loves strategy games, gardening, and making lembas bread. When not writing, she's working for Enclave Publishing, The Christian Writers Institute, or drawing maps to Cair Paravel. She lives with her awesome husband, hyperactive spawnling, dragon, and wolfpack in the Texas hill country. More at www.jamiefoley.com

Crystal D. Grant is a daydreamer who strives to instill a love of books within her young students. When she's not reading stories that sweep her away, she writes them. She's had multiple short stories published and her fantasy novel, *Shadowcast*, is releasing in 2023 from Quill and Flame Publishers. More at www.crystalgrantauthor.com

S.D. Grimm writes young adult fantasy and sci-fi that's magical, mythical, and a little grim. She is a proud Gryffindor, loves second breakfast, and identifies as rebel scum. Her office is anywhere she can curl up with her laptop and a few dogs. Learn about her novels at www.sdgrimm.com

Tanager Haemmerle is an author/illustrator. Her heart lives in young adult science fiction (the more cyborgs, the better!). But she also crafts nerdy picture books about spooky unicorns. Tanager enjoys walking her calico cat and doing handstands to see the world from a different point of view. More at www.dreamoffire.wixsite.com/mysite

Julie Hall is a USA Today bestselling, multiple award-winning author. She writes YA paranormal / fantasy novels, loves doodles, and drinks Red Bull, but not necessarily in that order. Julie currently lives in Colorado with her four favorite people—her husband, daughter, and two fur babies. Find her books at www.amazon.com/stores/Julie-Hall/author

Cassandra Hamm is a psychology nerd, art collector, jigsaw puzzler, and hopeless romantic who spends most of her time lost in another realm. Her award-winning work appears in various anthologies. A mental health advocate with a passion for social justice, she writes about shattered girls finding their way in the world. Learn more at www.cassandrahamm.com

A people-loving introvert, Lauren Hildebrand loves to tell stories that mingle humor, hardship, and hope. She lives in always-windy Kansas, considers Asian cuisine a primary food group, and can usually be found devouring classics or planning her next cosplay. Soli Deo gloria! Learn more on her Instagram at @laughterandlonging.

Ronie Kendig is a bestselling, award-winning author of over thirty books. She grew up an Army brat, and now she and her Army-veteran husband have returned to their beloved Texas after a nearly ten-year stint in the Northeast. They survive on Sonic runs, barbecue, and peach cobbler that they share—sometimes—with Benning the Stealth Golden. Ronie's degree in psychology has helped her pen novels of intense, raw characters. Learn more at www.roniekendig.com

Ellen McGinty is an author, editor, and story aficionado. Her debut YA fantasy trilogy releases with Quill & Flame Publishers in 2024. She lives in the Greater Tokyo Area with her husband and three wild boys. Learn more at www.ellenmcginty.com or on Instagram at @ellenmcginty_author.

Carrie Anne Noble writes fantasy fiction infused with fairytales and folklore, including *The Mermaid's Sister*, winner of the Amazon Breakthrough Novel Award for YA Fiction and the Realm Award for Book of the Year. She resides in the woods with her frolicsome half-Corgi but can be lured out with chocolate. Follow her on Instagram at @carrieannenoble7.

Jessica Noelle is a dreamer and reader who loves Jesus. She spends her days playing with her dog, drinking tea, and spending time with her friends and family and her nights spinning stories, editing for Havok Publishing, and devouring new books. More at www.jessicanoellewrites.com

R. M. Scott lives in the mountains of Idaho with her husband and two children. She is the author of Unseen, a YA Fantasy novel, and Slowpoke and the Guardians of Atopa, a Chapter Book. She tries to be as brave as a Gryffindor but is more Ravenclaw. Learn more at www.rmscottauthor.com

AJ Skelly is an author, reader, and lover of all things fantasy. She lives with her husband, children, and many imaginary friends who often find their way into her stories. They all drink copious amounts of tea together and stay up reading far later than they should. More at www.ajskelly.com

Callie Thomas is an indie author who loves all things fairy tales. She is inspired by the beautiful scenery where her family lives in Fredericksburg, Virginia. Her serial story, *A Forest of Stolen Memories*, is a YA sweet romance that has been on the Top Faves List since September 2021. More at www.authorcalliethomas.com

Elizabeth Van Tassel is a Graduate Gemologist who loves jewelry, creates artwork, and writes kidlit fantasy. She spent a decade in marketing, has been on CBS and Fox News sharing her wildfire survivor story, and speaks about building a diamond-resilient life in schools, inspirational gatherings, and corporations. Connect at www.elizabethvantassel.com

Nicole Wheeler loved words even before she could read or write them, and has since become fascinated by how we're formed by the stories we love. When she's not writing, she's dreaming of the next family vacation, or hopelessly multitasking. Nicole lives in Idaho with her husband, daughters and pomapug puppy, Winchester. More at www.Nicole-Wheeler.com

A.C. Williams is an author and writing coach with fifteen published books. A senior partner at Uncommon Universes Press, she is a Realm Award Winner and the 2022 Arise Daily Writer of the Year. She also contributes to two blogs ranked in Writer's Digest's Top 101 sites for authors. More at www.amycwilliams.com

Jill Williamson is an award-winning fantasy author of over two dozen books including *By Darkness Hid*, which won several awards. She has also written books on the craft of writing and teaches at www.goteenwriters.com, one of *Writer's Digest*'s "101 Best Websites for Writers." Visit her online at www.jillwilliamson.com

Laura L. Zimmerman lives in Pennsylvania with her family and four kitties. Her passions are loving Jesus, Star Wars, coffee, yoga, and reading. Check out KEEN and LAMENT, her YA fantasy Banshee Song Series, and her middle grade mystery R.A.D. Detectives: The Case of the Missing Robot. Learn more at www.instagram.com/lauralzimmauthor

never give up